THE ASCENDANCY VEIL

Book Three of The Braided Path

Also by Chris Wooding in Gollancz

The Braided Path:

THE WEAVERS OF SARAMYR
THE SKEIN OF LAMENT

THE ASCENDANCY VEIL

CHRIS WOODING

The right of Chris Wooding to be identified as the
author of this work has been asserted by him in accordance
with the Copyright, Designs and Patents Act 1988.

First published in Great Britain in 2005 by
Gollancz
An imprint of the Orion Publishing Group
Orion House, 5 Upper St Martin's Lane,
London WC2H 9EA

This edition published in Great Britain in 2006 by
Gollancz

1 3 5 7 9 10 8 6 4 2

A CIP catalogue record for this book is
available from the British Library

ISBN 0 57507 769 7
ISBN 9 780 57507 769 0

Typeset at The Spartan Press Ltd,
Lymington, Hants

Printed in Great Britain by
Clays Ltd, St Ives plc

The Orion Publishing Group's policy is to use papers that
are natural, renewable and recyclable products and made
from wood grown in sustainable forests. The logging and
manufacturing processes are expected to conform to the
environmental regulations of the country of origin.

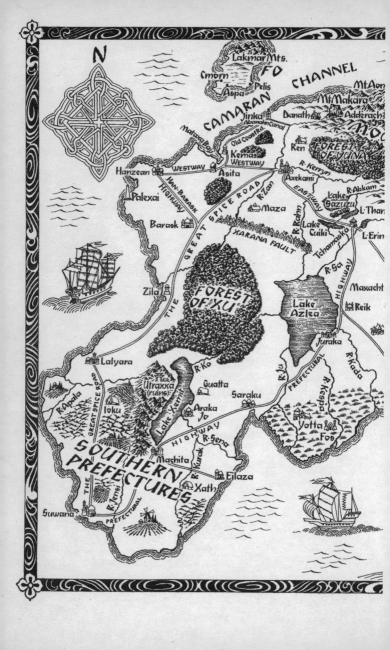

ONE

They loomed through the smoke, shadows in the billowing murk. In the instant before they came charging into the hall, they seemed as demons, their forms huge and vaporous. But they were not demons. The demons were still outside.

The pitiful scattering of defenders met the assault with grim stoicism. Some had taken up station on the balcony that ran around the room, but most were arranged at ground level behind a barricade they had assembled from toppled statues, plinths and the few small tables they had found. The Saramyr tendency towards minimal furniture had not worked to their advantage here. Still, they took what cover they could, aimed their rifles, and filled the air with gunfire as the ghauregs came pounding towards them.

Once, the entrance hall had been exquisite, a cool and echoing chamber intended to impress dignitaries and nobles. Now it had been stripped of its finery and ornaments, and the walls were scorched. The floor had been cracked by the same explosion that had set fire to the hangings and tapestries near the doorway. A dozen or so monstrous corpses were scattered there. One well-timed bomb had dealt with the first wave of creatures; the rifles would take care of a portion of the next. But beyond that, the defenders' cause was hopeless.

The ghauregs thundered across the wide open space at the centre of the hall and were cut down, their thick grey pelts ribboning with red as the rifle balls punched through them. But for each one that died there was another behind it, and several that fell got up again, their wounds only enraging them further. Eight feet high at the shoulder and apelike in posture, they were savage ogres of fur and muscle. Pain and death meant nothing to them, and they raced through the crossfire with suicidal fury.

The defenders managed to reprime fast enough for a second volley before the creatures crashed into the barricade and began tearing it apart, clambering over the top to reach the men behind. Rifles were dropped and swords drawn, but against the sheer size and power of the ghauregs there were too few blades. They knew this, and still they fought. They had been ordered to hold the administrative complex and they would do so with their lives. Saramyr soldiers would take death before the shame of disobeying orders.

The ghauregs punched and grabbed at their targets. Where the defenders were not quick enough to evade, they were bludgeoned to pulp or snatched up to be flung through the air like broken mannequins. Those who dodged away struck back with their swords, slashing at tendons and hamstrings. In moments, the floor was slippery with blood, and the cries of men were drowned by the bellowing of the beasts.

The soldiers on the balcony picked their targets as best they could in the melee, but they had problems of their own now. For behind the ghauregs had come several skrendel: slender, nimble things with long, strangling fingers that swarmed up the pillars. What little support the soldiers could give the men below dissipated swiftly as they struggled to keep the newcomers away.

The beasts had destroyed the barricade now and were sowing mayhem. Outsize jaws bit and snapped, crunching through bone and gristle; enormous shoulders strained as they rent apart their small and frail prey. In less than a minute, the remaining half-dozen ghauregs had decimated the tiny force holding the entrance hall, and only a few soldiers were left, their deaths merely an afterthought. But as the ghauregs' small yellow eyes fixed on the final, defiant dregs of resistance, one of their number burst into flames.

The two Sisters of the Red Order swept into the hall from

the back, an arrogant lethality in their stride. Both wore the sheer dark dress of the Order, both the intimidating face-paint of their kind: the black and red shark-tooth triangles across their lips, the twin crimson crescents curving over their eyes from forehead to cheek. Their irises were the colour of smouldering coals.

The other ghauregs shied away from the heat of their burning companion, and in that moment of hesitation the Sisters took them apart. Two of the beasts fell, spewing blood from every orifice; two more burst into white flames, becoming pillars of fire and smoke and bubbling fat; the last was picked up as if by some invisible hand and pulverised against the wall with enough force to shatter the stone. The skrendel began to scatter, winding back down the pillars and making for the entranceway. One of the Sisters made a casual gesture with a black-gloved hand and maimed them, popping and cracking their thin bones and leaving them flailing weakly on the floor.

In seconds, it was done. All that was left in the wake of the conflict was the restless industry of the flames, the mewling of the dying skrendel and the cries of wounded men. The remnants of the defenders regarded the Sisters with ragged awe.

Kaiku tu Makaima surveyed the scene before her. Her vision was poised on the cusp of the world of natural light and that of the Weave, overlaying one on top of the other. She looked past the battered and bloodied figures gazing at her, past the corpse-strewn hall to the doorway where smoke from the fire plumed angrily into the room. But beneath that veneer of reality she saw a golden diorama of threads, the stitches and fibres of existence: the whole hall rendered in millions of tiny, .endless tendrils. She saw the inrush and exhalation of the stirred air as the living drew it into their lungs; the curl and roll at the heart of the smoke; the stout, unwavering lines of the pillars.

She flexed her fingers and tied up the frantic threads of the flame, wrapping it tighter and tighter until it choked and extinguished itself.

'Juraka has fallen,' she said, her voice ringing out across the hall. 'We retreat south-west to the river.'

She felt their disappointment like a wave. She had not wanted to tell them this. Their companions lay dead around them, dozens of lives sacrificed to defend this place, and she was the one who had to inform the survivors that it was all for nothing. Perhaps they hated her for doing so. Perhaps, in their breasts, they harboured a bitterness that she had arrived and made their struggles meaningless, and they thought: *filthy Aberrant.*

She cared little. She had greater concerns.

She left her companion, Phaeca, to explain matters in more sensitive terms while she walked through the dispersing smoke of the snuffed-out fire and out into the warm and bright winter's day.

Juraka had been founded on a hillside overlooking the shores of the colossal Lake Azlea, an ancient market town that had begun as a stop-off point for travellers making the long trek from Tchamaska to Machita along the Prefectural Highway. In time, it had evolved a fishing and boatmaking industry, and sometime during the bloody internecine wars following the death of the mad Emperor Cadis tu Othoro it had been fortified and garrisoned. Latterly, it had become a vital part of the line which the remnants of the Empire had held for years against the Weavers and the hordes at their command.

But by the time Nuki's eye sank below the horizon today, it would be in the enemy's hands.

Kaiku swore under her breath, an unladylike habit picked up from her long-dead brother and never shed. She knew that the stalemate would have to end sooner or later, that eventually one side would devise an advantage over the other. She just wished the Weavers had not got there first.

The administrative complex was a sprawling, walled

enclosure of several grandiose buildings in a circular formation. To her right, houses ran up the hill to the fringe of a small forest; to her left, streets and tiny plazas fell away in a clutter of ornamental slate rooftops to the vast expanse of the lake, which glittered sharply in the crisp daylight until it was lost to the haze of distance. Ships were battling out there in a slow dance, the sporadic crack of gunfire and the bellow of cannons drifting up to her. The shore was crowded with jetties and warehouses, most of which were smashed and burning now. Smoke rose in indistinct columns, cloaking the lower streets in a fug.

Kaiku's gaze roamed across the town, across the broken shrines and sundered houses, the streets where men and women fought running skirmishes with shrillings and furies and worse. Gristle-crows soared high on the thermals overhead, providing a literal birds-eye view for their Nexus masters. But these were enemies she knew, creatures she had dealt with many times in the four years since this war had begun. She turned her attention to the authors of the town's downfall.

There were two of them, one down by the shore and another rearing over the treeline on the hilltop. *Feya-kori*: 'blight demons' in the Saramyrrhic mode used for speaking of supernatural beings. They were forty feet high: drooling, lumbering, foetid things in a mocking approximation of human shape, distorted figures with long, thick arms and legs, that walked on all fours and seethed a dire miasma as they moved. They were formed of some kind of noisome, roiling sludge that dripped and spattered, and where it touched it spread fire and rot, causing leaves to crinkle and wood to decay. They had no faces, merely a bulge between their shoulders, in which burned incandescent orbs that trailed luminous gobbets. They moaned plaintively to each other as they went about their destruction, their mournful cries accompanying the slow, idiot savagery of their actions.

As Kaiku watched, one of them waded out into the lake.

The waters hissed and boiled, and a black patina began to spread from where its limbs plunged. She felt her stomach sink as she saw its intention. It forged its way towards one of the Empire's junks, and with a doleful groan it raised one stump of a hand and brought it crashing down onto the vessel, breaking it in half and setting men and sails aflame. Kaiku closed her eyes reflexively and turned away, but even then she could feel the force of the demons' presence through the Weave, a blasphemous dark pummelling at her consciousness.

The other feya-kori was surging out of the forest, leaving a vile scar of browning foliage and collapsing trees in its wake. It smashed an arm into the nearest rooftops, wanton in its malice. Five of Kaiku's Sisters had already died attempting to tackle the feya-kori. All over Juraka the order to retreat was spreading, and the forces of the Empire were pulling back to the south-west.

Then she sensed the spidery movement of a Weaver down in the streets below, heard the distant screams of soldiers, and the rage and sorrow in her heart found a target.

If I cannot stop this, she promised herself, *I will at least take one of them in payment.*

She stalked away from the administrative complex, out through the prayer gate with its eloquent paean to Naris, god of scholars, and into the narrow, sloping streets beyond.

Blood ran in chain-link trickles between the cobbles, inching slowly downhill from the bodies of men and women and the foetally curled corpses of Aberrant predators. Kaiku experienced a moment of bitter humour at how Aberrants, which were created by the Weavers in the first place, were simultaneously their greatest resource and their greatest opponents. She and all the other Sisters were a product of the same process that had spawned monstrosities like the ghauregs. She was certain that the gods, watching from the Golden Realm, never tired of laughing at the way events had turned out.

She passed swiftly between the newly scarred buildings,

little fearing the creatures that ran amok in the alleys. Wooden balconies and shop-fronts gaped emptily as if in shock at how they had been deserted. Carts and rickshaws were left where they had been abandoned in the rush to evacuate the townsfolk. A crackle of rifle fire sounded up the hill as dozens of soldiers wasted their ammunition in a futile attempt to hurt the demon that was battering its way towards the lake from the treeline.

The screams she had heard were louder now. She sensed the stirring of the Weave like coiling tentacles, the Weaver's ugly manipulation of the invisible fabric beneath the skin of the waking world. She hated them, hated their clumsiness in comparison to the Sisters' elegant sewing, hated their brutal way of forcing nature to their will. She fed her rage as she approached, concealing her presence from the Weaver with a few deft evasions.

The street opened out into a junction of three major thoroughfares. The heart of the junction was a cobbled area in which stood a bronze statue of a catfish, depicted as if swimming upward towards the sky, its torso curved and fins and whiskers trailing. It was the animal aspect of Panazu, god of rivers, storms and rain and – by extension – lakes. An appropriate choice for a town on the shore of the greatest lake on the continent. Two-storied buildings leaned in close, their shutters hanging open, cracked plant pots outside and wooden walls riven by holes from rifle balls.

This had been one of the critical defensive points of Juraka, and had been fortified accordingly with barricades and a pair of fire-cannon. But such measures were useless against Weavers. Without a Sister of the Red Order to counter him, the Weaver had muddled the soldiers' minds and thrown them into rout. Aberrants had overrun the unmanned positions and were tearing into their panicking prey. The Weaver was nowhere to be seen.

Kaiku did not waste time considering how this pre-dicament had come about. There should have been a Sister here to protect the soldiers, but the Red Order was in disarray across the town. Instead she stood brazenly at one end of the junction and opened up the Weave. The air stirred around her, rippling her dress and ruffling her tawny hair where it lay across one side of her face. She surrendered herself to the ecstasy of Weaving.

The pure joy of disembodiment, of witnessing the raw stuff of creation in an endless profusion of glittering threads, was enough to drive the untrained to madness. But Kaiku had been there many times, and she had mantras and methods of self-control that anchored her against that first tidal wash of narcotic harmony. She saw the tears and rents left by the Weaver's passing, felt his influence extending into the golden stitchwork dolls that were the soldiers, twisting their perceptions, making them confused and helpless.

He was unaware of her yet, and she used that. She slipped closer, winding along fibres, darting from strand to strand so that the emanations of her approach would be subtle and widely spread, faint enough to be missed in amongst the throb of the demons' presence. She could locate him with ease: he was in the upper storey of an old cathouse overlooking the junction. This Weaver was young and careless, for despite his power he did not notice her until she was close enough to strike him.

She did not strike him, however. Even angry as she was, she knew the risks that facing a Weaver entailed. Instead, she slid into the fibres of the beams that held up the roof of the cathouse, securing herself along their length to obtain the necessary mental leverage. The best way to kill a Weaver, she had found, was to do it indirectly.

In one violent twist, she ripped the beams apart.

The explosive detonation caused by shredding the fibres of the Weave created enough concussion to blow the shutters of the cathouse off their hinges. Flame billowed from the topmost windows; boards splintered and went spinning end over end through the air. The roof caved in, crushing the

Weaver beneath it. The reverberations of the death flashed out across the Weave in a frantic pulse and slowly faded away.

One less of you, then, Kaiku thought, as the Weave faded from her vision.

The soldiers were coming to their senses, disorientated at finding themselves in the midst of an attack. Some were too slow to react, and were cut to pieces by the Aberrants that swarmed among them; but others were faster, and they brought their swords to bear. There were enough remaining to put up a resistance yet, and they did so with sudden and fierce anger.

Kaiku walked among them, slaying Aberrants as she went. With a wave of her hand she burst organs and shattered bone, tossed the creatures away or burned them to tallow and char. The soldiers, shouting hoarse rallying cries to one another, fought with renewed heart. Kaiku joined the cry, venting a deep and nameless hatred for what had been done to her, to her land, to these people; and for a time she steeped herself in blood.

Presently, there were no more enemies to fight. She came to herself as if from a vague and shallow trance. The junction was quiet now, a charnel house of bodies rank with the stink of gore and ignition powder. The soldiers were congratulating themselves and watching her warily, suspicious of their saviour. One of them took a step towards her, as if to offer her thanks or gratitude, but his step faltered and he turned aside, pretending that he was shifting his feet. She could see them arguing quietly as to who should do the honourable thing and acknowledge her help, but the fact that no one would do it of their own free will rendered it hollow. Gods, even now she was *Aberrant* to them.

'We should go,' said Phaeca, who had appeared at her shoulder. When Kaiku did not respond, the Sister laid a hand gently on her arm.

Kaiku made a soft noise of acknowledgement in her throat,

but she did not move. The feya-kori from uphill was coming closer, its funereal moans preceding the jagged sounds of the destruction it was wreaking.

'We should go,' Phaeca repeated, quietly insistent, and Kaiku realised that she had tears standing in her eyes, tears of raw fury and disappointment. She wiped them with the back of her hand and stalked away, overwhelmed by a prescient feeling that the desperate war they had been fighting for their homeland had just turned fundamentally, and not in their favour.

TWO

Sasako Bridge lay a little over thirty miles south-west of Juraka, spanning the Kespa as part of the winding Prefectural Highway. The terrain was hilly and forested right down to the banks of the river, and the road skulked its way between great shoulders of land that, in days gone by, had provided perfect points of ambush for bandits and thieves preying on the trade caravans which used this route in times of peace. The bridge itself was a hidden treasure: an elegant arch of white, supported by a fan of pillars that emerged from the centre of the river on either side of the thoroughfare like the spokes of two skeletal wheels. It had been worked from an extremely hard wood that had weathered little with time, and the careful etchings and votive iconography on the pillars and parapets were still clear after many centuries, though some of the scenes and characters and beasts they depicted had been lost to all but the most scholarly minds.

Now, with the retreat at Juraka, Sasako Bridge had become the key point in holding the eastern line against the armies of the Weavers.

The rain began at dusk, soaking the canvas tents of the army of the Empire. Sasako Bridge was the fallback point if Juraka was lost. A defensive infrastructure had been built here long ago against just this eventuality. Stockade walls and guard-towers were already in place; fire-cannons and mortars lay hidden among the folds of the hills. Sasako Bridge was the only spot where an army could cross the Kespa, unless they cared to head seventy miles south to Yupi Bridge – similarly guarded – or even further into the swamps, where the city of Fos watched over the Lotus Arch. If they were coming – and they undoubtedly were – then they would be coming through here.

Kaiku stood in the songbird-house, high up on the flank of a forested slope, and looked out over the hills to the river. The embroidered wall-screens had been opened to the west, for the cool breeze was blowing the rain against the opposite side, and the pale light of the moon Neryn bathed the view in spectral green. Lanterns glimmered down there among the glistening boughs, evidence of the sprawling camp hidden below the canopy of the foliage. The Kespa was just visible through the overlapping flanks of land, making its way steadily from Lake Azlea in the north towards the swamplands in the south and the ocean beyond. The air was alive with the restful hiss and patter of the downpour, and the insects had fallen silent under the barrage.

The troops of the Empire had found the songbird-house abandoned when they first began to set up fortifications here, and taken it as their own. It was a tender memory of days that already seemed impossibly distant, when the high families' domination of the Empire was unchallenged, as it had been for a thousand years until the Weavers had usurped them and thrown them into a savage war to preserve their own existence. Then, noble families often owned a songbird-house, a secluded love-nest bedecked with romantic finery – including songbirds – which was employed by newlyweds or young couples, or parents who wanted a little peace from their offspring.

Kaiku gave a small, involuntary sigh. It had been four years since the war began; but her war had begun almost a decade ago. Would she have even recognised herself if she had met the woman she was to become? Would she have ever imagined she might be wearing the make-up of the Red Order? She remembered a time when she had found it ghoulish. Now she enjoyed painting it on. It gave her a new strength, made her feel as fearsome as she appeared. Strange, the effect that wearing such a Mask could have; but if she had learned one thing in these ten years, it was that there was power in Masks.

She thought of the True Mask that had once belonged to her father, its leering face blazing in her mind like the sudden appearance of the sun. It came to her unbidden, as it always did, but as she forced it away it tugged at her with promises that would not easily fade.

Needing to distract herself, she turned back to face the room, where others were gathering for conference. It was wide and spacious, empty of furniture but for a low, oval table of black wood in its centre, upon which vases of guya blossoms and silver trays of refreshments were set. The screens were adorned with depictions of birds in flight and landscapes of lakes and mountains and forests, and mats for sitting on were laid across the polished wood floor. Servants hovered in the corners of the room, where twisting pillars cut from tree boughs held charms and superstitious knick-knacks. Even at a hurriedly assembled meeting such as this the rules of etiquette were not ignored.

She could identify most of the people here. It was the usual mishmash of generals sent by different Baraks, a scattering of Libera Dramach, a few representatives of other high families. She sought out the people she knew well: Yugi, clapping someone heartily on the shoulder and laughing; Phaeca, talking gravely with a man that Kaiku did not recognise; Nomoru, sitting alone at one side of the room, looking as scruffy as ever and wearing an expression that indicated she would rather be elsewhere.

When all were present, they seated themselves around the table, except for Nomoru, who remained on the periphery. Kaiku gave her a scowl. She was unable to understand why Yugi always included her in gatherings like this. Nomoru was so unrelentingly rude that Kaiku felt embarrassed being around her. Even now she radiated surliness and drew the gazes of the generals and highborns, who wondered what she was doing here but were too polite to ask.

The man at the head of the table was General Maroko of Blood Erinima. He was thickset and bald-headed, with a long black beard and moustache that hung down to his collarbone and made him look older than his forty-five harvests. He was in ultimate command of the forces that had been stationed in Juraka, elected through the usual process of squabbling and jostling between the high families that attended such matters.

'Are we all here, then?' he asked, a little informally considering the occasion.

'There is one more,' said Kaiku. She had barely finished her sentence before the latecomer's arrival was heralded by a stirring in the Weave. The air thickened, and Cailin tu Moritat manifested herself at the opposite end of the table from Maroko.

She was a ghostly haze in the air, a white smear of a face atop a long streak of black that tapered away to nothing several inches above the floor. The vague impression of features could be made out, but they blurred and shimmered. Kaiku sensed the unease of those who looked upon her and allowed herself a private smile. Cailin could make herself appear in perfect clarity if she liked, almost indistinguishable from the real thing. But she loved her theatrics, and she was much more menacing as an oblique, half-seen entity hanging vulture-like over the proceedings. She preferred to frighten people.

Kaiku announced her for those who did not already know, adding the correct honorific: Pre-Eminent of the Red Order. She was the official head of the Sisterhood now, having taken the title when the Sisters declared themselves publicly in the wake of the Weavers' great coup. Though the Red Order had never operated as a hierarchy, Cailin had long been their leader in all but name, and she declared it necessary to sanction her position if they were to be taken seriously. Kaiku could not argue with her logic, but as with much that Cailin did, it left her with an uneasy suspicion that what seemed apparently spontaneous had in fact been set up long before, and was merely part of a greater plan of which she was not aware.

Maroko went curtly through the pleasantries of greeting and welcome, then settled to the matter at hand. 'I have read your reports, and I know of our losses,' he said. 'I am not interested in apportioning blame or merit at this point. What I want to know is: what in Omecha's name were those *things* in Juraka, and how do we beat them?'

It was clear that the question was addressed to the Sisters. Kaiku was the one to reply.

'We call them feya-kori,' she said. 'I say *we* call them that because we dubbed them ourselves: they are not like any demon we have heard of, in living memory or in legend.'

'You knew of them *before* they attacked us?' jumped in one old general. Kaiku remembered him: he was ever quick to throw accusations at the Sisterhood. Did he distrust them because they were Sisters, or Aberrants, or both? He would be far from alone in any case.

'No,' she said calmly. 'Our information reached us only during the assault. Sadly, the intelligence came too slow, or the Weavers moved too fast, for us to forewarn you. Even so, I think you will agree that the loss of five of our number is ample evidence that we were taken as much by surprise as you were.'

'Ample,' agreed Maroko, with a pointed glare at the general. 'Nobody here questions the loyalty of the Red Order.' He looked back to Kaiku. 'What information do you have?'

'Very little,' Kaiku admitted. 'Much of what we have is speculation. The Weavers have summoned demons before, but nowhere near the magnitude of the feya-kori. Even with the new witchstones they have awoken these past years, none of us had imagined that their abilities had increased so much.'

'Then how have they managed to do it?' asked another general, leaning forward on his elbows in the lanternlight. 'And how can we stop them?'

'To both questions, I have no answer,' she replied. 'We know only that they came from Axekami.'

'*Axekami?*' someone exclaimed.

'Indeed. These demons did not come from the depths of a forest, or a volcano, nor any other wild or deserted place where their kind might usually be found. These came from the heart of our capital city.'

There was consternation at this. The generals began to argue and theorise amongst themselves. Kaiku and Phaeca used the time to communicate with Cailin. Some of the generals threw them distasteful glances, noting the telltale coloration of their irises as they strung and sewed the Weave. The Sisters constructed patterns of impression and intent and flashed them across the four hundred miles that separated them from their Pre-Eminent. Kaiku took care of the security of their link, monitoring the vibrations of the threads for roaming Weavers who might listen in, but nothing threatened them that she could find.

'I think the first and most obvious thing we should do,' Yugi was saying, 'is to send someone to Axekami.'

His proposition silenced the murmurings that were going on across the table. Though he had no power in any official capacity, he was the leader of the Libera Dramach, the organisation founded to protect the disenfranchised Heir-Empress Lucia tu Erinima. The fact that both Lucia and the Red Order were closely tied in with them made them as much a force to be reckoned with as any of the high families of the Empire.

'I'm sure you are aware of how dangerous such an undertaking would be,' General Maroko said; but as he did so, he was stroking the end of his drooping moustache with his fingertips, a habit which indicated he liked what he was hearing. 'The capital is deep in the Weavers' territory, and reports indicate that it has . . . changed quite drastically.'

Yugi shrugged. 'I'll go,' he said.

'I doubt that we can afford to risk you,' Maroko replied, raising an eyebrow.

Yugi had expected such a response. 'Still, somebody must,' he said, absently taking a sip of wine from the cup on the table before him. 'These feya-kori represent the greatest danger we have faced since this war began. We have no idea how to deal with them. They're too powerful for the Red Order, and artillery seems to have little effect if the assault on Juraka is any measure. Someone needs to go to Axekami and find out what these creatures are and where they are coming from.'

'I agree,' Maroko said. 'But such a decision is not under my authority. Our responsibility is to hold the eastern line. However, we can pass our suggestion back to the councils at Saraku . . .'

'We need answers, not more arguments!' someone called, to which there was a smattering of laughter and a grim smile from Maroko.

'Then I'll handle it myself, as a Libera Dramach matter,' said Yugi. 'With your permission, of course,' he added, even though he had no real need of it.

'See to it,' Maroko replied. 'Inform us of your findings.'

Kaiku was forming a request to Cailin when she received the pre-emptive response. Cailin knew her prize pupil well.

((Go with them. Both of you))

Kaiku and Phaeca went to see Yugi after the conference had disbanded. They found him in his tent, which had been pitched in the grounds of the songbird-house, where paths wound between weed-choked ponds and overgrown gardens. The boughs nodded with the impact of the rain, drizzling thin ribbons of water from their leaves onto the soldiers below as they hurried back and forth busily like ants in a nest. It took some effort to locate the tent among the crowded grounds, but once outside they knew that they had the right place by the lingering scent of burnt amaxa root that clung to it.

There was no chime nor any method of gaining the attention of those within, so Kaiku simply opened the flap and stepped inside, with Phaeca close behind her.

Yugi looked up from the map spread on the table before him. He was sitting cross-legged on a mat. The rest of the tent was a clutter of possessions that he had not yet unpacked. In the wan light of the paper lantern above him, Kaiku thought how old he looked, how deep the lines on his face and how haggard his cheeks. He had not coped well with the pressures of leadership. Though his exterior was still as roguish and bluff as it had always been, inside he was deteriorating fast. His amaxa root habit had increased in proportion to his decline, the symptom of some inner turmoil the exact nature of which Kaiku was unaware. For long years, even before she had known him, he had smoked the narcotic in secret and it had never got in the way of his efficiency as a member of the Libera Dramach. He had always been able to take it or leave it, a biological quirk or facet of his character that allowed him to somehow sidestep the addiction that snared most users of the drug. But now, more and more often, she found him with that slightly too-bright edge in his eyes, and smelt the lingering fumes in places where he rested, and she feared for him.

There was an instant of incomprehension on his face as he looked upon the two black-clad Sisters, who had come in from the rain and yet were not even damp. Then the grin appeared, a somewhat sickly rictus in the jaundiced light. 'Kaiku,' he said. 'Come to volunteer?'

'You sound surprised,' she observed.

He got to his feet, running a hand through the brown-blond quills of his hair. 'I would have thought Cailin would not let you go.'

'We have more than enough Sisters to defend a single bridge against the Weavers. And as to the feya-kori . . . well, you know as well as I. One Sister or a dozen will make little difference there.'

'I meant that I didn't think she would let *you* go,' he said. 'You are something of a valued possession of hers nowadays.'

Kaiku did not like the implication of that phrase, but she deflected it with a smile. 'I do not often do what I am told anyway, Yugi. You know me.'

Yugi did not take up the humour. 'I used to,' he murmured. Then his eyes went to Phaeca and he made a distracted noise of acknowledgement. 'You too?'

'It'd be nice to see home again,' Phaeca said.

He paced slowly around the periphery of the tent, deep in thought. 'Agreed. Three of you, then. That will be enough.'

'Three?' Kaiku asked. 'Who is the third?'

'Nomoru,' he replied. 'She asked to go.'

Kaiku kept her expression carefully neutral, allowing neither her dislike of the wiry scout nor her surprise that Nomoru had volunteered to cross her face.

'She's from the Poor Quarter,' Yugi said. 'She knows people. I want to test the water there, make contact with our spies. Those poor bastards in the capital have been living under the Weavers for four years now. They were happy enough to rise against Lucia taking the throne; maybe a little taste of the alternative has taught them the error of their ways. Let's see if the conditions have kindled any of that old fire.'

'A revolt?' Phaeca prompted.

He gave an affirmative grunt. 'Test the water,' he said again.

There was a silence for a moment, but for the dull percussion of the rain on the canvas.

'Is that all?' he asked.

Kaiku gave Phaeca a look, and Phaeca took the hint. She excused herself and slipped out of the tent.

'Ah,' Yugi said wryly, scratching under the rag around his forehead. 'This seems serious. Am I in trouble?'

'I was about to ask you the very same thing,' Kaiku replied. 'Are you?'

'Only as much as all of us,' he replied, looking around the tent at everything but her. He picked up a scroll case and began absently fiddling with it.

She hesitated, then tried a different approach. 'We have not seen each other as often as I would like these past years, Yugi,' she said.

'I imagine that's true of most of those you once knew,' he returned, glancing at her briefly. 'You've been otherwise engaged.'

That was a little too close to the bone for Kaiku. She knew her old friendships had suffered neglect, partly because of the war, mostly because she had devoted herself to Cailin's tutelage, which allowed time for little else. Lucia had become distant and alien, worse now than when she was a child. Mishani was ever absent, always engaged in some form of diplomacy or another. She had heard nothing of Tsata since he had departed for his homeland just after the war began. And Asara . . . well, best for her not to think about Asara. As much as Kaiku hated her, she was haunted in the small hours of the night by an insidious longing to see her erstwhile handmaiden again. But Asara was far to the east now, and likely would remain there, and that was best for both of them.

'The war has changed many things,' she said quietly.

'And none more so than you,' Yugi replied with a faintly snappish edge to his tone, looking her over.

She was hurt by that. 'Why attack me so? We were friends once, and even if you do not believe that any more, we are certainly not enemies. What has turned you into this?'

He laughed bitterly, a sudden bark that made her start. 'Gods, Kaiku! It's not as it once was between us. I look at you now and I see Cailin. You're not the woman I knew. You're different, *colder*. You're a Sister now.' He waved a hand at her in exasperation. 'How do you expect me to confide in you when you're wearing that damned stuff?'

Kaiku could barely believe what she was hearing. She

wanted to remind him that she had become a Sister to fight for *his* cause, that without the Sisters the war would have been over in a year and the Weavers victorious. But she held her tongue. She knew that if she opened her mouth, she would begin an argument, and she would likely destroy whatever slender bridges still existed between them. Instead, she swallowed her anger with a discipline which the trials of the Red Order had instilled in her.

'I suppose I cannot,' she said calmly. 'Please let me know the arrangements for our departure to Axekami.'

With that she left, stepping out into the rain where Phaeca waited for her, and the two of them walked through the crowded grounds of the songbird-house, back towards the river. For the first time in some while, Kaiku noticed how the soldiers unobtrusively moved aside to let them pass.

THREE

The triad of moons hung in a sky thick with stars. Two of them had matched orbits low in the west, descending towards the crooked teeth of the Tchamil Mountains, the flawless green pearl of Neryn peeping out from behind the huge blotched disc of her sister Aurus. Iridima glowered at them from the east, her white skin marbled with blue. Beneath, from horizon to horizon, lay the desert of Tchom Rin, an eternity of languid waves desiccated on the point of breaking. A cool wind brushed across the smooth, shadowy humps, dusting their crests. It was the only sound that could be heard in all the vastness.

Saramyr was riven north to south by the spine of the Tchamil Mountains, dividing the more populous and developed lands to the west from the wilder places in the east. The south-eastern quadrant of Saramyr was dominated by the continent's only desert, stretching over six hundred miles from the foot of the mountains to peter out a little short of the eastern coast. It was here that the settlers had come over seven hundred years ago, to begin the colonisation of the eastern territories.

Stories of those pioneer days were rife in Tchom Rin legend: tales of those who chose to stay while others went on to the more fertile Newlands to the north, those who made a pact with the bastard goddess Suran to live in her realm and worship her in return for being taught the ways of this cruel new world. Suran was kind to her followers, and she showed them how to thrive. In the wasteland of the desert, they built sprawling cities and gargantuan temples, and they chased out the Ugati and their old and impotent gods. The settlers took the desert as their own, and the desert changed them, until they had become like a people unto themselves, and the ways of the west seemed distant.

One of the greatest of the cities that the early settlers founded was Muia. It lay serene and peaceful in the green-tinged moonlight, in the lee of an escarpment that stretched for miles along its western edge. Tchom Rin architecture, so popular history told, had been invented by a man named Iyatimo, who had based his constructions on the bladed leaves of the hardy chia shrub, one of the few plants capable of surviving in the desert. Whatever the truth of it, the style proliferated, and the buildings of the Tchom Rin became renowned for their smooth edges and sharp tips. Bulbous bases flowed into needle-like spires; windows were teardrop-shaped, tapering upward; the walls that surrounded the city were made impressive and forbidding with rows of knife-like ornamentation. Though the lower levels of the complex, twining streets rose in orderly stepped rows of broad dwellings, the upper reaches were a dense forest of spikes, a multitude of stilettos thrust at the sky. Everything was drawn into the air as if the gravity of the moons overhead had sucked the cities of Tchom Rin out of shape and made them into something new and strangely beautiful to the eye.

Muia slept beneath the fearsome auspices of a statue of Suran some two hundred feet high. She was seated in an alcove carved out of the cliff face, a lizard coiled in her lap and a snake wrapped around her shoulders to symbolise the creatures that fed her in the desert cave where she was abandoned by her mother Aspinis. The belief in western Saramyr that it was arrogant to depict deities in any way other than through oblique icons or animal aspects had never taken in Tchom Rin, and so Suran was portrayed as the legends told her to be: as a sullen and angry adolescent, her hair long and tangled, with one green and one blue eye picked out in coloured slate. She was dressed in rags and holding a gnarled staff around which the snake had partially wrapped itself.

Suran did not have the grandeur of the majority of the Saramyr pantheon, nor the benevolence. The people of Tchom Rin had chosen a goddess that needed to be appeased rather than simply praised, a tough and bitter deity who would overcome any adversity and believed vengeance to be the purest of emotional ends. It suited their temperament, and they worshipped her with great fervour and to the exclusion of all others, scorning the passive and elastic religious beliefs of their ancestors. Though those outside the desert saw her as a dark goddess, the bringer of drought and pestilence, those within adored her because she kept those evils from their door. She was the guardian of the sands, and in Tchom Rin she reigned supreme.

Tonight, the city slept peacefully in the blessed respite from the heat of the day. But here, as anywhere else, there were those who needed the darkness of night for their business, and one such was on his way to assassinate the most important man in Tchom Rin.

Keroki flowed like quicksilver along the rope that stretched taut between two adjacent spires, heedless of the fatal drop onto the flagged and dusty streets below. Vertigo was a weakness he could not afford to have, and like the other minor frailties that he had possessed as a child, it had been beaten out of him during his cruel apprenticeship in the art of murder.

He reached the end of the rope, where it looped around the pointed parapet of a balcony, and slipped onto solid ground again. He allowed himself a flicker of humour: Tchom Rin architecture was pretty enough, but it did provide a lot of places to snag a rope. He left it where it was, strung between the two thin towers and invisible against the night sky. If all went well, he would be returning this way. If not, then he would be dead.

He was a short and thickset man, his appearance at odds with the grace with which he carried himself. His features were swarthy and his skin tanned dark by the desert sun. He was dressed in light green silks which hung loosely against his skin, tied with a purple sash: the attire of one of the servants of Blood Tanatsua. Often the simplest disguises were the best. He marvelled at how often he had heard of assassins masked and dressed in black, advertising their profession to anyone who saw them. His life had been saved more than once by the simple expedience of an appropriate costume for his task.

There were three guards inside the tower, but all were dead at their posts. His employer had promised it would be so. He had another man on the inside, for whom poisons were something of a speciality.

Blood Tanatsua's Muia residence was not an easy place to get into. In fact, had it not been for the virtually limitless resources of Keroki's employer and the amount of time they had had to prepare, it would have been impossible. He had already evaded or despatched at least a dozen sentries and avoided numerous traps on his way up the tower from which he had reached this one. The only way he had a hope of getting to his target was via this most circuitous route, and even then he was relying on the removal of some of the obstacles in his path.

But he was not a man to consider the possibility of failure. No matter what the difficulties and dangers that Keroki had to face, Barak Reki tu Tanatsua would meet his end tonight.

He slipped into the tower, through the rooms where the guards were slumped, victims of a slow-release venom that was so subtle they had not even realised what was happening to them, much less connected it with the meal they had eaten hours before. In contrast to the unadorned exterior of the tower, the chambers he passed through were lavish and ornate, with lacquered walls, lintels of coiled bronze, and wide mirrors duplicating everything. Globular lanterns of gold-leaf mesh hung from the ceiling, casting intriguing shadows.

Keroki did not appreciate the subtleties of the decor. His

sense of aesthetic appreciation had gone the way of his vertigo. Instead, he listened for sounds, and his eyes roved for clues that things were not entirely as they should be: a pulse at a guard's temple to indicate he was only faking death; a screen positioned to conceal an attacker; evidence of the bodies being disturbed by someone who had happened upon them and gone to raise the alarm. As an afterthought, he considered cutting the throats of the three men so that suspicion would not fall upon the poisoner, but he reasoned that they would not bleed enough to fool anyone with their hearts long stopped, and he dismissed the idea. Let the poisoner take his chances. He would undoubtedly have covered his own trail well enough.

Keroki headed down the stairs. The tower was made up of a succession of circular chambers, apparently innocuous, decorated as small libraries, studies, rooms for relaxing in and enjoying entertainment and music. Keroki's practised eye saw through the disguise immediately. These were false rooms, which nobody used except those guards who had spent weeks learning where the multitude of lethal barbs and alarms were hidden. They were placed here to protect the heart of the residence from thieves entering the way he did. Embroidered boxes on elaborate dressing-tables promised jewellery within, but anyone opening them would have their fingers scored with a poisoned blade or caustic powder puffed into their face to eat their eyes away. Valuable tapestries were attached by threads to incendiary devices. Stout doors – much more common here than in the west, where screens and curtains were used instead – were rigged to explode if they were not opened in a certain fashion. Even the stairs between the rooms were constructed with occasional breakaway steps, where the stone was a crust as thin as a biscuit and concealed spring-loaded mantraps beneath.

Keroki spent the best part of two hours descending the tower. Even with the information provided by the insider, detailing the location and operation of the traps, he was forced to be excessively cautious. He had not lived to thirty-five harvests by trusting anyone with his life, and he double-checked everything to his satisfaction before risking it. Additionally, there were some secrets which the insider had not been able to obtain, and certain traps which could not be simply avoided but had to be puzzled out and deactivated with his collection of exquisite tools.

He thought on his mission during that time, picking it over in the back of his mind as he had done for weeks now, examining it for anything which might compromise him. But no, it was as straightforward now as it had been when he first received the assignment. The morning would bring the great meeting of the desert Baraks, the culmination of many days of negotiations, treaties signed and agreements made. Presiding over all would be the young Barak Reki tu Tanatsua. It would be a unification of the Baraks of Tchom Rin; and with it, the cementing of Blood Tanatsua's position as the dominant family among them.

But if Keroki succeeded tonight, then the figurehead of the unification would be dead, and the meeting would collapse into chaos. His employer – the son of a rival Barak – believed that it shamed the family for his father to submit to Blood Tanatsua in this matter. And that was where Keroki entered the equation.

He had just made his way clear of the last of the false rooms when he heard voices.

His senses were immediately on alert. There should not have been guards here at the foot of the tower: the ones at the top and the gauntlet of lethal chambers in between were more than enough protection. A last-minute doubling of security? A failure on the part of his informant? No matter now; he was committed.

The men were beyond the door that he listened against. They were static, and judging by the tone of their voices and their conversation they were not particularly alert. But still, they presented something of an inconvenient obstacle.

He lay down with his eye close to the floor and drew out two tiny, flat mirrors attached to long, thin handles. By sliding them under the door and angling them in sequence he was able to obtain a view of the room. It was a large atrium with a domed and frescoed ceiling and a floor of clouded coral marble, overhung by a balcony which created a colonnade all around its edge. In the day, they would be lit by the light shining through the teardrop apertures in the walls, but at night they were cool and dark. Perfect cover.

Now that he had judged it was safe to dare, Keroki was able to ease open the door without a sound, lifting it on its hinges so that they would not whine. Once there was enough space to fit his head through, he peered out. Three guards, talking amongst themselves in the centre of the atrium, dressed in baggy silks of crimson and with nakata blades at their belts. The lanterns that hung from slender golden chains in the central space cast a dim and intimate illumination. The edges of the room were brightened with free-standing lamps of coiled brass, but it was not enough to dispel the patches of shadow.

Deciding that the guards could not see the doorway well enough to notice that it was slightly ajar, he slipped out and behind one of the broad pillars of the colonnade. His heartbeat had barely sped up at all with the proximity of danger; he trod with the calm ease of a jungle cat. The guards' voices echoed about the atrium as he glided from pillar to pillar, timing his crossings to when their talk would become particularly animated, or one of them would laugh, so as to cover even the slightest noise he might make. He knew how to move in such a way that he could evade the eye's natural tendency to be drawn to an object in motion, so that unless they were looking directly at him they would not detect him passing along the dim recesses of the cloisters.

His intention was to skirt the room and leave undetected through the door on the other side, which would bring him near to Barak Reki's bedchamber. In all probability he would have managed it had he not triggered the pressure plate that was hidden behind one of the pillars.

He felt the infinitesimal give in the stone beneath his foot, the fractional slide and click as he depressed it. His body froze, his pulse and breath going still.

Nothing happened.

He exhaled slowly. He was not foolish enough to think that trap had malfunctioned, but it appeared to be designed in such a way that it triggered when it was released. Standing on it merely primed the mechanism. Stepping off would activate it. Most people would not even have noticed the tiny shift that betrayed its presence; but Keroki was sharper than most people.

He cursed silently to himself. The colonnade had been left dark to tempt an intruder, and at its most inviting point a trap had been laid. Keroki's informer had known nothing about it. He should have realised that it was too easy.

Despite himself, a chill sweat began to form on his brow. He assessed his predicament. He was safely concealed from the guards, but he was also stuck here. Taking the weight of his foot from the pressure plate would undoubtedly not be pleasant for him. But what kind of trap was it? He could not imagine it would be anything fatal or overly dangerous, since this was a functional room and hence visited by people who would not know about the trap. Perhaps it was only rigged at night? Even so, he found it hard to believe that anyone would run the risk of accidentally killing a guest. An alarm, then; most probably a loud chime struck by a hammer that was cocked by putting weight on the pressure plate. But an alarm was just as fatal to him, for he had little chance of escaping alive if his presence was discovered.

The sweat inched down his cheek, and minutes crawled by against the background murmur of the guards. He had already wasted enough time negotiating the deadly false rooms in the tower; he could not afford to lose any more. Too soon the dawn would be upon them, and he had best be gone by then if he wanted to see another one.

He was still searching for an answer when the tone of the guards' voices warned him that they were ending their conversation. Then they fell silent, and he heard their soft footsteps heading away in different directions. It took him an instant to realise what they were doing.

They were splitting up and patrolling the colonnade.

He felt a dreadful flood of adrenaline, and mastered it. Years of brutal training had made him ruthlessly discliplined, and he knew when to take advantage of his body's reflexes and when to suppress them. Now was not the time for excitement. He needed to be calm, to think. And he had only seconds in which to do it.

When the guard found him, he was lying flat on his back and in such a way that the shadow of the pillar and the dim light combined to make him hard to see. The guard did not spot him until he was several feet away, and then he had to squint to be sure. It appeared to be a house servant by the garb, unconscious at the base of the pillar as if laid low by an intruder. And if the servant's foot happened to be still pressing down hard on the invisible pressure plate, then the guard was too surprised to notice.

He gave a peremptory whistle to his companions and leaned closer to investigate. Foolishly, he did not imagine any threat from the prone figure. He assumed that the threat had already passed on and left this poor servant in its wake. The assumption cost him his life.

Keroki twisted his body, bringing the small blowpipe to his mouth and firing the dart into the guard's throat. The poison was so fast-acting as to be nearly instantaneous, but even so, the man had a moment to let out a grunt of surprise before his vocal cords locked tight. By the time he had thought to draw his sword, the strength had left his body, and he was slumping. Keroki shifted to catch the falling guard's arm, pivoting on the foot which was still holding down the pressure plate. He pulled the man's weight so that he fell towards his killer, and Keroki muffled the sound of the impact with his own body. The guard was dead by the time Keroki pulled him onto the pressure plate. He sent a silent prayer to his deity Omecha that the mechanism was not especially sensitive, and then slipped his own foot off the plate.

There were no alarms.

The other two guards were calling in response to their companion's whistle now. Keroki slipped another dart into his blowpipe. Looking round the edge of the pillar, he saw one man starting across the atrium from the colonnade, and another in the shadows who had not reacted quite so decisively. Keroki aimed an expert shot and fired across the width of the chamber. The dart flitted invisibly past the first guard in the gloom and hit the man behind him, who slid to the floor with a groan. The sound was loud enough to make the remaining guard turn around. He saw his collapsed companion, swung back with his sword drawn, and took Keroki's third dart just below his eye. He managed a few seconds of defiant staggering before he, too, went limp and thumped to the ground hard enough to crack his skull.

Keroki stepped out from behind the pillar, glanced around the room, and clucked his tongue. The inside man who had provided the poison for his darts really did have a remarkable talent.

He dragged the corpse of the last guard behind the colonnade and used a piece of fabric to wipe away the smeared trail of blood and hair that he left behind him. Then, satisfied that the bodies would not be seen if anyone should casually enter the room, he headed onward. Dawn was pressing on him, and he still had to get back out through the trap-laden false rooms before the household awoke.

He found no more holes in his informer's knowledge. He negotiated the opulent corridors of the residence without another mishap, though twice he had to conceal himself to avoid a patrol of guards, and at one point he needed the assistance of a cleverly stashed key to allow him through a certain door that was always locked. Mirrored figures slunk alongside him in the silent corridors, where the cool air hung still as a dream, bereft of moisture. The night's hue became a deeper green as Neryn glided out from behind her larger sister and cast her full glow. Statues of Suran regarded him from spiked niches in the lacquered walls. Once a cat padded past, keeping to the corners, on its own mission of subterfuge.

There were no guards on the door of Barak Reki's bedchamber. His wife, so it was said, could not abide the idea of armed men so close as they slept. It was a foible that Keroki thought she would have cause to regret.

He put his hand to the door, resting it against the patterned surface, his other hand reaching for the blade of his knife. He got no further.

It was not the needle-bladed dagger that drove into his arm which truly stunned him, nor the hand that clamped around his mouth and drew his head roughly back. Simply, it was the fact that he had not heard them coming. He was tripped to the floor before he had a chance to react, and he hit the cold marble with enough force to take his breath away.

Now he found himself lying flat on his back once again, looking up at the ceiling, with a terrible numbness spreading like ice through his body. He tried to move, but his mind had been divorced from his muscles and his thoughts did not translate into action. Poison on the blade. Real panic filled him for the first time since childhood, a terror of paralysis that was raw and fresh and untested, and it pummelled him and made him want to scream.

Standing astride him in the darkness was a woman of almost supernatural beauty, with dusky skin and deep black hair, clad in a thin veil of a dress that was belted with silk. Keroki had purged all thoughts of lust from himself a long time ago, but even so a creature like this would have been enough to shatter his resolve, had the situation been different. But he felt far from ardour now.

She knelt down over him, straddling his waist with her hips. Delicately, she plucked the dagger from his arm and laid it aside, then brought her face close to his. Her breath smelt of desert flowers.

'Your friend with the poisons is outstanding, is he not?' she purred. 'Before I killed him I persuaded him to give me the one you are enjoying at the moment.' A slow smile, cruel and mesmerising, touched her lips. 'I thought perhaps I would handle this matter myself. No need to trouble Reki; there would be so many . . . repercussions. And besides,' she added, her voice dropping to a whisper, 'I like my prey alive. And I am so very hungry tonight.'

Keroki, believing himself to be in the clutches of some demon, tried anew to scream; but all he could force from his body was a whimper.

She laid a finger on his lips.

'Sssh,' she murmured. 'You will wake my husband.'

That was when Keroki finally realised who his assailant was. He had not recognised her at first, for he had never seen her face, and artistic renderings did not do her justice. Reki's wife. Asara.

She put her lips to his and sucked, until he felt something wrench free inside him and the rushing, bright flow of his essence came sparkling and glittering from his mouth into hers. His last thoughts as he felt the tidal pulses of his life retreating into darkness were strangely unselfish. He wondered what would be the fate of his land, the land that he loved although he had never known it till now, if a monster such as this stood at the right hand of the most powerful man in the desert.

FOUR

The unification of the Baraks of Tchom Rin was made official at mid-morning, in the western courtyard of the Governor of Muia's residence. It was a suitably grand venue for a day so momentous, set high up above the surrounding houses, protected by a wall whose top had been moulded into spiked cornices. The white flagstones and the pillars that ran around the edge of the interior were dazzling where the sunlight struck them. Verdant troughs of lush flowers were arranged around the central space; vines dangled through the wooden trellis that reached from the top of the pillars to the outside wall, forming a roof for the shaded portico. Steps went up to a dais at the western side, where the treaty was laid out, and beyond that it was possible to see to the cliffs where the enormous seated figure of Suran watched over proceedings with her odd-eyed gaze.

It was a remarkably sedate affair considering the importance of the occasion: merely a half-dozen speeches and a little pomp as the Baraks filed up with their retinues to sign the agreement. But then few people felt that this was truly a cause for celebration. Pride had been swallowed and old enmities grudgingly put aside, and the sting of it was bitter. Even as whole portions of Saramyr were overrun by the Weavers, even when Aberrants poured from the mountains to threaten their own homes, they had still squabbled and jostled between themselves for four years before finally accepting that they needed to band together for mutual survival in the face of the greater threat. It was not an easy matter to put their differences aside; they were buried deep in the grain.

One person who *was* celebrating was Mishani tu Koli. She stood near the back of the sparse gathering, holding a glass of chilled wine, as the last of the signatures were put to the treaty and Reki delivered the final speech. The rays of Nuki's eye slanted across the courtyard and the clean heat on her pale skin was pleasant and soothing. She felt lighter of spirit than she had in a long time. The treaty was completed, and her work was done here.

She had been in the desert almost a year in an ambassadorial role, for the Libera Dramach specifically and the western high families generally. Not that the time had darkened her complexion at all, but it had given her a taste for Tchom Rin fashion. Her dress was airier than she would have worn back home, a deep orange-brown like the last minutes of the sunset. Her black hair had been coiled and arranged with jewelled pins to fall in a multitude of braids down to the backs of her knees. She wore a dusky eye shadow, and small silver ear-ornaments. If not for her skin, she could have passed as a woman of the desert.

'Mishani,' said a soft voice in greeting. Mishani turned her head to see Asara standing next to her, watching the events on the dais draw to a close. As always, it took a fraction of a second to connect her with the Asara that she had known in the past. Even after all the time they had spent in each other's company trying to arrange the treaty that was being signed today, she could not reconcile this woman with the one who had been Kaiku's handmaiden. Something fundamental and instinctive in her rebelled against it, and had to be mastered by intellect. After all, they were physically *not the same*. Nothing by which she might recognise the old Asara existed in this new form.

Had she not known better, she would have said she was looking at a purebred Tchom Rin woman from the noblest desert stock. Her skin was tanned and flawless, her hair – blacker even than Mishani's – tied back in a simple ponytail that accentuated the elegant bones of her face, and drew attention to her almond-shaped eyes whose natural hue had been complemented by sea-toned eye shadow. Her pale blue robe was clasped at one shoulder with a brooch and clung to her figure, fluttering slightly in the warm breaths of wind that came from the west. She had dressed with the minimum of ostentation so as not to outshine her husband on this day, and yet all it served to do was to highlight how beautiful she really was.

But it was a false beauty. Mishani knew that, even if nobody else here did, except the Sister of the Red Order that observed from one side of the dais. Asara was an Aberrant, able to change her appearance to suit her desires. Her talent was unique among her kind, and Mishani was thankful that it was so. One of her was dangerous enough.

'You must be proud, Asara,' Mishani commented.

'Of Reki?' she appeared to consider this for a moment. 'I suppose I am. Let us just say I still find him interesting. He has come a long way since I met him.'

That was something of an understatement. Though they had never met, Mishani had heard accounts of Reki as an adolescent: bookish, timid, lacking the fire of his older sister the Empress. Yet when he returned to Jospa to take the title of Barak after his father's death, he had been a different person. Harder, more driven, ruthless in the application of his natural intelligence and cunning. And in four years he had not only made Blood Tanatsua into the strongest high family in the desert, but today he had succeeded in bringing the other families under his banner.

Mishani sipped her wine. 'You must be proud of yourself, also.'

'I do have a way of landing on my feet, don't I?' Asara smiled.

'You have heard, I suppose, about the events at Juraka?'

'Of course.' The Sister by the dais had told them both about it, having received the message from other Sisters who were present at the fall of the town.

'This treaty comes not a moment too soon,' Mishani commented. 'We cannot afford to be divided now.'

'You are optimistic, Mishani, if you think that the unification of the desert tribes will benefit the west,' Asara told her. 'They will not go to your aid.'

'No,' she agreed. 'But while the Weavers divert their resources in their attempts to conquer the desert, their full attention is not on us. And with this treaty and the collaboration of the desert Baraks, they might never take Tchom Rin.'

'Oh, they will, sooner or later,' Asara said, plucking a glass from a servant who was passing with a silver tray. 'They have the entire northern half of the continent and everything in the south-east outside of the desert. We hold the Southern Prefectures – barely – and Tchom Rin. We are encircled, and we have been on the defensive ever since this war began. Behind their battle lines, the Weavers have leisure to put into practice any scheme they can imagine. Like these . . . feya-kori.' She made a dismissive motion with her hand.

'I do not share your fatalism,' Mishani said. 'The Weavers are not in such a strong position as it would seem. Their very nature undermines their plans. Their territories are famine-struck because of the influence of their witchstones, and we hold the greatest area of cropland on the continent. They must feed their armies, and their armies are carnivorous, and need a great deal of meat. Without crops, their livestock die, and their armies falter.'

'And what of your own crops?'

'We have enough to feed the Prefectures,' Mishani said. 'The fact that we are driven into a corner means we have enough food to go around; if we had the whole continent to take care of, we would be starving. And since the fall of Utraxxa, I am told the blight is lessened slightly.'

'Is that so?' Asara sounded surprised. This was recent news, and she had not heard it, wrapped up as she was in foiling the inevitable attempt on her husband's life. 'That implies that it may retreat altogether. That the land might heal itself if the witchstones were gone.'

'Indeed,' Mishani said. 'We can only hope.'

Mishani and Asara stood side by side as the speech ended and the nobles and their retinues mingled and talked among themselves. The usual machinations and powerplays seemed subdued now, although there was an unmistakable wariness in the courtyard. Asara made sure the man who sent last night's assassin knew she was looking at him, then stared coolly until he broke the gaze.

'Will you be travelling west again, now that the treaty is signed?' Asara asked Mishani, looking down over her shoulder at the diminutive noblewoman.

'I must,' Mishani replied. 'I have been away too long. There are others here who can take my place. Yugi needs my eyes and ears among the high families in the Prefectures.' In truth, she was reluctant to leave, though she could not deny a keen pang of homesickness. But the journey across the mountains would be dangerous, and the memories of her trip here were not pleasant.

'I almost forgot,' Asara said. 'I have a present for you. Wait here.'

She slipped away, and returned a few moments later with a slender black book, its cover inlaid in gold filigree that spelt out the title in curving pictograms of High Saramyrrhic.

Mishani's time in the courts of Axekami had taught her how to conceal her reactions, to keep her face a mask; but it would be rude not to let her delight show at such a gift. She took it from Asara with a broad smile of gratitude.

'Your mother's latest masterpiece,' Asara said. 'I thought you might like it. This is the first copy to reach the city.'

'How did you get it?' Mishani breathed, running her fingertips over the filigree.

Asara laughed. 'It is strange. We have shortages of so many things that cannot get through to us due to the war, and yet Muraki tu Koli's books seem to find their way everywhere.'

Her laughter subsided, but there was still an amused glimmer in her eye. 'I know of a merchant who smuggles fine art and literature, most of which I suspect he steals from the Weaver-held territories where they have scant need of it. I asked him to look out for your mother's works.'

'I cannot thank you enough, Asara,' Mishani said, looking up.

'Consider it a fortuitously-timed reward for helping us achieve what has passed today,' Asara returned. 'At least now you will have something to read on your way home.'

Asara caught somebody's eye then, and excused herself to go and talk to them, leaving Mishani alone with the book. She stared at it for a long while without opening it, thinking about her mother. After a time, she left the courtyard unob-trusively and made her way back to her rooms. Her appetite for celebration had suddenly deserted her.

Reki and Asara made love in the master bedchamber of the Muia residence, mere feet from where Asara had killed a man the night before. The silver light of the lone moon Iridima drew gleaming lines along the contours of her sweat-moistened back as she rode him to completion, gasping murmurs of affirmation. After they both had peaked, she lay on his stomach, face to face with him as she idly twisted his hair through her fingers.

'We did it . . .' she said softly.

He nodded with a languid smile, still luxuriating in the satisfaction of the afterglow. She could feel his heart thump a syncopation to hers through his thin chest.

'We did it,' he echoed, raising himself up on his elbows to kiss her.

When he had laid his head back on the pillow, she resumed stroking his hair, her fingertips tracing the white streak amid the black, then down his cheek to where the deep scar ran from the side of his left eye to the tip of his cheekbone.

'I like this scar.'

'I know,' Reki said with a grin. 'You never leave it alone.'

'It is interesting to me,' she offered as an explanation. 'I do not scar.'

'Everybody scars,' he returned.

She let it drop, and for a long while she just looked at him, enjoying the heat of their bodies pressed together. He was no longer the boy she had seduced back in the Imperial Keep years ago. The loss of his father and sister, the sudden impact of responsibility upon him, had broken the chrysalis of adolescence and revealed the man inside. No longer able to hide from the world in books, nor under the repressive disapproval of Barak Goren or overshadowed by the vivacious Empress Laranya, he had been forced to cope and had surprised himself and everyone else with how well he had done so. The boy whom most had perceived as a weakling, while still not physically strong, had a fortitude of will beyond that which anybody had expected; and all his time spent in books had made him crafty and learned. His confidence in himself had multiplied rapidly, helped not least by the breathtaking woman who – to his bewilderment – had stayed with him through all his trials and supported him tirelessly. He was wondrously, madly in love with her. It was impossible not to be.

Of course, he still had no idea that she had murdered his sister Laranya and, by doing so, precipitated the death of his father Goren. Nobody knew that but Asara, and she, wisely, was not telling.

Blood Tanatsua had always been one of the strongest of the Tchom Rin high families, even after the slaughter in the Juwacha Pass that had claimed Barak Goren's life. The small advance force that had lost their lives there had not crippled the family, for the bulk of their armies had still been in Jospa, unable to respond fast enough to the news of Laranya's death. But under Reki's astute guidance, they had risen over the space of four years to the prime power in the desert.

It was not, however, all his doing. Circumstance had worked in his favour. The desert had remained a hard territory for the Weavers to conquer because the Aberrant predators that formed their army were not adapted to the sands and were at a great disadvantage there. But in recent months, a new type of Aberrant had appeared, one which might have been born for the desert, and it had begun decimating those territories near the mountains. Jospa, the seat of Blood Tanatsua, was in the deep desert and had yet to be threatened by this, but the other families had suddenly realised just how much danger they were in, and it was this that had spurred the sudden desire to unify. Blood Tanatsua had not been weakened by these attacks as their rivals had.

Then there was Asara. More than once a stout rival or an insurmountable obstacle to Reki's ascent had disappeared quietly and mysteriously. In the desert the use of assassination as a political tool was a little more overtly acceptable than in the west – hence their more thorough security – and Asara was the perfect assassin. Reki knew nothing of this: she took care to spend time away from him often, so that it would not occur to him that these instances of good fortune always coincided with her absences. Nor did he notice the occasional vanishing of a servant or a dancing-girl from their lands. He lived in ignorance of the nature of his wife; but then, he was far from the first man to ever do so.

'Reki . . .' Asara murmured.

'I recognise that tone,' he said.

She sighed and slid off him, lying on her back and looking up at the ceiling. He rolled onto his side, his hand on her smooth stomach, and kissed her softly on the neck.

'You are going away again,' he said.

She made a noise low in her throat to indicate he was correct. 'Reki, this will not just be for a week, or even several weeks,' she said. She felt him tense slightly through his fingers on her skin.

'How long?' he said, his voice tight.

'I do not know,' she replied. She rolled onto her side to face him; his hand slid over to her hip. 'Reki, I am not leaving you. Not in that way. I will be back.'

She could see his distress, though he fought to hide it from her. She even felt bad about it, and guilt was not something that Asara was used to feeling. Like it or not, this man had got under her skin in a way nobody but Kaiku ever had before. She could not have said if she loved him or not – she was too empty and hollow to find that emotion within herself – but she did not despise him, and that to her was as good as love considering that she secretly despised almost everyone.

'I have to go with Mishani to the Southern Prefectures. To Araka Jo,' she said.

'Why?' he asked, and in that one word was all the pain of the wound she had just dealt him.

'There is something I must do there.'

It was as blunt an answer as he had learned to expect from her. Her past was off-limits to him, and he had been forced to accept that before they married. Though she seemed little older than him, she had a wealth of knowledge and experience far beyond her years, and she forbade him to pry into how she had obtained it. It was a necessary stain on their relationship. Even Asara might be caught out with a lie if she had to invent a watertight past for her new self and maintain it over years of intimacy. The truth was, she was past her ninetieth harvest; but her body did not age, renewing itself constantly as long as it was fed with the lives of others. To admit that was to admit that she was Aberrant, and that would ruin everything she had worked to achieve even if it did not result in her immediate execution.

Reki was bitterly silent. After a few moments, she felt she had to give him something more.

'I made a deal, a long time ago. It is something that we both want, Reki. But you must trust me when I tell you that you *cannot* know what it is, nor how much it means to me.' She ran a sculpted nail along his arm. 'You know I have secrets. I warned you that one day my past might affect our present.' Her fingers twined in between his and held his grip. 'Please,' she whispered. 'I know your frustration. But let me go without anger. You are my love.'

Tears were in her eyes now, and answering tears welled in his. He could not bear to see her cry, and Asara knew it. The tears were a calculated deceit; they melted him. He kissed her, and the sobs turned to panting, and they joined again with something like desperation, as if he could salve the grief in his breast by dousing it in her throes.

By the time they were spent, he had already resigned himself to sorrow. She could always make him do as she wished. She had his heart, even if sometimes he suspected that he did not have hers.

FIVE

Nuki's eye was rising in the east as the barge lumbered downstream, following the river Kerryn towards Axekami. Paddle-wheels churned the water, driven by the groaning and clanking mechanism deep in the swollen belly of the craft. Vents on either side seethed a heavy black smoke that tattered and dispersed in oily trails. Once, there had been wheelmen to drive the paddles, swart and muscular folk who would labour below decks during those times when the barge headed against the flow or when the current was not strong enough to carry it. But their day was passing; many of the vessels that plied the three rivers out of Axekami had replaced the wheelmen with contraptions of oil and brass, pistons and gears.

Kaiku stood on the foredeck, the morning wind stirring her hair, watching the land slide by with a sickened heart. She was no longer dressed in the attire of the Red Order; her clothes were simpler now, unflattering and tough, made for travelling in. Her face was clean of the Sisters' paint. The cares of the past decade had not seamed her skin, though they told in the bleakness of her gaze sometimes. And it was bleak now.

The world had lost its colour. The plains that stretched away to the horizon on either side were not the sun-washed yellow-green she remembered. Even in the pale light of the dawn, she could see that they had been drained of something, some indefinable element of life and growth. Now they were doleful, and the occasional trees that grew in copses seemed isolated in a dull emptiness. Even the hue of the river water was unsettlingly altered to her eyes: once a blue so deep it was almost purple, it now seemed greyer, its vigour robbed. In days gone by birds would have circled the barge and settled in its rigging in the vain hope that it was a fishing vessel; but here there was not a bird to be seen.

This is how it begins, she thought. *The slow death of our homeland. And we do not have the strength to prevent it.*

She looked to the west, along the river, and there she saw a dim smear on the horizon and realised what it must be. She had heard the tales from their spies and from the refugees who had made it to the Prefectures from the Weaver-held territories. But nothing could prepare her for the sight of what Axekami had become.

The once-glorious city was a louring fortress, shadowed under a gloomy veil of fumes. The great walls bristled with fire-cannons, and other devices of war which Kaiku had never seen before. A huge metal watchtower squatted outside the south-east gate, dominating the road and the river alike. Scaffolding and half-constructed buildings patched the exterior of the capital. Kaiku remembered how she had been thrilled as a child to see this place, the wonder of their civilisation, the cradle of thought and art and politics. She was appalled to find it turned so, a forbidding stronghold steeped in a dark miasma that drifted slowly up to sully the sky.

The shanties of the river nomads on the approach to the city proper were deserted, their stilt huts empty. The nomads were gone. No longer would they crowd the banks and squint suspiciously at the barges passing by, no longer would they sew or string beads or pole out into the river for fish. The roofs of their huts were collapsing, crushed by the slow grip of entropy, and the supports on their rotting jetties tilted as they sunk into the mud. The clatter and growl of the barge's mechanisms disappeared into the silence as it slid by.

'What's been done to this place?' murmured Phaeca, who had joined her on the foredeck while she had been lost in reverie.

Kaiku glanced at her companion, but did not reply. She

always found it strange to see Phaeca bereft of the accoutrements of the Order. Perhaps it was because she was more used to seeing her with the make-up than without it, but Kaiku thought it suited her better when she was painted. It shifted the emphasis of her face favourably; when it was not there, she looked too thin, and forfeited some of her mystery and character. Still, what she lost she more than regained through her natural style. She had grown up in the River District of Axekami, and had a flamboyancy about her that Kaiku faintly envied. Her hair was always a masterpiece, her deep red locks twisted through elaborate arrangements of hair ornaments, here hanging in a tress, there coiled or bunched or teased into a curl. Her clothes were outrageous in comparison to Kaiku's, and though she had toned herself down today so as not to attract too much attention in the city, she still trod the thin line between elegance and gaudiness that characterised the fashions of the River District.

'Where is Nomoru?' Kaiku asked distractedly.

Phaeca made a noise that indicated she did not really care. Nomoru had, predictably, failed to endear herself to the Sister on their long journey from the Southern Prefectures. Even Phaeca, who was the soul of tolerance, had grown to dislike the scout's unremitting rudeness.

'Be aware,' Kaiku said after a time. 'The Weavers may be searching. Do not let your guard rest until we are out of the city again.' She looked again at the grim cloud seeping upward from the city and felt nausea roll in her stomach. 'And do not use your *kana* if you can possibly help it, except to hide yourself from their attention. It will draw them down onto us.'

'You're nervous, Kaiku,' Phaeca smiled. 'There's no need to remind me what to do; I know well enough.'

Kaiku gave her an apologetic look. Phaeca's ability to see through people was second only to Lucia's; she had an extraordinary talent for empathy. 'Of course I am nervous. What kind of fool would I be if I was not?'

'The kind of fool who volunteered for the mission in the first place,' Phaeca said dryly. Kaiku could not muster the humour to laugh. Her spirits had been too depressed by the ghastly shape of the unfamiliar city that loomed up before them.

The enormous stone prayer arch that had straddled the gate where the Kerryn flowed into the city was chiselled blank, the blessings gone. The grumbling, fuming barge took them steadily towards it. Kaiku feared to think what would be beyond that smooth maw, what she would find when they were swallowed.

If it had been a matter of preference, she would not have set foot on the barge at all. But the roads were carefully guarded by Weavers, and it was easier to slip into the city undetected at a crowded dock, so they had left their horses in a small town on the south bank of the Kerryn and taken this route. She despised every moment she spent aboard this craft with its mechanical core. It was a Weaver contraption, and Weavers created with no thought for consequence. She watched the greasy smoke venting from the barge with flat and desolate eyes.

Yet even they are not the real enemy, Kaiku reminded herself, *only puppets of a greater master.*

'Kaiku,' Phaeca murmured suddenly, a warning in her tone. 'Weavers.'

She had already sensed them, their consciousnesses purposeful as sharks, slipping beneath the surface of the world. They were hunting for Sisters, seeking any disturbance in the Weave that might indicate the presence of their most dangerous foes. The chances were slim that Kaiku and Phaeca would be noticed, but it was never wise to rely on chance. The Weavers' abilities had been unpredictable of late. Each witchstone they awakened increased their powers, and they had surprised the Red Order more than once. The feya-kori were only the latest example of that.

Phaeca and Kaiku sewed themselves into the Weave, blending with the background, becoming as inert to the

Weavers' perception as the boards of the deck beneath their feet. Such a technique was second nature to them, and required only a small amount of concentration and a minuscule exertion, not enough even to trigger the darkening of the irises that came as a side-effect of *kana* usage. They stood together as the Weavers passed over them, unseeing, and faded away to search elsewhere.

The barge slid beneath the desecrated arch and into the city proper, and Kaiku felt her chest squeeze tight in anguish at the sight.

Axekami had *withered*. Where once the sun had beat down on thronging thoroughfares, on gardens and mosaic-addled plazas, on shining temple domes and imposing galleries and bathhouses, now it filtered onto a place that Kaiku would not have thought was the same city had it not been for the familiar layout of the streets. A funereal gloom hung over the scene, a product of something deeper than the smoke that shrouded Nuki's eye. It exuded from the buildings themselves, from their shuttered windows and discoloured walls: a sense of exhaustion, of resignation, of defeat. It bore down on the Sisters like a weight.

The temples had gone. Kaiku searched for them, seeking out points of recognition from long ago, and found that where once the gaudiest and grandest buildings had stood there were strange carapaces of metal, humped monstrosities that sprouted pipes and vast cogs and vents seeping fumes. As her gaze travelled up the hill to their right towards the Imperial Keep at the top, she saw that the stone and gold prayer gate which had once marked the entrance to the Imperial Quarter had been pulled down. Even the small shrines in the doorways of the riverside houses were gone, the wind-chimes taken away. Without the religious clutter that adorned their façades, they seemed hollow and abandoned.

To their left, the archipelago of the River District was a shell of its former brightness and vivacity. Kaiku heard Phaeca suck her breath over her teeth at the sight of what her home had become. The great temple of Panazu had been destroyed and left to ruin. The cathouses and narcotic dens were empty, and those few people who walked its narrow paths or poled boats between the splintered islands were drab and went with their eyes lowered. The bizarre and whimsical architecture of the houses had not changed, but now it seemed foolish rather than impressive, a folly like an old man's last, sad snatch at youth.

Kaiku heard the catch in Phaeca's throat as she spoke. 'I think I'll go and change,' she murmured. 'Even this dress is too much for a city so dour.'

Kaiku nodded. It was a wise enough decision, but she suspected it was really an excuse to retreat and compose herself. Phaeca's sensitivity to emotions was a double-edged sword, and she was undoubtedly feeling the oppressiveness of this place far more than Kaiku was. She departed hastily.

'Find Nomoru,' Kaiku said absently after her, and Phaeca made a noise in acknowledgement before she was gone.

By the time they reached the docks, the fug in the air was thick enough so that it was palpably unhealthy to breathe, and Kaiku felt dirty just standing in it. The streets were crowded around the warehouses. Barges and smaller craft unloaded at piers amid the hollering of foremen; carts and drays pulled by manxthwa creaked by, heaped with netted crates and barrels; merchants argued and haggled; scrawny cats wound in and out of the chaos in the hope of spying a rat or two. But for all the industry, there was no laughter, no raucousness: cries were limited to instructions and orders, and the men worked doggedly with their attention on what they were doing. Heads down, concentrating only on getting through their tasks, as if existence was an obstacle they had to surmount daily. They were simply enduring.

Nomoru joined them as they disembarked. There were formalities: a passenger register to be signed with false names, faked papers of identification to be shown, a search for weapons. An officer of the Blackguard asked them their business, and reminded them of several rules and regulations that they were to abide by: no private gatherings of more than five people, no icons or symbols of a religious nature to be displayed, a sunset curfew. Phaeca and Kaiku listened politely, half their attention on shielding themselves from the Weavers who lurked nearby and monitored the docks. Nomoru looked bored.

They found their contact in the Poor Quarter as arranged. Nomoru led them, having grown up among the endless gang warfare that consumed the shambolic, poverty-stricken alleyways of this section of Axekami. Even here, the change in the city was evident. As squalid as it was, its occupants had always been angry, their tempers quickly roused, railing against their conditions rather than meekly submitting to them; but now the alleyways were quiet and doors were kept closed. Those people that they saw were thin and starving. The famine was biting even in the capital, and as always, the underprivileged were the first to suffer.

The sight made Kaiku think of Tsata, with his alien views on her society, and she wondered what he would make of all this. The memory of him brought a twinge of sadness. He had almost entirely slipped her mind over the years, buried as she was in studying the ways of the Red Order under Cailin; but his influence had lasted, and she often found herself trying to think of things from his viewpoint to lend herself a measure of objectivity. It was because nobody questioned the way things were that the Empire was in this situation in the first place: the ingrained belief that society could not do without the Weavers had allowed them to wrest the Empire from the hands of those who created it. Tsata had helped her see that, but then he had left her, returning to his homeland to warn his people about what was happening in Saramyr. As they walked through the dereliction of the Poor Quarter, she wondered vaguely if he would ever come back.

Their contact lived on the second storey of a tumbledown building, and they had to climb a set of rickety steps propped up with makeshift kamako cane scaffolding to get to the door. Kaiku's uneasiness had grown during their journey. Distantly she could hear the rumble and clank of one of the Weavers' beetle-like buildings in the eerily subdued quiet. The atmosphere here was an effort to breathe and tasted foul. If it were not for the fact that she knew her body was subtly and instinctively neutralising the poisons she was inhaling, she would have worried what damage it might be doing to her. Gods, what must it be like to *live* in this miasma?

Nomoru struck the chime and the door was opened by a sallow, ill-looking man. His eyes widened in recognition as he saw the scout. After an awkward instant, they exchanged passwords and he let them inside. He took them into a threadbare room where tatty mats lay on the floor. Sliding doors were left half-open to expose cupboards of junk crockery and chipped ornaments, and thin veils were draped over the window-arches, obscuring the view and making the room dim. An imposing, shaven-headed figure had moved one of the veils aside a little and was peering out at the street below. As they entered, he let the veil fall and turned to face them. He was ugly, with thick lips and a squashed nose and a brow that fell in a natural scowl.

'Nomoru?' he said. 'Gods, I never thought I'd see *you* again. You haven't changed a bit.'

Nomoru shrugged without replying.

He looked at the Sisters. 'And you must be Kaiku and Phaeca then. Which is which?'

They introduced themselves properly, despite his informality, bowing in the correct manner for their relative social stations.

'Good,' he said. 'I imagine you've guessed me by now. Juto en Garika. And that's Lon in the doorway. There's more of us, but we don't gather here. For now, you deal with me and Lon, and that's all.'

Kaiku studied him closely. His accent and manner all bespoke a life in the Poor Quarter. Like many here, he had no family name, but he took in its place the name of his gang, and the Low Saramyrrhic *en* prefix meaning literally 'a part of'. His sheer physical presence was intimidating. Ordinarily, Kaiku would not have felt threatened by that – not now she was a Sister of the Red Order – but the shock of seeing how Axekami had fallen and the fact that she could not use her powers within its walls had combined to make her feel on edge.

He sat down cross-legged on a mat without inviting anyone else to, but Nomoru sat down anyway and the Sisters followed her lead. Lon slipped unobtrusively away. The room was haphazardly set out with no thought to aesthetics, which mildly offended Kaiku's highborn sensibilities, but she told herself not to be priggish. If this was as much as she had to deal with during her time in Axekami, she would count herself blessed by Shintu.

'Let's get to it, then,' Juto said. He cast a glance at the Sisters. 'First thing, though: we all know who you are and your particular . . . abilities.' Kaiku was pleased to note that the familiar note of disgust when referring to her Aberrant powers was absent in his tone. 'It'd be best if none of us mentioned them aloud. Plots and schemes come and go, but anyone catches a whiff of you and they'll trip over themselves to sell you to the Blackguard.' He caught Phaeca's glance towards the doorway. 'Lon knows. You can trust him. Nobody else, though.'

'Do you two know each other?' Phaeca asked, referring to Juto and Nomoru. Kaiku had been wondering the same thing ever since Juto had first spoken.

Juto grinned, exposing big, browned teeth. 'We don't forget our own.'

'You were part of the same gang?' Phaeca prompted her. Nomoru just gave her a sullen glare in reply.

'Some time ago now,' Juto said. 'We'd given her up.' His gaze flickered to Nomoru. 'I went looking for you. Tracked you to the Inker that did you last. He said you—'

'Juto!' she snapped suddenly, cutting him off. 'Not their business.'

His eyes blazed for a moment, and then an expression of dangerous calm settled on his face. 'You haven't been Nomoru en Garika for a long while,' he said with an unmistakable threat in his voice. 'You be careful how you speak to me.'

She just stared at him, a challenge in the set of her shoulders, a scrawny creature with hair in spiky tangles levelling with somebody twice her bulk. There was no fear in either of them.

'How are things in the city?' Kaiku asked, in an attempt to break the stalemate. It worked better than she intended, for Juto bellowed with laughter and shook his head.

'Were you wearing blinkers on the way here?' he asked in disbelief. 'The people are crushed. The Lord Protector has the city under his boot heel and he'll keep on grinding until all that's left is powder and bone. Axekami is the lucky recipient of most of the remaining food in the north-west and still hundreds starve to death every day. The only good thing I can say is that at least we don't have the nobles siphoning all the supplies as we would have done under the *magnificent* government of the Empire.' His sarcasm was obvious and scathing. 'The workers get the food. And the Blackguard and the Weavers' damned Aberrant army, of course; that goes without saying. But the Poor Quarter suffers as ever, because some of us would rather die than go to labour in those gods-cursed constructions they've built in place of our temples.'

'And what do they do in there?' Phaeca asked. The Sisters had never been able to establish the purpose of the Weavers' buildings in the cities.

Juto curled his lip. 'No idea. Each worker only knows his own task, and what all those tasks amount to, nobody seems to be able to work out. They don't seem to *produce* anything. That's the cursed mystery of the things.'

He got to his feet and went to the window-arch again, looking out past the veil. When he spoke again, it was more measured. 'Then there's this murk. Old men cough themselves to death, mothers miscarry, the sick don't get better and cuts gets infected. What kind of people take over a city and then poison their own well? What idiocy is that?'

The question did not seem directed at any of them, so they stayed silent. He turned around and leaned against the wall with his arms crossed. 'They've outlawed the gods,' he went on. 'All of them. They're crippling any chance of rebellion by not allowing us to gather and coordinate. That's the reason everybody thinks they took down the temples. But heart's blood, it doesn't make sense! Letting the people have their faith would keep them calm, *discourage* revolt.' He scratched his ear and snorted. 'Some say they just want us to know that we haven't any hope. I don't believe that. I just think they hate the gods. Either that, or they're afraid of them.'

'And has it worked?' Kaiku asked. 'Do you think Axekami could be persuaded to rise against their oppressors?'

Juto sat down again, shaking his head as he did so. 'You could march an army up to the gates and they wouldn't dare to open them. It's not only a matter of spirit, though there's little enough of that left. We're weak and sickly. The Blackguard are fed and strong and there's more of them each month because people join up all the time. They see their families dying and their principles fade like mist in the morning sun. Then you've got informers and spies, all working to fill their bellies. The Weavers seem to know everything, whether by the cursed powers they possess or by the folk who've sold themselves. As fast as rumours start spreading about a new leader there are rumours that they've died or disappeared. And on top of all that, there's the Aberrants. The Weavers just have to say the word and the streets are full of them.'

'What about Lucia?' Nomoru interjected. 'Could rouse them then. If Lucia came.'

'Lucia?' Juto mocked. 'I won't deny the people would welcome *anyone* in place of the Weavers, Aberrant or not, but a legendary figure's no good if they're not here. I won't believe she's real till I see her with my own eyes, and even then she'd have to be in golden armour with the gods themselves singing her praises from the skies before I'd count myself safe enough to turn on the Weavers.' His tone was becoming bitter now. 'You think you can even *get* to Axekami with an army? I don't. The Weavers would crush you before you got north of the Fault.'

Kaiku took the disappointment stoically. She had expected such a response anyway. It did not take someone of Phaeca's skills to divine that Yugi's faint hope of picking up the scent of revolt would be thwarted; Kaiku had guessed that as soon as they entered the city. She did not think he had seriously entertained the possibility anyway.

'Enough of our troubles,' said Juto, hunkering forward and giving them a smile that was more like a snarl. 'What about yours? How goes the battle in the south?'

'That is a puzzle,' Kaiku said, brushing her hair behind her ear. 'It is much as we left it almost a fortnight ago. The Weavers have occupied Juraka, but there has been no move to cross the river as yet, and the feya-kori seem to have disappeared.'

'Ah, there's the meat of it,' said Juto. 'The feya-kori.'

'They came from Axekami,' Phaeca said. 'Do you know where?'

'I have my suspicions,' Juto said. 'But I've been waiting for you to arrive so we can take a look.'

'When can we go?'

'Tonight,' he said. 'After curfew.'

Kaiku considered this for a moment, then a small frown crossed her brow. 'What exactly do the Blackguard do to enforce this curfew?'

Juto grinned nastily. 'They let the Aberrants out.'

SIX

The Lord Protector Avun tu Koli trod warily through the chambers of his home. Despite Kakre's assurances that he would not be harmed, he could never be even slightly at ease in the areas that the Weave-lord had taken to inhabiting. The upper levels of the Imperial Keep had become an asylum.

The great truncated pyramid stood atop a bluff on the crest of the highest hill in Axekami. It was a masterpiece of architecture, arguably still unsurpassed since the fourth Blood Emperor Huira tu Lilira began building it more than a thousand years ago. The complex sculptures of gold and bronze that swarmed across its tiered sides had stunned visitors for a millennium with their intricacy and power, while the four slender towers that stood at its corners, linked to the main body of the Keep by ornate bridges, were as impressive now as they were all that time ago.

Throughout history, there had always been large sections of the Keep that were empty, simply because no high family had enough members to fill a building so huge, nor needed a retinue so large as to take up the spare room. Avun wondered distastefully what his ancestors might make of things now that the new occupants had arrived, and the Keep was finally filled.

The route to the Sun Chamber took him through room after gloomy room of depravity and madness. Weavers gibbered and rocked in clusters, hunched together, their Masks iridescing subtly as they shared the ecstatic bliss of their unseen world. Walls were smeared in blood and excrement, or scrawled with arcane languages which had sprung whole from the subconscious of the author. Abstract mathematics and diagrams, nonsense mingling with insights of staggering genius, were scored into priceless marble pillars or daubed across artwork that was hundreds of years old. The flyblown corpse of a servant, his lips and jaw eaten away by a roaming dog, lay in the centre of a room surrounded by strange clay sculptures, each precisely a foot high. An exquisitely clean and orderly bathing-chamber was guarded by a lunatic Weaver who spent his time obsessively tracing the grains of the wooden floor with his eye, and who screamed and flailed at anyone who entered.

Yet among these horrors other Weavers shuffled and limped, younger ones who had not yet fallen prey to the insanity of their kind. They were Kakre's lieutenants and aides, an assortment of bizarre figures who maintained their own private domains amid the chaos of the upper levels. Their own depravities only emerged after Weaving, when the trauma of withdrawal would trigger their particular manias, which were as varied and repulsive as imagination would allow.

The Weavers had always been careful to conceal the true extent of the damage that their Masks did to them, hiding away their worst casualties in their mountain monasteries; but here the inexorable and terrifying erosion of their minds was appallingly obvious. At least, Avun thought, the famine had provided plenty of victims for those Weavers who liked to kill or rape. He tried not to waste his trained servants when he could help it, preferring to use peasants or towns-folk culled from the Poor Quarter, but the necessity of navigating through this bedlam to attend to the whims of the Weavers had claimed the lives of many of them. It seemed that Kakre's decree of protection extended only to Avun, and anyone else was fair game.

The Sun Chamber had once been beautiful. The roof was a dome of faded gold and green, with great petal-shaped windows following its contours down from the flamboyant boss at its centre. It was rare enough to see glass in Saramyr windows anyway, but these were magnificent creations of many different colours whose designs had caught the light of Nuki's eye in days past and shone down onto the enormous circular mosaic on the floor. Now the light was weak and grim and flat, and what it fell on made Avun wish for darkness.

Kakre had taken the Sun Chamber for his own, and decorated it with the products of his craft. In the three galleries of wood and gold, where in ancient times councils had stood to attend to a speaker or watch a performance on the floor below, malformed and disturbing shapes hid in the gloom. Avun tried not to think about them. Here was where Kakre came to display some of the appalling art he made in his chambers many levels below. Every creation here was sheathed in skin taken from men and women and beasts while they were still alive, arranged as if in audience.

They had been moved around since last time Avun visited, and he unconsciously sought out the figures that had stuck most in his mind: the hunched figure whose left side was stitched from the skin of a man and whose right side from a woman; the winged being whose feathers were made of tanned and leathery sinew; the shrieking man from whose gaping mouth another face peered. There were animals and birds too, and other things not humanoid, frames overlaid with patchwork epidermis of many shades to form strange geometric shapes, or forms so repellent to the eye that they could not be classified. The accumulation of torture and pain and terror this room represented was more than even a man as cold as Avun could bear to consider. The faint shrieks of the tormented Weavers in nearby rooms only served to disconcert him further.

The Weave-lord Kakre was there, of course. He seemed to have lapsed into some sort of trance, standing immobile just off-centre of the mosaic that covered the floor. Avun approached quietly, watching him for any sudden movements. He had learned to be careful around the Weave-lord of late. Kakre's mental health had taken a dangerous slide in recent months, and Avun never quite knew where he stood with his master these days.

He studied the hunched figure before him. Like all his kind, the Weave-lord was clad in heavy, ragged robes sewn haphazardly together from all manner of materials – including hide and skin, in Kakre's case – and hung with ornaments: knucklebone strings and twists of hair and the like. The voluminous cowl partially covered the stretched, ghastly corpse-face that was his True Mask; the Mask concealed the even fouler visage beneath. Avun had never seen Kakre's real face, and never wished to.

'Kakre?' he prompted. The Weaver started a little and then slowly turned his dead face to the Lord Protector.

'You have come,' he wheezed, a faintly disorientated and dreamlike tone to his voice. Avun wondered whether he had accidentally interrupted Kakre's Weaving.

'You asked to see me,' Avun pointed out.

Kakre paused for a little too long, then shook himself and recovered from whatever befuddlement had been upon him. 'I did,' he said, more decisively. 'The feya-kori are ready once again. What is your advice?'

Avun regarded Kakre with his drowsy eyes. His permanent expression of disinterest belied a mind of uncommon ruthlessness. He did not look the part of the most important non-Weaver in Axekami, with his gaunt frame and balding pate, but appearances could deceive. He had rode the chaos of the Weavers' coup to make Koli the only high family to come out on top while the others went under, and in a short time had worked his way from being a mere figurehead for the Weavers – the human face of their reign – to becoming utterly invaluable to them.

'Zila,' he said.

'Zila?' Kakre repeated. 'Why not attack? Go straight for their core, straight for Saraku?'

'They expect you to move on and try to take the Sasako

Bridge, to push towards their heartland from Juraka. Do not do so. Let them know we can harry them all along their front. They will be forced to divide their armies, not knowing where the next assault will come from. Attack Zila with the feya-kori, take it, and fortify.'

'What good will that do?' Kakre asked impatiently. 'To chip away at them one town at a time?'

'War is not conducted in a headlong charge, Kakre,' Avun said. 'I would have thought you had proved that yourselves by now. Remember the early days, Kakre? That first sweep across the country after taking Axekami? Your only strategy was to fling as many troops as possible at your targets, counting your numbers as unlimited. You were beaten back time and again by forces one tenth your size. Because they used *tactics*. They knew how to fight wars.' He raised an eyebrow. 'As do I.'

He could feel the hatred in Kakre's glare from behind the shadowed eyes of the Mask. It was necessary to remind the Weavers of his worth now and again, lest they forget, but it was a risky business. Kakre was apt to lose his temper, and the consequences for Avun were usually painful.

'Tell me the details,' Kakre said eventually, and Avun felt the tightness in his chest slacken a little. He began to explain, recalling troop locations and the size of armies from memory, laying out the plan for his master. And if, long ago, he might have felt a twinge of guilt at betraying his fellow man this way, he felt nothing of the sort now.

The beginning of the war had not gone at all the way the Weavers had wanted it to. They had envisioned a complete collapse of the Empire, allowing them to overwhelm the disorganised opposition with their superior numbers and suicidal troops. But they had known nothing of the Sisters. With the Red Order knitting themselves across the gap that the Weavers had left and protecting the nobles from the Weavers' influence, the high families put up an unexpectedly efficient resistance. They were quick to recognise that their opponent had no knowledge of military strategies, and capitalised on it. The Weavers had the advantage in numbers; but the skilful generals of the Empire, well-studied and practised in the art of war, made them pay dearly for every mile gained. In time, it became obvious that even the apparently endless armies of the Weavers could not support such losses, and the Empire began to counterattack.

That was when Avun stepped in to lend his services. The Weavers were not generals: they were erratic, most of them were borderline maniacs, and they had no interest in history and so had not learned its lessons. Avun was shrewd and clever, and under his direction the armies of the Weavers became suddenly far more effective, and the Empire's counterattack was battered into a stalemate.

But by then the advantage had been lost. The forces of the Empire had retreated to the Southern Prefectures and held it tenaciously. The damage caused by the Weavers' ineptitude and the vast areas that they now had to keep occupied meant that the Aberrant armies were stretched thin, and the breeding programmes would take years to catch up. Time was both on their side and against them, for every witchstone unearthed made the Weavers stronger, but it accelerated the blight that was killing the crops.

The Weavers were impatient. They were afraid of their armies starving. Avun could understand that. But what he could not understand was what method lay in the Weavers' madness. A desire to conquer he could appreciate. The thirst for power through Masks and witchstones he could sympathise with. But the witchstones were *causing* the blight. It had been a secret for so long, but only the blind could fail to see the connection now. What use was a poisoned land to the Weavers? Even they had to eat.

Kakre would provide no answers, Avun was sure of that. But for his part, as ever, he would seek advantage for himself and his own, and as long as he was Lord Protector he had leisure to manoeuvre. Let the other nobles fight their hopeless battle against the Weavers' tide. Avun had made betrayal a science, and it had served him well. When the time came, he would betray the Weavers too.

But for now, he spoke his soft words of advice, teaching Kakre the best way to kill those he had once counted as allies, while distantly there came the hoot and gibber of the inmates of the madhouse that surrounded him.

He found his wife in her chambers. It was hardly a surprise to him. She almost never left them.

Muraki tu Koli was quiet, pale and petite, an elegant ghost whose voice was rarely raised above a whisper. Her long black hair fell in an unadorned centre parting to either side of her face, and she wore an embroidered lilac gown and soft black slippers because she did not like the noise that shoes made on the hard *lach* floors of the Imperial Keep. Her quill was scratching as Avun entered the room, inking vertical chains of symbols on a paper scroll.

She appeared not to notice Avun. That, too, was hardly a surprise. She spent a great deal of her time in her fantasies, and when she was there it was as if the real world did not exist. She had once told him, back when they were in something approximating a normal marriage, that she could not tell what her hands were doing when she was in that fugue state, that they set down words with a will of their own, as if she were a medium and others were speaking through her. He did not pretend to understand. He had marvelled at his wife's gift back then. Now it infuriated him. She used it as a retreat, and more and more she refused to return.

'Is it going well?' he asked, referring to what she was writing. He did not need to ask the nature of it. It was a Nida-jan book. It always was.

She ignored the question while she finished off a line and then put down her quill and glanced at him briefly through her curtains of hair.

'Is it going well?' he asked again.

She nodded, but gave no more answer than that.

He sighed and took a seat nearby. Her writing room was small and stuffy and lantern-lit, with no windows to the outside, only small ornamental partitions on the top edge of the wall to provide a throughflow of air. It was exactly the opposite of the kind of open and sunny place she liked to work. She hated this room, and resented working here. Avun knew that, and she knew he did. She was martyring herself in protest at being forced to remain in Axekami when she wanted to be home in Mataxa Bay. In such indirect ways she expressed her displeasure to him.

Avun regarded her for a time. She was not looking at him, but was staring into the middle distance. 'Are you sure you would not be more comfortable in a larger room?' he asked at length.

'The local air does not agree with me,' she replied softly. 'Did your meeting with Kakre go well?'

He told her about what had been said, pleased to have something to converse about. Muraki usually took little interest in anything he did, but they could talk politics at least. Or rather, he could talk to *her* about it; she never gave anything back. But she listened. That was better than nothing.

He exhausted that topic and, feeling the conversation was going unusually well, he went on with a new one.

'This cannot continue, Muraki,' he said. 'Why are you so unhappy?'

'I am not unhappy,' she whispered.

'You have been unhappy for ten years!'

She was silent. Contradicting him twice in a row would be too much for her, and she was plainly lying anyway. He knew exactly why she was unhappy, and wanted to draw her into a discussion. She did not like confrontations.

'What can I do?' he said eventually, seeing that she was not rising to the bait.

'You can let me go back to Mataxa Bay,' she replied,

meeting his eye at last. Then she broke his gaze and looked intently down at the paper before her, fearing she had gone too far.

But Avun was cold-blooded as a lizard and slow to anger. 'You know I cannot do that,' he said. 'You would be in danger there. You are the wife of the Lord Protector; there are many who could kill or kidnap you, use you as a bargaining chip against me.'

'Would you bargain for me, then?' she murmured. 'If I was captured?'

'Of course. You are my wife.'

'Indeed,' she said. 'But we have no love.' She glanced at him again, her face half-hidden by her hair. 'Would you sacrifice for me?'

'Of course,' he said again.

'Why?'

He gazed at her strangely. He could not see why she was finding this difficult to understand. 'Because you are my wife,' he repeated.

Muraki gave up. She had learned long ago that Avun's views on marriage and fatherhood had nothing to do with the finer points of emotion. Their own joining was one of political advantage, like many in Saramyr high society. There had been an element of attraction at the start, but that had long died, and they had been virtually strangers ever since.

Yet there was no possibility of annulment, even now, when the political advantage had become meaningless since the courts of the Empire had disbanded. She would not ask, and he would not countenance it. It would be shameful to him, a failure on his part. Just as he still refused to cut off Mishani from Blood Koli, even so long after he had driven her away. He would not admit to the dishonour of a wayward daughter, and yet he certainly would not reconcile with her.

'I am in the midst of writing,' she said after a time. 'Please let me finish.'

Avun took the dismissal with weary resignation. He got up

from his seat and walked to the doorway. Once there he paused and looked back to where his wife was already freshening the ink on her quill.

'Will you *ever* finish?' he asked.

But she had already begun scratching her neat rows of pictograms, and she did not reply.

More than six hundred miles to the southeast, high in the Tchamil Mountains, Mishani was reading her mother's words.

She sat sheltered in the lee of a rock, wrapped in a heavy woollen cloak with the wind blowing her hair across her face. She had put it into one enormous braid for the journey, tied through with blue leather strips, but some errant fronds had escaped and now tormented her. She brushed them away behind her ears; they worked free and came back.

Asara was nearby, feeding the manxthwa while the others went off and hunted. They jostled for their muzzle bags, nudging her with their heads. Mishani was surprised to hear her laugh at their impatience, and she looked up from her book as Asara playfully berated one of them. A smile curved Mishani's lips. The manxthwa's drooping, ape-like faces made them look mournful and wise, but they were in reality docile and stupid. They stared at Asara in incomprehension before beginning to butt her again.

The manxthwa had carried them from Muia, across the rocky paths of the desert and up into the mountains. They were seven feet high at the shoulder, incredibly strong and tireless, with shaggy red-orange fur and knees that crooked backwards. Since their introduction to Saramyr, they had become the most popular mount and beast of burden in Tchom Rin. Their spatulate black hooves, wide and split, dealt with smooth or uneven ground just as easily, and spread the manxthwa's weight well enough for them to walk on the dunes; they had evolved in the snowy peaks of the arctic wastes where the ground was soft and treacherous.

Though slow, they were nimble enough for narrow passes, they could go for days without rest as long as they were fed often, and they could survive extremes of heat without discomfort even beneath their thick pelts.

Once Asara had fixed on all their muzzle bags, she sat down next to Mishani and began rummaging in her pack. She was wearing furs, for winter at this altitude was cold even in Saramyr. Presently, she pulled out a small, round loaf of spicebread, tore it down the middle and offered one half to Mishani. Mishani put her book aside, accepted it with thanks, and the two of them ate companionably for a time, looking out across the hard, slate-coloured folds to where Mount Ariachtha rose in the south, its tip lost in cloud.

'You seem in high spirits,' Mishani remarked.

'Aren't you enjoying this?' Asara replied with a grin, knowing full well that Mishani hated it. She had been born a noble, and unlike Kaiku she disliked giving up the luxuries of her position.

'I can think of better ways to spend my day. But you seem glad of the journey.'

Asara lay back against the rock and took a bite of spicebread. It was baked with chopped fruit inside, and made a refreshingly sweet snack. 'I have been in the desert too long, I think,' she said. 'I need a little danger now and again. When you get to be ninety harvests, Mishani, you will know how jaded the old thrills can get; but risk is a drug that never gets dull.'

Mishani gave her an odd look. It was not like Asara to be so effusive. She usually avoided mention of her Aberrant abilities, even with those, like Mishani, who already knew about them. 'The gods grant I get to ninety harvests at all,' she said. 'Still, we have been fortunate so far. Our guides have kept us out of trouble. We may yet cross the mountains without running into anything unpleasant.'

'The Tchamil Mountains are a very big place, and I think there are not so many Aberrants out there as the Weavers would have us believe,' Asara said. 'But I was thinking of the danger at our destination.'

'That cannot be the only reason you chose to come with me,' said Mishani. 'There is danger enough in the desert.'

Asara gave her a wry smile. 'It is not the only reason,' she replied, and elaborated no more. Mishani knew better than to persist. Asara was extremely good at keeping secrets.

'Do you like my present?' she asked, out of nowhere.

Mishani picked up the book again and turned it in her hand. 'It is strange . . .' she said.

'Strange?'

Mishani nodded. 'My mother's books . . . have you ever read any?'

'One or two of her early works,' Asara said. 'She is very talented.'

'Her style has changed,' Mishani went on. 'I have noticed it over the previous few books. For one thing, she now produces much smaller tales, and has them printed faster, so that it seems a new Nida-jan book arrives every few months rather than every few years as before. But it is not only that . . .'

'I have heard they have become much more melancholy since your disagreement with your father,' Asara said. 'There are few that doubt she is expressing her own woe at your absence.'

Mishani felt tears suddenly prick at her eyes, and automatically fought them down. Her conditioning at the Imperial Court was too deep to allow her to show how Asara's comment affected her.

'It is not the subject but the content,' Mishani explained. 'Nida-jan has taken to poetry to express his sense of loss in his search for his absent son; but the poetry is ugly, and nonsensical in parts. Poetry was never her strong suit, but this is very crass.' She turned the book over again, as if she could find answers from another angle. 'And the books seem . . . hurried. She used to take such time over them, making every sentence exquisite. Now they seem hasty and haphazard in comparison.'

Asara chewed her spicebread thoughtfully. 'You think it reflects her situation,' she stated. 'Her writing became sad when you left. Now it has changed again and you do not know why.' She drew out a flask of warming wine and poured some for Mishani, who took it gratefully.

'I fear that something awful is happening to her,' Mishani admitted. 'And she is so far away.'

Asara settled herself next to Mishani again. 'May I offer you some advice?'

Mishani was not used to Asara being this friendly, but she saw no reason to refuse.

'Take wisdom from one who has been around a lot longer than you have,' Asara said. 'Do not always seek cause and effect. Your mother's words may not reflect her heart in the way you think. Forgive me for saying this, but you cannot help her. She is the wife of the most dreaded man in Saramyr. There is nothing you can do.'

'It is *because* there is nothing I can do that I lament,' Mishani replied. 'But you are right. I may be concerning myself over nothing.'

Asara was about to say something else when they heard the sound of scraping boots and voices from upwind, heralding the return of the guards and guides that were crossing the mountains with them.

'Be of good cheer,' Asara said, as she got up. 'In a few weeks you may be reunited with your friends. Surely that is something worth looking forward to?' Then she headed away to meet the men.

Mishani watched her go. She did not trust Asara an inch; her eagerness to travel west only made Mishani wonder what kind of business she had there. From what she knew of Asara's past, she had an unpleasant suspicion that it would be something to do with Kaiku.

SEVEN

The curfew in Axekami was heralded by an ululating wail from the Imperial Keep that set the teeth on edge and sawed at the nerves. Its source was the cause of much grim speculation among the people of the city. Some said it was the cry of a tormented spirit that the Weavers had trapped in one of the towers; others that it was a diabolical device used to summon the Aberrants from their slumber and to send them back when dawn came. But whatever the truth of it, there was no questioning that it was dreadful, both in itself and in what it represented. After the curfew, anyone found on the street who was not a Blackguard, a Nexus or a Weaver would be killed. There was no reasoning with the Aberrant predators, no pleas for clemency that would stay them in their purpose. They attacked on sight.

Juto cinched tight the straps on his boots and looked up to where the others waited by the doorway. They seemed nervous. Even Lon seemed nervous, and it had been his idea, his information that they were acting on tonight. Obviously wishing he had kept quiet about it now, Juto thought. Only Nomoru did not seem affected by the prevailing mood. She was slouched against one wall, checking the rifle she had borrowed, occasionally casting surly glances at the group in general. The newcomers had not been able to smuggle weapons into the city, so they were forced to use what was provided. Nomoru was clearly unhappy about it.

Juto stood up and studied the ragtag assembly. Gods, he was glad he was getting paid well for this. Patriotism, liberation, revolution: fools' games. Whatever agenda a man cared to operate under, Juto had found nothing put steel in the spine like the papery crinkle of Imperial shirets. If not for that, he would have been content to batten down and ride out the storm. But he needed money to survive in these hard times, and if there was one thing the forces of the old empire were not short of, it was money. As one of their best-placed informers in Axekami, he demanded his share of that wealth. It was unfortunate that sometimes he had to risk his neck in the interests of his continued employment, but that was the way of things.

They waited for the remnants of Nuki's light to draw away over the horizon, for the city's smoky shroud to choke the streets into darkness. Outside the silence was eerie. No footstep sounded, no cart creaked, no voices could be heard. Axekami was a tomb.

To break the silence, Juto suggested that Lon bring the newcomers up to date on events. 'And stop acting so godsdamned jumpy,' he added.

'Right, right,' Lon murmured, his eyes flickering over the assembled group. 'You all know the content of the communiqué I sent?'

'That's why we're here,' Phaeca replied. 'There was some confusion as to the author, though. Our information usually comes from Juto.'

Juto grinned, an expression which looked hideous on him coupled with his omnipresent scowl. 'Lon was very keen to claim the credit on this one,' he said. 'He wants to be sure I don't forget whose work it was when the money comes.'

'I was the one that saw them,' Lon protested in rough and ugly Low Saramyrrhic tones. He turned back to the sisters, as if seeking their support. 'And it was me who found out where they live as well.'

'Where they *live*?' Kaiku prompted, looking at Juto.

He nodded. 'That's where we're heading tonight. Out to the pall-pits.'

Kaiku's brow crinkled at the unfamiliar term.

'You'll see,' Juto promised, laughing.

'You said they lived there . . . ?' Phaeca inquired of Lon.

'I saw them. After they left Axekami and I sent you that message, after that they came *back*. After they'd been to Juraka.'

Kaiku did not trouble to ask how he knew about that. 'And you saw them?'

'I was right near the pall-pits. They bring a murk with them; it covers everything so you can't see, so they can move in secret. It covered the city, worse even than what we have now. But I was close enough; I saw them go to the pits. *Into* the pits.'

'There wasn't any . . . *murk* at Juraka,' Phaeca observed to Kaiku.

Kaiku shrugged. 'It would have hampered their own troops in Juraka. Perhaps they *wanted* us to see them. To let us know what we were up against.' She turned her attention back to Juto. 'And that is where we are going? These pall-pits?'

'Unless you have any other suggestions?' Juto replied.

'We will need to get close if we are to determine the veracity of Lon's information.'

'My lady, I can get you so close you can jump right in if the mood takes you.'

She let his irreverence slide off her. 'Have the feya-kori emerged again since you saw them return?' she asked Lon.

He shook his head and coughed ralingly into his fist.

Juto leaned out of the window and looked down into the street. A few lanterns burned in the depths of the houses, but none outside. Shadows were thickening. 'It's nearly time.' He turned back to them and gave them another of his nasty grins. 'Whatever gods you've got, pray to them now and hope they can still hear you in Axekami.'

The night was shockingly dark. With moonlight blanketed by the miasma that the city seethed under, and without street lighting, it was difficult to see anything at all. What illumination there was came from the feeble candle-glow that leaked from the buildings of the Poor Quarter.

Juto took them up onto the flat roof of the building, which was cluttered with debris and bricks, and made them stop there while their eyes adjusted. For the Sisters, there was no such need: their *kana* modified their vision, without any conscious thought on their parts, until they could see as well as cats. They waited for the others to catch up.

Beyond the Poor Quarter the hillside was crowded with pinpricks of brightness, topped by the clustered windows of the Imperial Keep. It might have been possible to look on such a sight and imagine the Axekami of old, but even at night the Weavers' influence was evident. The streets were black and quiet where once they had teemed with people in the lanternlight, and around the city the Weavers' buildings were islands aglow in their own industry, a red illumination from within that seeped through slats and vents: the glare of the furnaces. They stood out like sores, angry coronas limning the surrounding buildings that they hid behind. The air tasted of metal, thick with corruption. It did not seem to bother the others, but the Sisters found it made them claustrophobic, penned in by the threat of suffocation.

'I'm worried, Kaiku,' Phaeca said quietly.

'As am I,' Kaiku replied.

'No I mean . . . about *them*.' She motioned with her head to indicate the others; they had drifted a little way apart from the group.

'Juto and Lon?'

'And Nomoru.'

'Nomoru?' Kaiku was surprised. 'Why?'

'There's something between them. Something they don't want to reveal to us.'

Kaiku was inclined to agree. While Cailin's teaching left her less and less time to see her friends, it brought her into closer contact with the other Sisters, and of them Phaeca was her natural ally in temperament. Through sharing the trials of the Red Order's apprenticeship, they had come to understand one another very well, and Kaiku knew better than to dismiss Phaeca's intuition where people were concerned.

'They used to be in a gang together,' Kaiku murmured. 'It could be anything.'

'They're not pleased to see Nomoru.'

'Who is?' Kaiku returned dryly.

'But Nomoru volunteered . . .'

'Which is entirely unlike her.'

'Exactly,' Phaeca said, clapping her fingertips against the heel of her other hand. 'They didn't know she was coming, but she knew that they would be here. There's a history between them, that much is certain. And it's Nomoru who has chosen to dredge it up.'

Kaiku sighed, rubbed the back of her neck. 'We must be careful.'

'You ready?' Juto said, walking over to them. 'We'd better go. It will take us most of the night.' Behind him, Lon was manhandling a plank into place with Nomoru's help, lowering it to form a bridge across the narrow alley to the next rooftop.

Juto caught Kaiku's gaze and smiled. 'We're not going down to street level until we don't have any other choice. Not scared of heights, are you?'

Lon scampered across the plank and secured the other side as they approached. Kaiku looked over the lip of the alleyway into the empty street below. Nothing moved.

'Get on with it,' Nomoru hissed.

Kaiku gave her a disdainful stare and stepped up onto the plank. It was thick and solid, wide enough so that she would have thought nothing of walking its length if it were not suspended above a bone-breaking drop. Taking careful steps, she crossed the alleyway and stepped past Lon onto the next rooftop, which was similarly flat. The others followed without mishap, and then Juto and Lon hefted the plank between them and went to the other side of the roof.

'There, that wasn't so bad, was it?' Juto grunted as he passed. 'We're great improvisers here in Poor Quarter.'

In that way, they began to head round the hill on its westward side. Juto's preparations were certainly thorough. Though most of the rooftops were not flat but made of patchy slate, he had mapped out a route that meant there was always one adjacent roof or balcony that they could use. It was circuitous and indirect, certainly, but caution was needed over speed, and his method did not require them to touch the ground for the greater portion of their journey. The buildings of the Poor Quarter were crowded close enough that it was often possible to jump the alleys without needing the plank, and they began to spot other people doing the same thing as them, passing by stealthily in the distance.

As they went, Juto explained how this kind of travel had evolved in response to the curfew, and was used all through-out the Poor Quarter, which was the only place in Axekami where there were enough flat roofs to make it viable.

'It's a sort of truce,' he murmured, as they darted quietly across another dark expanse littered with derelict shacks. Men idled there, watching them as they passed. 'There's people who live in these buildings who'd cut my throat in the daylight; but at night, they give us free passage, and our gang will do the same for them. We might be dirty bastards, but we'll be gods-damned if we'll let the Weavers imprison us in our own territory.'

'Could we not have got closer to the pall-pits during daylight, and gone from there?' Phaeca asked. 'We would not have had so far to travel then.'

Nomoru snorted a laugh. Juto's lips twitched in response.

'You don't know the Poor Quarter,' he said. 'Believe me, that dump where you met us was as close as any of our gang could safely get. The pall-pits aren't far; it's just slow going.'

And it got slower, for the Aberrant predators were appear-ing in numbers now. More and more often Juto froze as if in response to some signal, and they crept to the edge of their rooftop or balcony to see the dark, sleek shape of a shrilling loping through the street below, its soft pigeon-warble drifting up through the night to them. Eventually Kaiku realised that the clicks and taps that she had thought were the sounds of boards settling in the night were being made by the men and women who lounged on the rooftops: they were lookouts, communicating in code, warning each other when Aberrants were nearby. She found herself marvelling that such a disparate group of antagonists could be so united in purpose against a greater enemy. It was like the battle for the Fold, when the people of the Xarana Fault had joined against the Aberrant army. Perhaps Juto was wrong; perhaps there *was* hope for an uprising, if the folk of the Poor Quarter were willing to put aside their differences and resist their new despots.

Eventually they came to the great thoroughfare that delineated the western edge of the Poor Quarter. They rested on the rooftop, overlooking the wide street, a river of deep shadow separating them from the more affluent districts on the other side.

'That was the easy part,' said Juto, hunkering down close to them. 'From here on in we have to go through the streets. We have to be fast, and quiet; and *don't* fire your rifles unless you have absolutely no other choice. Understand?'

'Is that it over there?' Phaeca asked, looking west to where an infernal red glow leaked into the sky, underlighting plumes of slowly roiling smog.

'That's it,' Juto said. 'We're close. But it only takes one Aberrant to see us, and it's over. Now you all know about shrillings, right?'

'Echo location,' Nomoru said. 'Helps them see when it's too dark for their eyes. Only forward, though. Can't see behind them.'

'It's mostly shrillings we'll be dealing with, though there's skrendel out here too, and they're hard to spot. Not so dangerous, but they'll put up a racket if they see you. Maybe ghauregs, but they can't see too well without any light. Chichaws, feyns. Assorted other types.'

Kaiku felt a strange thrill. She and Tsata had christened those creatures, among others, back in the Xarana Fault; it made her feel unaccountably dislocated to hear those names used here, hundreds of miles away. She found herself in a fleeting recollection of the Tkiurathi man with whom she had shared that feral existence for a time. They had seemed sweeter days, somehow.

They slipped down to ground level via a series of unsteady ladders and balconies on the north side of the building, after checking that the thoroughfare was clear. Kaiku felt her pulse begin to accelerate as soon as she touched the street. Suddenly the rooftops seemed a haven which she was reluctant to forsake. She clutched the barrel of her rifle, but it gave scant comfort, for like her *kana* it was a weapon of last resort and more likely to cost their lives than to save them.

'Stay here,' Nomoru hissed to the group at large. 'I'll go ahead.'

Lon made a noise of protest, but before he could speak Juto grabbed her arm. 'You won't,' he said. 'We stick together.'

She shook him off, her thin face angry, eyes glittering. 'I'm a *scout*,' she snapped. 'Wait for my signal.' Then before he could say another word, she flitted across the thoroughfare and disappeared into the black slash of an alley.

Lon swore in frustration. Juto motioned the others back against the wall, and slid to the corner of the building where he could get a better view of anything approaching. The clicks and taps of the lookouts were fainter here, but Kaiku still had the distinct impression that Juto was listening to them keenly, keeping track of the beasts that stalked their streets.

Time passed, marked by the thump of Kaiku's heart. She glanced at Phaeca, who managed a wan smile of reassurance and clutched her hand briefly. The night was full of small movements: rats scuttled along, hugging close to the buildings; part of a wall would crumble in a soft patter of dust, seemingly of its own accord; a stone bounced into the street from a rooftop, making them jump in fright.

'Enough,' said Juto. 'She'll find us. Let's move. It's too dangerous to stay here.'

Nobody protested. They slipped out of the Poor Quarter and across the street, where they were swallowed up by the alleys on the other side.

Lon took the lead now, moving with a purpose. They hurried through the narrow ways that lay between the main thoroughfares, pausing at every corner, scrambling into cover at the slightest hint of motion. There were more lighted windows here, but they were shuttered tight and only a tiny glow fought through to brighten the night. No lookouts aided them now; each turning could bring them face to face with the beaklike muzzle of a shrilling. Periodically they would stop and listen for the telltale warbling that the creatures made, which might give them a few moments' warning; but that did nothing to counter the threat of the other Aberrants who prowled more silently. Kaiku found her hands trembling with adrenaline.

'Back! Back!' Lon was whispering suddenly, and they flattened against the wall. They were in the middle of a long and narrow lane between residential houses, façades blank and featureless without the shrines and votive ornaments that they used to display. Dead plants straggled from clay pots, poisoned by the atmosphere.

A soft trilling coming from the end of the alley. Lon looked in alarm the other way, but it was too far to run. Kaiku felt a sinking feeling in her stomach, and gripped her rifle hard enough to bleach her knuckles.

'Here!' Juto snapped, and they scrambled behind a set of stone steps that descended from the porch-front of a house. It was pitifully inadequate as a hiding place: the four of them could barely cram behind it. Then Kaiku saw what Juto was up to. There was a cross-hatched grille there, covering the opening to the house's basement. He was pulling at it frantically.

Phaeca drew her breath in over her teeth. She was peering down the alley, where the lithe shape of a shrilling was silhouetted against the lighter street. It paused, head swinging one way and then the other, deciding which way to go next. The seconds it took making up its mind were agony for the Sister, who was praying to all the gods at once that it should go on its way and leave them alone.

But the gods, if they heard her, were feeling malicious that day. It turned towards them, and into the alley.

'It's coming,' she warned.

Lon cursed. 'Get that grille off!' he urged Juto, who gave him a roundly offensive oath as a reply. He had given up trying to pull and was shaking it instead, trying to work it loose from its setting. He had made some progress, for the stone was crumbly and weak, but it was still firmly in place.

'How close?' he murmured.

'Close,' Phaeca replied.

'*How* close?' he hissed.

'I don't know!' she said. She had never been good at judging distances.

Kaiku began to look over the edge of the step, but Lon pulled her down, and Phaeca with her. 'It'll see you!'

The warbling they could hear was merely the lower end of the aural spectrum of the shrilling's calls, which rebounded from objects and were picked up and sorted by sense glands in their throat, in a manner analogous to that of bats. The Sisters had captured live specimens in the past and studied them well.

Juto had freed up the grille a little, but not enough. The warble of the shrilling was becoming louder. He shook the grille hard. It was breaking away the stone bit by bit, scraping out dust and tiny pebbles, but it was still not coming free.

'Sweet gods, come *on*,' he pleaded. The shrilling was

almost upon them now, they could hear it, as if it were standing right beside them . . .

Phaeca grabbed his arm.

And they were still, all of them, like statues hunkered together. A moment later, the shrilling's head appeared, its long skull curving back to a bony crest, its sharp teeth bared beneath its rigid upper jaw. It came slowly forward, bringing its scaled, jaguar-like forequarters into view, and there it stopped, cooing softly, looking up the length of the lane.

The creature was mere feet away from where they crouched motionless in the shadow of the steps. They could see the rise and fall of its flanks, hear the hiss of its breath. They were paralysed, some ancient and primal biological response freezing them to the spot like a mouse in sight of a cat. It seemed ridiculous that the thing was *right in front of them* and it had not yet pounced.

But it did not see them. The darkness was too deep for its peripheral vision to pick them out, and its echo location system was too directional to detect them. At least, until it turned its head.

Still it did not move. The outsize sickle-claws of its forepaws tapped softly on the cobbles. Some animal intuition was pricking it, a sensation of being watched, of the nearness of other beings.

Go, Kaiku urged silently. They were close enough so that she could see the glistening black nexus-worm buried in its neck. *Heart's blood, go!*

She could sense Lon reaching for his dagger, moving slowly, slowly. She wanted to tell him to stop, but she dared not make a noise, fearing that even the movement of her lips or the disturbance of her exhaled breath would tip the balance here and bring the creature down upon them. Her *kana* was on a hair-trigger, coiled inside her, ready to burst free in an instant.

The shrilling padded onward.

Kaiku could barely believe it. They watched it go, prowling

up the lane, its sinuous form exuding a deadly confidence, its tail dragging behind it. She thought it was a trick at first, and she kept thinking that right up until the point where the Aberrant turned out of the end of the lane and was lost from view.

They sagged with ragged sighs of relief.

'I think we all owe Shintu a year's worth of thanks for that one,' Phaeca murmured, invoking the trickster deity of luck.

Lon was chanting a mantra of swear-words that were lurid enough to make even Kaiku uncomfortable.

Juto, visibly rattled, got to his feet and kicked the grille he had been trying to loosen. It broke free and fell into the basement.

'Come on,' he said in disgust. 'The sooner we're out of this gods-damned place, the sooner I get paid.'

They came upon the pall-pits not long afterward.

Nomoru had still not returned, and Kaiku was worried despite herself. She did not like the surly scout – nobody liked her, as far as she could fathom, though she and Yugi did seem to have a tacit connection – but she had become used to her, enough so that her disappearance made Kaiku concerned for her well-being. Phaeca was more pragmatic: she was only hoping that Nomoru had not got herself caught or killed and alerted the enemy to their presence. But the Weavers seemed quiet now; in fact, there was a curious absence of them, for when Kaiku and the others first arrived in the city there had been periodic sweeps across the Weave to look for Sisters or other anomalies, and in the last few hours there had been none.

The pall-pits were set into the hillside at a slight angle, and from where the intruders hid at the edge of the housing district they could see the whole terrible scene. A great swathe of the city had been levelled to make space for the pits, and rubble still surrounded them, half-standing walls and split beams and spars of metal piled in heaps or leaning against each other to form bizarre and discomfiting sculptures of ruin.

Beyond the waste ground the disorder ceased: the pall-pits themselves were built with ruthless precision. They were two sets of concentric circles side by side, enclosed by a wall of metal. Each circle was stepped lower than the last as they progressed inward to the gaping holes at the centre, colossal black maws that exuded turgid, oily smoke in vast columns. Wide, smooth ramps led from the inner pits to their outer edges. The red light of furnaces blazed along the tiers, trapped behind grilles and slats and vents, painting the pits the colour of dirty blood. It sheened across a grimy warren of pipes.

They paused for a time in the shadow of the houses, surveying the cluttered waste ground. The glow from the pall-pits pushed back the darkness; they would be exposed when they broke out into the open. Lon was more nervous than ever now, glancing here and there, his fingers twitching as if playing some invisible instrument. He kept on choking back coughs, occasionally eliciting an annoyed glare from Juto.

'We'll never make it across that,' he murmured. Then, tangentially: 'Where *is* that *bitch?*'

Kaiku felt irritated that he should be abusing a companion of hers, no matter how disliked she was; it made her feel cheap and disloyal to tolerate it. 'Will you be quiet?' she hissed sharply, and he gave her a resentful glare and held his tongue.

'We'll make it,' Juto said, responding to Lon's first comment. 'The fog's coming. Let's wait a while.'

Juto was right. There was indeed a thickening in the air, the murk drifting down in veils too heavy to stay aloft. The rank taste in Kaiku's mouth that had been there since they had arrived in the city became more pronounced, an unhealthy metallic tang.

'Could have done with this earlier,' Juto observed, scrunching up his face.

'Does it happen often here? The fogs?' Phaeca asked.

'Once in a while. Not often. Seems we really do have Shintu on our side tonight.'

The haze sank into the streets quickly, concealing the pall-pits and turning the waste ground into a red mist, in which shadowy shapes hulked like the carcasses of wrecked ships. At Juto's signal, they scuttled out into the disconcerting light, running low towards a heap of rubble and rusty iron beams. They skidded into cover in a scramble of loose stones, and Juto was just scanning to be sure all was clear for their next run when Lon grabbed his arm.

'We can't go,' he whined.

'What?' Juto said. 'Why not?'

'The fog. It's the demons. It's the *demons!*'

A spasm of disgust passed across Juto's face. Lon was cringing, his eyes darting about.

'Don't be an idiot,' Juto snarled. 'It's just fog. It doesn't mean it's the feya-kori's doing.'

'It's the demons!' Lon cried, trailing off into a strangled whimper as Juto grabbed him by the throat and pulled him closer, so that they were eye to eye.

'It's just fog,' he said menacingly. There was a moment when they held each other's gaze, and then Lon looked down and away. Juto released him. 'You're the one who knows the way into this place. Get moving, or I'll shoot you myself.'

With that, he broke cover, dragging Lon with him. The Sisters followed close on their heels. They charged through the dense red miasma, hid, looked around, ran again. Once Phaeca saw a dark shape lumbering at the limit of their vision, a mist-ghost that she swore was a ghaureg; but it did not appear again, and they had no choice but to go on. There would never be any better conditions for an infiltration.

Eventually they reached the wall of the pall-pits. It loomed out of the red fog before them, resolving into detail as they neared, a grotesque hybrid of stone and plates of metal. With Lon in the lead, they skirted round the curve of the wall, eyes straining for any sight of Aberrant guards in the swirling murk.

But fortune was with them once again: they reached Lon's secret entrance without being spotted. It was a square hole in the wall, where a panel had either come loose or been ripped off, hidden behind a pile of rubble and joists. Lon paused at it, looked pleadingly at Juto.

'It's the demons,' he whispered.

'Get inside!' Juto snapped, and they crawled through and into the pall-pits.

EIGHT

The murk was so heavy inside the pits that it was all Kaiku could do not to retch. Her eyes teared and became bloodshot, and her skin crawled. Her *kana* was ridding her body of the impurities she was breathing, and it was literally seeping out of her pores. She wanted nothing more than to be gone from here; but she had a task to complete, and there was no turning back now.

The tiers were mazed with huge pipes, or cut through with trenches. While it made picking their way to the centre a complicated task, it also kept them well hidden as long as they crouched. It was barely possible to see the next tier down anyway, and the pits themselves were only visible as a fierce red haze. They headed to the right side of one of the ramps that ran from the edge to the smoking abyss. While it would provide the most direct route, it was too exposed to travel on, and they found themselves wondering why it was so smooth and featureless when every other part of the pall-pits was so densely packed.

Lon knew his way, it seemed, however reluctant he was to follow it. He led them between bellowing furnaces that made the Sisters shy away; down steps of metal that clanked underneath their shoes; past slowly rotating cogs that rumbled threateningly. Kaiku had been near Weaver machinery before, but the din threatened to overwhelm her. She would have clapped her hands over her ears to shut it out, if she thought it would have done any good.

The murk seemed to be getting thicker as they descended, and with it a steadily growing sense of something . . . *other*. The Sisters exchanged a glance; they both felt it. Lon had not been lying: there were demons here. Even keeping their *kana* reined tightly, it was impossible not to register their presence in the Weave. It became more pronounced as they neared the centre of the pit; a vast and infantile malevolence, beyond human understanding, brooding in the depths. The feya-kori.

'They're here,' she said quietly.

'As promised,' Juto replied.

Phaeca was getting as jumpy as Lon now; Kaiku could see her out of the corner of her eye, starting violently whenever a swirl in the fog suggested the shape of an enemy. Despite her nausea and the fear of her surroundings, Kaiku was more experienced at this kind of thing than Phaeca was, and she held her nerve more steadily.

'Be calm, Phaeca,' she murmured. 'I will do the work. You have only to conceal me.'

'Gods, there's something wrong,' Phaeca replied, her angular face rendered sinister by the light. 'There's something wrong.'

'I know,' Kaiku replied. 'Let us do what we have to and be gone.'

They clambered down a ladder onto the lowest tier, and their surroundings opened out fractionally. There were fewer pipes here, only a few hulking metal chambers of some kind, and just visible across a short expanse of metallic flooring was a railing, beyond which a raging torrent of red smoke churned upward. The bellow of the furnaces all around the interior edge of the pit was deafening.

'Close enough for you?' Juto cried over the noise.

Kaiku gave him a look and disdained to respond. She walked to the railing, Phaeca trailing at her heels, and looked down. The smoke stung her eyes abominably. She blinked and turned away to Phaeca.

'Are you ready?'

Phaeca nodded.

'Then let us begin.'

They eased into the Weave together, subtle as a needle into satin.

This time, there was little of the euphoria that usually attended entry into the golden stitchwork of reality. Instead, a cold ugliness swamped the Sisters, emanating from all around, dimming the shine of the threads that sewed through their surroundings. The pall-pit before them was a black abyss of corruption, a dreadful tangle of fibres that sucked and boiled, concealing all within. Here in the Weave, the presence of the demons was more terrifying still: immense, dormant monstrosities just below the surface of their sight.

Dormant, and yet becoming less so. For now the Sisters realised that their growing awareness of the feya-kori had not been because they were getting nearer to their targets. It was because the demons were waking up.

'Oh, gods, Kaiku,' Phaeca said aloud.

((Stay with me)) came the reply across the Weave, phrased without words. *((We have time))*

Phaeca, despite her terror, did not falter. She knitted the Weave around them, blending them into its warp and weft, deadening the faint emanations of their presence. Kaiku was going to have to use her *kana* if they were to learn anything about the demons, and while she would make every effort to be as delicate as possible, it would still draw Weavers. Phaeca's job was to disguise them as best she could.

Kaiku fought to keep her composure amid the swelling awareness of the feya-kori. A part of her was sorting the implications of their situation even as she sent her *kana* into the pall-pit. The feya-kori could not have known they were here; they were not even using their powers to any appreciable degree when the murk began to descend. She refused to believe that the creatures were waking up in response to the Sisters' presence. Part of her thought that it was a trap, that the demons knew they were coming; but who could lay such a trap? Certainly not Lon, who was plainly terrified, and not Juto, who was in as much danger as all of them if the demons emerged before they had time to get away.

Nomoru?

She did not dare to think about it further. Gently, she subsumed her consciousness in the greasy plethora of the pall-pit. It cloyed and stroked at her, making her feel befouled. She ignored the discomfort and concentrated on reading the threads, following thousands of them at once, mapping the contours of their movements, picking them apart to understand their composure and purpose. She could feel Phaeca's presence behind her, brushing away her trail with consummate artistry. And in the depths, she could sense something massive stirring, and prayed it was only a murmur in the demon's sleep.

The belching smoke in the pall-pit was heavy with metals and poison. Kaiku set herself to tracing it, seeking out its source. She slid through vents, down black, churning pipes, spreading out across the city. Phaeca sent her a warning resonation, indicating that she would not be able to disguise Kaiku if she dispersed her *kana* so widely. Kaiku drew back, limited herself to following only a dozen or so routes. She felt suddenly irritated that she had been checked by her companion: she had a scent, and a suspicion was growing in her mind that she was eager to prove.

She followed it back to the factories, the grub-like buildings of the Weavers where men laboured, uncertain as to what they were producing. But Kaiku saw now. What they were producing was the smoke. It was piped from the buildings to the pall-pits, into a steam-driven system of gates and vents and airlocks and furnaces that regulated pressure and heat and refined the raw pollution into an even more concentrated form. And what ended up in the pall-pits was not like normal smoke.

It was *congealing*.

The awakening of the feya-kori was sudden and terrible. Kaiku felt the Weave bunch around her, drawing inward around the pall-pit, and a huge and baleful mind uncovered itself as if an eye had blinked open, drenching the Sisters in a wave of hostility. Kaiku pulled away, caring nothing for subtlety now, only wanting to escape the pall-pit before her *kana* became ensnared in the demon. She could not be sure whether they had noticed her or not, so minuscule was she to its attention; but their course was clear either way. They had to go. The smoke in the pit was thickening to a solid, and the feya-kori were coming.

She and Phaeca returned to themselves at the same moment. Perhaps seconds had passed in the world of human perception: Juto and Lon were still watching them expectantly. The Sisters twisted away from the barrier, their *kana*-reddened eyes wide in alarm, and in that instant a colossal arm of rank and foetid sludge reared out of the pall-pit behind them. Kaiku saw the horror on the faces of the two men, felt the sickening weight of inevitability as the arm descended . . .

It crashed down on the edge of the pall-pit, several metres to their right.

Kaiku did not even have time to feel relief that it had missed her. The need to escape was overwhelming. She could hear the hissing as the demon dripped and spattered over the metal, could sense the force of its presence emanating from the pall-pit. It was climbing out.

Juto and Lon had already turned to run, but they stopped still even as the Sisters did. Someone was blocking their escape.

Nomoru.

She stood at the foot of the ladder to the next tier, her rifle at her shoulder, trained on Lon. Thin and dishevelled as she was, the hateful expression on her face in the red light convinced them that hers was not a threat to be taken lightly. Juto's own rifle was up in a heartbeat, trained on the scout.

'What's this?' he demanded.

'Nomoru!' Kaiku cried. 'We have to get out of here!'

'Not him,' she said, tipping her head at Lon. 'The rest of you go.'

Behind them, a dreadful moan issued from the depths of the pit. The blunted arm-stump of the demon compressed as it took the weight of the body below. From the second pall-pit, away to their right, an echoing answer came.

'Heart's blood, Nomoru, we will all die here! Deal with this later!'

'Won't be a later,' she said, her voice steely calm, her tangled hair flapping around in the updrafts. 'Weavers and Aberrants everywhere. He knows.' She narrowed her eyes as she looked at Lon. 'Sold us out. Like he sold me out before.'

Kaiku went cold. Lon staggered, his knees suddenly going weak.

'Thought I didn't remember?' Nomoru called over the bellow of the furnaces. 'Thought I was too drugged on root to realise? You *gave* me to them.'

'Put it down, Nomoru!' Juto said through gritted teeth. 'Whatever you think he's done, if you fire that rifle, you'll be dead before he hits the ground.'

'Never thought you'd see me again, did you?' Nomoru continued, ignoring Juto, focused only on Lon. 'Didn't expect me back. Thought maybe you'd be able to get rid of me. At the same time you got rid of all the others. Juto included.'

'Nomoru . . .' Juto warned.

'Fixed the obstruction in my rifle,' she said to Lon. 'It'll fire now without blowing up and killing me. Thought you should know.'

'It didn't happen like that!' Lon cried. 'They came for *me!* I got away, but you were too drugged. You'd smoked too much! I never sold you.'

Phaeca jumped with a shriek as another of the feya-kori's massive arms crashed onto the lower tier of the pall-pit. Through the murk they could see the second one as an enormous silhouette, swelling from the ground as it pulled its body up. The position of the nearer demon's hand-stumps showed that it was clambering out to their right, far too close. At the bottom of the ramp which, they realised in a belated flash, was the the feya-kori's way in and out of the pit.

'Come on!' she shouted at Kaiku over the din. 'Let's go!'

'Not without her,' Kaiku replied, her hair lashing about her face.

'What do you care about *her?*' Phaeca howled.

'She is one of us,' Kaiku said simply.

'*Put it down!*' Juto roared, even as Lon tried again to explain to Nomoru what had happened that day, when she had been taken as an adolescent and brought to the Weave-lord Vyrrch, whom she had evaded for days before fortune allowed her to escape during the kidnapping of Lucia from the Imperial Keep.

'You want proof?' she said to Juto. 'Had to wait till I had proof. Went looking around. Weavers are hiding here. Waiting for his signal. He led us to them.'

'No, no!' Lon cringed, almost in tears. '*He* sold you! *He* did!'

He was pointing at Juto, whose face was a hideous rictus of anger. 'Why you gods-damned cur! You'd lie to save your own skin?'

'He's not lying,' Phaeca said.

'What do you know, you cursed she-Weaver?' he hollered over his shoulder.

'You're not a good liar. It's in your eyes,' she replied. 'He's telling the truth.'

A great, dreary moan rose from the pall-pit, and metal screeched as it took the strain of the demon beneath. Nomoru's gaze had moved from Lon for the first time, and was on Juto now. Kaiku dared not look away, but she could sense the massive shape of the feya-kori rising from the pall-pit over her shoulder, could smell its abominable stench.

'You?' Nomoru hissed.

Juto deliberated for an instant, then decided that pretence was not worth it any more. 'You were becoming a root addict, just like your mother. A liability. We could spare you, and it never hurts to be on the Weavers' good side.' He grinned. 'And since your friends over there can't use their powers without giving themselves away, and their rifles are useless like yours was, I think that gives me the advantage.' And with that, he squeezed the trigger and fired.

Kaiku did not even think. Time crushed to a treacly crawl. She was in the Weave before the ignition powder had sparked, was flashing across the distance between them before the ball had left the end of the barrel, and had caught it and torn it apart before it reached Nomoru.

She only just made it. The ball exploded a few inches from the side of Nomoru's face, peppering her in burning fragments of iron and lead. The shot that had fired from her gun towards Lon suffered no such intercession: it hit him dead centre in the forehead and blew out through the back of his head in a crimson spray.

Time snapped into rhythm again. Nomoru flailed backward into the ladder, her hand flying to her face, one side of which was a lashwork of blood. Lon fell to the ground. Juto looked shocked, unable to understand why his target was still on her feet. Then he turned to the Sisters in realisation.

And from above them, a doleful groan, and the Sisters looked up to see the feya-kori towering to their right, half-out of the pit, a slimy mass in the suggestion of a humanoid shape, with a mere bulge for its head in which two yellow orbs fizzed and blazed. Those eyes were turned upon them now.

'Gods,' Phaeca whispered. '*Run!*'

Nobody needed another prompt this time. Juto shoved Nomoru aside and clambered up the ladder and away; Nomoru scrambled after him in enraged pursuit, and the Sisters followed. They ran low, hiding themselves in the maze of obscuring pipes, shrinking under the dread regard of the demon. Nomoru was screaming at Juto, who was darting away ahead of them; she was still bent on revenge, apparently careless of the danger they were all in.

The feya-kori dragged its hindquarters out of the pall-pit, emerging from the column of red smoke, rising to its full height of forty feet at the shoulder. Its companion gave a cry, and it responded; then, with a slow and langourous movement, it swept one enormous arm down to crush the four little humans that fled from it.

They felt it coming, sensed the fog sucked away to either side as the stump came towards them, and they scattered. Nomoru threw herself beneath some enormous pressure chamber that was like a barrel of metal in a cradle; the Sisters flattened themselves against a rack of pipes; Juto ran on, seeking to outdistance the blow. The hand slapped down, spraying its acid vileness across the tier. It crashed into furnaces that buckled with the force and blasted steam and burning slag out in furious plumes. But its aim was poor, for they were hidden and it was only guessing where they were; though iron was bent and melted mere feet from Kaiku and Phaeca, they were unharmed.

The Weave was suddenly alive, heavy with activity. Nomoru had not been wrong: it was an ambush. Weavers were here, close by. Phaeca and Kaiku had not noticed them till now, since they were reining in their *kana* and the Weavers were hiding themselves. The Sisters knitted themselves into their surroundings, trying to become invisible to the searchers; but Kaiku's violent use of the Weave in saving Nomoru had given the game away, and they could not hide for long when the Weavers were on the scent.

Yet across it all was the huge and disorientating presence of the feya-kori, throwing the Weave into disarray. They were simply too massive to work around; they influenced everything with an overwhelming force, confusing the Weavers and the Sisters equally.

The Sisters did not dare to move. They could feel the

feya-kori searching for them, like a piqued child looking for ants to squash, its gaze sweeping the pall-pits. Kaiku's heart pounded in an agony of expectation.

Then she saw Juto, spotted him through the buckled pipes before them. He was climbing up to the next tier, still running from the demon. And there at the top of the steps Kaiku saw a pair of Weavers, their Masks turning as they scanned for their quarries. If there had been any doubt as to Nomoru's story, it was dispelled by the sight of Juto heading up towards them, hailing them as he went.

The feya-kori lumbered past them to their right, its steps accompanied by a shriek of metal as it stamped the landscape of the pall-pit flat. It had stepped off the ramp and onto the tiers. Heading for Juto.

He looked back in alarm, clambered up the last of the stairs so he was standing near the Weavers. It was evident that he thought it would provide some kind of sanctuary. He was wrong. The feya-kori's stump crashed down onto him in a geyser of sludge, turning Juto and the Weavers alike into burning pulp.

The Weavers' death-cry rolled across the Weave like thunder. Kaiku and Phaeca used its wake to dig themselves deeper into concealment, evading the frustrated minds that searched for them. The Weavers were distressed by the loss of two of their number. Kaiku found strength in that. She remembered Lon's reaction to the descending fog, and Juto's strange and mistaken certainty that it was nothing to do with the feya-kori. Matching that with the circumstances of the Weaver's ambush, she could only draw one conclusion. Neither the men who had betrayed them nor the Weavers who lay in wait had known that the demons were going to emerge.

Still they did not dare to move. They could sense the feya-kori waiting for them to show themselves. The Weavers had turned their attention to it now, lulling it, cajoling it in some fashion that Kaiku did not understand. After an agonising minute, the Sisters heard it turn and climb back onto the ramp. Kaiku dared a glimpse through the piping at their back, and saw it retreating into the red smoke. The second demon was visible as a ghostly blur beyond it. They were heading up the ramp, towards the Emperor's Road, a wide thoroughfare that led to the west gate. Gradually, the stench of their presence began to diminish, and with it their violent influence on the Weave.

'We have to go,' Kaiku said. If they did not take advantage of the Weavers' disarray now, it would be too late.

Phaeca was shivering, her pupils pinpricks in her red irises. She jumped at Kaiku's touch, startled back into the real world. Kaiku repeated herself, and Phaeca nodded tersely. They got to their feet and hurried to where Nomoru had hidden; but when they arrived, there was no sign of her, except for a rusty spattering of bloodstains.

'She can take care of herself,' Phaeca murmured. When Kaiku hesitated, her companion gripped her arm hard. 'She *can*, Kaiku. It's us they're after. She's safer on her own.'

Kaiku realised that they were still carrying their rifles, and she threw hers aside. She would not dare to fire it after what Juto had said. Phaeca did the same.

The steps that Juto had climbed had been melted by the touch of the demon, so they headed around the tier to find another way up. Without a guide, their path was tortuous, and they found dead-ends more often than not. As the demons retreated, the Weavers were returning to their search in earnest, but the Sisters were harder to find now that they had moved on. It was not only the Weavers they had to worry about, however: through a break in the miasma they spotted the tall, black-robed shape of a Nexus on a higher tier, and that meant there were Aberrants hunting for them too.

But the feya-kori's fog worked in their favour. As foul as it was, it was keeping them hidden. They made their way up two tiers in quick succession without encountering anything, and with distance the Weaver's probing grew less accurate.

Kaiku gave her companion a nervous glance. In the red light, without her make-up and dressed in dowdy peasant clothes, she barely recognised her friend. Nor did she recognise the expression of abject terror on her face. Kaiku, frightened as she was, had been hunted before, and she had survived then as she was determined to survive now. But this was new to Phaeca, and her talent for empathy made her mentally frail. The unrelenting expectation of running into a Weaver or an Aberrant – both of which would result in an excruciating death – was pushing her into the edge of something like shock. Her Weaving was suffering too, becoming clumsy and distracted; she was not disguising herself well.

Kaiku grabbed her suddenly, pulling her aside into the niche between two sets of pipes. She was only just fast enough. Her eyesight was better than the ghaureg's, and she had spotted its silhouette in the mist before it had registered hers. Kaiku clutched her friend close to her as the massive Aberrant trod slowly towards them, then on and past, leaving only a fleeting glimpse of a shaggy, muscular body and over-sized jaws packed with teeth. Phaeca's breath fluttered as she released it, and Kaiku saw that her eyes were squeezed tightly shut.

'We will get out of this,' she whispered. 'Trust me.'

Phaeca managed a nod, her red hair falling untidily across her face. Kaiku brushed it back, unconvinced.

'*Trust* me,' she repeated with a smile, and through her fear she actually felt confident. They would not die here. She would see to that, even if she had to take on every Weaver in the area.

She pulled Phaeca into motion, and they slipped away in the direction the ghaureg had come from. The air crawled with the attention of the Weavers, the threads of the Weave humming with their resonance. They were sending vibrations between themselves, throwing a net for the others to catch and hold, hoping that the Sisters' presence would interfere with the pattern. It was a technique Kaiku had never seen before: ineffective, to be certain, but it meant that the Weavers had begun devising ways of working together, and that was dangerous.

The Sisters cringed as something jumped across the aisle right in front of them, a shadow darting out of the murk and away. They froze, but it did not come back; it had not seen them. Phaeca was a wreck after that, but Kaiku urged her up another set of steps and onto a higher tier. They were hopelessly lost, navigating only by the brighter glow in the mist that was the pall-pit's centre. The plaintive wail of the feya-kori came to them distantly.

Kaiku said a quick prayer to Shintu – she could not decide whether he was on their side or not tonight, but with what she knew of the god of fortune it was probably both and neither – and an instant later she turned a corner and almost ran into the outer wall of the pit.

She blinked in surprise.

'It's the wall . . .' Phaeca said, a slowly dawning hope in her voice.

Kaiku gave her a companionable squeeze on the arm. 'See? Have faith.' She looked up at it. It was only nine feet high. Scalable. They would not have to waste time looking for the way in that Lon had provided for them.

'Help me up,' Kaiku said. Phaeca glanced around, seeing only the swirling mist – which was gradually beginning to lift with the departure of the demons – and the dark bulk of the Weaver contraptions that hummed and tapped. Convinced that there was nothing immediately nearby, she made a stirrup with her hands for Kaiku to step into. Kaiku boosted herself up onto the wall, and Phaeca jumped as her friend unexpectedly shrieked. Her fingers came loose and Kaiku fell back down, landed on her heels and collapsed onto her back. She scrambled to her feet, and her forearms were running with blood.

Phaeca was frantic. The Weavers' attention had devolved upon them suddenly, drawn by the scream.

'Again,' Kaiku said through gritted teeth.

'But it's—'

'*Again!*'

For she knew that her cry had given them away, and if they did not get out of there now they were not getting out at all. Phaeca hurriedly knitted her fingers again and Kaiku threw herself up before her instinct for self-preservation could stop her. The thin bladed fins atop the wall cut into her arms in a dozen different places, slicing across the existing cuts, bringing tears to her eyes. Her *kana* was racing to repair the damage, awakening without her volition; she forced it down, for it would bring the Weavers more surely than her scream had. She lifted her weight, driving the blades deeper into her flesh, tiny razors that ribboned her skin agonisingly. She got one foot to the top of the wall, holding her body clear, and then she stood in one convulsive movement. The blades slid clear of her, and the pain was so exquisite that she almost fainted.

'Kaiku!'

It was Phaeca's cry that brought her back from the brink. She staggered, and the blades cut through the sole of her boot and pricked into her heel. With a moan, she bent down, holding her arm out, and only then did she catch sight of the thing thumping towards Phaeca from the right. It was a feyn, an awful collision between a bear and a lizard, with the worst features of each. Phaeca's expression was desperate, frantic: she saw Kaiku leaning down and she jumped. Kaiku braced just in time, her adrenaline pumping, and she caught Phaeca and hauled her up and over the wall. Phaeca's legs dragged across the blades as she went, carving through her trousers and darkening them in red, but she somehow got them under her again in time for Kaiku to drop her over the other side of the wall.

Kaiku had one last glimpse of the enraged monstrosity before she pulled her foot free and jumped down next to Phaeca, who was picking herself up, tears blurring her eyes.

She was whimpering; Kaiku, whose wounds were much worse, was silent. They staggered across the waste ground towards the city, and the fog swallowed them, leaving the fruitless questing of the Weavers behind them like the buzzing of angry wasps.

Kaiku did not remember the journey back to the Poor Quarter, and the sanctuary of the rooftops. She did not know what Phaeca said to the men that they found there. She remembered rough faces and an ugly dialect, questions which frightened her; and then dirty bandages, mummifying her arms and enwrapping her feet. They were little more than strips of cloth. At some point her ability to suppress her *kana* had slipped: she could feel her body healing itself restlessly.

She never exactly lost consciousness, but she slipped out of the world for a time, and when she came back to it she was in a bare room, and a grey dawn was brightening outside. Her head was on Phaeca's breast, and she was being held like a baby. Her arms burned. She became aware that Phaeca was Weaving, concealing the activity within Kaiku's body as the power inside her repaired the damage done to its host. She felt hollow, as if there was a vacuum in her veins where the lost blood should be. But she was alive.

'Kaiku?' Phaeca's voice came simultaneously from her mouth and reverberantly though her breastbone.

'I am here,' she said.

There was a silence for a time. 'You faded away for a while.'

'It takes more than that to kill a Sister,' she replied, with a faint chuckle that hurt too much to continue. Then, because the bravado felt good, she added: 'I told you to trust me.'

'You did,' Phaeca agreed.

Kaiku swallowed against a dry throat. 'Where are we?'

'The building belongs to a gang. I don't know their name.'

'Are we prisoners?'

'No.'

'Not even . . . did they see our eyes?'

'Of course,' Phaeca said. 'They know we're Aberrants. I could scarcely conceal it from them.'

Kaiku sat up slowly and felt lightheaded. Phaeca put out a hand to help her, but Kaiku waved her off. She steadied herself, took a few breaths, and raked her tawny hair back.

'What will they do? What did you tell them?'

'I told them the truth,' said Phaeca simply. 'What they will do is up to them. We're in no state to do anything about it.'

Kaiku frowned. 'You are very calm.'

'Should I be scared of *men*? After what we saw in the pall-pits?' Phaeca's face was wry. 'I think they already knew of us. I believe they believed me. Aberrants are the least of their worries here in the Poor Quarter. And now we are not the scapegoat for all the world's ills, people like these have found somewhere new to put their hate.'

Kaiku looked around the room. It smelt of mildew. The wooden walls were greened with mould, and the beams were dank. A few dirty pillows were thrown in one corner, and a heavy drape hung across the doorway. No lantern burned here; they must have been sitting in the dark.

Kaiku noticed then the bandages around her friend's legs, beneath the bloodied tatters of her trousers. 'Spirits, Phaeca, you're hurt too.' She remembered what had happened as she said it.

'Not as badly as you were,' she replied, and there was something in her eyes, some depth of gratitude that words were inadequate to express. She looked away. 'I'll deal with it later. Until then, you rest.'

Kaiku sagged, and Phaeca put her arm round her friend again, letting her rest her head. 'I am tired,' Kaiku murmured.

They heard footsteps, and the drape was pulled back. Kaiku did not even rouse herself from Phaeca; her muscles were too heavy. Two men came in: one was very tall and thickly bearded; the other had shaggy brown hair and a rugged, pitted face, and when he spoke Kaiku saw that his teeth were made of brass.

'We've been talking,' he said, without introduction or preamble.

Phaeca looked at him squarely. 'And what have you decided?'

The brass-toothed man squatted down in front of them. 'We've decided that you look like you need a hand.'

NINE

Yugi tu Xamata, leader of the Libera Dramach, awoke in his cell at Araka Jo to find Lucia standing at the window, looking out onto the lake. His head was thick with amaxa root. His hookah stood cold in the corner, but the sharp scent remained in the air, evidence of another night of over-indulgence. He sat up on his sleeping-mat, the blanket falling away from his bare shoulders. It was chilly in winter at these altitudes, and there was no glass in the windows, but he had been burning up with narcotic fever last night.

He blinked, frowning, and squinted at Lucia. Whether by a trick of the morning light or his own mind, she looked ethereal, her slender form transparent, her thin white-and-gold dress a veil. Yugi had never known Lucia's mother, but he was told that she resembled Anais strongly in her petite, pretty features and the pale blonde colour of her hair. But there the similarity ended: the hair was cut short and boyish, revealing the appallingly trenched and rucked scar-flesh at the back of her neck, and her light blue eyes told a story that nobody else could share. She was eighteen harvests of age, and the child he had watched grow had gone, replaced by something beautiful and alien.

He coughed to clear his throat of the taste of last night's excesses. When Lucia did not react, he dispensed with politeness. 'What are you doing here, Lucia?'

After a long moment, Lucia turned her head to him. 'Hmm?'

'You're in my room,' Yugi said patiently. 'Why are you in my room?'

She seemed puzzled by that for a moment. She glanced

around the cell as if wondering how she got there: great blocks of weathered white stone draped with simple hangings, a wicker mat covering the floor, a small table, a chest, other odds and ends scattered about. Then she gave him a smile as innocent as an infant's.

'We want to see you.'

'We?'

'Cailin and I.'

Yugi sighed and sat up further, the blankets sloughing to his waist. His upper torso was almost smooth of hair, but several long cicatrices tracked over the skin, old wounds from long ago. He did not like the way she phrased her words, the implication that Lucia and Cailin had decided to summon him together. Cailin was held in altogether too high a regard by this girl, and that was dangerous. He knew what Cailin was like.

'What's this about?'

'News from Axekami,' she said, and did not elaborate. 'We'll be by the lake.'

Yugi decided not to bother asking her any more questions. 'I'll come and find you.'

Lucia gave him another smile, and turned to leave. As she did so, the hookah overturned with a crash, spilling ash and charred root onto the mat. Yugi jumped.

'He doesn't like the way you make his room smell,' Lucia said, and then went out through the drape.

Yugi got up and dressed himself. The cold chased off the tatters of sleep. He set the hookah back upright and tidied the ash away, annoyed. The spirit had never managed anything quite so violent before. He could sense it there, a tall black smudge just on the edge of his vision, but he knew that if he looked at it directly, it would be gone. It was a peripheral thing, seen only from the corner of the eye. A weak ghost, like the hundreds of others that haunted Araka Jo, clots of congealed memory that dogged the present.

Outside his cell was a walkway of the same ubiquitous

white stone that formed the bones of the complex. On one side was a long row of cells like his own, simple rectangular doorways; the other was open to the view.

It was something to wake up to, he had to admit that, even though the dregs of last night were somewhat blunting his appreciation. The ground sloped down to a wide road, again of white and aged stone, and beyond that it swept up, to where the scalloped slate roofs of the temples showed among the jagged green treetops. The swoop and swell of the mountainside hid dozens of them, all linked by dirt paths or flagged walkways that wound through the pines and kijis and kamakas. They were solid and crude in comparison to modern temples, but their form gave them a gravity that was primal and brooding, and the bas-relief friezes on their entablatures depicted scenes heavy with forgotten myth.

Araka Jo was ancient and in partial ruin, several of the temples little more than outlines of their original floorplan surrounded by mossy rubble. Despite the unfamiliar presence of inhabitants again – it had become the Libera Dramach's home these past few years – it still felt as if they were intruders there. The spirits never let them forget it.

There was a stone basin near his doorway, from which he splashed icy water on his face to wake himself. Once he was done, he removed the dirty rag from his forehead and wet his hair, smoothing it back into untidy spikes before reattaching the rag. He had slept in it, as usual.

That done, he went to find some lathamri. People were up and about even at this early hour, travelling to and fro along the roads of the complex, on visits and errands and business. Several people he greeted on his way, the cheery façade snapping into place automatically. Everyone knew him as the leader of the community. Unlike their previous hideout in the Fold, the Libera Dramach did not operate in secret in Araka Jo. Everybody here knew about Lucia, and the organisation that had been built around her. Everybody here was Libera Dramach by allegiance. Anybody who had not been able to stomach that had gone elsewhere in the Southern Prefectures.

He turned off the thoroughfare to where a side-road was lined with wooden stalls, feeling exhausted even by that short journey. The tiredness was not physical – he had always been healthy as a mule – but a weariness of spirit that weighed him down. His smile felt false now, more so than ever before: he was forced to use it too much. The people needed him to be positive, looked to him as an indicator of their fortunes. He could not afford to show weakness. He could not afford to let them know that he did not want to lead them any more.

Between the stalls were rows of stone idols, strange crouching things that had been smoothed by centuries of rain and wind. Their slitted, blank eyes stared across the side-road at each other, over the heads of the people who milled between them. Some kind of guardian spirits? Nobody knew. Araka Jo had been built in the early years after landfall, the result of a splinter religion taking advantage of the new freedom to explore their beliefs. They must have been particularly numerous and industrious to have created a complex of temples the size of a small town. Perhaps it was a mountain retreat, a place of prayer and meditation. But its purpose and its creators had been lost to history, and it had been abandoned. The folk of Saramyr were not interested in ruins.

Yugi bought a mug of lathamri from a merchant and drank it while staring at the statues. Frightening how easily the past could be forgotten. He wondered how the previous inhabitants might have felt, labouring towards what they thought was a great work, if they knew that mere centuries later nobody would know or care what they had done it for.

Perhaps they would have appreciated the irony, he thought. It was Saramyr's blithe ignorance of its past that now threatened its future.

The hot, bitter drink awakened him enough to face dealing with Cailin and Lucia, so he returned the mug to the merchant with a coin inside it and left. It was an old tradition: if the drink was not drained then the coin would be wet, so it was only polite to finish it all. Strange, Yugi thought as he walked away, that traditions linger long past the time that their origins had been lost to memory, yet the lessons of history can fade in a generation.

He headed back towards the building where his cell was, and over to the other side, where the lake lay. It was a bracingly cool and crisp day, and while there was no dew on the grass the air felt moist. He slept in what had once been the living-quarters of the worshippers who had built the place. There were about twenty of that type of building scattered around the complex, identically white and rectangular, differentiated by the carvings and sculptures on their corners. They were spartan and austere inside, being merely corridors and cells with a central atrium for cooking and washing, but Yugi did not overly mind. Some days he thought about moving down into the village that had been built around the lower slopes of the complex to house the overflow, but to do so would cause gossip, and now was not the time for rumours. Everything he did was political, whether he wanted it or not. He wished he had Mishani's faculty to enjoy that kind of life.

Beyond the building there was a long, grassy slope down to the shore of Lake Xemit. A dirt path led to a large boathouse from which fishermen issued across the water. Trees encroached in copses here and there, but not enough to obscure the magnificent view. Folk were scattered about, some talking, others on their way from one place to another. It was easy to forget the famine even existed here, in the heart of the Southern Prefectures. Life went on, regardless.

Yugi spotted Cailin and Lucia and made his way towards them. As he went, he looked out over the lake to the horizon. Lake Xemit was colossal: forty-five miles across and nearly two hundred and fifty long. It was the second largest inland body of water in Saramyr after Lake Azlea, cradled between two mountain ranges.

He had been to the other side once before, during the assault on Utraxxa. It had been one of the most famous victories of the last four years. An ancient Weaver stronghold, deep in the heart of the Southern Prefectures. Though cut off from the other Weavers after the forces of the Empire had consolidated, it still exuded its foulness into the earth, still spawned more Aberrant predators to harry the troops of the Empire from within. Protected by the mountains, it took two years before the high families, led by Barak Zahn, managed to penetrate the monastery. Though the Weavers destroyed everything of value, even the witchstone itself, it was a triumph in the eyes of the people.

It was that, more than any other incident, that gave the men and women of the Empire the strength to fight on through the long years of war. The Weavers, who for so many generations had been held as mysterious and unfathomable beings by the common folk, were only mortal. They could be beaten. The fight could be won.

They needed another victory like Utraxxa, Yugi thought. *He* needed one.

Lucia and Cailin were walking together slowly, talking. It irked him that Cailin was the only one whom Lucia ever seemed attentive to; with most people she had a frustrating air of distraction. Yugi could not help noticing the odd behaviour of the wildlife as he approached: the way the ravens in the trees never stopped watching her, the cat that unobtrusively tracked her from downslope, the rabbits who would hop and hide, hop and hide, yet always keeping abreast of her. Natural enemies, yet with Lucia about they were not interested in each other.

Cailin noticed him coming and they stopped to let him catch up. She was a little taller than he was, her face painted like those of all the Sisters, her black hair drawn back through a jewelled comb into twin ponytails and a thin silver circlet set with a red gem placed around her forehead. Her sheer black dress and ruff of raven feathers lent her a somewhat predatory aspect, adding to the air of cool superiority she exuded. Yugi wondered how well her arrogance would stand up in bed, whether her icy exterior would shatter in the throes of orgasm; then he caught himself, and forced the thought away.

'Daygreet, Yugi,' Cailin said. 'Did you sleep well?'

It was a weighted question. Yugi made a neutral noise to evade it. 'Lucia said there is news.'

'Kaiku has made contact.'

'She is safe, then?' Yugi asked. Despite their estrangement, he had been worried for her these past weeks; it was only now, at the point of discovery, that he realised how worried.

'She is safe,' Cailin said. 'Though she very nearly did not make it out at all.'

'Where is she now?'

'Heading down the Zan towards Maza.'

'And the others?'

'Phaeca is with her. Nomoru is gone.'

'What do you mean, *gone?*'

'She disappeared. They do not know where she is.'

Yugi held up a hand. 'Start from the beginning, Cailin, and tell me what Kaiku told you.'

So Cailin relayed the story of the investigation of the pall-pits, of their betrayal and how Nomoru had second-guessed it, and how they had escaped the city.

'A gang from the Poor Quarter helped them?' Yugi repeated in frank disbelief.

'Smuggled them aboard a barge.'

'And what did they want in return?'

'Apparently nothing.'

Yugi grimaced. 'Gods, they were lucky, then.'

'Perhaps so. But the people of the Poor Quarter are not stupid. The Sisters may be Aberrants, but even we are not so despised as the Weavers. Things are turning, Yugi. They know we are on their side.'

'Are you really?' Yugi said skeptically.

Cailin did not reply, and Yugi left it at that. He glanced at Lucia, who was looking away across the lake, apparently oblivious to their conversation.

'My Sisters learned a lot from the pall-pit,' Cailin said at length. 'The implications are grave indeed.'

Yugi felt a cold eel of nausea turn gently in his stomach, a remnant of last night's excesses. He did not want to hear any bad news now.

'The Weavers have modified the old sewers into a pipe network. They are channelling the miasma that their buildings produce.'

'Into the pall-pits,' Yugi guessed. He scratched his stubbled cheek. 'Why?'

'Because that is where the feya-kori are.'

'Because that is *what* the feya-kori are,' Lucia corrected, over her shoulder.

Yugi cocked his head at Cailin, expecting elaboration.

'They are composed of the Weavers' miasma,' Cailin said. 'Without it, they are formless. They draw it around them like a shroud, and build their shape from it. When we called them blight-demons, we did not know how right we were.'

Yugi was quick to latch on to a potential upside. 'Would that explain why they returned to Axekami after the assault on Juraka? That they need to . . . replenish themselves? Like a whale can dive for hours, but has to come up for air?'

'Exactly,' Cailin said, raising an eyebrow. 'An apt analogy.'

'Could that be the reason the Weavers are poisoning Axekami in such a way?'

'Perhaps,' came the careful reply. 'But let us not tie all our threads to a single revelation. There is much we do not understand yet.'

'But this gives us hope, surely?' Yugi said. 'The feya-kori have a limit, a weakness.'

'You do not yet see the grander scale,' Cailin replied. 'It is not only Axekami that the Weavers are choking. There are pall-pits in various stages of completion in Tchamaska,

Maxachta and Barask. More are being built on the north side of Axekami, and in Hanzean to the west.' A chill wind off the lake rippled through the grass and hissed through the trees. 'These two feya-kori are only the first. The Weavers will bring more. We cannot stand against them.'

Yugi sighed and rubbed at his eye. 'Gods, Cailin, does it get any worse?'

'Oh yes,' she said. 'Two nights ago, the feya-kori left Axekami again.'

The fortified town of Zila had seen its fair share of conflict. Since the time it was built over a thousand years ago it had weathered assaults from the native Ugati, from renegade warlords, and from the Empire itself; and still it stood, grim and dark upon a steep hill to the south of the River Zan. It was a strategic linchpin, commanding both the estuary and the thirty-five mile strip of land between the coast and the western edges of the Forest of Xu, a thoroughfare vital for travel between the affluent northwest and the fertile Southern Prefectures. Now it had become a bastion against the Weavers, denying them the passage along the Great Spice Road.

Barak Zahn looked over his shoulder at the town, a crown of stone, the roofs of its houses sloping back to the narrow pinnacle of the keep at its tip. That wall had never fallen to an enemy, not in all the history of Zila. Not even when the town was overrun, when Zahn himself had been one of the invaders; they had surmounted the wall, but they had not breached it. Then, he had left Zila smoking and battered. It was in considerably better shape now: the ruined houses had been rebuilt, the keep repaired, the streets set back in order. Troops of the Empire walked behind its parapets; fire-cannons looked out over the river. But its air of invulnerability was gone, its power diminished.

His horse stirred beneath him, and he turned his attention back to the estuary, where four huge junks swayed at anchor.

The wind was brisk and the light crisp and sharp: they were heading into midwinter now, and though it was still warm the breeze off the sea could be biting.

He was a lean man, his hair grey and his stubbled cheeks uneven with pox-scars. He wore a brocaded jacket with its collar turned up, and his eyes were narrow as he stared across the water. Around him and before him were hundreds of mounted men in the colours of their respective houses. Most of them were his own Blood Ikati, clad in green and grey. To his right, wrapped in a fur cloak, the head of Blood Erinima sat in her saddle, plump and wizened. Lucia's great-aunt Oyo.

It was over a week since Kaiku and Phaeca had escaped Axekami, but Zahn knew nothing of that. He had, however, heard the news that the feya-kori were on the move again. The Red Order were few in number and stretched thin, but Cailin tried to ensure that there was at least one in every frontline settlement. The warning had spread within minutes. Not that it concerned Zahn overly: the feya-kori, like the Aberrant armies, moved too fast to keep up with, and the news that they had been deployed simply meant they were at large again, and Saramyr was a very big place. They could be up to anything. Besides, he had more immediate concerns.

The first was the woman next to him. It seemed that even in the face of the greatest threat the Empire had encountered since its inception, the wranglings of the courts went on. Though they were all ostensibly united against the Weavers, the old powerplay of concessions and arrangements and oaths continued. Oyo was annoyingly persistent, even following him up to Zila where the greater portion of his armies were garrisoned along with those of Blood Vinaxis. Her demands were simple: she wanted his daughter.

Zahn had known it would be impossible to keep Lucia's parentage a secret forever. She was so obviously affectionate towards him, and that coupled with the rumours of the Emperor Durun's infertility and Zahn's close relationship with the Empress Anais was all that anyone needed to draw the correct conclusion. Once he had become convinced that it was hopeless concealing it any longer, he let it be known that he was the father, and hoped to have done with it. But Blood Erinima – the mother's family – were not satisfied. They disputed his claim. They wanted her back, to bind her to Blood Erinima where they believed she belonged.

Zahn did not want to trouble himself with it. He believed their loyalty towards their kin was genuine – and indeed, he had never prevented them seeing Lucia – but it was also painfully transparent that they were thinking towards the outcome of the war, for if victorious then Lucia was by far the most likely candidate for the throne, and Blood Erinima wanted to ride with her to power again. However, Zahn's claim on her complicated things immensely, for as the only surviving parent she was legally his child before the family of the deceased mother. If that claim could be proved to be genuine.

But Zahn was not the biggest problem: Lucia was. She had no interest in such matters. She was happy to acknowledge her relatives, but she would not talk politics with them. Zahn was her father; it was that simple. As far as matters of Blood went, she needed neither Blood Ikati nor Blood Erinima. The Libera Dramach were at her beck and call, an army to rival any of the great houses and independent of them. She did not care about becoming Empress. She did not care about being a leader, or a figurehead, or anything at all of that nature. It was difficult to tell *what* she cared about. That frustrated women like Oyo immensely, and they fumed and said that the child did not realise what was good for her, and that she should be with her family. But Zahn knew his child, as well as anyone *could* know her, and he believed her a thing apart from the grubby machinations that Oyo wanted to drag her into. He loved her, and he let her go her own way. But he would not renounce his fatherhood, no matter how Blood Erinima cajoled and promised and threatened.

A rowboat was sliding across the estuary towards the southern shore; it was time to deal with the second and more recent concern. Zahn spurred his horse through the ranks of his men and trotted down the shallow incline at the base of the hill. Oyo watched him go with an unfriendly gaze. A small guard of twenty fell in behind at the command of one of his generals. A Sister joined them, appearing unobtrusively at his side like a shadow, her face still. They passed through the army to the stretch of clear grass where the water ended, and there they stopped.

The rowboat had reached the shore now, and the new-comers were dragging it out of the water, all four of them together. Zahn tried to establish which one of them was the leader, but it was hopeless. They were all dressed in simple hemp clothes, their hair varying in colour from blond to black; all had the same yellowish skin tattooed head to foot in curving tendrils of pale green. Tkiurathi, from the jungle continent of Okhamba, so his aides informed him. Savages, they said.

The question was, what were the savages doing in Saramyr?

The boat secured, one of them approached Zahn, walking fearlessly towards the forest of soldiers. Zahn glanced up at the junks. They were of Saramyr make. The gods knew how many other Tkiurathi were in there, but they had better hope they could swim: one signal from him and Zila's fire-cannons would blow them to flinders.

The stranger stopped a short way from Zahn. His orange-blond hair was smoothed back along his skull and hardened there with sap. Okhamban *kntha* – called 'gutting-hooks' in Saramyrrhic – hung from either side of his belt: double-bladed weapons with a handle set at the point where they met, each blade kinked the opposite way to the other.

'Daygreet, honoured Barak,' said the Tkiurathi, in near-flawless Saramyrrhic. 'I am Tsata.' He bowed in an ambiguous manner, in a style used between men who were unsure of their relative social standing to each other. Zahn could not decide if it was arrogance or accident. The name was faintly familiar to him, however.

'I am the Barak Zahn tu Ikati,' he said.

Tsata gave him a curious look. 'Indeed? Then we have a mutual acquaintance. Kaiku tu Makaima.'

Zahn's horse crabstepped with a snort; he pulled it firmly back into line. Now he knew where he had heard the name before. This was the man who had travelled with the spy Saran into the heart of Okhamba to bring back the evidence of the Weavers' origins; the man who had helped Kaiku destroy a witchstone in the Xarana Fault. He looked down at the Sister who stood to his right.

'Can you confirm this?'

Her irises had already turned to red. 'I am doing so.'

Zahn regarded the foreigner with frank suspicion on his face. 'Why are you here, Tsata? This is not a good time to be visiting Saramyr.'

'We come to offer you our aid,' said Tsata. 'A thousand Tkiurathi, to fight alongside you against the Weavers.'

'I see,' Zahn said. 'And what would you do if we did not *want* your aid?'

'We would fight anyway, whatever your wishes,' Tsata replied. 'We come to stop the Weavers. If we can do it together, so be it. If not, we shall do it alone.'

'He is who he says he is,' the Sister said. 'I have contacted Kaiku tu Makaima.' She bowed to Tsata in the appropriate female mode. 'She sends you greetings, honoured friend. The Red Order are pleased that your path has set you upon our shores again.'

Zahn felt a twinge of irritation at being undercut. His unfriendly stance was somewhat robbed of force now that Tsata had the Sisters' approval. The Red Order considered themselves above political loyalty; they knew they were invaluable, and took advantage of it. They might have been easier on the eye than the Weavers were, but they were not so different as they liked to think.

He slid down from his horse and handed the reins to a nearby soldier. 'It seems I have been ungracious,' he said, and bowed. 'Welcome back.'

'I am only sorry I could not come sooner, or bring more of my people,' Tsata said, dismissing the apology. 'Ten times this many would have come, if we had the ships.'

'I had not known the Tkiurathi were a seafaring folk,' Zahn said, embedding an implied question in an observation.

Tsata smiled to himself. Such a Saramyr thing to do, to be so indirect. 'The ships came from Blood Mumaka, as did the crew.'

'I thought they had fled Saramyr when the war began.' What Zahn thought of that was evident in his voice.

'To Okhamba, yes. They sailed their fleet away. But they still desire to help their homeland in such ways as they can. Mishani tu Koli came to me before I left and asked me to pass on news of Chien os Mumaka's death to his mother. I found them only hours before they left Hanzean, ahead of the Aberrant armies that were spreading through the northwest. In return for my news they allowed me to travel with them back to Okhamba. I have kept in contact with Blood Mumaka ever since; when the time came, they offered their aid.'

'Four ships?' Zahn said disparagingly.

'They need the others to conduct their trade with,' Tsata replied. 'The rest of the Near World goes on as ever, no matter what the state of matters here. They cannot see that if Saramyr falls, they will be next. But my people can. I have shown them.'

Zahn considered the Tkiurathi for a moment. On the one hand, any aid was welcome in these times, and he was not such a fool as to turn away a genuine ally; but on the other, it was difficult to believe that a thousand men – *ten* thousand, if Tsata was to be believed – would willingly sail to another continent to fight for people they had virtually no contact with.

'Our ways are not your ways, Barak Zahn,' Tsata said, his

expression serious. He had guessed the other man's thoughts. 'We will not wait at home until it is our turn to be attacked. The Weavers threaten the whole of the Near World. We will stop them at their source, if we can.'

Zahn was about to reply when the Sister touched him on his arm. She was looking to the north, over the river. The line of the horizon was hazed. Zahn's eyes went to the junks: they seemed ghosted slightly, blurred at the edges. He blinked, feeling faintly myopic.

'Is it usual for fog to come so quickly in these parts?' Tsata asked, as the air thickened around them.

TEN

The walls of Zila had held back the enemies of the Empire for a thousand years and more. The feya-kori went through them like children kicking over mudcastles.

They approached under the cover of the fog, but nobody was deceived. Kaiku had warned the Sisters about the demons' methods, and the murk had gathered too quickly and smelt too foul to be natural. Yet, somehow, knowing that they were coming only made it worse: the sickening inevitability of their arrival weighed on the defenders' hearts.

The troops had already begun to prepare the town for evacuation by the time the feya-kori appeared. They lunged suddenly out of the miasma, emerging as if from nowhere within a few dozen metres of the wall. Men howled as the demons loomed up towards them; the sharp slope to the north of the town made them seem as if they were coming from below, surfacing from a sea of mist. They grabbed hold of the lip of the wall, the stump-ends of their arms smashing down onto the stone in a hissing mass of black ooze, crushing and dissolving those soldiers not quick enough to get out of the way. Then, with a long, protracted groan, they hauled, and the top third of the wall gave way in an avalanche of bodies and bricks and mortar.

Alarm bells clanged from the murk; men fought to decline their fire-cannons far enough to hit the enemy. But the feya-kori were too close. They punched and tore and smashed, their movements slow and massive, destroying a great section of the wall in minutes while rifles and arrows pocked them ineffectually.

They lumbered into the town, crashing through buildings

as if they were made of sticks and paper. The Aberrant predators and Nexuses were not far behind them.

Tsata raced through the ruined streets left in the demons' wake. A dozen Tkiurathi were with him, their gutting-hooks held ready, eyes darting about for signs of the enemy. Behind them they could hear the cries of the feya-kori, disembodied moans drifting through the swiftly thinning fog; before them, distantly, was the sound of combat, where the troops of the Empire had knitted across the gash in the wall and were putting up a bloody resistance against the Aberrant horde. Tsata was concerned with neither: his purpose was the area in between, where the smoking, charred trail of the demons had left houses collapsed into rubble, with men and women and children trapped and maimed or out of their wits with fear.

The Tkiurathi dispersed at his suggestion, fracturing into groups of two and three and hurrying in different directions. They filtered off into the narrow spoke-roads and cross-alleys of the town, heading away from the main swathe of destruction – where nothing was left alive, and the cobbled thoroughfares were a melted quagmire – to the edges, where there were people to be helped.

Tsata tasted bile: the very air was bad here. The sight of the feya-kori still burned in the forefront of his mind. For the month that it took to cross the sea from his lands, he had been experiencing a steadily growing elation at the thought of returning to Saramyr. Four years he had been gathering his people, tracking them down and persuading them to his cause; four years of hunting through deep jungle, of tireless diplomacy, of bringing together men and women who had scattered over hundreds of miles of nearly impenetrable terrain. And though he might have only managed four ships to carry them, those four could go back and forth as many times as was necessary to transport all the Tkiurathi to Saramyr.

But he had been here mere hours before he witnessed how much worse things had become in his absence, and now he wished he had listened to his heart instead of his head and got here sooner.

He scrambled over a slope of rubble, where the dusty guts of a building had spilled out across the street, to where a pair of women were heaving at a beam to uncover the supine man beneath. He did not give them time to react to his appearance, to act on the flicker of fear and uncertainty at the sight of him. He grabbed the beam and lifted, and after a moment's hesitation the women added their strength to his, and two more Tkiurathi appeared and joined in. The beam moved, and the man scrambled free, delirious with agony, his foot crushed inside his boot. One of the women helped him stand one-legged.

'Find a crutch and get away from here,' Tsata told them. 'Through the south gate.' Then he rapped a few words in guttural Okhamban to his companions and they were running again.

The mist had faded to a fine haze, burnt off by the sharp light of the winter sun. The demons were abandoning their concealment; they had no need of it now. One of them had reached the town's keep, the highest and most central point, hub of Zila's wheel-like layout. Burning and broken buildings traced the creature's path from the gap in the north wall to where it was smashing into the keep's brickwork. The other one had rampaged towards the western wall.

Tsata hoped the ships had got away. There had barely been time for the Tkiurathi to gather their communal belongings and swim for shore; he had last seen the junks turning in the estuary, their prows pointing towards the open sea. A few Tkiurathi men had stayed, along with the crew. They would return and tell others what they had seen today. What the Weavers were now capable of.

For the Tkiurathi who were on Saramyr, the protection of their *pash* was now the priority. Okhambans did not think in the way Saramyr did: they had no concept of personal ownership, and their society had evolved around a group dynamic which meant, at its most basic level, that they considered individual needs less important than those of the many. *Pash* was their name for whichever 'many' they were involved with at the time, a fluid and multilayered concept of overlapping priorities which was how the Okhamban people – including the Tkiurathi – assigned importance to a situation. At this moment, at this time, their *pash* included the people of Zila; and so they had headed into the town without a second thought, to help with the retreat, to save lives when they could, heedless of any risk to themselves.

A cry for help drew them into a small square where one side had collapsed inward. The façades of the buildings had shaken away from their superstructures and opened the rooms to the sky. Smoke was seeping from beneath the rubble on the ground floor of what had once been a cobbler's shop, where something was ablaze. An old, bearded man was frantically working to clear away the stones there. He caught sight of Tsata and his companions, wasted a moment on uncertainty, then called to them.

'There's someone under here!'

They joined him in his work, hefting the heavy, uneven stones and flinging them away. There was a frantic knocking noise coming from beneath.

Tsata's survival instincts kept him fitfully glancing about as he laboured, honed by generation upon generation of jungle life. Without even thinking about it, he knew where the feya-kori were by their dreary, yawning voices; they were too far away to be a threat. He could tell by the cadence and timbre of the battle to the north that the forces of the Empire were still holding out. But there were Aberrant predators loose in the city, those that had slipped through the gap in the wall before it could be sealed. He had seen their handiwork, and one or two of their corpses.

They had just uncovered the corner of a trapdoor, from which the smoke was coming, when something moved in the square.

The three Tkiurathi were on their feet, gutting-hooks in hands, before the pair of ghauregs even noticed them. They ran out from the cover of the building and into the square, drawing the eyes of the beasts, leading them away from the old man. The Aberrants snorted at the sight of prey, growling deep in their chests. One of them bellowed a challenge, shaking its head, its grey shaggy pelt flailing with the movement; then slowly they advanced.

Tsata circled around the square, keeping his gaze on the predators. His companions were fanning away from him, treading soundlessly across the rubble-strewn cobbles. Coherent thought had fallen away, succeeded by the quicker and more direct reactions of a hunter. The ghauregs clacked their jaws together with a bony snap like a crocodile's, wary of their opponents. Their muzzles were streaked in blood.

There was a banging from the trapdoor, louder and more urgent than before now that it was not muffled by so much rubble, and the ghaureg's heads snapped around to fix on the old man who crouched there. He paled.

The three Tkiurathi moved together, taking advantage of the instant of distraction to cross the distance between them and the predators. Their hide shoes were so soft and their tread so light that the ghauregs did not hear them coming; they turned back only just in time to react to the attack.

Tsata saw the fist swiping towards him early enough to duck beneath it. He rammed one of his gutting-hooks into the ghaureg's ribs with as much force as he could muster. It bit deep, but the thick muscles of the beast were too tough to cut easily, and the blade wrenched free of his hand as he darted past. The ghaureg overswung, roaring in pain, and one of the other Tkiurathi took its hand off at the wrist with a brutal downward stroke; but he had been too eager at the sight of an inviting target, and he did not see the ghaureg's other hand until it grabbed his shin in an unbreakable grip. He slashed across the beast's muzzle, slicing through its lip, but the blade jarred against bone and glanced off. It flung him away, whipping him by his leg with a cracking of bones to send him flailing through the air. He crashed in a heap against the rubble, but even before he had landed Tsata had made his second strike. Occupied with one enemy, the ghaureg had no time to deal with the other, and Tsata plunged his second gutting-hook into the creature's back with all his strength.

This time he found something vital. His enemy lurched away spasmodically for a few steps, trying to paw at its back but unable to reach; then it collapsed, and blood ran over its lower teeth with its last bubbling breath.

Tsata had never lost sight of the second ghaureg in the time it took to despatch the first one. That one was still engaged with the remaining Tkiurathi. He did not spare a moment to check on his fallen comrade, but instead he carefully approached the body of the ghaureg, ready to leap away if it should move. He wrenched his weapons free and then went to the aid of his beleaguered kinsman.

That man – his name was Heth – had been fighting tactically. Instead of going up alone against a stronger enemy he had been drawing it after him to allow the others time to finish off the first ghaureg. Now he saw Tsata coming, and the advantage turned his way. He switched to the offensive, ducking in low to hack across his enemy's knees. The strike was inexact, hitting its calf instead, but it was enough to send a flood of red soaking through the grey fur. Heth pulled back faster than the counterpunch could follow, and in that moment Tsata got in behind the beast, close enough to chop a deep blow into its tricep before retreating out of its reach. Enraged, it swung back to snap at him, and once again Heth slipped inside its guard and raked a cut along its thigh.

They harried it for several minutes, each time leaving a wound, each time escaping its grasp. Finally, when its pelt was drenched crimson and blood loss had made it sluggish, Heth took advantage of an ill-executed lunge to take it through the throat, and it went down without another sound.

Tsata exchanged a breathless smile with Heth. 'We must be quick,' he said in their native tongue. 'Others may come.'

They sheathed their blades. Heth went to see to their companion, who was beginning to scream as the shock wore off. Tsata went for the trapdoor. Fumes were coming thickly from beneath it now. The knocking had stopped, and the old man was long gone. Tsata cleared away the remainder of the debris and pulled the trapdoor open, keeping it between himself and the hatchway. Flame billowed out, then retreated and settled to an insidious purr.

He took a breath, held it, and looked down into the hatchway. His eyes began tearing immediately: the smoke was too hot to bear for long. Unable to see, he instead reached in, trusting to his senses to tell him if he was getting too close to the fire. His hand touched fabric and muscle. He found a purchase, guessing it to be the upper arm of the person who had been knocking, and pulled.

The man was surprisingly light for his size, but even so Tsata had trouble with the dead weight. He dragged the limp figure across the rubble a little way and laid him down, but by then it was already apparent that he was too late.

Tsata looked down on him for a moment. His skin was white, his features so small as to be almost vestigial. There were little gill-slits at his neck, and his glazed eyes were bulbous, with pupils like crosses. An Aberrant.

He had been hiding in the city, perhaps sheltered by the cobbler. Tsata had heard that Aberrants were no longer executed on sight as they had been before the civil war began. Priorities had changed now, and with both the Red Order and Lucia fighting on their side, it seemed inappropriate to allow the killing any longer. But prejudice could not be erased as easily. Though it was unlawful to murder them, they were still reviled in the main, still forced to hide or to take shelter in their own remote communities. People like the Red Order were the lucky ones; they had the outside appearance of normality, at least. This man would have been treated as a freak.

Tsata's eyes tightened in disgust at the thought. There was

so much hate in this once-beautiful land. He wondered if this man had had a family, for unlike Tsata's home, pair-bonding and the exclusive possession of offspring was the way in Saramyr. Then he glanced over at the hatchway, where flames were licking out. He decided that he would rather not know.

Barak Zahn sat on horseback near the south gate of Zila, overseeing the rabble of townsfolk fleeing for their lives. He was flanked by several bodyguards, and nearby a group of Blood Vinaxis soldiers fought to herd the crowd and keep them calm. Like panicked animals, they were liable to stampede. The noise was terrible, and the air still lingered with the smell of the feya-kori's fog, mingled with the infectious odour of fear.

He looked up the hill at where one of the demons had almost finished smashing the keep to rubble. The other one was tracking about at random, pounding houses and shops and warehouses to pieces with slow and methodical blows. The sound of tumbling stone and the demon's cries rolled across the town.

His blood burned: he was furious at his own impotence. Gods, it felt so fundamentally *wrong* to abandon a strategic outpost like this. He had men ranged along the riverbank and along the walls, but they were only putting up as much resistance as was necessary to evacuate everyone they could, keeping the Aberrants out for as long as possible. This was a lost battle the moment the feya-kori appeared. There simply was no defence against them. And this is what it would be like in the next town they attacked, and the next, until the Southern Prefectures had fallen and the Weavers had swallowed the land.

Still, even in the face of such abject defeat, he salvaged what positive aspects he could to pass on to his allies. They were holding back the Aberrants along the river to the west and east with relative ease. Apparently the attack had relied on the feya-kori breaking down the wall and the Aberrants flooding over the water north of the town. But the feya-kori had broken through and then gone on a rampage, and the troops of the Empire were quick enough to seal the breach behind them. If there had been any kind of tactical thought applied by the demons, they would have made a bigger hole, or at least stayed there to ensure that enough Aberrants had got through to keep the passage open. Zahn doubted that the Weavers had more than a rudimentary control over their terrible creations, and that, at least, was something worth knowing.

He looked up at where the gristle-crows circled high above, out of rifle range. As always, the Nexuses were nearby, hidden and protected, directing the battle from afar. The gristle-crows were their eyes, the Aberrant predators their puppets. If they could get to the Nexuses they could throw the animals into disorder; but the Nexuses had learned to stay scattered since Zahn had routed them at the battle of the Fold, years ago. And even if they did, even if they slew every Aberrant here, they still could not win. It came back to one immutable fact: they had no weapon against the blight demons.

A rider drew up before him: a young and handsome man with a thick head of brown hair, wearing Blood Ikati colours. 'What news of our allies?' Zahn asked. He remembered this man; he had sent him into the town to keep tabs on the Tkiurathi. He had been uneasy about letting them leave their ships, but in the chaos that followed the gathering of the demon fog he had been loth to spare the men necessary to prevent them. Now they were loose in the town, and though they appeared to be a help rather than a hindrance, long experience had taught him to mistrust such apparent altruism.

But the young man's report shed no new light. The Tkiurathi were indeed doing their best to speed the retreat, rescuing the injured and aiding stragglers, hunting down those Aberrants that were loose in the streets. Some of them were dying in the process. Perhaps a ploy to win his trust, then?

The young man was coming to the conclusion of his report, but Zahn was not really listening any more. He was gazing up at where the feya-kori rose seething above the slate rooftops of the town, thinking about the strange folk from the jungle continent. It was probably what saved his life.

He saw the rifleman in the upper window of a ramshackle house an instant before the muzzle flash, and only because he happened to be looking that way. It gave him that extra minuscule fraction of a moment which was the difference between the ball hitting his heart or his shoulder. The force of it knocked him out of his saddle, sending him crashing to the ground, his feet tangled in his stirrups. His horse neighed and bucked wildly; he was dragged thrashing across the cobbles. The horse's hooves clattered as it stepped back over him. Shock swamped his senses, making everything distant and slow and remote. He was dimly aware of a man lunging for him, the young messenger, a knife in his hand; but then the messenger's hand was gone, and a moment later his head, as the swords of Zahn's bodyguards cleft through him. Another stroke, and the stirrups that tethered Zahn to the horse were severed. Suddenly, he saw the sky again; the horse danced away, kicking, and someone shot it.

There were men surrounding him, and angry cries as others rode towards the building to flush out the sniper. But the sniper would be already dead, having taken his own life. Nobody would know who had sent him, nor the messenger that had been the backup; but Zahn knew. Of course he knew.

As he lay there panting and white with his men looking into his eyes and speaking incoherently to him, he cursed the name of Oyo tu Erinima, who wanted her grand-niece back.

ELEVEN

Kaiku spun and sewed, looped and knotted, moving on a thousand fronts at once as she darted through the labyrinth of the Weave. Her opponent was fast as she, *faster*, blocking her, confusing her, burrowing into her stitchwork defences; but Kaiku would not relent, would not allow even the most fractional lapse of concentration. For every gain her opponent made, they lost an equal amount. Tangles frayed, nets were strung, traps laid and avoided; a scurrying combat like an army of tiny spiders warring on a golden web so complex that it stunned the mind.

Kaiku used every trick she knew, and improvised some she didn't. Sinkholes that sucked threads into an insoluble muddle; scatter-stitch that created an endless and disorientating array of possible routes across the battlefield, ultimately heading nowhere. She plucked strings like a harp and meshed them with other resonances to set up interference patterns, disguising her movements. Sometimes her methods were effective, sometimes not; but then, the same applied to her opponent's attempts. This battle had raged for long minutes in the world of human senses. In the Weave, it seemed like it had been going for years, and still neither combatant flagged, neither wavered. They were evenly matched. Stalemate.

Then, finally, her adversary withdrew. Kaiku did the same. They hung there, disembodied, exhausted and wary, like bloodied tigers at bay. On the edge of her perception, she sensed the shift and glide of the leviathans that haunted this glittering world, ever elusive, unreachable. They were calling to each other in their fashion, concussive pops and creaks passing back and forth along the Weave. Kaiku knew that her senses were only interpreting the sounds to accommodate her human mindset, for there was no sound at all in this place; but even so, it was eerie and magical to hear. The leviathans spoke more and more often now.

At the signal, she drew her *kana* back, retreating into herself like the tentacles of an anemone, and opened her eyes. She was kneeling on a wicker mat in the centre of a wood-panelled room. A paper lantern hung overhead, casting shadows in the cool gloom, half-illuminating the charcoal etchings that hung on the wall, the tiny tables with their vases of dark blossoms. An incense burner filled the room with the scent of kama nuts, bitter and fruity and smoky all at once. Opposite Kaiku was Cailin, regarding her approvingly, her irises a rich red. Both were breathing hard, their skin glistening with sweat in the lantern-light. Both wore the attire of the Order.

Cailin smiled. 'Congratulations,' she said.

Kaiku could not suppress a short laugh of exultation. She had fought her tutor to a standstill for the first time ever. She had taken on the most powerful Sister alive, the Pre-Eminent of the Red Order, and not been beaten by her. It felt magnificent.

Cailin stood up, and Kaiku with her. 'Walk with me,' she said.

Kaiku was a little unsteady, but she obeyed, flushed with success. They walked through the building that housed those Sisters who lived in the village downslope of Araka Jo, and went out into the night.

The village was haphazard and a little ramshackle, as had been the town of the Fold where most of its inhabitants had come from. The Libera Dramach had taken Araka Jo as their own after being driven from the Xarana Fault, since nobody else appeared to want it. The nobles and high families, used to their luxury, had retreated to cities like Machita and Saraku; the latter had become the unofficial capital of the Empire's territories while the war raged.

They followed dirt paths between stilt-legged dwellings. Lights glowed on porches in the darkness; candles flickered in small shrines of stone and metal. Chikkikii popped and cracked in the bushes; mountain rodents sang to each other as they darted in quick bursts from shadow to shadow. Aurus hung high and full in the east, massive and looming.

They did not speak for a time, except to acknowledge the occasional hail from the villagers. The Sisters were well regarded here, and Kaiku enjoyed the attention. Eventually, the houses became sparser, the trees crowded close to the paths, and the gentle sound of the village faded behind them and left only the sounds of the night, riotous and yet strangely restful.

'You have been something of a trial, Kaiku,' Cailin said, then looked at her. 'I hope you see now why I persevered with you.'

'You were right,' she said. She had to admit that, at least. 'It took me a long time to understand, but you were right.'

The taller woman smiled indulgently. 'You have no idea how it felt to let you go, knowing what a talent you had. To watch you throwing yourself into anything and everything with scarce an inkling of your abilities. The gods forbid I ever have children, if they cause me such worry as you.'

Kaiku laughed softly. 'Muleheadedness is one of my less admirable traits.'

They walked on for a time.

'Would you?' Kaiku asked. 'Have children, I mean?'

'None of us should,' Cailin replied. 'Not yet.'

'None of us? You mean the Red Order?'

'We do not know what might happen if we did. We dare not think what might come of it.'

'But surely someone has tried? An accident, even?'

'Nobody has tried. Accidents have occurred, but they have been dealt with.' She saw the expression on Kaiku's face, and added: 'They chose to do it. They knew that now was not the time.'

Kaiku did not like what she was hearing. Children were something that had barely even occurred to her – she assumed herself lacking in the maternal instinct – but to have the choice taken away from her was not something she would condone. Cailin sensed that, and attempted to explain.

'We are long-lived in the Red Order, Kaiku. We are few, but we are tightly knit. More so, perhaps, than any other faction in Saramyr. The nobles continue their internecine squabbling even in the face of famine and destruction. Look at what has happened to Barak Zahn. But the Red Order remains united, and that is because our highest priority is *ourselves.*'

'Then perhaps we are the most selfish of all, then,' Kaiku murmured.

'That is your Tkiurathi friend talking,' Cailin snapped. The warmth had fled from her now. 'Need I remind you that not even ten years ago any of us would have been killed for manifesting the abilities we possess? That most of us died through burning ourselves alive or committing suicide for shame at what we had become? This is *still happening* in the Weaver territories, Kaiku. Children are still manifesting *kana* and dying for it, and we can only get to a small fraction of them. Were it not for our selfishness, you would not be here and nor would I, and the Weavers would have had this land long ago.'

Kaiku lapsed into angry silence. She could not argue with that, but Cailin's tone made her furious. The mention of Tsata only made things worse: it reminded her of the news they had received from Zila, which told only of the destruction of the town and the fact that the Tkiurathi were there, but not whether Tsata had survived it. Beneath her carefully suppressed exterior, she was frantic.

'We are a breed apart,' Cailin went on in a softer tone. She laid a hand on Kaiku's shoulder to stop her walking. 'The first of an upward step in humanity. It is our duty to preserve ourselves, our purpose to make a world in which we can live.

That is why we fight the Weavers. When that threat is gone, when this land is stable and we have found our place in it, then perhaps children will come. But until then, Kaiku, they are too uncertain.' She sighed, bowing her head, and closed her painted eyes. 'Look how dangerous we are; it is only through the Red Order that we even know how to cope with the gift we have been given. What if our offspring possess power greater than ours? What if they begin to manifest that power from birth instead of adolescence? A child who could annihilate half a town in a fit of pique? What would we do with such a creature? Kill it? *Could* we? And what would the mother say to that?'

Kaiku would not meet her eyes. She would not concede, though she saw the sense in the argument. But nobody would choose for her on a matter such as this, not even Cailin.

'We have enough troubles to contend with for now,' Cailin said. 'We remain focused and united, and nothing must jeopardise that.'

'Enough!' Kaiku replied tersely. 'You have made your point. I do not wish to discuss it.'

The triumphant glow of their battle had faded now and left her feeling irritable. She began to walk again, not caring whether Cailin came with her or not; but the Pre-Eminent joined her after a few steps.

'I have something to show you,' she said.

'Indeed?'

'You have earned it, I think.'

This caught Kaiku's interest. She brushed her hair back from her face and gave Cailin an expectant look.

'Not here,' she said. 'Come with me.'

They walked on a little way. The path they were taking turned and sloped upward. Kaiku knew where they were heading: a small and remote building that had presumably been some kind of temple in past ages, hidden amid the trees in a tiny dirt clearing. There was a dry stone font at the entrance to the clearing, and beyond was a mound-shaped structure with sealed doors at each point of the compass, topped with a cone of concentrically tapering discs that ended in a small gold bobble at the tip. Around its base were fashioned symbols in a dialect of High Saramyrrhic too old for Kaiku to understand.

'This?' Kaiku asked. She had often wondered what was inside. It exuded a faintly watchful emanation.

'No,' Cailin replied. 'I only wanted to be sure we were alone. I would have it that we kept what I have to show you between ourselves. Only a select few know of it.'

'More secrets?' Kaiku asked wearily. Deception did not sit easily with her; it went against her character.

'It is better to always have something with which to surprise those who might turn on you,' Cailin said. 'Look at the Weavers. They must have spent centuries developing their crafts, and still we have not the barest idea of what may yet lie unrevealed.'

'We are not the Weavers,' Kaiku replied.

'Do not be obtuse, Kaiku.' Cailin's velvety voice was frosting over again. 'I ask that you keep this matter secret. Even from Phaeca. It is a small favour, but important to me. Do we understand each other?'

'I understand,' Kaiku said, but she fell diplomatically short of agreeing.

'Watch, then.' Cailin closed her eyes and took a long, slow breath.

Kaiku felt the Weave stirring, tiny currents across the unseen realm. Her sensory powers had increased dramatically since she had applied herself to her studies, and now she was always aware of the Weave even when she was not actively Weaving. Like her Sisters, she could tell an Aberrant just by looking at them, and she could perceive the trails left by spirits and the imprints of strange places that most people could only feel as a kind of sixth-sense unease, if at all. With a little more effort, she could sense bonds between family and friends and even enemies, charting the physical and emotional response between their bodies.

Cailin had once told her, Tane, Asara and Mishani that they walked a braided path, that they were fated to be drawn back together no matter how far they were apart. Kaiku had asked her then how she knew; now she had the answer. Cailin had seen the insoluble ties: Kaiku's friendship with Mishani; Tane's love for her; the link that existed between her and Asara through sharing breath. But Cailin did not know all, it seemed. Tane had died, and none of the Sisters' vaunted powers could do a thing to predict that.

Then, before her eyes, Cailin disappeared.

She blinked. It was if a shadow had passed before the moon across the tall, thin figure of the Pre-Eminent, and when it was gone, so was she.

And yet . . . and yet she was *not* gone. Kaiku could still feel her there, her imprint on the Weave. Her eyes were just not seeing her.

She slipped into the Weave herself, and there was Cailin, contoured in innumerable strings of light.

((How?)) She was aghast with wonder.

((There is more. Touch me with your hand))

Kaiku did so, reaching slowly towards the Pre-Eminent, using her Weave-imprint to see her. She rested her hand on Cailin's shoulder: but where she should have found flesh and bone, there was nothing. She inhaled a sharp breath in surprise. Again she tried, again she failed. She passed her arm through where Cailin's body should be, and apart from a faintly glutinous drag on her fingertips, she touched only air.

((Impossible . . .)) Kaiku felt foolish as soon as she had transmitted the thought, but she could find no other way to express it. Cailin was in the Weave, and *only* in the Weave; her physical body was . . . *gone*.

((We have arts of which you have only scratched the surface, Kaiku)) Cailin's communication came without words, phrased instead in a semantic blaze. *((New techniques of manipulation*

that we have laboured on in secret for decades. You are ready to begin learning the inner mysteries of the Red Order))

The Weave warped, flexing inward and knotting into a singularity that existed for the slenderest of instants before bursting back into shape; and there was a leviathan.

Its very presence was enough to stun them. Distance had no meaning in the Weave except in how human minds interpreted it, but until this moment the leviathans had been far, far away, unfathomably aloof. Now one of them appeared in such close proximity that the backwash almost scattered the Sisters' consciousnesses, shaking them out of coherence. They regrouped, overwhelmed; but the entity was still now, and calm descended.

Its size, its sheer *impact* on the Weave was colossal. The Sisters were motes in its presence: it dominated utterly the world of golden threads. It was a white void, an aching, blazing split that burned the eye with its brilliance. There was no shape to it, for it seemed to exist in many shapes all together; yet the human mind could not allow that, and so they put their own shape to the leviathan, fixed it in their perception. It was vast and smooth and streamlined, something like a whale in form but so alien to any creature they knew that analogy was impossible; and they were plankton against its flanks.

They regarded it in utter terror, not daring to do anything but hang there, motionless, while their Weave-senses fought to cope with what was happening.

It regarded them, too. They felt its attention brushing them as the hull of some dark, gargantuan ship sliding past, a crushing force missing them by inches. It could destroy them with the weight of that scrutiny. Kaiku had once faced the Children of the Moons, spirits so old that it was not within humanity's grasp to comprehend them; yet they were children indeed compared to this. This was a factor of magnitude so far beyond those spirits that sanity would not hold long enough to consider it.

A moment passed, and then, without warning, the Weave furled like a flower into a knot of infinite density, and then sprang back. The leviathan was gone, but the resonation of its passing rang like a bell.

Kaiku and Cailin left the Weave together. Cailin was visible again. For a long minute, they stood listening to the banal night, breathing, feeling the touch of the wind on their faces and in their hair.

Questions were lancing back and forth beneath the skin of reality. The other Sisters had sensed the leviathan. But neither Cailin nor Kaiku could respond. They stared at one another, and did not say anything. They did not have the words.

A few days later, Mishani arrived at Araka Jo.

She found Kaiku by a small lake a little way east of the temple complex. She was standing at the edge of a wooden viewing-platform, looking out across the carpet of lily pads and floating blossoms of white and red. The lake was surrounded by kamaka trees, their leaves hanging over the water in long drowsy chains. Nuki's eye had that peculiarly sharp winter's quality; it was pleasantly warm in his gaze, but where the shade obscured it there was a faint chill.

Kaiku was not wearing the attire of the Order. She had dressed in a thick robe, purple and blue and lavender, belted with a green sash. To Mishani, who was used to her friend's tomboyish tendencies, it was an unexpectedly feminine choice of clothing. Mishani watched her for a time from the end of the viewing-platform, simply enjoying the sight of her in contemplation.

'I know you are there, Mishani,' she said, a smile in her voice. 'I am long past the stage where you could sneak up on me.'

Mishani laughed, and Kaiku turned around to embrace her.

'Gods, I am glad to see you safe,' she murmured.

They talked for a long while, for they had much to tell. It had been over a year since they had last met, just before Mishani departed for Tchom Rin. Kaiku's talk was mostly of her training, for she had not travelled so far as her friend had. Mishani carried the bulk of the conversation; Kaiku was eager to hear all about the desert cities.

'And look at you now!' Kaiku said, plucking at Mishani's sleeve. 'You look like a desert noble yourself!'

'I will confess a certain fondness for the fashion,' Mishani grinned. Then she sobered and said: 'I have to tell you this, Kaiku: Asara is here.'

Kaiku's mirth flickered like a guttering candle. 'Asara?' For an instant, she was reliving that moment in the Fold, when she had seduced a man named Saran Ycthys Marul, not knowing that it was Asara in another shape. The sheer *betrayal* still scorched her. Then her smile returned, a little forced now. 'She can wait. Come, let us walk.'

They followed a trail around the edge of the lake, a dirt path scattered with worn stones that had mostly sunk into the ground with the passing of centuries. Ravens and jays hopped about the undergrowth, or took off in a startled flap of wings, blasting leaves and twigs in their wake. Most of the foliage in Saramyr was evergreen, but the people held some residual genetic memory of the time when their ancestors dwelt in temperate Quraal, and even more than a thousand years after they had come to this land there was a faintly disjointed feel to the wintertime. A sensation that something should be, and was not. The majority of the trees here never bared themselves, and that jarred with old instincts.

Kaiku felt happy to be with her friend again. There was an ease between them that nobody else in her life shared. As always, she was surprised that she could forsake that feeling so easily, that she could forget how it was when they were together; and yet she knew that when they were next parted, she would forget anew.

As they walked, Mishani told Kaiku of her journey back across the mountains.

'My impression was that the peaks were swarming with Aberrants, but we saw scarcely any, and those at a distance,' she said. 'Even when we got to the plains, and we had to cross the South Tradeway and skirt north of the marshes, our journey was unhindered. I had thought I was fortunate not to have encountered any trouble when I first crossed into the desert, but I am beginning to think that fortune had nothing to do with it.'

'Our scouts report the same,' Kaiku agreed. 'The Weavers are concentrating their forces in the cities, and fewer of them are roaming the countryside. There is speculation that even they do not have the numbers to stretch adequately across all that territory. They lost hundreds of thousands in the early months of the war, before they learned to fight tactically. Maybe they cannot breed enough, or capture enough – or however they are replenishing their armies – to cover the shortfall.'

'In that, at least, we can take heart.'

There was a pause, filled with the soft tread of their shoes and the rustling of the leaves, long enough to elicit a new subject.

'I read your mother's new book,' Kaiku said.

'So did I. Several times.'

'There is something odd about it. About those last lines, especially.'

Mishani nodded sadly. 'The words Nida-jan says to the dying man? They are the first stanza of a lullaby she used to sing to me, one that she wrote herself. We were the only ones that knew it in its entirety.'

'*I* know it,' Kaiku said. 'You sang it to me once, when you were telling me how you discovered Chien was working for your mother.'

'You remember that?' Mishani asked in surprise. She had

not thought of the unfortunate merchant for a long time now. He had been poisoned by her father's assassins during the siege at Zila; but not before Mishani had found out that he had been charged by her mother in secret to protect her from those same assassins.

Kaiku's lip twitched at the edge. 'She does have a gift for words. It sticks in the mind.' She kicked at a branch that lay across their path. 'After I read those lines, I could not shake the sensation that she meant something by them.'

'That is plain enough,' said Mishani.

'So I began to read her earlier books. The ones since her style changed, since your father became Lord Protector. Trying to divine what her intention might be, what she was trying to express.'

'And did you come to any conclusion?' Mishani was fascinated by this, that her friend should have been thinking along exactly the same lines as her.

Kaiku tilted her shoulders in a shrug. 'Nothing, beyond a certainty that there is something there. The answers remain impenetrable.'

Mishani felt a twinge of disappointment. She had hoped her friend might have some kind of resolution for her.

'Tsata is back,' Kaiku said, apropos of nothing.

'Here?'

'In Saramyr. He is coming to Araka Jo with the Tkiurathi.' Kaiku had charged the Sister present at the attack to find out whether Tsata had survived. It had taken several days, for the Tkiurathi had departed from the main army some time before, and the Sister had other things to do; finding someone who remembered one man amid an army of people who looked identical to her eyes was not an easy task. But the answer had come that morning.

Kaiku had been almost giddy with relief: she had not realised how tautly she was wound until the tension inside her slackened.

'Strange days indeed,' Mishani said wryly, looking up at Kaiku, who was several inches the taller.

'Do not use that tone!' Kaiku laughed. 'I know what you insinuate.'

'He has crossed an ocean to come back to you, Kaiku,' Mishani pointed out.

'He has crossed an ocean to fight the Weavers,' she replied. 'You know his kind; it was the only logical course of action to him.'

'I do *not* know his kind,' said Mishani. 'Their ways are hard for me to understand. Not for you, though, it seems.'

Kaiku made a prissy little *moue* at her friend. 'Perhaps I should be the ambassador, then, instead of you.'

'Ha! You? We would be at open war within the day!'

And so it went. They meandered along the lakeside in the bright light of the winter's day, and for a time they forgot their cares in the simplicity of companionship. Such moments were all too brief, for both of them.

In the Imperial Keep at Axekami, the evening meal was served.

The Lord Protector Avun tu Koli knelt opposite his wife at the small, square table of black and red lacquer. Between them were woven baskets which steamed gently, separate ones for shellfish, saltrice, dumplings and vegetables. Little bowls of soup and sauces, tall glasses of amber wine. The servants ensured everything was satisfactory and then retreated through the curtained archway, leaving their master and mistress alone.

They sat in silence for a time. The room, though not so large, seemed cavernous and hollow; the sound of their breathing and their tiny movements were amplified by the empty space. It was not yet late enough to merit lanterns, but the murk over the city choked the sunlight that came in through the trio of floor-to-ceiling window-arches in the western wall and left only a drab gloom. Vases and sculptures were positioned in alcoves, but the central space was open, and only they were there, kneeling on their mats with the table and the food between them.

'Will you eat?' Avun said eventually.

Muraki did not respond for a few seconds. Then she began to slip on the finger-cutlery. Avun did the same, and they took food from the baskets and put it onto their plates.

'Did your writing go well today?' he asked.

'Well enough,' she replied quietly, an unspoken accusation in her voice.

'I thought you should get away from that room,' Avun said. 'It is not good for your health, to shut yourself away like that.'

Muraki glanced up at him through the curtains of her hair, then looked meaningfully out of the window and back to him. *Healthier than breathing this air*, her gaze said.

'I am sorry for having interrupted you, then,' he said, pouring a dark sauce over the shellfish, holding the bowl with his unencumbered thumb and forefinger. 'I wanted to have a meal with my wife.'

She did not reply to that. Instead, she began to eat, cutting portions with the tiny blades and forks set on silver thimbles that she wore on the middle and ring fingers of her right and left hand, taking small and delicate bites.

'The feya-kori are on their way back from Zila,' Avun said. He needed to say something to breach his wife's wall of silence. When she did not respond, he persevered: 'The troops of the Empire were driven out with barely any resistance at all. The Weavers are pleased with their new creations; more will join them soon, I think.'

The quiet became excruciating once again, but Avun had given enough to expect something in return. Eventually, Muraki asked: 'How soon?'

'A matter of weeks. It is uncertain.'

'And then?'

'We will overrun the Southern Prefectures, and after that we will turn to Tchom Rin.'

'And will you turn their cities into places like this?'

'I cannot see why the Weavers would do so,' he replied. 'There will be no need for feya-kori once they have control of the continent. And so, there will be no need for this miasma.'

'Will there be a need for us, do you think?' she asked softly. 'When they have control of the continent?'

Avun smiled gently. 'I am no fool, Muraki. I do not think they would keep me as Lord Protector out of gratitude. I will be invaluable to them still. The people need a human face upon their leader. They will never trust a Mask.'

'But they will trust you?'

'They will trust me because I will give them their skies back,' Avun said. He took a sip of wine. 'I do not want to live under this murk any more than you do; it is unnatural. But the sooner we are rid of the opposition, the sooner we can dispense with the feya-kori and dissemble the pall-pits.'

'And the temples?'

Avun was lost for an answer for a moment. His wife had a way of pricking his sorest spots in a tone so submissive that he could not take umbrage. 'The temples will not return. The Weavers do not like our gods.'

Muraki's silence was more eloquent than words. She knew he still prayed in the dead of night, in the empty interior of the temple to Ocha on the roof of the Keep. The dome still remained in all its finery, though the statues of the gods that had ringed it were gone, and the altars and icons stripped away. It had an appallingly wounded feel to it now, and Muraki would not go near it. But Avun did.

Muraki wondered how he reconciled his actions to himself: he was not the most pious of men, but he would not forsake his gods, even though he would tear down their temples. Did he expect forgiveness? She knew of no deity so divinely gracious as to provide him with that, after the crimes he had committed against the Golden Realm.

Avun dodged the subject in the end, returning to his previous point. 'In the end, the world will be as it was. The blight can be contained once the Red Order are overthrown, for the Weavers will not need so many witchstones. The miasma will be gone. And the land will be united once again.'

'That is what the Weavers say? I had not heard that before now.'

'I met with Kakre this morning. I persuaded him to divulge. It was not easy.' Avun seemed proud of himself; she had no trouble believing that it was a courageous thing to do. She knew what had happened to him in the past when Kakre was displeased.

'Why?' she asked, puzzled. 'Why did you do it? You have been content in ignorance until now.'

He gazed at her levelly. 'Because my wife does not like the air here,' he said. 'And I had to be able to tell her it would be pure again one day.'

Muraki's eyes flickered to his, and then back to her plate. It was the only outward sign of the flutter she felt in her breast. For a long while, she said nothing.

'Do you believe them?'

'It is the only way I can make sense of it. The alternative is to continue to poison the land. To do that would kill their own people, their own army. There is not enough food, and the famine will get worse.'

'Or perhaps we do not see the Weavers' greater plan,' she whispered, her voice softening with the terror of contradicting him. 'Perhaps Kakre is merely mad.'

Avun nodded. 'He is mad.'

Muraki looked at him in surprise.

'I have been watching his decline most carefully,' Avun said. 'It has steepened since he awakened the feya-kori. I think the effort of controlling them has hit him the hardest. His sanity is eroding fast.' He took a bite of a dumpling, chewed for a moment and swallowed, as if what he was saying was just idle conversation and not something he might be executed for. 'I suspect he would not have told me the Weavers' long-term plans if he had not been quite so addled.'

'But if the Weave-lord is mad,' Muraki breathed, 'who will direct the Weavers?'

'That,' he said, raising his glass, 'is the question.'

TWELVE

The desert city of Izanzai sprawled over an uneven plateau that rose high above the dusty plains. It was a forest of dark spikes, its buildings cramming up to the lip of the sand-coloured cliffs. Needle-thin towers speared towards the pale sky; bulbous temples tapered to elegant spires as they ascended; bridges looped above the hot, shadowy streets. At its southern edge there was a vast earthen ramp that was the only road up to the top of the plateau, built through years of toil and costing many lives.

Izanzai commanded an impressive view of its surroundings. To the south and east the plains were gradually swallowed by the deep desert, and in the distance it was possible to see the beginning of the enormous dunes that humped across central Tchom Rin. To the north and west the land was starker still, dry flats and mesas streaked with swatches of muddy yellow and deep brown, then suddenly rising hard, becoming the great barrier of the Tchamil Mountains. The mountains loomed grey and bleak, their sides flensed of life by hurricanes, innumerable peaks ranked one behind the other and stretching to infinity.

At their feet, men fought and died.

Barak Reki tu Tanatsua sat on manxthwa-back on the lip of a mesa, overlooking the battle. The warm wind plucked at his hair and clothes and ruffled the pelt of his mount. His eyes were narrowed, studying the form and movement of both sides, calculating strategies. The fight was all but over, and the desert forces were the victors, but he would not count it done until every last one of the enemy were dead. To his right and left, also on manxthwa, were a Sister of the

Red Order and Jikiel, his spymaster. Other bodyguards waited at a distance, keen and alert, though they were far from anything that could harm them.

The latchjaws had arrived in greater numbers than ever this time. Had they come up against the armies of the families of Izanzai alone, they would have crushed them. But the unification of the Baraks had changed things, and with old enmities laid aside, Reki had been able to direct a much larger force to defend the city. The alliance had come not a day too soon, it seemed.

But the battle had been costly. Those cursed Aberrant beasts were tough to kill, and more often than not they took a few men with them when they went. Unlike the majority of the predator species that the Weavers had deployed thus far, they needed little water or food and were all but immune to the heat. They dealt with shifting sand or hard stone with equal ease; and their deadly natural armour meant that the desert warriors' manic, close-up fighting style was effectively rendered suicidal. Too many were falling to them, snatched up in the mantrap-like jaws that gave them their name. Gods, if he didn't think it impossible, he would have believed that the Weavers had tailored this species for exactly this purpose: to overrun the desert.

It *was* impossible, wasn't it?

'Your men in the mountains have located some of the Nexuses,' the Sister murmured suddenly, relaying the information passed from her companions nearer the battle.

Reki made a noise of acknowledgement. He could have guessed that anyway. A section of the shambling monstrosities down on the plain had suddenly gone berserk, a sure sign that their masters had been killed. No longer under the control of the Nexuses, they reverted to being animals again, and animals were liable to react badly at finding themselves in the midst of a pitched battle of thousands.

'It seems that this day is ours,' Jikiel observed.

Reki looked askance at his spymaster. '*This* day,' he said. 'But how many more can we win?'

Jikiel nodded gravely. He was old and bald, brown and wrinkled as a nut, with a thin black beard and moustaches hanging in three slender ropes down his chest. He was robed in beige, with a nakata, the hook-tipped sword worn by the warriors of Tchom Rin, belted to his hip. 'Perhaps we should take action against the source,' he suggested.

'I was thinking the same,' said Reki. 'Each time they come, there are more. We are forced to spread ourselves thin, for the borders of the mountains are vast. By bringing the Baraks together, we have won a respite; but that is all. They will overwhelm us in time.'

'What are your orders, my Barak?'

'Assemble as many men as you need. Send them into the mountains. I want to know where these things are coming from.'

'It shall be done.'

They watched the battle for a little longer. The Nexuses were falling, and with them went their troops, collapsing into disorder and being shot down by the desert folk. The manxthwa stirred and grumbled, shuffling from side to side and scraping their hooves. The Sister delivered reports from time to time.

Half of Reki's mind was on the battlefield, but half had drifted elsewhere, to his wife. It always seemed to. She had been gone over a month now, but the anxiety of separation had not faded. He still yearned for her. And he still burned at the way she had left him: without an explanation, with only cryptic hints and emotional blackmail left in her wake. He was furious at himself for letting her go without demanding more. He wondered what she was doing now, what was so important as to take her over seven hundred miles to the west. In the time she had been gone, he had tormented himself with innumerable invented histories; but in the end, how could he guess? What did he really know about Asara's past? She was a mystery to him, as much as she had ever been.

And yet, was there really anything to fear? Was there

anything he could not forgive her for, anything that might stop him loving her? He could not believe that. And he could not bear the torture of possibilities when there were the prospect of certainties that he could deal with and overcome.

'Jikiel?' he murmured, turning himself so that he was out of the Sister's earshot.

'My Barak?'

'Find out about my wife.' It felt like the most exquisite betrayal, and for a moment he considered taking it back; but it was a risk he had to take. If Asara did not trust their love, then he would have to take matters into his own hands. 'Find out *everything* about her.'

A smile touched the corner of Jikiel's mouth. 'I thought you'd never ask.'

Asara came to Cailin in the small hours of the morning, in the house of the Red Order at Araka Jo. Cailin was drinking bitter tea, looking out through the sliding panels at the dark trees, watching owls.

'Asara,' she purred. 'It was only a matter of time.'

Asara was already inside the room, having glided through the drapes without a sound. 'Why else do you suppose I would come this far, if not to see you?'

Cailin put aside the delicate bowl that she was drinking from, stood up and faced her visitor. 'Kaiku, perhaps? You never did seem to be able to keep away from her for long.'

Asara did not rise to the bait. 'I saved Kaiku's life for *you*,' she said calmly. 'I have paid a price for it ever since. I expect a measure of gratitude for that.'

'Ah, gratitude,' Cailin replied. 'Why would I owe you that, Asara? You did what I told you to. You will get your reward when our deal is complete.'

Asara stepped a little further into the room. It was dark; there was no light but the white glow of the two larger moons. She stood there in the shadows, a disdainful arrogance in the tilt of her chin. She wore a white dress fastened with a brooch, delicate jewellery on her wrists and in her hair. Every inch the desert Barakess.

'Things are different now,' Asara said. 'I am no longer the woman I once was.'

'You think you have *changed?*' Cailin said in disbelief. 'You can change all you want on the outside, Asara, but inside you are just as empty as you have always been.'

'It is my situation that has changed.' Her tone had become edged with venom now. 'As well you know.'

They regarded each other across the room. It was the same one in which Kaiku and Cailin had been Weaving several nights before, on the second storey of the Red Order's house. The vases stood empty now, the incense burner cold. The charcoal etchings on the wood-panelled walls seemed to creep in the darkness.

'I must congratulate you,' Cailin said at length. 'Your seduction of the Heir-Barak showed impressive foresight. How you must have grieved when both his sister and his father died, making way for him to become head of his family.'

'His sister was ineligible to become head of the family, since she was wed to the Emperor,' Asara replied levelly. 'Her demise benefitted you more than me. You wanted the Weavers to succeed in their coup, you *wanted* them to take this land. And now you have your wish.'

'And you had nothing to do with her death, I suppose?'

'Maybe so, and maybe not,' Asara replied. 'If the former, it would have been another example of how I have given more on your behalf that anyone has a right to ask, and received nothing in return.'

'Such is the nature of our agreement, Asara. You will be paid in full when the time comes.'

'Then I am altering our agreement.'

Cailin raised an eyebrow. 'You are? How amusing.'

'I am the wife of a Barak now, Cailin,' Asara said, bridling a little. 'I hold the most powerful man in the desert in the palm of my hand. You cannot sweep me aside as you might once have done.'

Cailin's red-and-black lips were set in a mocking smirk. 'I see. And you think that because you have fooled a callow boy into marriage that you can use it as leverage to bully me? I had thought better of you, Asara.'

'I have been over a *decade* in your thrall, Cailin,' Asara spat, sudden rage igniting within her. 'Kept tied by your promises. You realised what I needed – the gods know how; your filthy *kana*-games, no doubt – and you have exploited me ever since. And all this time I have chased a dream that I am not even sure you are capable of fulfilling! Now I have the power in the desert, and I can turn Tchom Rin against you and your kind. I know what *you* desire, and I can make it much more difficult for you if you do not give me what I want *now!*'

'Enough!' Cailin snapped. 'What is ten years, twenty, *fifty* to such as us? We will not age, Asara. We do not run out of time as others do. Where is your patience?'

'I have been patient,' came the reply. 'But there is a line between patience and foolishness. Should I be your slave for another decade, and another, until you decide to release me? And even then, could you grant me what you say you will? *Would* you? One woman's word is a slender thread to hang such a weight from. And you have hardly been a paragon of trustworthiness in the years I have known you.'

Cailin laughed, the sound high and bright. 'Poor Asara,' she said. 'Poor, murdering Asara.' Her laughter faded, and her voice grew dark. 'You want sympathy? I have none. The Red Order's cause is as much in your interests as ours—'

'I doubt that,' Asara interrupted.

'—and however unwillingly, you are fighting for yourself when you fight on our side. We will make a world where Aberrants can live without fear. And you *will* aid us in that, whether you want to or not.'

'You are avoiding the issue,' Asara said, stalking closer. 'Give me what I want.'

'Release you from our compact? Hardly. You are, despite your faults, an extremely useful ally.'

'*Give me what I want!*' Asara cried.

'Or *what?*' Cailin shouted. 'What will you do, Asara? You think you can turn the desert against us? You think you can *stop* us? Your best efforts would be nothing more than a mosquito bite to the Red Order. We could kill you a thousand times over before you could even get back to your beloved Barak. And even Reki is not such a fool as to forsake the powers we lend him when the Weavers are even now trying to invade Tchom Rin. Yours is a poor bluff, Asara, and you tire me now.'

'It ends here, then!' Asara returned. 'It all ends here. If you cannot prove to me that you can do what you say, then I—'

Cailin cut her throat.

It was a swift, dismissive gesture with her hand, a disgusted flick of her fingers in the moonlight. She did not touch the other woman; they were too far apart. But Asara's neck opened from side to side in a red slit, as cleanly as if Cailin had been holding a sword.

Asara staggered backward, her eyes wide, making damp noises in her chest. Blood gushed, pulsing down the front of her dress, staining it a glistening black in the moonlight. Cailin watched impassively, sidelit by the moonlight, her irises gone crimson.

Asara tried to make a sound, but none would come. She tried to draw breath, but not even a gasp would make it through her severed windpipe. Panic swamped her, a terror like nothing she had ever known before: she was dying, dying unfulfilled, and when she was gone it would be as if she had never been here. Her legs went weak, her muscles leaden. She fell to her knees, clutching her throat with one hand, the other feebly propping her upright, her splayed fingers sliding in her own fluids. Her head was becoming light. So much blood, so much blood, and nothing she could do would staunch it.

Not like this, was all she could think with the last dregs of her reason. *Not like this*.

Cailin made a vague waving motion with two of her fingers, and Asara's throat sewed shut, fibres and tissues knitting seamlessly from side to side as if zipped. Eager nourishment slammed from her heart to her brain, and she hauled in a huge, sobbing breath. She had never felt such a divine sensation as the relief she experienced then, nor a hatred so pure as that which she had for the one who had hurt her this way. Still gasping, her dress sodden black, she raised her head and fixed Cailin with a gaze of utter malice.

The Pre-Eminent of the Red Order looked down on her coldly. 'Satisfied?' she asked, then walked out of the room, leaving Asara kneeling in a pool of her own blood.

An hour's walk northeast of Araka Jo, deep in the forested mountains, lay the glade of an ipi.

It was a place of preternatural stillness and tranquillity, a cavernous sanctum with a roof of interlaced branches and leaves through which the winter sun shone in bright, slanting shafts of light. Gently rolling hillocks and tuffets cradled pools as motionless and transparent as glass; rocks smooth and white like bleached bone hid half-buried in the earth. In the midst of the glade stood the ipi itself: a colossal tree, its bark black as char, rucked and gnarled with age. Its uppermost branches meshed with the canopy overhead, while the lower boughs reached out across the clearing like crooked arms, fingers shaggy with pine blades.

Lucia knelt at the base of the tree, her head bowed, clad in a belted robe of dark green. She was meditating, communing with the spirit of the glade. To talk to an ipi was easy for her these days. Her power had grown at a frightening rate since she had emerged from the shrine of Alskain Mar back in the Xarana Fault, and all but the most ancient spirits were open to her now. Yet with every step she took into the world of the spirits, she took one away from the world of humanity, and she was becoming more like them by the day.

Kaiku watched her from the edge of the glade. Somewhere in the trees, out of sight, were her Libera Dramach bodyguards. But in this place, in the ipi's serene presence, Lucia might have been alone in all the world. And it was true, in a sense. For there was no one like Lucia, nobody who could imagine what it was like to be as she was, poised halfway between two worlds and belonging to neither any more.

It pained Kaiku to see her so isolated. Mishani's visit had reminded her of Yugi's stinging words, how he had accused her of neglecting her friends while she subsumed herself in the teachings of the Red Order. Once, Lucia had been like a younger sister to her; now, Kaiku was not so sure.

Eventually, Lucia lifted her head and stood. She picked her way barefoot along the knolls, retrieved her shoes from where she had left them at the edge of the glade, and then joined Kaiku.

'Daygreet,' she said with a beatific smile, and then hugged Kaiku impulsively. Kaiku, faintly surprised, returned it.

'Gods, you are the same height as me now,' she said.

'Growing like a weed,' Lucia laughed. 'It's been too long since you came to see me, Kaiku.'

'I know,' Kaiku muttered. 'I know.'

Lucia put her shoes on and they began to walk back towards Araka Jo. Kaiku dismissed the bodyguards and sent them ahead: their charge would be safer with her than with twenty armed men, and they recognised her even without the makeup and attire of the Order. She and Lucia ambled along the narrow forest trails. Lucia chattered happily as they went. She was in an unusually ebullient mood, certainly not the state of dreamy detachment that Kaiku had come to expect from her.

'The blight is retreating,' she said out of nowhere, interrupting herself in the process of telling Kaiku about her day.

'It is?'

'The ipi can sense it. Since the witchstone beneath Utraxxa broke. The land here is recovering, little by little.' She watched a bird arrowing through the treetops as she spoke. 'We are not too far gone to go back. Not yet.'

'But that is wonderful news!' Kaiku cried. Lucia gave her a sidelong grin. 'No wonder you are so cheerful today.'

'It is wonderful news,' she agreed. 'And I hear you have news also.'

Kaiku nodded. 'Though I am not so sure whether it is good news or bad.' And she went on to tell Lucia about her and Cailin's encounter with the leviathan. The *Weave-whale*, as Cailin had come to call it.

'I am afraid of them,' she admitted. 'For too long we had ignored them as they ignored us, assuming them forever out of our reach. But we have attracted them now, I think. They have noticed what was once beneath their notice. Our meddling in the Weave is drawing creatures to which the Weavers' capabilities for destruction pale in comparison.'

'But what are they?' Lucia asked.

'Perhaps they are gods,' came the reply.

Lucia did not comment on that, but it sobered her. They walked on a short way in silence through the sun-dappled forest. A raven hopped from branch to branch overhead.

'Lucia, I truly am sorry,' Kaiku said at length. 'I have neglected you for some time now. I was so caught up in learning how to use what I have that I . . . . forgot what I had.'

Lucia took her hand. It was a gesture from the old Lucia, the child, before she became a young woman.

'It is the war,' she said. 'Do not be sorry, Kaiku. You are a weapon, as am I. What good is a weapon if its edge is not sharpened?'

Kaiku was shocked at the fatalism in her tone. 'Lucia, no! We are *not* merely weapons. If I taught you nothing else, I taught you that.'

'Then you believe we have a choice? That we can turn away from all this now?' She smiled sadly, and relinquished Kaiku's hand. 'I can't. And I don't believe you can, either.'

'You *have* that choice, Lucia!' she insisted.

'Do I?' Lucia laughed again, and this time it was bitter and made Kaiku uneasy. 'If I wanted to duck the expectations the world has of me, I should have done it long ago. Before the Libera Dramach reorganised; before the battle at the Fold, even. Too many people have died in my name now. I cannot go back. That time has passed.' She looked down the trail, and her eyes became unfocused. She was listening to the rustle of the forest. 'I've become what they wanted of me. I've become their bridge to the spirits, for what good it will do. I am a weapon, and a weapon is useless if it is not wielded. I cannot stay useless for very much longer.'

'Lucia—' Kaiku began, but was interrupted.

'You think I don't know about the feya-kori? How we have no defence against them, no way to strike back? How long before you all call on me, then? Your last resort? Your only hope?' They had stopped walking now, and Lucia looked fierce. 'Do you know how that is, Kaiku? To spend your whole life knowing that your options are narrowing day by day, that eventually you must deliver on this promise that you *never made!* They look to me as their saviour, but I don't know how to save anyone!'

'You do not have to,' Kaiku told her. 'Listen to me: you do *not* have to.'

Lucia looked away, not remotely convinced.

'In my life I have known people who are so selfish that they would sacrifice anything and anyone to bring advantage to themselves,' Kaiku said, putting her hand on Lucia's arm. 'And I have known a man so selfless that he was willing to throw away his life too cheaply for the good of others. I believe the right path lies somewhere in between. I have told you before, Lucia: you need to be a little more selfish. Think of yourself for once.'

'Even at the expense of this land and everyone in it?' Lucia replied scornfully.

'Even then,' said Kaiku. 'For as much as you think it might, the fate of the world does not rest on your actions.'

Lucia would not meet her gaze. 'I'm afraid, Kaiku,' she whispered.

'I know.'

'You *don't* know,' she said, and her expression revealed a depth of something that made Kaiku scared to see it. 'I'm *changing*.'

'Changing? How?'

Lucia turned from her, staring out into the forest. Kaiku's attention fell upon the burn scars on the nape of her neck. The stab of guilt at the sight would never go away, it seemed.

'I realise I am distracted sometimes . . . *most* of the time,' she said. 'I realise how hard it is to talk to me. I do not blame you for not coming to see me so often.' She raised a hand to forestall Kaiku's protest. 'It's true, Kaiku. I can't pay attention to anything any more. Everywhere I go, there are the voices. The breath of the wind, the mutter of the earth; the birds, the trees, the stone. I do not know what silence is.' She turned her face sideways, looking over her shoulder at Kaiku, and a tear slid down her cheek. 'I can't shut them out,' she whispered.

A lump rose in Kaiku's throat.

'I'm becoming like them,' Lucia said, her voice small and terrifying in its hopelessness. 'I'm forgetting. Forgetting how to care. I think of Zaelis and Flen, of my mother . . . and I don't *feel*. They died because of me, and sometimes I can't even recall their faces.' Her lip began to tremble, and her face crumpled, and she rushed into Kaiku's arms suddenly and clutched her so tightly that it hurt. 'I'm so *lonely*,' she said, and began to cry in earnest then.

Kaiku's stomach and heart were a knot of grief that brought tears to her own eyes. She wanted to reach Lucia somehow, to do something to make things better, but she was as helpless as anyone. All Kaiku could do was to be there for her, and she had been sadly remiss at that these past years.

And as they held each other on the narrow forest trail, the leaves began to fall. First one, then two, then a dozen and more, drifting down from the evergreens to settle on their shoulders and pile around their feet. Lucia was weeping, and the trees were shedding in sympathy.

THIRTEEN

The Tkiurathi appeared one morning soon afterward, on a slope south of Araka Jo. By the time anyone noticed them, they had already made cook-fires, strung up shelters of animal hide, and dozens of them were sleeping in the boughs like cats. A makeshift village of yurts and hemp hammocks had sprung up overnight amid the tree trunks. To all appearances, they might have been living there for weeks.

Tsata was sitting in the crook of a tree, where the branch met the bole, one leg dangling. He was idly sharpening his gutting-hooks on a whetstone, his attention elsewhere. From his vantage point at the north side of the village he could see up the dirt trail towards Araka Jo. He believed at first that he had chosen this spot at random, but he decided in the end that he was fooling himself. He was keeping an eye on the trail. Waiting to see if Kaiku would come to him.

A Tkiurathi woman called from below. She raised her blade, and he tossed her down the whetstone, which she plucked from the air with a grin of thanks before wandering back towards the centre of the village.

Tsata slipped his gutting-hook back on to the catch at his belt and relaxed, watching the activity around him. It was exciting to be here in Saramyr again, and the better because this time he was not alone, but surrounded by his people. They took the strangeness of the land in their stride. They were brothers and sisters, insulated within their *pash*, comforted by the knowledge of community. Tsata found himself smiling.

At the base of the trees, traditional three-sided yurts called *repka* had been built. They were communal places for living and sleeping, with splayed, tunnel-like arms around a large hub construction with a chimney-hole through which curls of smoke rose. Other fires had been made outside: the hunters had already caught some of the local wildlife, and Tsata had been busy indicating foods that were safe to eat. He was recognised as the authority on Saramyr within the *pash*, having been here before and having studied its language and its customs long before that.

It was the way among the Tkiurathi that they were all teachers, each one sharing what unique knowledge or abilities they had. It had been one such man who had taught Tsata Saramyrrhic, a man who had travelled and lived here for decades before returning to his homeland. Tsata had a particular gift for languages – he had already learned a good deal of Quraal, which was the lingua franca of the trading settlements dotted around the Okhamban coast – and he had been bewildered and fascinated by stories of Saramyr. He applied himself to learning Saramyrrhic with a singularity of purpose that impressed his teacher, and within a few years he was as skilled at it as any foreigner could be. The months he had spent here had improved his command of the language vastly, but even now he was not entirely fluent in the overwhelming multitude of modes and inflections, the tiny subtleties of High Saramyrrhic that only those born to it could hope to master.

When he looked away from the settlement and back to the trail, Kaiku was there. She was regarding him impishly, a wry expression on her face.

'Are you coming down here, or shall I come up there?' she called.

He laughed; he knew her well enough to tell that she was not bluffing. With monkey-like grace, he slipped off the branch and swung from it to the ground ten feet below. There was a moment of awkward hesitation as they met, as each tried to determine whether to greet the other in their native fashion or that of the foreigner; then Kaiku stood on tiptoes, kissed him on the forehead and embraced him. Tsata was warmly surprised: it was an unusual gesture of extraordinary intimacy for a Saramyr to bestow.

'Welcome back,' she said.

'It is good to be here,' he said. 'I wish all welcomes had been as pleasant.'

'The feya-kori,' Kaiku murmured, nodding slightly. 'I fear you could have timed your arrival a little better.'

'Perhaps we have arrived at just the right moment,' he countered. 'From what I have learned, there have been no darker days than these. And there is no further need to convince my people of the threat to us; the men who return to Okhamba will spread the word. Seventy-five of us lost their lives the day we landed, but the remainder will fight harder for their sacrifice.' His face cleared suddenly. 'But we can talk of such things later. Let me show you our new home. And you must tell me what has occurred in my absence.'

It was as if they had never been apart. They fell easily into the rhythms of conversation that they had established during their long period of isolation, when they had lived and hunted together in the shattered wilderness of the Xarana Fault.

He talked of the many obstacles he had faced in his mission to alert his people to the danger of the Weavers. Kaiku spoke of her induction into the Red Order and her training. She told him also of Lucia and Mishani; he had met them briefly before his departure from the Fold, but he knew them primarily through Kaiku's stories. And she spoke of her fears for Lucia, and about the Weave-whales, and the plight of the beleaguered forces of the Empire.

They wandered the village as they talked. Kaiku had chosen travel clothes over the attire of the Order for her visit to the Tkiurathi village, for she did not wish to appear intimidating. Now she was glad that she had. Amid the informality of the Tkiurathi, she would have felt self-conscious in her make-up.

The people were muscled and lean, their skin tough and their hands seamed through the rigours of their lifestyle. She often found herself identifying them as much from the unique pattern of their tattoos as by their features, for it was difficult to see past them at first: they were such an overwhelmingly prominent facet of their appearance. The women were strong and physically unfeminine by Saramyr standards, having little softness about them, though Kaiku found in some a kind of wild beauty that was appealing. They sat as equals with the men, their long hair bound with cord or left loose, wearing sleeveless garments of hemp or hide and trousers of the same.

Tsata sat with her around one of the campfires that had been built out in the open, along with a dozen other Tkiurathi who were eating. The men to either side of them handed them bowls and tipped a portion of their own bowls into those of the newcomers. It was a typically Okhamban gesture of sharing. Kaiku did not know how she was supposed to respond, for she had nothing to give back; but Tsata motioned to her not to worry, no response was needed, and he began to fill the remainder of both their bowls from a pot of stew that hung over the fire. It was the meat of some local animal mixed in with vegetables and unfamiliar spices: it smelt delicious, though not so delicate as Saramyr food, more laden with heavy flavour. By the time he had finished, they had been handed chunks of bread from others in the circle, torn from their own loaves. Kaiku could not help but thank them, even though she knew almost nothing of their language.

'You do not need to thank them,' Tsata told her. 'You do so by allowing them to share in *your* food, when *you* have some and they are hungry.'

'I know,' she said. 'But it is difficult to break the habits of a lifetime. Just as I would find it odd if some of your people turned up at the door of my house expecting to be fed.'

'It does not quite work that way,' he laughed. 'But I can tell there will be many such misunderstandings between your folk and mine in the days to come.'

One of the women, who had been studying Kaiku, said something to her in their rough, guttural dialect. She looked uncertainly at Tsata.

'She says your language is very beautiful,' he translated. 'Like birds singing.'

'Should I thank her for that?'

He smiled. 'Yes. *Ghohkri.*'

Kaiku repeated the word to the woman, by chance pronouncing it perfectly to murmurs of approval from round the fire. Encouraged by her response, others started to ask her questions or make observations, which Tsata translated rapidly back and forth. Presently Kaiku was drawn into the conversation around the circle, with Tsata murmuring condensed explanations in her ear as people spoke to each other in Okhamban. She began to interject with a few comments of her own, to which there was always a slightly uncomfortable moment of incomprehension until Tsata could provide the Okhamban; but they were polite and patient, and Kaiku began to enjoy herself greatly. They were clearly fascinated by her, and they thought that even the shabby travel clothes she wore were incredibly exotic.

'Gods, they should see the River District in Axekami,' Kaiku commented to Tsata, then remembered that Axekami was not as it once was, and saddened a little.

Eventually, they left the circle and wandered around the rest of the camp. Everywhere Kaiku looked, she found something out of the ordinary, whether it was the way the Tkiurathi fashioned their tools, the smell of their strange meals or the startling way they slept in the trees.

'It is an old instinct,' Tsata explained. 'There are many things on the ground that cannot reach us in the branches. Some people still prefer it, even in a safe forest like this one. The rest of us sleep in the *repka.*'

'No forest is truly safe,' Kaiku said. 'The animals have become steadily more violent as the blight has encroached on our land.'

'In the jungles that we come from, Saramyr animals would not last a night,' Tsata said. 'We are used to worse predators than bears or wolves. I doubt you have anything that would trouble us much.'

'Ah,' said Kaiku. 'But we have Aberrants.'

'Yes,' Tsata said, who had gathered a good deal of experience at hunting them on his last visit. 'Tell me about them. I hear things are different now.'

So Kaiku told him about the latchjaws in the desert, and about other new breeds they had identified and named. Nobody was sure if these species had recently appeared or if they had simply not been seen frequently enough to be noticed in the past. Certainly, there always seemed to be a few reports of Aberrants that nobody recognised, in among the usual ghauregs and shrillings and furies.

Then Tsata told her about the Aberrant man he had tried to rescue in Zila, and they were off on a new tack.

'Of course they still hate us,' Kaiku said, as they walked around the edge of the village. 'People have always been susceptible to the fear of difference. But things are progressing at a different pace in different areas. Aberrants who are outwardly freakish are despised more than those who look "normal." I do not think most people even think of Lucia as Aberrant any more: they have elevated her into something else, some nebulous and divine saviour to suit their purposes, and the high families appear content to encourage it. They need a figurehead, and if the price of winning back their Empire is to have Lucia on the throne, then so be it. At least she is of noble blood. Plus she has Blood Ikati and Blood Erinima on her side, and the Libera Dramach. Between them they form the strongest alliance by far, and nobody wants to be divisive and oppose them.'

'And what of the Red Order?' Tsata asked.

A brief look of frustration passed over her face. 'The high families do not like us, despite the fact that we saved them from destruction, despite the fact that we are the ones who protect them from the Weavers, who could otherwise simply reach into their heads from Axekami and kill them.' She snorted. 'The Red Order is mistrusted, as if we were another kind of Weaver.'

'And aren't you?'

She should not have been surprised: he was ever blunt. 'No!' she said. 'The Weavers killed Aberrants for centuries to cover the evidence of their own crimes. Their post-Weaving whims still account for more deaths than I would like to think. And they have taken the land from us.'

'As your people took it from the Ugati,' Tsata reminded her. 'I know the Sisters are not so foul nor so cruel as the Weavers, but you seek to fulfil their role within the Empire. Will you be content as servants? The Weavers were not.'

'The Weavers never intended to be. They always meant to dominate, whether they knew it themselves or not. The god that pulls their strings demanded it. It was the only way they could get to the witchstones.'

'You have not answered the question,' he chided softly.

'I do not *know* the answer,' she replied. '*I* do not intend to be a servant of the high families when this is done, but I do not know what plans Cailin has made. I have an oath to fulfil, and that oath requires the destruction of the Weavers. If I can make it that far, I will die content.'

'You must consider the consequences of your actions, Kaiku,' Tsata said, though it was evident by his tone that he meant it as general advice rather than referring specifically to the Sisters. 'You must look ahead.'

'What point is there in that?' she asked. 'There is no alternative. We have but one path in this matter. The Red Order are trying to help people achieve that.'

'This land has been stung once before by placing their

trust in beings more powerful than they,' Tsata said. 'It is understandable that they are wary of you.'

She let it drop at that. Tsata was a questioner, and she admired that in him – he made her examine herself, to scrutinise her own choices and opinions – but he was also tenacious, and she did not want to get into an argument now. Instead their talk drifted to other things. Surrounded by Tkiurathi, she found herself wondering about Tsata's childhood, and began to ask him about it. She was surprised that she had never done so before, but she had always been afraid to pry for fear of making him reveal something he did not want to: Okhambans were unfailingly obliging, but they did not like their generosity abused. He was perfectly open, however.

'We do not have parents in Okhamba.' He saw the smile growing on her face, and corrected himself. 'I mean, we do not assign responsibilities to the ones who give birth to us. The children are raised equally as part of whatever *pash* they are. Everyone takes a hand in child-rearing. I do not know which of them were my parents, though I had an inkling. The biological bond is discouraged. It would lead to favouritism and competition.'

They talked of gods and ancestors also. Kaiku had learned in the past that Okhambans did not revere deities, but rather pursued a form of ancestor-worship similar to Saramyr folk, if much more extreme. Whereas Saramyr respected and honoured their ancestors, Okhambans had a more ruthless process. Those who had achieved great things were treated as heroes, with stories told about them and legends spun so that their deeds might be passed on to inspire the younger generation. Those who had not were forgotten, and their names were not spoken aloud. Okhambans believed that a person's strength and courage, ingenuity and wit and inspiration came from themselves alone; that they were responsible for all that they did, that there was no deity to make reparations to or to blame when things went bad. Tsata saw deities as a kind of cushion against the brutal and raw realities of existence.

Kaiku, on the other hand, could not believe how an entire continent of millions could not see what every Saramyr saw: that the gods were all around them, their influence felt everywhere, that they might be capricious and sometimes terrible but that they were undoubtedly *there*.

'But Quraal has different gods,' he had said once. 'How can you both be right?'

'Perhaps they are merely different aspects ascribed to the same entities,' Kaiku had countered. 'We put our own faces on our gods.'

'Then who would they side with in a war between Quraal and Saramyr?' Tsata had returned. 'How do you know who is right if you do not know what they want?'

But Kaiku could only think how empty her life would be if she believed that the world as she perceived it was all that there was. She knew otherwise. She had looked into the eyes of the Children of the Moons. Tsata's ruthless practicality and realism failed to take into account the spirits that haunted both their lands.

'Spirits are beings that cannot be explained,' he had said, 'but we do not worship them, or ask them for forgiveness.'

'If you cannot explain spirits,' Kaiku had replied, 'then how much else can you not explain?'

'But what if your gods are merely spirits of a much greater magnitude?'

So it had gone on. But that was a debate that she had no wish to revisit, so she steered away from contention. She talked about her own beliefs, hopes and fears, and was surprised anew by how easy it was. For such a guarded soul, she found it remarkably effortless to lower her defences to this man. He was so honest that she could not believe him capable of deception, and deception was what she feared the most: she had been duped too many times in her life. So caught up was she that she did not notice Nuki's eye slipping westward through the trees. When she did, she gave a start and clutched his arm.

'Heart's blood, Tsata! It's late. I'd forgotten the other reason I came to see you. Will you come back to Araka Jo with me? Yugi has called a meeting, and he asked if you would attend.'

'I will come,' he said. 'May I bring others?' In response to Kaiku's puzzled frown, he said: 'I am not their leader, merely their . . . favoured ambassador. Others should come, to hear and decide. I will keep the number small. There will be three, including myself. Is that acceptable?'

'Three, then,' Kaiku said. 'We convene at sunset.'

The meeting was held in the rectangular central hall of the largest temple in the complex. It was open to the air, for what once had been a magnificent roof had crumbled under the pressure of ages, and the early-risen Iridima looked into the hall from overhead as Nuki's light turned the sky to copper and gold. It was built of the same white stone as the rest of the complex, and from that stone were carved a dozen enormous idols which lined the walls, four on each of the long sides and one at each corner. The roof had protected the idols for centuries from the worst of time's assaults before it fell, and they were better preserved than most: disconcerting, imposing beings that spoke to something subconscious in the viewer, some ancient memory long lost that still lingered in wisps in the deepest chasms of the mind. Their eyes were uniformly bulbous and slitted horizontally, exuding a dark hunger, and their forms were amalgamations of mammal and reptile and bird.

Lanterns had been placed in newly-set brackets, and an enormous wicker mat dyed with fine designs had been laid in the centre of the otherwise featureless floor, on which the debaters would sit. When Kaiku and Tsata arrived, most were already there, kneeling or cross-legged with their shoes or boots neatly set behind them, just beyond the edge of the mat. She recognised them all: Cailin, Phaeca and several other Sisters, Yugi, Mishani, Lucia, Heir-Barak Hikken tu Erinima, Barakess Emira tu Ziris, and assorted folk of the Libera Dramach. Kaiku was relieved to note that Asara was not present: she had been avoiding her ever since she received news of her arrival. Then she wondered if she *was* here, and Kaiku simply did not recognise her.

There were few nobles present, since most were content to stay in the cities, and this was primarily a Libera Dramach gathering. Hikken was here because he never strayed far from his niece Lucia, hovering like a vulture, and Barakess Emira had been at Araka Jo on a visit. She was an enthusiastic supporter of the Libera Dramach, but she was not powerful, having unwisely backed Blood Kerestyn during the last coup and suffering the loss of most of her army.

Kaiku led Tsata into the hall along with the two other Tkiurathi – a brown-haired, thickset man named Heth who spoke some Saramyrrhic, and the woman who had complimented her on her language back at the village, whose name was Peithre. Beyond the mat where the principal participants would sit, there were a few dozen others lining the walls to observe. Then she spotted Nomoru.

Kaiku's heart jumped in surprise as their eyes met. There she was, in the flesh, scrawny and unkempt and surly, half her face in shadow. Kaiku had almost given up on seeing her again, assuming that she had died in Axekami. How she had got out of the pall-pits and out of the city, Kaiku would probably never know. But she was tough as a rat, this one, and she had come through once again.

As Kaiku stared, she tilted her head, and the light from nearby fell on the side of her face that had been hidden. Kaiku caught her breath. Nomoru's skin was crisscrossed with scars, thin raised tracks like ploughlines streaking her from cheek to ear and along her neck. It occurred suddenly that Nomoru was *showing* them to her. She looked away, perturbed by this new thought. Did Nomoru hold her responsible? Kaiku had not thought fast enough when she saw Juto squeeze the trigger to shoot Nomoru: she should have killed the momentum of the rifle ball in the air instead of blowing it apart. Even though Kaiku had scarred her in the process of saving her life, did Nomoru blame her for her disfigurement? Gods, she did not want that woman as an enemy.

But then she was slipping her shoes from her feet and kneeling on the communal mat, and Tsata indicated to his companions that they should do the same. She was in full Red Order garb now, and it armoured her against the stares of the people in the hall, against the resentful presence of the idols and the restless flitting of the spirits that whirled invisibly in the recesses, stirred by the unwelcome crowd.

The appearance of the Tkiurathi caused some whispering around the room, but they seemed oblivious. When the meeting began and formal introductions were made for the benefit of all assembled, Kaiku stood and named the Tkiurathi, explaining their presence and apologising in advance for the necessity of translating. Heth murmured her words in Okhamban to Peithre.

Refreshments were laid between them as the formalities went on, small lacquered tables of drinks and silver bowls of finger-food. Heth immediately reached for one of the morsels but was arrested by a negative glare from Tsata, and retreated. The welcomes were done as the last light bled out of the sky and left Iridima hanging in a star-speckled winter night, and it was Yugi, leader of the Libera Dramach, who put forward the reason why they were all here.

'The question before us today is simple,' he said. 'What do we do now? The stalemate has been broken, and the Weavers have the advantage. If we do nothing, they will create more of the feya-kori, and they will sweep aside our forces as they have at Juraka and Zila. As yet we have established no defence against these demons, and though we have learned something of their nature it hasn't yielded any way to hold them back. It's only because they are forced to return to their pall-pits and recuperate that they have not been able to invade the Southern Prefectures with impunity; but though we have a little time, we don't have much of it. Soon, other pall-pits in other cities will be operational. If we can't stand against two feya-kori, what chance do we have against ten or more?'

And so the debate began. Opinions were put back and forth. Yugi mooted the option of marshalling their forces for a full-scale attack on Axekami, more to get it out of the way than because he believed it was a viable option. It was quickly dismissed by the council as foolhardy and pointless: even if they succeeded, it would leave them overstretched and vulnerable. Axekami was not the Weavers' power base, but the old Empire's, and hence it would not be a fatal blow to them; additionally, they still could not hold the city against the feya-kori, and it could be easily retaken.

'If Axekami is to be won, it must be won by the people!' Hikken tu Erinima declared, at which point Yugi called Kaiku and Phaeca to give an account of their recent movements in Axekami and how they gauged the mood of the people. It was not encouraging. Other spies that had reported to Yugi corroborated their opinion.

'We cannot allow ourselves to hope for revolt,' Cailin said. 'The scale is too big, and there is little hope against the Weavers. They can eliminate agitators at will. Without the Red Order to defend them, the people would not have a chance to organise, and there are barely enough of us to protect the forces of the Empire, let alone its citizenry as well.' Her eyes glided over the assembly. 'Passive resistance is the best we could hope for, and even then it is a slim hope. Disseminating the message would not be an easy task, and it would have to be done without the Red Order, for we dare not operate in the Weavers' cities. We cannot even allow Lucia to use her talent for dreamwalking to spy for us there. The risk is too great.'

'Then what do you propose?' Hikken demanded, barely hiding his contempt. 'Should we do nothing?'

'That is not so inadvisable as it sounds,' put in the Barakess Emira. She was a plain-faced woman somewhere near her thirtieth harvest, with dark brown hair worn long and straight. 'The Weavers' forces have seemed thinner of late. It is possible that their armies are starving due to the effects of their own blight. They are short of time, as we are. The question is, whose will run out first?'

'But our spies have been unable to confirm that their forces really are less than before,' Yugi pointed out. 'And we don't know the extent of their supplies. At best it's a guess.'

'However, if we could find some way to hold them off, to delay them, it might be enough to turn the tide,' Emira persisted.

'We *have* no way to hold them off,' Cailin said. 'That is the crux of the matter. The only limitation on the speed they can demolish our cities is their own need to revivify.'

'Perhaps a retreat to the mountains, then?' suggested a Libera Dramach man. 'If we cannot stand against them, we could disperse and strike at them like bandits.'

Yugi nodded. 'That's a last resort, perhaps. But I think that would be the end of us as surely as if we stood up to the feya-kori with only swords and cannon. And if the Weavers do to the Prefectures what they are doing to the territories they have already taken, then the famine will get far worse, and in the mountains there will be no food at all.'

'There is another alternative,' said Cailin. 'To strike at the witchstones.'

'It has been tried,' Hikken said. 'At Utraxxa. And it failed.'

'No,' Cailin replied. 'At Utraxxa we underestimated the Weavers. But their reaction indicates that we *would* have succeeded if we had been given a chance.'

'Perhaps you could explain for the benefit of our guests and our audience?' Kaiku prompted politely. The Tkiurathi had not spoken, except to mutter translations to each other.

They knew little about the state of affairs in Saramyr, and were content to listen and learn.

Cailin inclined her head in acknowledgement. 'When we finally mustered the strength to assault the Weaver monastery that lay in the mountains west of here, across Lake Xemit, the Red Order had another plan in mind beyond simply destroying the witchstone there and ridding us of the blight. We intended to engage the witchstone, to learn about it. Through our own observations of how the Weavers' power grew with each stone awakened, and the information Lucia gleaned from the spirit of Alskain Mar in the Xarana Fault, we had determined that all the stones were connected in a manner similar to a net or a web. We believed that we could exploit that link, trace it to the other witchstones and destroy them, too. Instead of one victory, we would win them all at once.'

The assembly did not make a sound; only the faint sussuration of the wind could be heard. The temperature was dropping now that Nuki's light had fled the sky, settling towards a level that was cool but not unpleasant.

'We never got the chance. Just before we penetrated the chamber where the witchstone lay, it was destroyed. We can only assume that the Weavers used explosives. It was something we would never have expected them to do: they had always prized the witchstones' welfare above even their own lives. They were protecting the network by removing our way in.' She swept her gaze across the assembly then, and her tone became fiercer. 'But I say it was *not* a failure. We were close enough to glimpse the witchstone's nature as it came apart. Two years have passed since then, and we have not wasted that time. We have studied what we learned at Utraxxa, and we are more ready than ever now to engage a witchstone again. And this time we will destroy them all.'

Kaiku felt a thrill at the determination in her voice. Gods, the promise of action after so long in hiding or retreat or stalemate was enticing to her.

'And how do you propose to stop yourself becoming . . . cut off, as before?' Mishani asked.

Cailin settled herself again. 'The Red Order have reconstructed the network we observed between the witchstones and examined it. There is no stone that cannot be sacrificed, but there is one which will seriously damage the structure if it falls: the hub, if you will. As the Nexuses are the anchor for the beasts they control, so this stone is the anchor for the other stones. The Weavers had plenty of time during our long assault on Utraxxa to prepare explosives. But I think they will be much more reluctant to destroy their hub, the most powerful node of them all. And if we catch them by surprise, they may not have *time* to destroy it. If we can get to it intact, we can use it as a way in to the network, and reach all the witchstones in one swoop.'

Kaiku's skin prickled at the thought. Was there a chance, even so slim, that they could end this? She had not been at Utraxxa, having been reluctantly kept back by Cailin, but she had heard of the horrors that her brethren had experienced within. Could it be done? To go through the veins of their power structure, spreading like a virus?

'Do you *know* this, or is it merely conjecture?' Hikken asked. He was a prickly middle-aged man, with a deeply-etched face and prematurely grey hair, and his manner of speaking was aggressive and confrontational.

'It is conjecture,' Cailin admitted, spreading her hands to indicate helplessness. 'But it is based on very educated guesswork. We have *seen* how these stones operate. This is not a wild theory, nor would we be rushing at this blindly. If it were to be done, it would be our second attempt, and we would not make the same mistakes twice.'

'Where is this . . . anchor-stone?' It was Tsata who spoke.

'It is the first stone that was awakened,' Cailin replied. 'The one that started it all. It lies beneath the mountain monastery of Adderach.'

Hikken laughed rudely. 'And how do you propose we *get*

to Adderach? Even if it were not deep in the mountains, it is surely the most fiercely guarded stronghold the Weavers have!'

'That is also conjecture,' Phaeca put in. 'We have no idea what awaits us at Adderach. Nobody has ever been there. I may remind the council that several times we have found the Weavers rely too much on their shields of misdirection and not on physical guards.'

'Those were in the days before the Red Order became known to them,' Mishani said.

'But they may think themselves protected by the mountains,' Phaeca argued. 'They may not be able to get enough food to such a remote place to sustain an army. Who knows what the Weavers think?'

'There are many ways to Adderach,' said Cailin. 'But none of them are easy.'

'And you think the Weavers will not notice an army marching towards Adderach?' Hikken cried. 'How exactly *do* you intend to do it?'

'We go quietly,' Cailin replied. 'And we—'

'This is pointless!' Lucia said suddenly. She had been customarily distracted up until this point, but she appeared entirely focused now. At the sound of her voice, everyone in the hall fell silent and looked to where she knelt.

'Pointless,' she repeated, softer this time. When she spoke, it was with surety and conviction, and she sounded like her mother the Empress. 'Even if we did attack Adderach, even if we succeeded, in our absence the Weavers would cut a swathe through the Prefectures and cause such murder as would make any victory too costly. And if the Weavers discovered our plan, they need only send one of the demons to defend Adderach and all would be lost. Whatever our other intentions, we need to be able to tackle the feya-kori. And the only way to stop an entity like that is with a similar entity.'

She stood up, and when she spoke, her voice was stronger

than Kaiku would have believed possible from such a slip of a woman.

'It has been ten years since I was taken from the Imperial Keep in Axekami. Ten long years, and in that time there has been more blood shed for me than I dare think of. You have placed such hope in me and I have given you nothing in return but death. Now the time has come to live up to your expectations.'

She paused for a moment, and Kaiku noticed that even the spirits had quieted, and the ancient attention of the idols was on her. *Do not say it, Lucia*, she thought. *Do not do this.*

'A friend once told me I was an avatar, placed here by the gods to do their will,' she continued. 'I do not know. But I know this: we can face these demons and beat them, but we can only do so with the aid of the spirits. The entities that have lived in this land since long before we ever came here. If the Weavers can raise an army of such beings, then so can I.' She took a breath, and there was an infinitesimal tremor as she drew in the air, the only flicker of uncertainty that she showed.

'I will go to the oldest and most powerful spirit that our lore knows, deep in the heart of the Forest of Xu. I will speak with that spirit, and rouse it to our banner. The soul of the land will rise to its own defence.' Her voice was rising to a crescendo now. 'We shall make such war as the gods themselves will tremble to see it!'

The explosion of noise from the crowd was earsplitting. Cheers and cries of support rang around the hall and floated up into the night sky. This was the sign they had waited for all this time: the call to arms, the moment when their saviour would enter the fray and turn the tide. They did not care whether such a plan was even feasible; all that mattered was that Lucia had taken a hand, and with that, she had become the leader they had so desperately needed.

But though the people around her rejoiced, Kaiku was silent. She knelt where she was, and looked up at where Lucia stood, so terribly frail in the face of this riotous adulation. A battle had been lost today. Lucia was theirs now, irrevocably; she had forsaken her last chance of turning away.

As if sensing her thoughts, Lucia's eyes met hers, and in them was such sorrow as made Kaiku want to weep.

FOURTEEN

After that, there was little else to say.

The assembly dispersed with a sense that things had been left unfinished. Lucia's announcement had effectively ended the conference. Kaiku saw Cailin muttering into Yugi's ear, and she suspected that the seeds of action put forward today had only just begun to germinate. But diplomacy was not her strong suit, and she was content to leave it to people like Mishani, who appreciated the subtleties. She looked around for Nomoru, still worried about the scout's intentions, but could not find her in the crowd. Instead, she led Tsata and the Tkiurathi out of the temple and into the cool night beyond.

'We will go with you, if you will have us,' Tsata said to Kaiku, as they came to the edge of the complex where the trail ran back towards the Tkiurathi village.

He was assuming that she would not let Lucia follow this course alone. And what was worse, Kaiku reflected, was that he was probably right.

'Xu is no ordinary forest,' Kaiku said. 'The spirits hold sway there, and have done since before my people ever set foot on these shores.' Her eyes were grave. 'There is no more dangerous place in all of Saramyr for our kind.'

'The more reason for you to take us,' said Tsata.

Kaiku felt too weary to try and argue. She thanked them all – though she suspected by Tsata's expression that she did not need to – and bade them farewell, leaving the offer open. She was not the one to make such decisions, and she had no intention of bearing the responsibility for their deaths inside the Forest of Xu. Only the gods knew what awaited them in there.

It occurred to her, as she walked back to her house in the Libera Dramach village downslope of the temple complex, that she was already thinking about the journey in terms of *when* she went, rather than *if.*

Heart's blood, where did all my choices go? she thought in a morose moment, then snorted with disgust at her own self-pity.

She shared a house with Mishani here at Araka Jo as she had in the Fold, though the two of them were rarely there at the same time, as turned out to be the case tonight. She presumed Mishani had gone elsewhere with other members of the assembly to continue their discussions privately. The house was near the building where the Red Order met and where most of the Sister had their rooms, but Kaiku had not felt comfortable with the idea of living there as Phaeca did: it felt too much like surrendering a part of herself. The place was relatively nondescript and a little cold in the wintertime, but Kaiku had given up on the idea of having a stable home at least until the war was over, and as long as she had a roof and a private space she was happy.

It felt empty tonight. She slid the outer door closed behind her and listened to the darkness for a time. Outside, night-insects were chirruping and clattering. She walked through to her bedroom. The glow of the lanterns rose gently as flames kindled in their wicks at her passing, sparked by a small and frivolous use of her *kana.* Cailin would have disapproved. Kaiku didn't care.

Her bedroom was small: she only came here to sleep. There was a comfortable mat of woven, springy fibres, upon which was laid a thick blanket, and then a further blanket on top of that. Simple, unadorned, utilitarian. On the wall facing the curtained doorway was a mirror, an old one of Mishani's; she caught her reflection, and thought how well the make-up of the Order hid the melancholy mood that had descended on her. Even now, she projected a certain aura of authority and aloofness. On the far side of her sleeping-mat were a pair of chests flanking a dressing-table with another mirror, and on one wall hung a scroll with a verse from Xalis, another donation from Mishani. Kaiku was terrible at decorating: it seemed so unimportant to her. Her interest was not in material things.

She had sat down at her dressing-table and was preparing to remove her make-up when she spotted the Mask. She saw it over the shoulder of her double in the small vanity mirror, leering at her from where it hung on the wall, and it startled her so badly that she jumped with a yelp and sent little wooden pots of lip-paint scattering noisily to the floor. She stared at it, meeting its empty gaze in the mirror. It stared back at her.

Her skin crawled. She could not remember putting it up there.

She got up and slowly walked over to it. Its face of red and black lacquer was mischievous, mocking.

'Gods curse you,' she whispered to it. 'Leave me be.'

She took it down from where it hung on the wall. The contact of her hand brought a faint sense-memory of her father, the indefinable warmth of his presence. She bit back tears and put the Mask back in its chest.

Why couldn't she just destroy it? Why put up with that malevolent, insidious lure night after night? She could not have said herself. Perhaps because it was the last piece of her father she had. Perhaps it was the practicalities involved: she had used it twice before to breach the Weavers' barriers, and since the Weavers were still no wiser as to how she had done it, there was no reason it could not be used again. Cailin had made a brief stab at studying it, but there was little to learn beyond what the Sisters already knew. As True Masks went, it was young and weak and unremarkable, but no Sister dared probe too far into the workings of a True Mask, even one such as this. That way lay insanity.

Perhaps she kept it to remind her of what she was fighting against, and why she was fighting them. For this Mask had started it all for her: it had cost the lives of her family and set her adrift in the world. Until she found the Red Order; until she found another red and black mask to wear.

She caught herself. Thinking like that was not a good idea in her current state of lassitude. Seeing Lucia give herself up to her followers had drained her somehow, and she felt beaten and defeated. What was worse, she was resigned to going to the Forest of Xu, because *someone* that Lucia trusted had to be there, and she was the only option: Yugi was too valuable to go, and Mishani would be no use as part of such an expedition. Her talents lay elsewhere.

So Kaiku would be leaving Mishani again, after so short a time. She swore bitterly. This war was taking everything from her, little nibbled increments of her soul being swallowed as the harvests passed by, leaving her with just enough hate and determination to go on surviving. Her own side did not even appreciate her sacrifices. Her friends were torn away from her again and again. And it seemed they had not gained ground on the Weavers once since this whole affair began, since the death of the Blood Empress Anais. The best they had managed was to stall their retreat temporarily.

Something had to give. She could not continue this way for another ten years.

Take heart, then, a sardonic inner voice told her. *The way things are going, the Weavers will have us all before the summer.*

The chime sounded outside the door of the house. Kaiku looked up. For a moment, she considered not answering, but the lanterns were lit so her visitor knew she was in. Eventually curiosity got the better of her. She arranged herself quickly in the mirror, walked to the door and slid it open.

It was Asara. Kaiku recognised her even though she wore the form of a stranger, a dusky-skinned Tchom Rin woman with black hair in a loose ponytail hanging over her shoulder. She was wearing a robe of silver-grey.

'What do you want?' Kaiku asked, but she could not

muster the effort to put any venom in her voice. It all seemed so pointless suddenly.

'Am I to take it, then, that you still resent me after our last encounter?' Asara guessed by Kaiku's tone that she had surmised her identity.

'A grudge worth holding is a grudge worth keeping alive,' she replied.

'May I come inside? I wish to talk.'

Kaiku thought about that for a moment, then she turned away and went into the house. Asara followed and slid the door shut behind her. Kaiku stood in the centre of the room, and did not invite Asara to sit.

'The attire of the Red Order does not suit you,' Asara said. 'It makes you into something you are not.'

'Spare me the criticism, Asara,' she said dismissively. 'If I had been a Sister when last we met, you would not have been able to deceive me as you did.'

'Perhaps that would have been better for both of us.'

'It would have been better for *me!*' Kaiku snapped, finding her anger.

But Asara did not rise to it; it seemed to slide off her. 'I came here to apologise,' she said.

'I am not interested in your apologies. They are as false as that skin you wear.'

Asara looked faintly amused. 'This skin is my own, Kaiku. It just happens that I can change it. I am Aberrant, just like you. How is it that you can celebrate your own abilities and despise mine?'

'Because I do not use mine to deceive other people,' she hissed.

'No, you use them to *kill* other people.'

'Weavers and Nexuses, demons and Aberrant animals,' Kaiku returned. 'They are not what I would call people. They are monsters.' She missed the hypocrisy of Asara's statement, for she had no knowledge of the lives that had been given to feed her, to fuel the metamorphic processes in her body.

'You killed several men on Fo; have you forgotten?'

'That was *your* fault!' Kaiku cried.

Asara raised one hand in a placating gesture. 'I am sorry. You are right. I do not want this to become an argument. But I would have you listen, even if you do not believe me.'

'Speak, then,' Kaiku said; but her arms were crossed beneath her breasts, and it was clear that nothing Asara said would appease her.

Asara regarded her for a moment, her gaze unreadable, made smoky by her eyeshadow.

'I have never meant to be your enemy, Kaiku. I did deceive you in the past, but I did not intend to harm you. Even that last time.' Her voice dropped a little. 'I would have stayed as Saran Ycthys Marul. You would never have known. We could have been happy.'

Kaiku opened her mouth to speak, but Asara stopped her.

'I know what you would say, Kaiku. It was foolish of me. I thought I could create myself anew, spin a new past: to wipe the slate clean. And you were ready to love Saran. You *were*, Kaiku.' She overrode Kaiku's weak protest. 'You would not love me, but you would love him.'

'He was not real,' Kaiku said in disgust.

'He was as real as Asara was. As I am now.'

'Then *you* are not real either,' Kaiku returned. 'The Asara I knew was only the face you wore, the role you took on, when first I met you. Is that who you are? How many faces had you worn before that? Do you even know?'

Asara saddened. 'No,' she said. 'No, I do not. Have you an idea what it is to be me? I do not even know what I should *look* like. Counterfeits are all I have.'

'You will get no pity from me,' Kaiku laughed scornfully.

Asara's face became stony. 'I do not want pity from anyone. But sometimes . . .' She looked away. 'Sometimes I do need help.'

This shocked Kaiku more than anything Asara had said so far. Asara had always been fierce in asserting her independence; this was a terrible admission for her. Despite herself, she softened for a moment. Then came the memory of Saran Ycthys Marul, looking at her with Asara's eyes as Kaiku, half-clothed, wept with the shame of betrayal.

'You do not deserve my help,' she said.

Asara glared across the room, her beautiful face cold in the lantern-light. 'I do, Kaiku. Honour demands that you discharge your debts, and you owe me your *life*. I did not merely save you from dying. I brought you back from the dead. Nothing you have done for me has ever come close to repaying that.' Her voice was flat with menace now. 'You nearly killed me, and I have never held you accountable. I watched over you for years before your *kana* emerged, and I rescued you from the shin-shin when they would certainly have had you. You think me so deceitful and cruel, but I have been a better friend to you than you realise. I have forgiven you everything, and asked almost nothing in return.'

Kaiku was unmoved. Asara tossed her head and made a noise of disgust. 'Think on what I have said. You count yourself honourable; well, honour does not extend only to your friends and your loved ones. The time has come to pay me back what is owed. Then we will be even, and I will leave you forever.'

With that, she walked to the door and slid it open. On the threshold, she looked back.

'I am going with you into the forest. We shall resolve this later.'

Then she was gone, and Kaiku was alone again.

Sometimes, when the fumes of the amaxa root had swaddled him in their plush and acidic folds, Yugi thought he could glimpse the spirit that haunted his room. It hid in the corner where the ceiling and two of the walls met, a spindly thing all bones and angles, black and beaked and half-seen. It was never still; instead it was in constant jittering motion, shivering and twitching with a rapidity hard for the eye to follow, making it blurred and unfocused. Yugi would study it while he lay on his sleeping-mat, puffing at the mouthpiece of his hookah. It was a part of the night to him, and night was where he found his peace, where he could be left alone and the jagged rocks of his memory could be blanketed in a narcotic fog.

He had been watching the spirit, lost in a haze, when he noticed a movement at his doorway. It took him a moment to establish who his visitor was. She came and squatted down next to him, laying her rifle aside.

'Bad habit,' she murmured.

'I know,' he replied. His mouth was dry and the words felt thick in his throat. He felt her hand grip his jaw gently, move his head left and right, looking into the cracked whites of his eyes.

'You're under,' she said. 'Thought you could handle this.'

'Want some?'

'No.'

She took the pipe out of his hand and put it back in its cradle on the hookah, where a wisp of smoke drifted up towards the white stone ceiling. Yugi tried muzzily to focus on her.

'I'm sorry about your face,' he mumbled.

Nomoru shrugged her narrow shoulders. 'Never the prettiest kitten in the box anyway. Besides, it makes Kaiku nervous. Can tell she thinks I want to kill her. Funny.'

Yugi grinned widely, then faltered, not sure whether it was appropriate. His hand came up, seemingly belonging to someone else, moving into his vision to touch her scarred cheek. At the moment of contact his fingertips exploded into sensation, bypassing his numb arm and going straight to his brain, islands of exquisite sensitivity free-floating before him. He felt the rayed tracks of the cicatrices that marred her skin, his face a comical picture of childlike wonder.

'It's a beautiful pattern,' he murmured.

Nomoru grunted a laugh. 'You're under,' she said again. 'You'd think mud was beautiful.'

Yugi did not appear to be listening. He took his hand away, suddenly unable to get comfortable on his mat. The curvature of his spine was annoying him. He got up into a cross-legged position with some difficulty, only to find that his knees were now causing him bother and he had merely shifted the ache from his upper back to his coccyx. He reached for the hookah, but Nomoru caught his arm and guided it back to his lap.

'Don't,' she said. 'Not going to watch you end up like my mother.'

'Come under with me,' he said, his pupils huge and bright though his face was slack.

She shook her head. 'You know what happened last time.'

'Weavers won't get you here. You can trust me.'

She looked away from him. 'I don't trust anyone.'

He was hurt by that. For a moment, there was nothing to say.

'Where did you go? In Axekami,' he asked at length. Sparkling shapes were whirring about the floor like translucent wriggling eels. 'I was worried.'

'No you weren't,' she said. She leaned back on her hands. 'Easier to get away on my own. Had to see an Inker.' She drew up her sleeve, where a freshly completed tattoo of a hookah with a dagger in it stood out against the paler pictures surrounding it. 'Paid the debt I owed Lon. Or Juto. Doesn't matter which.'

He was getting more lucid now. Amaxa root was short-lived in potency, and required a constant topping-up from the hookah to remain effective. The spirit that lived in the corner of his room was nothing more than a grey smear now, if ever he had seen it at all.

Suddenly he reached out and slipped his arm round Nomoru's waist, drawing her to him. He lay back as she moved with the pressure, uncrossing his legs so that she could slip onto his chest, her thin, hard body resting down the length of him. Her face was close enough to his so that he could feel her breath on his face, the sensation narcotically amplified to a rolling cloud of fire on his stubbled cheek. He studied the newly cut contours in her skin, his eyes flicking across them in fascination. Then he put his lips to hers. Her tongue was small and she tasted sour and kissed too hard, but it was familiar to him and he liked it. The amaxa root sent sparkling bursts from his mouth throughout his body.

She pulled away from him. 'Take that off,' she said, touching the trailing end of the rag tied round his forehead. 'Feels strange.'

'I can't,' he said, with a tired sigh. They had been through this before.

She was cooling again. 'She's dead. It's done. Take it off.'

'I *can't*.'

She looked down at him a moment, then shrugged. 'Worth a try,' she said, and fell to him once more.

The roof gardens of the Imperial Keep had withered and died. Where once they had been verdant and lush, planted with trees and flowers gathered from all over the Near World, now they were a brown, skeletal wasteland. The flowerbeds were a mush of detritus and spindly crinkles that were the remnants of bushes. The trees sloughed bark and oozed sap, and the leaves were all gone. It was a doleful and tragic place, and few came here now. The murk closed it in, a smoky grey canopy, and a bitter wind chased sticks and twigs across the flagstones.

Avun met the Weaver in a small paved area screened by a dense tangle of branches on all sides. At its south end, a double set of steps flanked by small statues of mythical beings led to paths set higher and lower in the gardens. There was a carved wooden bench, dull from lack of care, but Avun did not sit. He stood with a heavy cloak wrapped around him, for the lack of sunlight and the wind made it as cold as he could ever remember being in his life. The branches rattled a macabre and erratic rhythm as they tapped against each other.

The Weaver came slowly up the steps from below. He was young, not so raddled as others of his breed, and he moved with a slow and controlled gait. His Mask was all angles of gold, silver and bronze, his cowl hanging loosely over it. The patchwork robe was stitched and patterned crazily; there seemed to be some kind of order there, but Avun could not grasp it. He gave up looking. Perhaps it would be best not to work it out.

'Lord Protector,' he said, the voice made tinny by the metal Mask.

'Fahrekh,' Avun replied.

'I assume you have heard about Kakre's injudicious choice of victim today?'

Avun blinked languidly. 'He was a useful general.'

'He may still be alive,' Fahrekh said. 'Though I doubt he will be good for much any more.'

'He had been with Kakre too long before I found out,' said Avun. 'There is no point antagonising the Weave-lord now. My general would not lead the Blackguard so well without half his skin.'

'And without half his sanity, I suspect.'

Avun did not care to think about it. 'This has become intolerable,' he muttered.

'Indeed.'

There was a silence between them. Each was waiting for the other to say what they both thought. In the end, it was Fahrekh.

'Something must be done.'

'And what do you have in mind?' Avun said carefully, though he knew full well what it was. They had fenced around this before. Avun had no idea about Fahrekh's feelings, but he was gods-damned if he was going to incriminate himself by being the first to speak it out aloud.

'We will kill him, of course,' Fahrekh said.

Avun regarded the Weaver with hooded eyes. Could he trust this one? He still had a suspicion that Fahrekh was only faking complicity, that this was some test of loyalty by the Weavers. If he went along with it, would they treat him as a betrayer?

'You would kill one of your own?' he asked.

'It is necessary. We must cut off the spoiled right hand to save the arm.' Fahrekh's voice was an even and measured monotone. 'Kakre is a liability. For the good of the Weavers, he must be removed.'

'Will he stand down?'

Fahrekh chuckled. 'No Weave-lord has ever stood down before. Besides, he is too irrational now. He will not see things as we do. The Weavers need a new and clear-sighted leader, or our ambitions will go unfulfilled.'

Avun thought about this. He had learned a lot about the Weavers in his time as Lord Protector, through observation and conversation and by listening to Kakre's periodic fugues. Discovering the power structure of his allies was an important goal for him: their strength lay in secrecy, and Avun was determined to uncover them.

How was it that the Weavers were so united in purpose? And how could that be squared with the way they would kill each other in times past at the behest of their masters? At first he had believed that there was a coterie of Weavers in Adderach dispensing orders, but that was not good enough. In two hundred and fifty years he would have expected at least a few coups, power struggles, *something* like that. Yet there was no evidence of such. There were certainly disagreements about the way things should be done from time to time, but never about the ends, only the means.

Avun had not been able to understand it to his satisfaction, but he had established some things. The Weavers did not appear to know themselves where their direction came from: it was simply an instinctive drive towards the same goal.

Whatever provided this goal was vague and indistinct, not an absolute dictator or an entity that was in complete control of the Weavers; it was simply a *knowledge* that all of them accepted and did not question.

There had never been a usurper in the Weavers before; but then, they had never needed one until now. Weave-lords had become liabilities to their patrons in the past, but they had been mere inconveniences. Kakre was the first Weave-lord who had *command*: command of the Aberrant armies, the feya-kori, and through Avun, the Blackguard. And a commander who was insane worked against the best interests of the Weavers.

Avun had to decide: was Fahrekh genuine, or was this all a trick?

'How would you do it?' he asked.

'I will catch him after he has Weaved. During his mania, when he is vulnerable.' Avun could feel the Weaver studying him from behind his Mask. 'I will need you to help me,' he said.

This was what Avun had feared. To commit himself would mean his death, if Fahrekh was false.

'What would you have me do?'

'We must contrive a reason for him to Weave. Something very difficult. I will supply you with the task; you must persuade him to take it up. Once exhausted, I will strike.'

'And after he is dead? I suppose you will be the new Weave-lord?'

'For the good of the Weavers,' Fahrekh said. 'I shall expect your immediate support.'

The branches rattled as the two of them faced each other beneath the iron-grey sky. Avun knew there was no way to be sure of the creature before him. Who could tell what kind of madness lurked beneath that surface? But he also knew that Kakre was a liability, and becoming more so by the day, and sooner or later he might take it into his head to get rid of his Lord Protector. There was risk in both action and inaction, and in the end, he had to trust his intuition. And he was an expert betrayer.

'I will do as you ask,' he said.

Fahrekh nodded slowly, once. He turned and departed without a word. Avun watched him go, and then clutched his cloak tighter around him. It really was cold out here; he had begun to shiver.

FIFTEEN

Nuki's eye rose on a clear, chilly day, the grass trembling with dew; but Kaiku, Lucia, and their companions were up long before, and as they ate a cold breakfast, their eyes were on the trees. The endless wall of trees.

They had camped within sight of the southern edge of the Forest of Xu, on the north bank of the River Ko. Few of them had slept much that night. Those that did woke unrested, complaining of ill dreams. There were twenty-five of them in all: Kaiku and Phaeca, Lucia, Asara, the three Tkiurathi, and eighteen other men and women of the Libera Dramach. They were here to face the Forest, and to find that which lurked at its heart: the Xhiang Xhi, most ancient and powerful of all the land's spirits.

Kaiku returned to the camp, having washed in the river. Her teeth should have been chattering, but the autonomic reaction of her *kana* had raised her body temperature enough to cope. She was taking such things for granted now, her sense of wonder having faded over time. Perhaps she could not yet bring herself to believe Cailin's screed about how the Sisters and certain other Aberrants were superior to those who had not been changed by the Weavers' blight; but she could not resist a private smirk of amusement at the sight of the other soldiers hopping and flapping to warm themselves after dunking their stripped upper bodies in the freezing water.

She stood on the crest of the river bank and debated for a moment whether to dress herself as a Sister or to remain in her tough, sexless travelling attire. She decided on the latter, in the end. It felt somehow false to put on the face of the Red Order to go into the forest. The forest would not be fooled.

She stared grimly at the trees, the border between humanity's realm and that of the spirits. They stretched from horizon to horizon east to west, and rose upon hills in the northern distance. The Forest of Xu was the single largest feature of Saramyr west of the mountains, almost three hundred miles north to south and two-thirds that in width, bigger even than the colossal Lake Azlea which neighboured it. The only information about what lay within were rumours and legends, and none of them pleasant. The Saramyr folk had learned long ago that their land was big enough to live in without disturbing the spirits, and the Forest of Xu was the densest concentration of spirits in the land. Half-hearted attempts at exploration had been made, in advance of a foolhardy plan to build a road through the trees to facilitate trade between Barask and Saraku. Few who went in there had ever come out. Those that did escape left their sanity behind.

It would be suicide, then, to set foot in such a place. But this time, they had something new. This time, they had Lucia. And on her slender shoulders rested all their lives.

As if sensing her thoughts, Lucia appeared at her side. Kaiku glanced over at her, then back at the forest.

'It hates us,' Lucia whispered.

'I know,' Kaiku murmured. 'It has a right to.'

A line creased Lucia's brow. 'We are not the enemies, Kaiku. The Weavers are.'

'The Weavers were like us once,' Kaiku said.

'But it is their god that makes them what they are,' Lucia said. She sounded frail, ready to shatter, and part of Kaiku did not even want to respond to this. But she had to now.

'Their god never made anyone *join* the Weavers. Not after those first ones. The rest came of their own free will. He never made them put on the Masks. That was ambition, and greed, and the need to control and dominate. There is no depravity they commit that was not already there inside them. It is only that their consciences have withered.' She brushed her hair back from her face. 'They are just men. Men who wanted power, the way all men do.'

'Not all men,' said Lucia.

Kaiku looked over at where Tsata was sitting cross-legged, talking with his two companions. She nodded slightly. 'Not all men.'

'Don't despair,' Lucia said, laying a hand on her arm. 'Please. You have always been stronger than me. I can't do this if you don't believe.'

'Then do not do it,' Kaiku replied, turning to her. 'Go back, and I will go back with you.'

Lucia's smile was sad. 'You have always thought of me over everybody else,' she said. 'Even if it cost the world, even if it cost the Golden Realm itself, you would have me prize my own safety before others.' She embraced Kaiku. 'You, and you only.'

Kaiku felt a slow tightening in her heart; she knew by Lucia's tone that there was no dissuading her.

Lucia released her and looked into her eyes. 'Nobody is safe any more, Kaiku.'

They made ready to leave as the dawn light grew. Little was said. There was a palpable air of foreboding among them. A pair of manthxwa had been brought as pack animals, but like the ravens that had accompanied Lucia on her journey from Araka Jo they refused to go nearer to the forest than they already were. In the end the travellers were forced to distribute their supplies as best they could and turn the creatures loose. Only the Tkiurathi did not seem intimidated.

Kaiku caught Asara looking at her strangely. Asara did not break the gaze; in the end, Kaiku did. Gods, it was bad enough going in there at all, but with Asara's black hints at some debt to be discharged, she was not sure whether that woman was to be trusted. Why had she come? She was never one to recklessly endanger herself. What price would she demand of Kaiku in return for saving her life?

There was only one reason why the Aberrant spy was here,

risking her life with the rest of them. She had unfinished business.

When they were ready, they gathered at the edge of the trees. Beyond, the forest was a tangle of boughs and bushes, the ground knotted with hillocks and roots. Birds chittered, insects droned, distant animal cries could be heard. There was nothing out of the ordinary that they could see; but some prickling sense on the fringe of perception warned them against stepping past the ranked trunks of the border, something deep and primal.

They were waiting for Lucia. She wore no armour like the soldiers, only some time-stained peasant clothes that did not suit her frame and made her seem small. She carried a pack as the rest of them did, at her own insistence, though they had loaded it lightly. She stood with her head bowed, her short blonde hair hanging forward, the burned skin of her neck exposed. They wanted her to turn and rouse them, to give them some of that fire that had blazed during the assembly at Araka Jo; but she had none to give them. Instead, she hitched up her pack to make it sit more comfortably on her shoulders, looked up, and walked into the forest. Without a word, the others followed.

At Lucia's first step beyond the barrier of the trees, the forest fell silent. It spread outward in a wave, as if the tread of her foot had triggered some great ripple like a pebble dropped in a pond. As the ripple passed, the birds stopped singing, the insects quieted, the cries of the animals died in their throats.

The intruders found themselves subject to a hush so profound that it was unnerving. The creak of leather armour and the rustle of their clothes were the only sounds they could hear, beyond the faint stir of the wind across the plains and the distant hiss of the river. They felt subtly fractured from reality, bereft of the spectrum of background sounds which had surrounded them to some degree all their lives. The silence ached.

They went on. If they had harboured any doubt that the forest was aware of them, it had been discarded now.

The trees thickened as they went further inward. The bulk of the companions travelled in single file, threading their way around the rise of tuffets and rocks, hopping over dry ditches. The Tkiurathi took alternative routes, spreading out, reading the land. Though Lucia was their navigator they would not let her take the lead. She walked in front of Kaiku, occasionally shouldering her pack anew as it began to chafe. She was not strong: a sheltered childhood and adolescence had given her no experience of physical hardship. But though she struggled, she did not complain.

Nobody spoke for what must have been an hour at least. The sense of oppression in the air was heavy, and getting heavier. Kaiku could feel the presence of the spirits here; they pervaded the place like the scent of disuse in a vacant house. They were waiting, breathless with malice and appalled that these humans would dare to enter their realm.

Kaiku hoped that Lucia knew what she was doing. She was certain that Lucia could communicate with these spirits easily enough, but whether they would listen to her was another matter. And when – *if* – they got to the Xhiang Xhi which hid at the heart of the vast forest, would Lucia's abilities be up to the task?

She recalled trying to reason with her back at Araka Jo. Why here? she had asked. Why this? Of all the spirits in the land which inhabited the deep and high and empty places, why choose the Xhiang Xhi?

'Because the other spirits hold that one in awe,' she had replied, half-listening. 'Because no other could rouse them. This one dwarfs all the spirits in Saramyr. Even the Children of the Moons fear the Xhiang Xhi.'

At one point, Kaiku dropped back to talk to Phaeca. She had somehow managed to imbue even her drab travelling clothes with a touch of flair, and her red hair was as immaculately arranged as ever. Small details like this gladdened Kaiku; they helped to stave off the steadily growing sense of hostility and isolation.

'Why don't they get it over with?' she hissed, as soon as Kaiku was nearby.

'Have faith, Phaeca,' Kaiku said. 'Lucia will protect us.'

Phaeca gave her a quick look of disgust. 'Don't spin me such platitudes,' she snapped. 'You're as afraid as I am.' Almost immediately, the anger was gone, and she was aghast at her own reaction. 'Forgive me,' she murmured. 'This place is hard on my nerves.'

Kaiku nodded. Phaeca's particularly sensitive nature was both a blessing and a curse here. She wondered whether Cailin had been wise to send her; she suspected the Pre-Eminent had done so only because Kaiku was going, and Phaeca was her closest companion within the Red Order.

Phaeca, Asara, and possibly Tsata and the two other Tkiurathi were all here because she had come. And she had come because she could not let Lucia make this journey without her. Both she and Lucia, by risking themselves, had dragged others in their wake and put their lives in danger. Selfishness out of selflessness. There was no way to win. She thought she understood a little of Lucia's sense of being crushed by responsibility now.

The change, when it came, was sudden.

Phaeca cried out in fear at the sensation. It was like a thick tar that gathered in from all directions to engulf the mind. The Sisters spun defences automatically to preserve themselves; but the other members of the party had no such recourse. They were swamped by a glowering prescience of doom that manifested all around them. The sunlight that leaked through the leaf canopy thinned and died as if a cloud had passed before Nuki's eye; but then it began to darken beyond even the drabbest day, blackening to deepest night and worse, until all light was excluded and even those with the ability to see in the dark were rendered blind.

Panic ensued. The darkness was bad enough, but the terror they felt was out of proportion even to that. Their senses screamed danger at them: there were *things* nearby, and while their eyes were useless their imaginations took charge. Monstrous, fanged beings, hanging in the air or slinking along the ground, black creatures who could only be envisioned by the gimlet gleam of their claws and teeth. The only sound was the desperate voices of the party, somebody shouting that they must protect Lucia, men who wanted to run but did not dare.

It took Kaiku a few paralysed seconds before she had the presence of mind to switch her vision into the Weave. The darkness was merely physical, and had no power there. The world blazed into light again, the stitchwork contours of golden threads outlining the forest and the people within. She could see them stumbling, their arms out, eyes open but unseeing, pupils like saucers. Some had drawn swords, and were standing rigidly, listening for the approach of the enemy. The Tkiurathi had dropped into crouches, making themselves small targets; they appeared calm, though the pounding of their hearts and the rush of blood around their bodies told a different story. The threads of the Weave were churning, confirming Kaiku's suspicion: this terror was an artificial thing, a projection.

But it was not without cause. For the spirits were coming, manifesting in the air all around them, forming into shapes that mimicked the party's fears. They were vague and indistinct yet, but gaining coherence with every passing moment, their blurred forms separating into limbs, jaws, talons. Dozens of them. She and Phaeca could not hope to fight them all.

'Lucia!' she cried, but Lucia was not listening. She was kneeling on the ground, her hands buried into the grassy dirt, her head hung. Somebody shrieked, a voice that faded rapidly as if carried away at speed; Kaiku tried to locate them, but it had happened too fast for her. She cast about helplessly, unable to act. Lucia was talking to them. She could only hope that whatever she said was enough.

The spirits were bleeding from the air, slinking from the treetops, knotting and sewing into shape with deadly purpose. The blinded humans in their midst flailed, aware that something was coming for them and having no way to prevent it. Kaiku's *kana* was raging within her, desperate for release; but the enemy were too many, and there was nowhere to send it that would have any effect. She felt Phaeca across the Weave, felt her struggle to keep control against the choking terror. She could see, as Kaiku could. One of the Libera Dramach narrowly missed impaling a companion on the point of his drawn sword as he staggered about; another almost tripped over Lucia, his hands held out before him, eyes unfocused.

'Stand still, all of you!' she shouted, putting as much authority as she could muster into her voice. They did so, clinging to her words as a lifeline to control.

'What's happening?' someone called to her, fraying with hysteria.

'Lucia will see us through,' she replied, with more conviction than she felt. 'Wait.'

She glanced back at where Lucia knelt. There was another shriek somewhere among the trees, cut short. She squeezed her eyes shut – which did nothing to block her Weave-vision – and prayed. The spirits were looming now, nightmare caricatures of childhood terrors, prowling between the trunks of the trees, stalking the humans. Kaiku desperately wanted to lash out; maybe she could ward them off, make them think twice about their prey. But to do so would mean the death of them all, for whatever Lucia was saying to them, her negotiations would collapse at the first sign of hostility from Kaiku.

'Stand still and wait!' she said again, because she could

not bear the silence. The Tkiurathi had not moved. Asara was nowhere to be seen. And seeping towards them like mist came the spirits, their forms now shifting and warping as they moved, bending perspective to become elongated, then suddenly two-dimensional, now folding around a tree at an angle that had not seemed possible a moment before.

Closer, closer. Close enough to kill any one of them.

Something slackened, some constriction in the air that went loose. The oppressive hatred of the spirits seemed to retreat. Kaiku looked to Lucia, but there was no outward reaction from her. The spirits hung where they were. Some of them had risen up by their intended victims like malevolent shadows about to snatch the bodies that formed them. She dared not breathe. Here, at this instant, was the balance. If it tipped one way, they would all live; if the other, she would have no option but to fight, and there would be no hope for them then.

Then the forest sighed, and the spirits began to float backwards and away, bright eyes still fixed on the humans as they slipped between the trunks of the trees. Kaiku let out the breath she had been holding. The horrifying shapes were losing coherence now, dissipating into the Weave. And with their passing, the sense of malice and danger faded and the light returned. Slowly and by degrees, vision returned to them. It was like waking from a dream.

They stared at one another gratefully, their eyes thirsty for sight. Guilt and confusion flickered across their faces as they were revealed: some were caught still cringing, others brandished swords inches from their companions. All were ashamed of their fear. Those who had moved about or fallen over reoriented themselves, blinking. The Tkiurathi rose slowly to their feet. Asara reappeared, stepping into view from where she had hidden herself.

The forest had lightened back to normal now; Nuki's eye glowed through the canopy, and the world was green and brown and sane again. The silence was as great as before, but the spirits were gone.

Lucia stood up slowly, her hands still dirty. She looked around, but her gaze passed over them as if they were not there.

'They will give us passage,' she said simply.

Phaeca began to cry.

They went on, for there was little else to do; but their fragile confidence was shattered, and they crept like skulking children beneath the louring boughs of the forest.

Two of the soldiers had been lost in the darkness, vanished without trace. Had Lucia not been there, none of them would have been alive now. Far from reassuring them of their faith in their appointed saviour, the incident had reminded them of just how slender their chances really were. Even the Weavers were better than this: at least they were a physical enemy. In the Forest of Xu, they were allowed to survive only because the spirits chose not to kill them. If anything happened to Lucia, they would never leave this place.

Kaiku's thoughts were darker still. For she knew something the others did not, and it made matters worse than they already were.

'We're still not safe here,' Lucia had said in response to her prompting, once they were back on their way. 'These spirits suffer us to pass, but there are others that won't.'

Kaiku checked that there was nobody else within earshot. 'What are you saying?'

'As we go further towards the heart, we will find older spirits,' Lucia replied. 'They will not be so easily pacified.'

Kaiku was observing the shaken expressions on the faces of the party.

'Perhaps you had better keep that to yourself for now,' she muttered, hating herself for advocating dishonesty. 'For a while, at least.'

Lucia made a distracted noise, and seemed to forget that Kaiku was there at all.

Kaiku had walked with Phaeca for a time: she was affected worst of all of them. It hurt to see her in such a state, but some callous part of Kaiku wished that she had not been so indiscreet about her distress. Heart's blood, she was supposed to be a Sister. These people *needed* to believe that she was indomitable. Her own weakness was infecting the others, undermining everyone. She was concerned that Phaeca might pick up some of the impatience in her manner, but if she did, she said nothing.

As the day aged through evening to dusk, the forest became strange.

The change was slow and gradual. At first it was only an occasional incident: an unfamiliar flower, or a tree that looked odd. Then they found a remarkable rock that poked from the turf, a brilliant silvery lump of some kind of metallic mineral. Later they came across a cluster of dark magenta blossoms which nobody could identify, and a tree whose branches wrapped through the branches of other trees, twisting like vines. The green of their surroundings deepened and became mixed with purple and platinum.

Heading deeper into the forest, they began to see animals, silent and watchful, some unlike anything they had ever observed before. One of the soldiers swore that he had seen a white creature like a deer, out in the trees. Asara spotted a long-legged spider, carapaced like a crab and as high as a man's knee, sidling from its burrow. The terrain became rougher, hills and cliffs rising, ghylls and ditches deepening into chasms.

The sky was a sullen crimson when the leader of the party, a middle-aged Libera Dramach man known as Doja, called for a camp. The spot he chose was on the grassy lip of a stony gorge, where the trees drew back and left a fringe of clear ground, a gentle slope between the forest and the dizzying drop, where there was mercifully no canopy to hem them in.

Iridima was visible through the translucent veils of colour still hanging across the ceiling of the night. On the other side of the gorge there was a narrow and immensely high waterfall. The water was carved into three uneven streams by red-veined rocks, and plunged in thin, misty strings, joining together again halfway down in their rush to the river below.

When the camp was made, Kaiku stood on the edge of the precipice and looked down into the gorge. What river was this? A tributary of the Ko? Where was the source, and where did it end? Had anyone in living memory ever looked upon it until now? This river had flowed here, perhaps for thousands of years, and nobody had known it. If not for Lucia, it might have flowed for thousands more, untroubled by humanity.

She gazed into the middle distance, saddened by the indifference of the world. How small they were in the eyes of creation, how petty their struggles. The spirits guarded their territories, the moons glided through the skies, the seas remained bottomless. Nature did not care for the plight of humankind. She began to wonder if Lucia's task was not an impossible one after all. Could she really rouse the spirits, even to protect themselves? Did even the gods take notice of how they fought and died?

She turned away from the gorge. Such thoughts would only make her despair. And yet the idea of returning to the camp held no attraction for her, either. The party was subdued, still reeling from how easily they had been overcome. Asara was there; Kaiku was avoiding her as best she could. Phaeca was a wreck that she did not want to deal with. She did not feel like talking to Tsata or the Tkiurathi, either: somehow, what she felt was too private to try to explain to them.

She was deciding whether to get some rest when she spotted Lucia walking into the trees.

She blinked. Had she really seen what she thought she saw? She headed up the grassy slope towards the treeline. Her doubt evaporated as she went. Of course Lucia had slipped away on her own: it was just like her to disappear like that. Probably the people in the camp thought she had gone to sleep. Lucia needed solitude more than any of them, and she had the least to fear from the forest spirits.

The thought did not comfort Kaiku. She skirted the camp and reached the point where she had seen Lucia enter the trees. A pair of sentries were watching her from where the tents were clustered, evidently wondering what she was up to. She let them wonder. Better if she could get Lucia back without anyone noticing. On the heels of that thought came another: how had Lucia got away without being seen?

The forest seemed funereal in the moonlight. The silence and the still air gave it a tomblike feel, and the unfamiliar foliage put everything subtly off-kilter. Though Iridima's glow rendered everything in monochrome, these plants still reflected a kind of colour, some hue that she found hard to identify. She listened for a moment, and faintly she heard a tread heading away from her.

She was about to follow when something moved in the darkness, a shifting of some vast shadow. She paled. It was massive, as big as a feya-kori but wider, filling the space between the roots of the forest and its canopy. She could see it only as glimpses, obscured as it was by the boles of the trees in between; but glimpses were enough. Some colossal four-legged thing, there in the forest. Watching her.

She went cold as she found its eyes. Small and yellow, impossibly bright, and set far apart on a head that must have been bigger than she was.

It could not be there, her rational mind told her. It would knock over trees whenever it moved. It could not be there because it could not *fit*.

But yet she saw it, in defiance of sense, a hulking shape among the trees, wreathed in dark. If she set foot in the forest, it would come for her. And yet, if she did not, she left Lucia to its mercy.

The sentries were staring at her oddly now, as she stood

transfixed on the edge of the clearing. She did not notice. She was caught by the gaze of that dreadful beast.

Lucia, she thought. She took a step forward, and the beast was on her.

Mishani shivered suddenly at her writing desk. She frowned and looked over her shoulder. At the edges of the lantern-light the room was cool and empty. The unease persisted for a moment or two, but Mishani was too level-headed to give much credit to phantoms of the mind, and she was soon immersed in her task once more.

She was kneeling on a mat in the communal room of the house at Araka Jo which she shared with Kaiku. Before her, spread across the table, were rolls of paper, inkpots and quills and brushes, a glazed-clay mug of lathamri and a stack of books. She was dressed in a warm sleeping-robe and soft slippers, but she had no intention of sleeping just yet.

Her interest in her mother's books had become an obsession these past weeks. She was desperate to understand, dogged by the certainty that there was something she should *know* through these words, some message her mother was trying to communicate to her. It had been a growing suspicion for some time now, but with the publication of the last book she had realised that it was indisputably more than fancy on her part. The final lines that Nida-jan spoke were the first half of a lullaby that had been a private song between mother and daughter. Her mother had used it once before, with the merchant Chien, as a way to identify him as an ally to Mishani if all else should fail. Now she was using it again.

But to what end? That was the puzzle. And no matter how Mishani pored over the books, she could not see what it was she was supposed to work out.

She took a sip of lathamri and stared at the paper before her. After exploring several theories, she had returned to the area of the books that bothered her the most: the awful poems that Nida-jan had taken to reciting. Their appearance seemed to coincide with the point where her mother had begun producing smaller books at a faster rate, and her exquisite prose had become sloppy. Mishani had written out one of them with a brush on the paper before her, large calligraphic pictograms painted in black ink. As if by increasing their size they would give up their secrets. She had tried making anagrams for hours now, scratching the words she built from the symbols in tiny script at the bottom of the paper, but it all came out as nonsense.

She tutted to herself. She was getting frustrated, and it was late. She had drunk too much lathamri which was making her jittery, for she had a small frame and was not used to it. And she could not concentrate properly while she had the knowledge in the back of her mind that Kaiku and Lucia had most likely reached the Forest of Xu by now. Gods, she hoped their trust in Lucia was well founded. If she did not come out of there alive, all their hopes were gone. And if she did not come back, then Kaiku would not either . . .

Such thoughts bring you no profit, Mishani, she told herself. *Make yourself useful.*

Indeed, making herself useful was something she really should have been doing; but she did not want to leave Araka Jo until she had unlocked the mystery of Muraki's books. She had returned from the desert to lend her political skills to the Libera Dramach in the Southern Prefectures, but most of the nobles were in Saraku or Machita, and seldom visited here. She had heard about the assassination attempt upon Barak Zahn during the rout at Zila, and suspicion naturally fell upon Blood Erinima. She wondered what kind of retribution Zahn had in mind, and whether she should go to him and offer her help. Division was the worst thing at this time, and yet it did not surprise Mishani in the least that the nobles could not cooperate even in the face of such an overwhelming enemy. Blood Erinima sought advantage for themselves, just like every other high family. They were not thinking of the wider consequences, only the chance to win themselves the throne. Such was the way of politics.

She could sense the proximity of an answer in the pages before her. She knew she was close, but the solution still eluded her. Though she did not know what to focus on, where to look, she believed that if she persisted, the picture would gradually become clear. If only through sheer force of will.

An owl hooted outside. She stared at the paper. For a long time, she did not move; she was entirely consumed by the workings of her mind, turning possibilities over and over. Absently, she picked up her mug, took a sip, and put it back again.

The slight movement in her peripheral field of vision, the way the mug did not seem to sit quite right against her fingers as she replaced it: these were the tiny warnings that told her she had misjudged where to set it down, that the lathamri was tipping off the edge of the desk. She snatched at it, catching it before it could fall, and in doing so the trailing edge of her other sleeve caught the ink pot and tipped it over. She hurriedly set the drink down and righted the ink pot, but by that time a slick of black had spread in an ellipse over a section of her calligraphy.

She huffed out a breath, annoyed by the waste of ink. Her sleeping-robe was stained at the cuffs too. She reached to roll up the paper and discard it, but she was arrested halfway. Slowly, she drew her hand back and stared at the paper again.

The ink had spilled across several lines, but the one that caught her eye had escaped with only minor damage. Only two pictograms in the middle of a four-syllable word had been obscured. But what had caught Mishani's eye was that there was a new word made by taking out those two symbols. The first and the last, when contracted together, created a new meaning.

Demons.

Excited, she looked to the book where the original poem

had been, identified the missing symbols. Doing so shed no new light, but it did not diminish her sudden momentum. She laid aside the stained parchment and copied out the poem anew, then put two strokes across the two syllables to make *demons* again. On a whim, she hunted down any other instances of those pictograms. There was only one. She crossed it out, and it made the word senseless. Yet still she refused to believe that the appearance of *demons* was coincidence. She stared at the word she had mutilated. In its entirety, it meant *perhaps*. After a moment, she put a stroke through another of the pictograms. Now it said *by*, in the chronological sense. She studied the word for any other combinations that might make a meaning, but found none. She looked through the poem for other pictograms like this third one she had struck off, but it did not occur again. She examined the other words for symbols she might remove to make new meanings, but the possibilities were too many, and some words could not be contracted.

She was confounded once more, but the elation of progress would not let her stop. After a moment of listlessness, she began flicking through the books to find other poems, copied them out, and crossed through the three pictograms whenever she could find them. *Demons* appeared again, formed out of the same word as last time. It was nothing conclusive, but it was the possibility that was tantalising.

Finally, as night drew on, she found the word she needed. It was five pictograms long, and three of them were the three symbols she had marked for deletion. With quick strokes, she cut them out and looked at the result.

Mountain.

She was fractionally disappointed, having hoped for something more definite, something that could not possibly have been a random coincidence of syllables. But the disappointment lasted only a moment. It was a word, at least.

She needed to know more symbols to strike out. She needed a key to solve the code. Where would she find such a key?

The answer came to her immediately. She had had it all along; it was only a matter of asking herself the right question. The lullaby.

Snatching up a new roll of paper, she scribbled the lullaby down, then located the original poem she had been working on. Notes spilled from the edge of the desk, displaced by frantic activity. She went through the poem symbol by symbol, crossing out whenever she found a pictogram that matched a pictogram in the lullaby. And slowly, words began to emerge there. Some of them were nonsense, and some were impossible to contract at all, but these she ignored. She read only those words that she had altered to form a new meaning, and when she did so, she found the message.

New demons attack Juraka by midwinter.

She sat back on her heels, gazing at the page. For some time, she was blank, her mind scattered in the aftermath of revelation. Then she began to draw her thoughts together.

Mother, she thought in disbelief. *All this time . . .*

It had started not long after the war had begun. The poems, the bad writing. She had become sloppy because she was writing too fast. The books were short because she had to distribute them quickly enough for the information contained to be relevant. The poetry was terrible because it was hampered by the need to embed messages in it, and because she wanted to draw attention to it.

All this time, Muraki had been their spy in the heart of their enemy's camp, and they had not known it till now. *Mishani* had not known it till now. For it was only she who could have broken the code, only she – and Kaiku, though her mother did not know that – who possessed the necessary knowledge. But Muraki must have noticed that her warnings were doing no good, and finally, in her latest book, she offered a broad hint to her daughter, whom she must have believed was reading. For anyone else to decipher it meant death for Muraki. That was why it was only the first stanza of the poem: without both stanzas, the code was still gibberish.

Now Mishani thought back. There had been other clues. References to lullabies; Nida-jan's meditations on how his poetry had the cadence of a parent singing to their child; a passage where Nida-jan considered composing a song for his lost son, one that only they would know, which he would sing when he found the boy at last. Heart's blood, how many lives might have been saved, how many battles won, if Mishani had been clever enough to decipher this earlier? It was so obvious in hindsight that she could not believe she had been so dull-witted.

Her mother had been risking her life to help the Empire, drawing information from her husband the Lord Protector and passing it on through her writing. And nobody had realised.

Once Mishani had thought her mother weak, weak and uncaring. She felt tears pricking her eyes at the shame of her ungraciousness.

Spurred by that feeling, she went to work on the other poems. There would be no sleep for her tonight.

SIXTEEN

Kaiku awoke from a vivid dream of sweat and heat and sex, memory tattering with wakefulness, leaving only the face of the man who had been taking her. Tane.

She felt suddenly embarrassed as her eyes flickered open, and she saw the others in the tent, kneeling nearby. Asara and Tsata. Had her dream showed outwardly, in moans or in the languid movement of her body? She was still fully clothed, but no blankets had been laid on her, which made her feel exposed. And gods, why Tane? She had not thought of him for a long time.

Then she remembered the beast.

She jerked upright in alarm. Tsata held up his hands in a placating gesture.

'Be calm, Kaiku. No harm has come to you,' he said.

'No harm?' she repeated. 'And Lucia?'

'Lucia is perfectly safe. Why would it be otherwise?' Asara said.

Kaiku stared at her for a moment. She was remembering how the thing had *flitted* at her, a charge broken up into a thousand tiny and discrete increments: flash impressions of shadow, each one larger than the last as it neared, enacted in a fraction of an instant. It was so fast she had not even time to rouse her *kana*. It should have battered aside dozens of trees as it came. Then darkness, and dreaming.

Asara handed her a cup of water. She took it with a suspicious glance at the desert lady. Watching over her while she slept was far too compassionate an act for Asara: she cared only because Kaiku still owed her, and she intended to collect.

Asara sensed her mood, perhaps, for she rose into a crouch then. 'I am relieved that you are well,' she said. 'I must help with the preparations. We leave soon.' And she left, ducking through the flap.

Kaiku began to arrange herself, a little self-conscious at being seen straight out of bed with her hair mussed and eyes puffy with sleep; then she remembered the weeks she had spent in the wild with Tsata back in the Xarana Fault, and laughed at herself for her vanity. He had already seen her at her worst; it was scarcely worth concerning herself over.

He responded to her laughter with a look of bewilderment. 'You seem in good spirits,' he observed.

She sighed. 'No, it is not that,' she said. She thought about explaining, but decided it was not worth the effort. Tsata would not understand.

He let it drop. 'What happened to you?' he asked.

So Kaiku explained about the beast in the trees. She made no mention of why she had strayed from the camp. She meant to have a word with Lucia about her dangerous wanderings as soon as circumstances would permit.

Tsata listened as she talked. In contrast to Lucia, he had a wonderfully grave expression when listening, as if the object of his attention was the only thing in the world. Kaiku had found it mildly intimidating at first, but now she enjoyed it. When she spoke, she knew he thought her words important. It made her feel better about herself.

When she was done, he shifted himself so that he was sitting cross-legged. Tkiurathi could never kneel for long; it became excruciating for them after a while, unlike the folk of Saramyr.

'It appears that you were fortunate indeed. We lost two more soldiers last night. We can presume that they met the same creature that you did.'

'We *lost* them? How do you mean?'

'They are gone. Tracks lead into the forest, but beyond that all trace has disappeared.'

Kaiku rubbed her hands over her face. 'Gods . . .' she murmured. 'Lucia said that the spirits' agreement to let us pass was no guarantee of safety. I had hoped to keep that from the rest of the group, at least until our morale was better.'

'That was foolish,' said Tsata. From anyone else, it would have been rude, but Kaiku knew how he was. 'Perhaps we would have been more careful if we had been told.'

'More careful than we were? I doubt it.' She would not shoulder the responsibility for their deaths. 'Everyone was frightened last night; they were watchful, despite what Lucia had told them.'

'They are more frightened now,' Tsata observed.

'As well they should be,' Kaiku replied.

There was a beat of silence between them.

'You were writhing in your sleep. Who were you dreaming of?' he asked suddenly.

Kaiku blushed. 'Heart's blood, Tsata! There are some politenesses my people employ that you would do well to learn.'

He did not look in the least abashed. 'I apologise,' he said. 'I did not realise you would be embarrassed.'

She brushed her hair behind her ear and shook her head. 'You should not ask a lady such things.' She met his gaze, his pale green eyes devoid of guile, strangely like a child's. For a moment she held it; then she looked away.

'Tane,' she said with a sigh, as if he had forced it out of her. 'I dreamt of Tane.'

Tsata tilted his chin upward: an Okhamban nod, in understanding. 'I appreciate your honesty. It is important to me.'

'I know,' she murmured. Then, feeling she needed to apologise herself, she took his hand in both of hers. 'It was only a dream,' she said.

He seemed surprised by the contact. After a moment, he squeezed her hand gently and let go. 'We all dreamed last night,' he said. 'But you, it seems, were the only one who dreamt anything pleasant.'

'I am not so sure it was pleasant at all,' she said. Though she could remember nothing for certain except that Tane was in it, she was unsure whether the dream-congress was entirely consensual on her part. In fact, she had an uneasy intuition that he had been raping her. She looked up. 'What did you dream of?'

Tsata seemed uncomfortable, and did not reply. 'We should go; the others will be waiting for us.'

'Ah! You will not get away so easily,' she said, grabbing his arm as he made to rise. 'Where is your honesty now?' she chided playfully.

'I dreamt of you,' he said, his tone flat.

'Of me?'

'I dreamt I was gutting you with a knife.'

Kaiku stared at him for a moment. She blinked.

'I see your studies of Saramyrrhic have not yet encompassed the art of telling a woman what she wants to hear,' she said, and then burst out laughing at his expression. 'Come. We should be on our way.' When he still seemed uneasy, she said again: 'It was only a dream, Tsata. As was mine.'

They emerged from the tent to a crisp dawn. It was early yet, but from the faces of the group Kaiku guessed that few had slept well, if at all. They were wearily taking down the camp, wandering in pairs or eating cold food – no fires were allowed in the forest, on Lucia's advice. The silence that surrounded them was as oppressive as it had been the day before. It made the whole forest seem dead. Asara had packed her tent up and was sitting on the grass, watching Kaiku across the camp. Kaiku dismissed her with a glance. She did not want to worry about that one for now.

A sudden commotion from the treeline drew her attention. People were getting to their feet, running up towards where two men were emerging with a third being dragged between them.

'Spirits, what now?' Kaiku muttered, and she headed that way herself, with Tsata close behind.

They had dumped the man face down on the grass by the time she arrived, and soldiers were jabbering over the corpse. 'Who is this?' she demanded, putting enough of the Red Order authority into her tone to silence them. 'What happened to him?'

'He's one of those who went missing last night,' came the reply. 'We went to look for them. Didn't find the other.' He exchanged glances with his companion. 'As to what happened to him, your guess is as good as ours.'

With that, he tipped the body over with his boot, and it came to lie on its back with one arm awkwardly underneath it. The soldiers swore and cursed.

Though he seemed otherwise untouched, his eyes were milky white, no pupil or iris visible. The skin around them was speckled with burst blood vessels, and brilliant blue veins radiated out from the sockets, starkly protuberant. The man's expression was slack, his jaw hanging open in an idiot gape.

'I think you were more fortunate than we had guessed,' Tsata muttered, 'if this is what your beast does to its victims.'

Kaiku turned away, crossing her arms over her stomach, hugging herself. 'Then why did it spare me?'

She began to walk; the sight of the dead man was more than she could take at the moment.

They travelled round the gorge and onward, following Lucia's directions. She was their compass, for she could sense the Xhiang Xhi and headed unerringly towards it. The group were jumpy now. The forest had a way of tricking the eye, inventing movement from nothing, so that people would start violently and look down at their feet, or out into the trees, thinking something had scurried past. They began to hear noises in the silence now, strange taps and clicks from afar. The first time they occurred, Doja – the leader of the soldiers – called a halt and they listened for a while; but the sounds were random and monotonous, and eventually they tried to ignore them. It did little good. The tapping began to wear at them, much as the silence had before it.

The forest continued to change, darkening as they penetrated further. Purple was predominant now, as of deciduous leaves on the late edge of autumn, and the canopy thickened overhead so that they walked in twilight. A strange gloom hung in the air. The taps and clicks echoed as if they were in a cavernous hall, unnaturally reverberant.

The group threaded its way through terrain that became increasingly hard, up muddy slopes and through tangled thickets with branches they dared not hack aside for fear of retaliation. They went with swords and rifles held ready, in the faint hope that they would be any use.

Kaiku and Phaeca walked together, keeping close to Lucia. Phaeca seemed better today, despite having barely slept. Whenever she had closed her eyes she had been pitched into the same nightmare, something so horrible that she refused to speak of it. Still, she had artfully made herself up and disguised the shadows under her eyes, and it did not show on her. Kaiku had been concerned about how well she might hold up in this environment, but she felt a small relief at seeing her friend recovered.

'How is she?' Phaeca murmured, gesturing at Lucia.

Kaiku made a face that said: *who can tell?* 'I do not think she even knows where she is at the moment.'

They observed her for a time, and indeed, she had the look of a sleepwalker. She drifted along without paying attention to anything or anyone nearby.

'She is listening to them,' Phaeca said. 'To the spirits.'

'I fear for her, Phaeca,' Kaiku admitted. 'She said things to me, back at Araka Jo . . .' She trailed off, deciding that to speak of it to Phaeca would be breaking a confidence. 'I fear for her,' she repeated.

Phaeca did not pry. 'What is she, truly?' she mused.

'She is an Aberrant, the same as you and me.'

Phaeca looked unconvinced. 'Is that all she is, do you

think? I'm not so sure. It's her nature more than her abilities. And her uniqueness.' She glanced at Kaiku. 'Why aren't there more of her? There were many with our powers: the Sisterhood only accounts for a fraction of the total, those that were not killed or who did not kill themselves. Yet have you ever heard of anyone with Lucia's talent?'

Kaiku did not like where this was going. It came uncomfortably close to suggesting that Lucia was divine, and she had thought Phaeca above that. 'What are you saying?' she asked.

Phaeca shook her head. 'Nothing,' she replied. 'Just thinking aloud.'

Kaiku lapsed into silence, wondering about this. She had tried to talk to Lucia earlier in the day about her late-night excursion into the forest, but alarmingly she found it impossible to get through. Lucia was not only paying no attention, but she could not bring herself to focus enough to make any sense of Kaiku. She stared right through her as if she were some puzzling phantom, then her eyes would slide away elsewhere.

Whatever was happening to Lucia, she was, as ever, facing it alone. Kaiku was entirely shut out. She could do nothing but worry.

Another one of them fell by mid–afternoon.

It was Tsata's cry to his kinsman that alerted them. They did not catch the meaning, phrased as it was in Okhamban, but they understood the tone. Several men clustered around Lucia; the others hurried into the trees towards the source of the sound. Kaiku directed Phaeca to stay, haste making her peremptory, and then went after them. She clambered up a steep rise of land, using roots as handholds and odd gold-veined rocks as steps, and ducked through the foliage and past a thicket of tall, straight trees to where she could see the soldiers' backs in a circle. They made way for her as she arrived.

It was the Tkiurathi woman, Peithre. She lay in Tsata's arms, breathing in thin, rasping gasps, her skin pale. Heth broke through the circle a moment later, and demanded something of Tsata in their native language. Tsata's reply was clear without translation: he did not know what was wrong with her.

'Let me,' said Kaiku. She crouched down in front of Peithre. The ailing woman's eyes fixed on her, a mixture of desperation and pleading. Tsata looked around, searching for the source of what had done such harm, but nothing was evident.

'Tsata, tell her to be calm. I will help her,' she said, not taking her gaze from Peithre's. Tsata did so. Then Kaiku put her hand on Peithre's bare shoulder, and as the soldiers watched her irises changed from brown to bright red.

'She is poisoned,' Kaiku said immediately. She held her hand cupped beneath Peithre's chin, and a dozen tiny flecks, like bee-stings, popped from the skin of the jaw and throat and collarbone and fell into her palm, where they ignited in tiny pyres. 'That plant,' she pointed behind her, at where a patch of curved, thin reeds with bulbous tips rose out of the bank of a tiny brook.

One of the soldiers brandished his sword and took a step towards them.

'Do not touch them!' Kaiku snapped. 'You will kill us all. We will not harm the forest, even if the forest harms us.'

'Can you save her?' Tsata murmured.

'I can try,' she replied; and for a moment they were back in a fog-laden marsh in the Xarana Fault, and it was Yugi and not Peithre who lay dying. But then she had been a clumsy apprentice; now she was a seamstress of the Weave. She closed her eyes and plunged into the golden world, and the Tkiurathi and soldiers could do nothing but wait. Heth muttered to Tsata in Okhamban. They watched the patient closely, observers to a process too subtle for them to understand. Peithre began to sweat, giving off an acrid stink: Kaiku was hounding the poison from her body. Then gradually her breathing slowed. Her eyes drifted closed. Heth exploded into a guttural tirade, but Tsata held his hand up for silence. Kaiku was concentrating too hard to reassure him. Peithre was not dying, not now; but she would have to sleep.

Minutes passed before Kaiku's eyes flickered open again. The soldiers murmured to each other.

'She will live,' Kaiku said. 'But she is very weak. The damage the poison has done is too widespread and too deep for me to repair entirely.'

Heth spoke up in Saramyrrhic. 'I will carry her.'

'It is not that simple. She needs rest, or she may not survive. Her body is at its limits already.' She met Tsata's gaze. 'The poison was very strong,' she said. 'It is a miracle she lived long enough for me to get to her.'

She looked up, and caught sight of Asara standing there, watching her through the trees with singular interest. Then she turned away and was gone, leaving Kaiku faintly perturbed.

'Make her comfortable,' Kaiku said to the Tkiurathi. 'I will speak with Doja.' She got to her feet.

'You have my gratitude,' Heth said uncertainly, glancing at Tsata for approval. He found Saramyr customs as difficult as she found theirs.

'And mine,' Tsata said.

'We are *pash*, you idiots,' she said tenderly. 'No thanks are needed.'

'You mean we're staying here?' one of the soldiers called in disbelief. All eyes looked to him. He was a black-haired man around his twenty-fifth harvest. She knew him: his name was Kugo.

Kaiku fixed him a hard stare, made harder by the demonic colour of her eyes. She could feel the momentary warmth of cameraderie drain from her. 'That is what I am going to talk to your leader about.'

'We can't stay here!' he said. 'Heart's blood, four of us are dead already; you yourself were nearly a fifth; she was a hair's breadth from being number six. This is only our second day! How long do you think we're going to survive if we just wait around in the forest?'

Kaiku could feel herself tensing, readying for a confrontation. She should have just walked away from this, swept him icily aside. But something inside her would not allow her to let it go, because she knew where this was coming from, and she wanted to hear him say it.

'What would you have us do, Kugo? Abandon her? What if it were you?'

'It's *not* me. And if it were, or if it were any of these men, I'd stay with them whatever the consequence. We would not abandon our own.' There was a murmur of approval at this. 'But these are not our own,' he said. 'I won't risk my life for foreigners.'

Tsata and Heth did not react to this, but Kaiku did.

'Have you learned *nothing*?' she cried, walking up to Kugo until she was facing him. 'Why do you think we are fighting this war, you fool? Because we were so ready to let the Weavers scapegoat Aberrants that we never thought to question them! We let them kill children for more than two centuries because we held jealously onto the prejudices that they instilled in us! People like you joined the Libera Dramach to change that. And now, now that Aberrants like me have *saved your empire*, now that we are *following* an Aberrant into the heart of the most gods-damned dangerous place on the continent, now you say that these people who are willing to die alongside us are *not our own?*'

She was in a fury now such as she had rarely been, and the air tautened around her, the tips of her hair lifting in the palpable aura of her rage. Kugo's face was a picture of shock.

'This division is what kills us! Do you not see? You cannot throw away one set of arbitrary prejudices and still maintain another! You cannot decide to accept Aberrants like me and still regard foreigners as lesser than you! Your ignorance condemns us to repeat the same cycle, war after war until there is nothing left! Heart's blood, if your kind ran out of enemies you would start killing your friends! These people,' she gestured at Tsata and Heth, 'could teach you something about *unity*.'

She grabbed the side of his head with one hand; he was paralysed with fright now. Her voice dropped.

'You will afford the Tkiurathi the same respect you give these other men, or you will have me to deal with.'

With that, she shoved him roughly away and stalked into the forest. Silence reigned in her wake. Tsata watched her leave, his tattooed face unreadable; but he stared at the point where she was lost to the undergrowth for a long time after she was gone.

She went to see Doja when she had calmed down, and he agreed that they should stop here for the night and evaluate Peithre's condition anew in the morning.

'But if another of my men goes missing, we're leaving,' he warned.

'You must do what you will,' she said. 'But I am staying. And in the end, it is Lucia's decision whether you will leave or not: you would not last an hour in this place without her.'

Doja was angry, she could sense that, though he suppressed it well. He was a square-jawed man with a cleft chin covered in wiry black stubble, a sharp nose and small eyes. Kaiku respected him immensely as a leader, but she had undermined him and he resented that. Threatening one of his soldiers had not done her any favours in his estimation, and now her intransigence was a direct challenge to his authority. The relationship between the Libera Dramach and the Red Order had become more and more strained of late. Whereas before the Red Order had been an extremely useful secret weapon for their cause, now that they were out in the open they were too powerful to be trusted, and there was a general suspicion that they only fought on the side of the Empire because it coincided with their own agenda.

'I give you one night,' he said. 'After that, we will ask Lucia.'

A clamour arose before Kaiku could reply, coming from the direction where she had left Peithre. She broke off their conversation without another word and hurried back to that spot, and there she found the soldiers with their rifles ready, spread in a loose circle, aiming outward between the trees. Someone, made jumpy by his surroundings, sighted on her as she approached; she ducked instinctively, but thankfully he did not fire. She swept past him with a corrosive glare and he cringed away from her.

'What is it?' she asked Tsata. He and Heth knelt by Peithre, their own guns ready.

'Out in the trees,' he said, motioning with his head.

She looked, and as she did so, she glimpsed something. It was a flash of white, darting between the vine-strewn maze of trunks.

'Do not fire on them!' she said, raising her voice to include the whole group. 'Remember where we are! Shoot only if they attack.'

The soldiers muttered sarcastically between themselves. She glanced down at Peithre, still asleep on the forest floor with a blanket as a pillow, and then out into the trees again. Another movement caught her eye, but it was too quick, gone before she could find it.

((Are you with Lucia?)) she asked Phaeca, and received an immediate affirmative. ((Bring her here))

'There's one!' someone cried.

'Do not fire!' Kaiku shouted again, fearful of the excitement in the man's tone, as if he had just spotted game and was about to take it down. Kaiku saw where everyone else was looking, down a corridor of boles and bushes to where one of the things had frozen, caught in their eyes, watching them watching it.

It was beautiful and terrifying all at once. Its short fur was perfectly white, but for where shadows delineated the hollows of its ribs. It had elements in it of deer and fox – a brush for a tail; stubby, sharp antlers; a certain furtiveness of movement – and yet its musculature and bone structure were disturbingly human, as though it were a lithe and elongated man standing on all fours. Its face had something of the fox's narrow cunning, and something of the deer's alarmed docility, but its features were more mobile than either, and when it skinned back its lips it showed an array of close-fitting, daggerlike teeth that betrayed a carnivorous diet.

'Aberrant,' someone hissed.

'It is no Aberrant,' Kaiku murmured in reply. Even if she could not sense it by their Weave-signature, she would have known anyway. There was something about these creatures, some linearity of structure that bespoke an entirely natural evolution. They were somewhere between spirit and animal, a hybrid of the two.

Then it was gone, launching itself back into the trees. Phaeca appeared a few moments later, leading Lucia and a group of soldiers who acted as her bodyguards. Asara arrived, her own rifle ready.

'Lucia,' Kaiku said. She did not respond: her eyes were far away. '*Lucia!*'

She focused suddenly, but almost immediately began to drift again. 'What are these things?' Kaiku demanded. 'Can you talk to them? Do they mean to harm us?' She shook Lucia's shoulder and said her name again. '*Listen* to me!'

'Emyrynn,' Lucia murmured, staring over Kaiku's shoulder into the trees. 'They're called emyrynn in our tongue. They want us to follow them.'

'Follow them? Is this some kind of trap?'

Lucia made a vague negative noise in her throat. 'We have to follow them . . .' she said, and then she had slipped beyond rousing again, lost in some dreamwalk where Kaiku could not reach her. Kaiku bit her lip to kill the frustration at seeing her this way. This forest was too much for Lucia, overwhelming her, making her more distant than ever before. It was agony to watch, for Kaiku had no way of knowing if she could ever come back from this, or whether every moment within the borders of the forest was making her worse.

Doja was quicker to decide than she was, and his faith in Lucia was evidently greater. 'We can't move this woman yet. Three men, go with them. Come back and fetch us when you find whatever it is they want us to see. And heart's blood, *be careful.*'

'I will go,' Kaiku said, because she would do anything not to be around Lucia a moment longer.

'And I,' said Tsata.

Asara volunteered also. Doja was happy to accept: it meant he did not to have to risk any of his soldiers. Kaiku felt a flicker of uncertainty at the thought of having Asara along, but she had Tsata at least, and in him her trust was total.

'Where are they? Where are you seeing them?' she asked the group in general, and several men pointed, all in roughly the same direction. They set off into the trees; Tsata warned Asara about the reed that had poisoned Peithre, and she nodded in acknowledgement, not taking her eyes off Kaiku.

Rifles held close, they forged through the undergrowth, while ahead of them the emyrynn led onward, annoyingly elusive and yet never quite out of sight. None of them spoke; their concentration was bent on seeking out danger, waiting for the jaws of a trap to spring shut, hoping to predict it in time to evade.

But their journey was not a long one. They had not been travelling for more than ten minutes before they found what it was the emyrynn wanted to show them, and there they stood dumbfounded, and wondered what kind of beings they had stumbled upon in the depths of the Forest of Xu.

In the upper levels of the Imperial Keep, where the Weavers' lunacy had made it dangerous to tread, the dust lay thick and spiders webbed the windows.

Kakre's preferred room for Weaving was not the Sun Chamber that he had populated with his kites and mannequins of skin. He found the noise of the other Weavers distracting. Instead, he took himself to a section where he could be alone, a morose and silent place too out of the way for the Weavers or the frightened servants to trouble themselves with. The floor was rucked with wide, overlapping trails, paths carved in the powdery dust by the threadbare hem of his robe as he wandered. Weak daylight filtered through the miasma that cloaked the city, and the air was heavy and oily.

Avun had been here for three hours now, talking with spectres. Seven Governors of the major towns and cities within the Weavers' territory hung in a circle around the centre of the empty room, blurred apparitions, with Avun the only solid one among them. They were discussing the interminable minutiae of their respective situations, the state of the land, the course of the famine. Kakre was the link that held them all together, a junction through which all eight participants could see each other as murky avatars. Avun had insisted that it be so, for drawing eight people together in a country the size of Saramyr was impractical at best, especially as some lived in the distant Newlands to the east.

Kakre was getting angry. He had allowed himself to be persuaded to achieve this feat, and yet so far he had heard nothing that could not have been done by individual conferences, which were far less taxing. If he did not believe that Avun had been sufficiently cowed by past punishments, he would have thought the Lord Protector was beginning to take his masters for granted.

The conference dragged out while the light of Nuki's eye began to fade. Kakre was the greatest among the Weavers – certainly in his own estimation, anyway – but the strain of maintaining so many links for so long was beginning to wear on him. Pride forbade him to buckle, but he cursed Avun's name inwardly, and began to think of myriad discomforts he might wreak upon the man when this was done.

Finally, Avun began to wrap up the proceedings, enacting elaborate rituals of farewell to each of the participants in turn. Kakre cut the connection when Avun was finished with them, and the spectres faded away. At last it was over, and only Avun remained. Kakre staggered slightly, his knees weak. Avun's quick glance indicated that he had noticed, but he wisely forbore to mention it.

'You have my deepest gratitude,' Avun said. 'A face-to-face conference, or as near as we can get it, makes all the difference in government. Many valuable ideas can be mined when our heads are put together.'

Kakre was not convinced anything had come out of that meeting beyond a few status reports and vague allusions to methods of progress, and Avun's thanks sounded facile. But he was not in a very coherent state of mind at the moment, and he mistrusted himself. The mania would surely strike him after such a long and strenuous period of Weaving; he could already feel himself itching for the knife he kept beneath his robes.

'You would be best to leave now,' Kakre snarled. 'If you wish to avoid being harmed. I shall have words for you later. Oh, indeed.'

Avun bowed and left. Kakre shakily sat down on the floor; dust rose in a languid puff around him. He was thankful now that he had insisted Avun come to him for the conference, instead of holding it in a state room. At the time, it had been a whim, a reminder that Avun was his servant and not vice versa; but now he found his solitude a balm, for there was nobody to see his weakness.

The post-Weaving mania was spreading slow tentacles through him like blood dripped into water. He wanted to do some skinning, but he felt too weak to procure himself a victim, and he had used up his last canvas a few days ago. The urge and the lethargy were growing at the same pace, putting him in an impossible situation. He breathed a cracked curse and gritted what was left of his teeth. He would have to ride this one out, at least until he had the strength to do something about it. He briefly fantasised about torturing Avun, but in the face of his growing need the visions he conjured seemed pallid and childish.

Instead, he was blinded by a rare window of clarity upon himself, a moment in which he saw what he had become, free of delusion and madness. His bladework had been steadily deteriorating for years now. Most of the sculptures that he kept had been cut in the days before the Weavers shattered the Empire. His arthritic hands trembled as they held the knife, and he was more a butcher than a surgeon of late. But it was not only his coordination: his mind had rotted too. The effort of summoning and controlling the feya-kori had battered the frail mush of his physical brain, turned him addled and senile, and he saw now the damage it had wreaked and how much more it would do next time he roused the blight demons from their pall-pits.

For a short time, he knew what he was, saw the ruin he had visited on his body and mind, and he screamed and cried and clawed himself; but it passed, and the thoughts became too hard to hold on to, and dissipated like smoke.

Fahrekh found him like that: curled up, a heap of rags and hide, the dead-skin Mask pressed to the floor, caked with grey dust. He stood in the doorway for a time, his angular face of bronze, silver and gold expressionless.

'Weave-lord Kakre,' he said. 'You seem unwell.'

'Get out,' Kakre croaked.

'I think not,' came the reply. He walked into the room, until he was standing over the Weave-lord, who strained his neck to look up at the younger Weaver.

'*Get out!*' he hissed again, and was racked with spasms.

'We have matters to discuss, you and I,' Fahrekh said slowly. 'Matters of succession. Specifically, mine.'

Kakre's head snapped up, suddenly lucid. Fahrekh's impassive Mask gazed back at him.

They plunged into the Weave together, and battle was joined.

It was in the abyss that they met, the endless, watery dark which was Kakre's preferred visualisation of the fabric of reality. Whether by accident or design, it was Fahrekh's too, and he was equally happy with the interpretation. As they attacked each other, their interactions with the Weave took on the form of fish to fit their surroundings. Thousands of individual strings of thought became shoals of piranhas, riding the invisible cross-currents which flowed in mazy twists all around them. On either side of the fray, the masters of the conflict floated, maintaining their positions amid the whip and slide of the Weave. Kakre was a ray, Fahrekh a massive black jellyfish, its tentacles deadly purple streamers. These were the representations of their physical bodies, the core of their presence in the Weave. The piranhas were their fighters, a dizzying multitude of mind-strands that darted through the space between them, seeking for a way through the enemy shoal. They savaged one another, bursting into bright blooms of scrabbling gold threads as they hit, illuminating the darkness with brief globes of light that knotted inward to infinity and collapsed.

The squabbling of the piranhas was enacted faster than the eye could follow. They arced and looped in squads of dozens, thrusting or retreating or laying decoys. Smaller fish darted around the periphery of the thrashing battlefield, trying to circumvent the conflict and reach the enemy: some would be caught by their opponent's defences, others dashed to pieces in the cross-currents. The Weavers had innumerable tricks: using fish to shield other fish, slingshotting off the edge of invisible whirlpools, laying sluggish bait which would explode into an insoluble labyrinth of tangles when engaged. It was a dizzying tableau of astonishing viciousness, hidden beneath a thin skin of illusion to protect the minds of the combatants from the raw and maddening beauty of the Weave.

And Kakre was losing.

Though less than a second had passed in the world outside the Weave, where time was governed by the sun and the moons, the private battle had passed through a multitude of shifts and phases, as of a military campaign enacted at extreme speed. Kakre was canny, and had tricks learned from long experience; gaining mastery of the feya-kori had taught him some things that Fahrekh had yet to fathom. But he was making mistakes. Little slips, infinitesimal blank spots in his mind where once a reaction would have been instinctive, sinister patches of forgetfulness that drifted across his psyche, robbing him of focus. Fahrekh was young and burning with energy; his vigour made up for his relative lack of finesse. Kakre's shoal was losing ground, becoming tattered. Holes were opening in his defences faster than he could stitch them shut.

But there was worse. Kakre was exhausted. His physical body was tearing itself apart under the stress of the combat. He could feel his systems wrecking themselves in an effort to provide him with the strength to fight, and there would soon be nothing left for him to draw on. Fahrekh, who would have been a difficult opponent even when they were on equal footing, had caught him at his lowest ebb. Kakre could not win; he was only delaying the inevitable.

Well, if that was so, it was so. Kakre would never relinquish himself. He would fight till his dying breath.

His moment of defiance was his last thought before Fahrekh outmanoeuvred him totally. His enemy had been gathering forces behind a knitted ball of decoys, and now they suddenly shot out and round, engulfing Kakre's shoal like a hand closing into a fist. Kakre abandoned them immediately, knowing they were lost, and began creating a new shoal; but he had no vitality to give them, and they were sickly and slow. Fahrekh's ravening horde swept them aside and tore towards Kakre's unprotected ray to rip him apart.

And in that instant, the Weave-whale appeared.

It burst out of nothingness, filling the black abyss, overwhelming them with its sheer scale. The impact of its arrival blasted across the Weave like a detonation, scattering Fahrekh's shoal, buffeting them with a shockwave. Fahrekh managed to hold his coherence, but Kakre tattered away, losing his grip on the Weave, dissipating back into his physical body again.

It was sheer insane fury that saved him. There was no confusion as he was wrenched back to the world of human senses, no hesitation, and no conscious thought involved. Riding a wave of rage, a scream ripping from his throat, he lunged at Fahrekh, drawing his skinning knife from his belt. Fahrekh, stunned by the Weave-whale, was not fast enough to react. Kakre drove the blade beneath his metal Mask, ramming it deep into the soft flesh under his chin, through his palate and up into the front of his brain. The force of it took Fahrekh off his feet, and he collapsed to the floor in a billow of dust with Kakre on top of him. Still screaming, Kakre plunged the knife into Fahrekh's throat and chest again and again, drawing spurts of blood into the air, hacking flesh to moist ribbons. Finally, in one last, disgusted motion, he tore off Fahrekh's Mask and buried the knife up to the hilt in his eye; and after that, he was done.

He slid off the corpse of his enemy, his patchwork robe wet with blood, and lay there for some time, the only sound the laboured wheeze of his breath, slowing and slowing until he fell asleep.

SEVENTEEN

There was a village inside the Forest of Xu.

At least, when they had first laid eyes on it, they had *assumed* it was a village. They still were not entirely certain even now, as dusk approached on their second day in the forest. It was something so utterly alien to their experience that they had no adequate parallels to draw.

It was built around the existing trees with no apparent boundaries, sprawling up the trunks into the canopy and spreading along the ground in a curiously organic fashion. The constructions were formed of a glistening substance, hard as rock and smooth to the touch, predominantly an icy blue-white, but sometimes shaded brown or green. It had a subtle iridescence and a maddening quality that was not quite translucence but more a chameleon-like mimicry of colour: it seemed to change its hue to whatever lay behind it, depending on where the viewer stood. When Kaiku laid her hand on it, she left a hazy pink imprint which faded after a time.

Tsata, particularly, had been fascinated by how this strange village had been built, and it was he that found the key, and uncovered the secret at least partially. The substance was sap, bled from the trees and hardened through some unknown art into a multitude of shapes. Every construction, no matter how remote, was eventually linked to a tree bole at some point, though no evidence of cutting could be found. And now that they had established this, it was possible to see a certain flow to the architecture, a kind of glacial creep around which offshoots had been moulded with exquisite artistry. Kaiku had the uncomfortable sensation that the village was still growing; indeed, she found evidence of channels in which glistening sap still lay, oozing with excruciating torpidity towards the tips and edges of the existing constructions, which were wet with the stuff. She guessed that this would be moulded and hardened too, in time, to form another offshoot.

The village was an exhibition of dizzying variety. Wide discs buried in the bark of the trees were set in irregular patterns, sometimes growing in size as they ascended, sometimes diminishing. Spiky sprays erupted into the air. Gossamer threads were stitched through the branches, or formed twisting, unsupported bridges that defied physics. Some of the dwellings were like uneven pagodas, others smooth semicircular domes, still others jagged starbursts of colourful sap. Many of them had no visible means of entry. Some were up in the trees: inverted cones of three-quarter circumference growing out from the trunks. Venous tubes like tunnels ran between them, sometimes fracturing into smaller capillaries that tapered away to nothingness as they ran like shatter-cracks along the bark.

Different building styles were evident in different parts of the village, one graduating into another as the eye followed the lines of the dwellings. Some had been sculpted like coral, hulking accretions of sap that branched and overlapped in a dozen different formations and colours; others were thin and needle-like, white clusters of stalagmites rising high overhead; still others were cloudlike and billowing, rounded shapes heaped together like a pile of snowballs.

Kaiku, Asara and Tsata were the first to see it, and it was only afterwards that Tsata pointed out they were probably the first humans ever to have done so. The impact of that had made Kaiku lightheaded, and she had to sit down for a short while.

They had to assume that it was built by the emyrynn, but their only basis for that was the way the creatures had led them here. Once Kaiku and her companions had arrived, the emyrynn disappeared entirely. Upon exploration, there was no sign of life here, nor any indication that anyone or anything had ever occupied these bizarre abodes. Either that, or the inhabitants had deserted this place on their approach, taking everything with them, leaving it preternaturally spotless.

Tsata returned and led the rest of the party to the village. Lucia seemed to believe the spirit-beasts were trustworthy, and they had little alternative but to take her word for it. If that was the case, then had they been provided this place for shelter, somewhere to rest their wounded? Was it possible that these creatures were benevolent rather than hostile? Though many of them suspected a trap, for spirits were notoriously tricky, they settled themselves for the night. The disconcertingly alien surroundings were made more ominous by the eerie quiet and failing light. Doja insisted that they camp in the open and not sleep inside any of the sap-buildings. His men were only too glad to comply.

Neryn was waxing tonight, casting a soothing green light through the interknit branches overhead. Aurus was low in the northern sky, visible only by her glow on the edges of the leaves. Kaiku wandered through the camp amid the restless murmur of the troops, distracted by the architecture. The troops cast unfriendly glances at her. She was alone, and content to be so. Lucia was asleep; Phaeca had also retired, complaining that she felt ill; Tsata and Heth were tending their fallen comrade and would not leave her side.

Kaiku had spotted Asara earlier that evening, leaning against the side of one of the emyrynn dwellings, watching her while she absentmindedly cleaned her rifle. Kaiku, suddenly tired of her manner, had strode over to her to have this out; but she had picked up her rifle and gone before Kaiku got there. Obviously she did not want to talk then.

But now, suddenly, she appeared at Kaiku's side. 'I wish to speak with you,' she murmured.

'And I with you,' Kaiku replied.

'Not here,' said Asara. 'Come with me,'

Kaiku followed as Asara led them away from the camp. The village spread and towered around them, the silent edifice of an unknown species, aloof and impenetrable. They went some way from the camp, until they were sure there was nobody around, and there Asara stopped. For a moment, she did not turn; her shoulders were tight with suppressed emotion. Then she seemed to make a decision, and she faced Kaiku.

Kaiku studied her expectantly. The almond-shaped eyes painted in soft green, the dark skin, the achingly exotic beauty of her all belonged to a stranger, but under that she was still Asara; wonderful, treacherous Asara, whom she loved and hated in equal measure. The woman who had given her life, and taken for it a piece of Kaiku's essence and left a piece of her own, little splinters of desire that had lodged in their hearts and never quite worked free. Each wanted what the other had: that sliver of themselves that had been lost in the transaction.

Eventually, for Asara seemed so uncertain, it was Kaiku who spoke first. 'What is my debt, Asara?' she asked. 'What would you have me do to redress the balance between us?'

'You admit that you owe me, then?' Asara said quickly.

'I do owe you,' Kaiku said. 'But do I owe you enough to do as you ask? I will hear what you have to say before I decide.'

'Very well.' Asara still seemed wary. 'But you must swear first that what I have to ask you will never be repeated by you to anyone. To *anyone*. Whether you agree or not.'

'You have my oath,' said Kaiku, for she knew that Asara would go no further without it, and she wanted this done.

Asara regarded her carefully in the darkness, her eyes glittering. Debating whether to trust her.

'Asara,' Kaiku snapped, impatient. 'You have followed me this far. Do not fool yourself into thinking you are making a choice; you made it some time ago. You have shadowed my footsteps too long. What do you *want*?'

'I want a *child*,' Asara hissed.

There was silence between them. Asara retreated, spent by the effort of the admission. Kaiku stared.

'I want a child,' she said again, quieter. 'But I cannot bear one.'

'Why not?' Kaiku asked, slightly dazed. *This* was her secret longing?

'I do not know why not,' Asara replied. 'I can . . . change myself, but only to an extent. I can take on the forms of men and women, but not of beasts, nor of birds. I can alter my skin and my shape, but I have limits. What I can do, I do by instinct. I do not know how it happens. I cannot see inside myself. I cannot *fix* myself.'

It made sense to Kaiku then. 'You want me to make you fertile.'

'You can do this!' Asara said, and there was naked hunger in her voice. 'I have heard of the deeds you and your kind are capable of. I have seen Sisters bring men back from the brink of death, healing with their hands. I watched you save that Tkiurathi woman's life just hours ago! You have the power to repair whatever is wrong with me.'

'Perhaps,' said Kaiku.

'*Perhaps?*' Asara cried.

'I am not a god, Asara,' Kaiku said. 'I cannot create what is not there. I do not know what kind of changes Aberrancy has wreaked in you. What if you have no womb? I cannot give you one.'

'Then look! Look inside! You can tell me!' Asara was desperate now; her hopes had been vested in this for so long that the possibility of them being dashed was too much for her to take. For so long, lonely and empty; ever outcast, ever unable to fill the void that yawned inside her. There were none like she was, even among the Aberrants. In all ninety of her years, she had never found another. And it was Shintu's cruellest trick indeed to make her ageless and yet rob her of the power to procreate.

But Kaiku's brow was creased in a frown. 'I will have to think on this, Asara.'

'You *owe* me,' Asara spat, her fear turning to fury. 'I gave you a life; now you give me one!'

'And what would you do with it, Asara?' Kaiku asked. Her hair hung across one eye, but the other one regarded Asara steadily. 'What would I be unleashing if I allowed more creatures like you into the world?'

'It is the right of every woman! I was denied!'

'*Are* you even a woman?' Kaiku asked. 'Were you one to begin with? I wonder.' She had lapsed into the tone she used when she wore the make-up of the Sisterhood: stern, authoritative. 'Perhaps the gods had a reason to deny you. Perhaps one of you is enough.'

'Do not pronounce moral judgements upon me!' Asara raged. 'Not when you and your Red Order plot and scheme towards the throne. Your conscience is not unstained, Kaiku. Ask Cailin why your kind let the Weavers take the Empire. Ask her if hundreds of thousands, if *millions* of lives were worth sacrificing so that the Sisterhood could rise!'

Kaiku gazed at her levelly. 'Perhaps I will,' she said, and she turned and walked away. She could sense Asara's hateful glare prickling against her nape, and was half expecting the spy to attack her out of sheer thwarted anger; but Asara let her go.

Kaiku let the quietude of the forest envelop her, broken only by the sinister ticks and taps in the distance. Once her mind was still, she began to consider what Asara had said.

They spent an uneasy night within the emyrynn village, but when dawn came they were still all there. None of them were in good shape, however. Terrifying dreams haunted them, and the early watches had been punctuated by the shrieks of waking men. Most gave up trying to sleep, too afraid of what lurked just beneath the skin of unconsciousness. Those that persevered caught snatches of slumber, a few minutes at a time, before awakening in a worse state than they had been before. Tempers were fraying among the men. They resented the forest and the spirits and so, lacking targets, they snapped at each other.

What was worse, it became clear soon afterward that they would not be going anywhere that day. Peithre had improved a little, but Phaeca had become sick. Kaiku talked with Doja, who admitted that it was foolhardy to go on with one of the Sisters down and the other one determined to stay. He broke the news to his men, sweetening it by pointing out that he believed they were safe from the forest in the emyrynn village.

Kaiku was dubious about this last statement, but it served her purpose. The soldiers accepted their fate with stoic expressions, though later there would be dissent amongst them. The spirits were bad enough, but the sleeplessness was getting to them too. There was something in this place that poisoned the mind, and they did not want to linger a moment more than necessary. She knew how they felt. There was no telling how much longer it would take them to get to the Xhiang Xhi, and every day there was a day back.

She visited Phaeca. Against Doja's wishes, Phaeca had moved herself out of her tent and inside one of the emyrynn dwellings, where she had unrolled her sleeping-mat. It was warm and oddly sterile there, an irregularly shaped room with the curve of a tree bole as one wall. Protuberances of sap were moulded from parts of the floor and ceiling, things that could have been sculpture or which might have had a mundane and utilitarian purpose. A thin tunnel, too small for anything bigger than a mouse, opened out into the room. From what Kaiku could determine, it wound all the way up the tree until it was lost in the branches, but she could not imagine what it was for.

Phaeca was making little sense. She was babbling as if feverish, but she had no temperature, and though she was agitated she was not sallow. She slapped Kaiku's hand away when it was laid on her cheek, and muttered unpleasant things about her as if she was not in the room. Kaiku knelt by her for a time, deeply concerned. There was no healing possible: she had defences to keep others out, even other Sisters. Besides, the more she studied her companion, the more Kaiku worried that the affliction was not physical at all. Her shrieks had been the loudest last night. Like Lucia, the forest was battering her, and Kaiku did not know how well her sanity would hold.

Gods, why did we ever come to this cursed place? she thought to herself, but she already knew the answer to that one. They came here because it was their last chance.

She glimpsed the emyrynn a few times that day, flitting among the trees in the distance. Each time, she stared out into the blue and green folds of the forest and wondered about the nature of their curious hosts. She went to see Peithre, who was very weak but awake, and spoke with Tsata for a time. But he seemed odd to her today: there was something in his manner that she could not fathom, and eventually she gave up on trying and left him alone. The atmosphere in the camp depressed her, but she was stuck here, as they all were.

She took to wandering around the village, to give herself space to think. The charge laid on her by Asara was a heavy one. At least she knew now why Asara had followed her into the forest: she had an investment to protect. But even if Kaiku could do it, the question was: *should* she? Did she dare allow a being like that to procreate?

It was not the same to her as being asked to stop Asara having children. That she would never do. That was taking something away from her. But giving her the ability to breed seemed another matter entirely. It was action rather than inaction: every deed of her offspring, every result would be because of Kaiku.

What if they all grew with Asara's abilities? What if they were all as deceitful as their mother? How could they fail to be? Gods, she would be making Asara the progenitor of a new race. A race of beings who could take on any face, any human form; the perfect spies, lethal mimics, with unguessable life-spans. Only the Sisters would be able to penetrate their disguise.

She caught herself. Her imagination was running away with her, perhaps. There was no guarantee that Asara's off-spring would inherit her gift. And even if they did, there was no reason why they should become the beautiful and dreadful creatures that Kaiku envisaged. Asara's nature would not necessarily be theirs.

But the possibility was there. She could not deny that.

She wanted to talk it over with Tsata. It was frustrating that he was so close by and yet she was oath-bound not to speak of it. She admired his incisive mind and his honesty. He would have been able to help her untangle the knots. He would have told her that action and inaction are the same in this matter, that if she was prepared to deny Asara the gift of fertility for fear of creating a race of monsters then she should be prepared to prevent her from conceiving too, and vice versa. He would have cut through the deceptions that she made for herself, the double standards and smokescreens of etiquette and belief. He would have told her that the real reason she was debating this was because she did not want the responsibility of having to make that choice.

She knew all this, but it did not make the deciding any easier.

Night stole across the land again, and this time there were no moons to leaven it.

The soldiers had come to dread the darkness. The prospect of sleep was worse than the exhaustion of being awake, and many were too afraid to even try; yet always they were dragged down towards unconsciousness. Sentries nodded at their posts; heads lolled, and their owners were startled awake with a cry as the nightmares leaped hungrily upon them. The forest was a place that tricked the eye anyway, but deprived of sleep as they were, they were constantly seeing movement and fleeting hallucinations.

'We have to set out tomorrow,' Doja had growled at Kaiku. 'These men can't take this any longer. We'll carry Phaeca and the Tkiurathi woman if necessary.'

Kaiku had not flatly forebade it, but she was reluctant. In the end, she agreed that if Peithre's condition improved overnight enough to safely move her, then they could fashion stretchers and set off again. She, too, was concerned about the state of mind of the party. Her *kana*-ministered metabolism meant that she was not so exhausted as the others, but she feared that accidents were bound to happen if there was much more of this. There were altogether too many rifles and jumpy trigger fingers in this camp.

But there was one ray of hope among it all: just after the last of the dusk had fled the sky, word came to Kaiku that Lucia was awake and lucid. Kaiku hurried to her, and found her outside her tent. She gave Kaiku a fleeting smile and invited her to walk. They wandered a little way from the camp, among the nacreous wonders of the emyrynn, and Kaiku was relieved to see that she was indeed clear-headed and attentive.

'The Xhiang Xhi is not far,' Lucia said.

'Is that so?' Kaiku asked in surprise. 'We cannot have penetrated very deep into the forest yet.'

Lucia cast her a slyly amused look. 'This is a place of spirits,' she said. 'We could walk forever and never reach the other side, or we could emerge there within an hour's march. Distance is fluid here. Don't you think it a coincidence that this village happened to be so close to where Peithre fell? In a forest this size, wasn't that extraordinarily convenient?'

'It had occurred to me,' Kaiku admitted.

'If the Xhiang Xhi did not want to be found, we would never find it,' Lucia said. 'But it does.'

'Then why does it not appear? Why put us through this?'

237

'I don't know. The ways of the spirits are strange. Perhaps it's testing us. Perhaps it's curious about me, and wishes to study me first.'

Kaiku did not like that thought. 'You could still turn back, Lucia,' she said. 'It is not too late.'

Lucia gave her a sorrowful look. 'Oh, it is. *Far* too late.' She looked away, out of the village through the dark trees and unfamiliar foliage. 'Besides, if we turned back now we would never get out of the forest. The Xhiang Xhi wants to see me. It's intrigued, I think. If not for that, we would not have survived even this long.'

'If it wants to see you, why is it allowing us to be harmed?' Kaiku asked rhetorically.

Lucia answered anyway. 'It wants to see *me*,' she replied. 'The rest of you are expendable, perhaps.'

Kaiku felt a slow chill creep through her.

Lucia turned with a suddenness of movement that made Kaiku stop walking. The younger woman gazed at her with an unfamiliar purpose in her eyes.

'Lucia, what is it?'

'There are things I must say to you,' she said. 'In case I never again get the chance to speak them.'

Kaiku frowned. 'Do not talk that way.'

'I'm serious, Kaiku,' she said. 'I don't know if I'll ever be this clear-headed again.'

'Of course you will!' Kaiku protested. 'Once we get out of the forest, you will—'

'Let me speak!' Lucia snapped. Kaiku was shocked into silence. Lucia softened. 'Forgive me. Let me say this. That is all I ask.'

Kaiku nodded.

'I want to thank you. That is all. You and Mishani. I want you to know that . . . I appreciate everything you have done for me. For being like sisters to me. And you have always, always been on my side. When all this is done, I . . .' She trailed off. 'I just wanted you to know. You have my love, and you always will.'

Kaiku felt her eyes welling, and she gathered Lucia up in an embrace. 'Heart's blood, you make it sound like a farewell. We will come through this, Lucia. You will live to tell Mishani that yourself.' Lucia clutched her closer. 'I will protect you, even if it means my life.'

'There are some things that even you cannot protect me from,' Lucia whispered. And then she looked up, over Kaiku's shoulder, and some aspect of her body language told Kaiku there was somebody there. She turned, and it was Heth.

'Is Tsata with you?' he asked without apology or preamble.

The tone in his voice killed the caustic reply Kaiku was about to make. 'I have not seen him,' she replied instead.

'But he left to go after you,' Heth said, his features animate with confusion as he wrestled with the unfamiliar Saramyrrhic syllables. 'Into the forest.'

'I have not been out of the village,' Kaiku said.

'He saw you leave,' Heth persisted. 'I was with him. I did not see you, but he did. He said he must talk with you.'

An odd foreboding was settling into Kaiku's marrow. 'When was this?'

'A few minutes ago. Peithre has worsened; I came to fetch him.'

Kaiku looked at Lucia. 'Three nights past, the night I was attacked by the spirit in the trees . . . I saw you walk out into the forest, and I went to follow you.'

Lucia looked blank. 'I didn't leave my tent that night. I was asleep, and there were guards outside.'

'Gods!' Kaiku hissed. 'Go back to the camp! Heth, show me where he went!'

Heth obeyed without hesitation, while Lucia hurried away, alarmed. Kaiku followed the Tkiurathi for a short distance, until he stopped and pointed. 'That way.'

Kaiku's irises turned red. She would never be able to track a Tkiurathi through conventional means, even if she had the necessary skills; but in the Weave she could still hunt him.

She could see his scent-trail, the faint agitation of air in his wake, the memory of his breath and the reverberation of his heartbeat.

'See to Peithre,' she murmured. 'You cannot help me now.'

And with that, she plunged into the forest.

It swallowed her eagerly. Hanging vines and tendrils of blue plants brushed at her as she ran. The ground was treacherous, a tangle of roots and glittering rocks; it rose and dipped and twisted, making her speed reckless. But she read the ground as she read the air, predicting its contours through the threads of the Weave, and she was sure-footed.

She cursed herself as she went. If only she had pushed Lucia a little more, if only she had thought to investigate further the incident when she had seen her walking away from camp. But Lucia had been impenetrable, her mind elsewhere, and Kaiku had not wanted to cause more trouble among the soldiers before she heard the story from Lucia's own lips.

Now she knew that there was no story. Lucia had not gone anywhere. Whatever it was she had been following that night, it was not Lucia. And Tsata had fallen for the same trick.

If he died because of her stupidity . . .

She was genuinely, utterly terrified. Not for herself, but for the incomplete half of that thought. She was afraid of the void that would be left in the wake of his passing. Adept at armouring her own heart, she had not realised how much she had missed him while he was away, how much it gladdened her to talk with him, to fence with his foreign mindset, to simply have him near her. Not until now, not until she thought she might be about to lose him again, and permanently this time.

She accelerated to a sprint, following his invisible trail, her boots sliding on the ground, her shoulders clipping trees that she failed to dodge entirely. There was a panic welling within her, something that threatened her with madness. She dared not think about what would happen if she found him dead, his eyes milky white and his face a map of swollen veins like the other man they had found. Even if she had to face down that massive shadow, that half-seen beast that had attacked her before, she would not falter.

The sound of her passing was loud in the silence of the forest, the lashing of fronds against her body and the dull sound of her boots on the dirt. Something was whispering to her, some premonition that told her every second was precious, every instant she delayed could be the crucial one, the difference between facing the awful emptiness of Tsata's death and the joy of finding him alive and well. Fighting her way through the golden tapestry of the forest, she cried out his name, hoping to warn him somehow, praying that he could hear her and that it was not too late.

And then she burst through a screen of leaves and into a tiny patch of open ground, and there was Tsata, his outline a million glowing threads, turning towards her in surprise. And over his shoulder she saw *something*, some black and twisted entity that shared her shape in the physical world but not here in the Weave: a spirit that mimicked others, leading its victims away to kill them. Its illusion failed it then, and it turned its face upon her, and she saw there a doorway to the secrets of the spirit realm, a sight so incomprehensible that it would turn a man's mind inside out and slay him on the spot. But she was a Sister of the Red Order, and she had seen things that no man had.

'*Do not look at her!*' she screamed, grabbing Tsata's head and pulling it down into her shoulder. Her other arm she threw out at the spirit, and her *kana* burst free and tore into it. It howled, an unearthly shriek as Kaiku shredded through its defences and ripped into its essence, and then it was rent into tatters.

The silence returned, and there was only the two of them. Kaiku became suddenly conscious of the nearness of their bodies. She released Tsata's head and he raised it, a question in his pale green eyes. Though he did not understand, he knew by what he had heard that Kaiku had saved him from something. Their faces were a fraction too close still: he had not drawn away past the point where proximity could still pull lips and tongues together. They trembled there for an instant, on the cusp of that; and then she kissed him, and he melted into her, his arms sliding around her back.

For a time, there was nothing but the sensation of it, the rhythm of their mouths meeting and parting, the pressure of their contact. Then, as their kisses became shallower until they were mere brushes of the lips, thought began to intrude once again. Kaiku opened her eyes – still blood-red in the aftermath of her *kana* – and saw Tsata looking back at her. Her gaze roamed him uncertainly, afraid of the blow that would shatter the fragile state they had found themselves in. She traced the lines of the tattoos on his cheeks, the orange-blond sap-stiffened hair, the line of his jaw; and she saw in him the antithesis of all she hated in her life, all the deceit and subterfuge and secrecy that had killed her family and torn her world apart. And yet she waited in terror for him to break the spell, to tell her that this was only a mistake of passion, that his brutal self-honesty would not allow him to go on with this if his heart was not in it.

He seemed about to speak; but in the end, he moved to kiss her instead. She pulled away fractionally, and he stopped, confused.

'Peithre has worsened,' she murmured. 'You should go to her.'

His pale green eyes flickered across her face. Then he was gone, disappearing without a word into the forest, leaving Kaiku alone.

When Nuki's eye next rose in the east, it found Mishani sitting on the shore of Lake Xemit, looking out over the water.

It was a cold dawn, and around her she had a heavy

crimson shawl, embroidered in gold. Her hair pooled on the cloth that she had laid down to prevent her dirtying her hem. She had been here most of the night, thinking, chasing herself in ever tighter circles until she was left with a conclusion. It was an unwise course, one that she dreaded to take, and she did not want to accept it; yet she knew in her heart that it was inevitable, and her protests were weak and failing fast.

Presently she heard the tread of approaching feet on the dewy grass slope that led down from the temple complex of Araka Jo. She guessed it to be Yugi even before he walked into her line of sight.

'Daygreet, Mishani,' he said. 'May I join you?'

'Daygreet, Yugi. Please do.' She moved across to make space for him on the cloth, and he sat down heavily next to her.

'No sleep for you, then?' he said.

'Nor for you, it seems.' She studied him. He looked dishevelled as ever, and he reeked of amaxa root. It was obvious what had kept him up.

'I begin to wonder how many more nights I have left,' he said. 'Sleeping seems such a waste of precious time.'

'That sounds a fast route to madness,' Mishani said, half-seriously.

Yugi scratched the back of his neck. 'This whole land is in the grip of madness, Mishani. If I were mad, I might at least have a chance of understanding it.'

They looked out across the lake for a time, before Yugi spoke again.

'There is word that your mother will publish another book soon. Cailin speaks of plans in the wake of the information you have given us,' he said, and coughed. 'She's still agitating for an assault on Adderach when Lucia returns. Depending on what news comes from this latest tale.'

'Foolish,' Mishani said with a sigh. 'An army would be cut to pieces in those mountains.'

'Perhaps,' Yugi replied.

She glanced at him. He was unshaven and gaunt. 'You are overfond of the root, Yugi,' she said. 'Once you controlled it; now it controls you. You are the leader of many men and women. Their lives are your responsibility. Stop this idiocy before you lose your judgement.'

Yugi seemed a little surprised, apparently deciding whether to take umbrage or not. Then he sagged, and merely looked weary. 'You're far from the first to tell me that. It's not so simple.'

'Cailin could help you overcome the addiction, perhaps,' Mishani suggested, brushing her hair over her shoulder.

Yugi snorted a laugh. 'I'm not addicted, Mishani. I smoked amaxa root for years and it never got a hold on me. The root is only a symptom of the cause.'

'What, then, is the cause?' she asked.

He did not answer for a while, debating whether to tell her or not. Mishani was no confidante of his. But she waited patiently, and finally he shrugged and sighed.

'I was a bandit, once,' he said. 'I imagine you know that.'

'I had surmised as much from things Zaelis said,' she admitted.

'Did you also know that I had a woman back then?'

'A wife?'

'As near as can be. We had little use for marriage, and no priests.'

'That I did not know.'

Yugi was tentative, ready to abandon this conversation at the slightest hint of sarcasm or mockery from Mishani. She gave him none. This was important to him, and that made it important to her, for he was the leader of the Libera Dramach and any knowledge about his state of mind could be advantageous.

'Her name was Keila,' he said. He opened his mouth to say more, perhaps to describe her to Mishani, perhaps to talk of what he felt for her; but he changed his mind. Mishani understood that. Words seemed mawkish that were most deeply felt.

'What happened to her?' Mishani asked.

'She died,' Yugi said. He looked down at the ground.

'Because of you,' Mishani said, reading his reaction.

He nodded. 'There were perhaps a hundred of us at our height. And we had a reputation. We were the most feared bandit gang from Barask to Tchamaska.'

'And you led them, back then?' Mishani guessed.

Yugi nodded. 'Gods, I'm not proud of some of the things I did. We were bandits, Mishani. That made us killers, thieves, and worse. Every man had his morals, every man had . . . things he wouldn't do. But there was always someone who would.'

He gave Mishani a wary glance. She watched him steadily, showing nothing. He was searching for condemnation from her, but she would not condemn him. Her own past was hardly unstained.

'A man can . . . detach himself,' Yugi murmured. 'He can learn to see people as obstacles, or objects. He can learn to shut out the crying of women and the look in his enemy's eyes as he dies. They are just animal reactions, like the thrashing of a wounded rabbit or the twisting of a fish on a hook. A man can persuade himself to the necessity of any-thing, if he has the will to.' The lake was grey and still in the dawn light. He gazed into it. 'The world of bandits was a ruthless one. We had to be more ruthless still.' He smiled faintly, but it was bitter and there was no joy there.

'Does it disturb you?' he asked. 'To know that the leader of the Libera Dramach is a thief and a murderer?'

'No,' said Mishani. 'I ceased to believe in innocence long ago. A bandit may kill a hundred men, but those we choose to govern us kill many times that number with their schemes and policies. I learned of such things at court. At least your way of murder is honest.' She watched a bird winging its way across the lake, south to north. 'I cannot speak for others, but I do not care about your past. I did not know those you harmed, and to be outraged at you would be false sentiment.

We are all of us guilty of things that make us ashamed. Good men do evil deeds, and evil men can become good. I care only what you do now, Yugi, for you hold the reins of many lives.' The bird disappeared at last, vanishing in the distance, and she shifted herself where she sat and turned her eyes to him again. 'Go on with your tale.'

'We made enemies, of course,' Yugi said after a time. 'Other bandit gangs wanted to topple us, but none of them had a chance against our strength. I became overconfident.' He began to pick at the cloth between his knees. 'There was word of a gathering of our rivals. I led my men out to ambush them. But it was a trick. One I should have seen coming.'

'They ambushed you?'

'Not us. They raided our camp, where we had left our women and children. There were only a dozen fighting men there. I didn't think they knew where we hid, didn't think they'd dare to attack us even if they did know. Wrong on both counts.' His eyes tightened. 'Gods, when we got back . . .'

Mishani was silent. She pulled her shawl a little tighter around her to fend off the cold.

'She wasn't quite dead when I found her. I'll never know how she held on that long. But she waited for me, and . . . we . . .' His voice failed him. He swallowed. 'She died in my arms.'

He stared furiously out across the lake, taut with a festering anger. 'And do you know what my first thought was after she had died? My very first? I'll tell you. I *deserved* it. I deserved for her to die. Because I realised then that every person who died on my blade had a mother or a brother or a child who felt the grief that I was feeling. And I tore a strip from the hem of her dress and I wrapped it around my head, and I swore I'd wear it always to remind me of what I'd done, and who I'd lost because of it.' He touched the dirty rag around his forehead. 'This.'

'And what happened afterward?' Mishani asked. She did not offer sympathy. She did not think he wanted any from her, nor would she have given it if he had.

'The others were already screaming for revenge,' he said. 'But I knew how it would be. Our retribution would spark other retributions, as it always had and always would. Running around in circles, getting nowhere, an endless back and forth of blades and bleeding bodies. And so I walked away from there. They thought to give me space, to let me grieve for my woman. They thought I would be back.' His eyes were flat. 'But I never came back.'

Mishani knew the rest from Zaelis: how Yugi had drifted into the Libera Dramach; how his natural leadership skills and experience had made him more and more invaluable until he had become Zaelis's right-hand man; how, after Zaelis had died at the Fold, he had become the head of the Libera Dramach. And she understood him now.

'You do not want to lead these people, do you?' she asked.

Yugi looked at her for a long moment, then tilted his head in affirmation. 'I'm no general like Zahn. I don't have the vision and ambition that Zaelis had. I led a hundred men and I led them well, but in the end I failed and it cost me the only thing I ever . . .' He looked away. 'Ah, what use is talking?'

'You could step down,' said Mishani.

'No, I couldn't. Because I'm still the best gods-damned leader they've got. Zaelis may have picked his men well, but he couldn't get generals, he couldn't get war-makers. They belong to the noble houses, and the moment one of them get near the Libera Dramach, the moment *politics* becomes involved, then it's over for us. They all want Lucia.'

Mishani nodded. 'There is sense in what you say. Even Zahn would be a danger. But can you lead thousands to war, Yugi? Your skills were of great use in the Fold, but then you were fighting as bandits fight. It may come to a moment when you must be a general, and your choices on the battlefield will cost many lives. Will you be able to make those choices? Or will you hide in your drugged dreams?'

Yugi looked grim. 'If it's my punishment that I must suffer to lead these men and women, then I'll bear it because I have to. The gods certainly have a sick sense of humour, to make revenge on me for my past misdeeds by giving me *more* lives to ruin.'

'They do indeed,' said Mishani.

Yugi got to his feet then. Nuki's eye had risen a little more by now. The lake was blue, and the air was warming. 'Thank you for hearing me out, Mishani. I don't know why I chose to talk to you of all people, but I'm glad I did.' He looked up the slope, to where the white temples of Araka Jo stood crumbling. 'How is it that our past dictates our future?' he wondered aloud. 'Where's the sense in that?'

And then he was gone, walking away from her, and she was alone again.

She sat for a long time and thought on what he had said. Then she returned to her house and began to pack what things she needed.

She was going to see her mother.

EIGHTEEN

Few slept in the forest that night, but for Kaiku it was not out of fear of dreams.

She wandered the emyrynn village alone after Tsata had left her, traipsing listlessly between the iridescent columns and swirls and spikes that clung to the trees and sprawled along the ground. Fretfully replaying the moment in her mind when they had kissed, picking it apart to find what meaning she could therein. What had been in his eyes when she had halted him? Would it have been better to have let him kiss her again before giving him news of his ailing kinswoman? Did he interpret it as an excuse for rejection? And indeed, in Kaiku's intention, had it been that? Did she shy from him on purpose, using Peithre as an excuse to get herself out of it? Gods, she did not even know herself what she had wanted then; but retrospect was a hard eye to cast upon her actions, and she was full of regrets and uncertainties.

She had achieved no resolution by the time dawn came, and she heard Phaeca's scream.

Her meanderings had almost brought her back to the camp when the sound reached her. It took longer to process than it otherwise would, for the sleeplessness was beginning to tell. She wasted a second on incomprehension before breaking into a run, sprinting around the tent cluster where others were getting to their feet. She reached the alien dwelling where Phaeca had been resting, pushed aside the soldiers who crowded around the entranceway and went inside.

Phaeca was still screaming. She was hunkered against the tree bole that formed one wall of the room, her possessions and bedding scattered across the floor. Blood ran from the walls and lay in pools on the floor, smeared at the edges where her heels had slipped in them. Chunks of smoking flesh and blackened bone were strewn about. Some of them were whole enough to still have the fur on. White fur, soaked in red.

Kaiku stared at the scene, aghast. 'Phaeca, what have you done?' she breathed. Her voice rose in anger and disbelief. 'You *killed* one of them? You killed an emyrynn?' She crossed the room and grabbed hold of Phaeca's shoulders, shaking her roughly. 'Why? *Why?*'

'It was trying to kill *me!*' Phaeca shrieked. 'It was in my room! I woke up and it was in my room!'

Kaiku squeezed her eyes shut. The scene as it might have happened played across the darkness: Phaeca, awakening from a nightmare to find an unfamiliar creature before her, lashing out with her *kana*. She was already in a state of questionable sanity, driven to raving and feverish mutterings by the malevolence of the forest. The sight of the emyrynn must have been too much for her. Or maybe it *had* attacked her. Maybe she was telling the truth. It didn't matter, in the end. She had killed one of them.

'This is not *your* room,' she said, her voice quieter now. 'You were sleeping in its home.'

A cry of alarm went up in the camp, and those soldiers at the doorway turned back to look. 'There's something moving out in the trees!' came the shout.

'Do you know what you have done, Phaeca?' Kaiku said, her tone heavy with despondency. 'Your actions will be the death of us all.'

At that, Phaeca's face twisted into a snarl, and she launched herself at Kaiku.

Kaiku did not expect it in the least. Perhaps, had she thought on it, she would have been more careful in her words. She knew how fragile her friend was in this place. But though she had worried about Phaeca's state of mind over the past few days, she had never once thought that she might become violent. Even in the wake of what she had just discovered, she assumed the killing of the emyrynn was an accident, a reaction rather than a premeditated act. The sight of the Sister's face twisting into a contortion of such utter hatred made her quail; and then she was being carried out of the doorway of the dwelling by the weight of the attack, scattering the soldiers there, and she fell onto the blue-green grass outside with Phaeca atop her.

The savagery of Phaeca's assault stunned her; she only resisted at all because instinct drove her to. Phaeca raked her face with her nails, slapped and punched at her head, shrieking and screaming oaths and curses in a coarse Axekami dialect that was entirely unlike her usual mode of speech. Two of the soldiers, unable to credit what they were seeing, reached down to pull the crazed Sister from her victim; they were flung back and away by an invisible force that flattened the grass and cracked the sap wall of the emyrynn dwelling.

It was the outrush of Phaeca's *kana* that brought Kaiku to her senses. The wrenching of the Weave sparked an answer in her own body, a surge of energy that she fought to curtail before it broke out of her, fearful of hurting her friend.

She should not have done so. It took her too long to realise that Phaeca's *kana* was not only directed at the soldiers, it was also directed at her. Phaeca was attacking her in the Weave, and that made her intent lethal.

She surrendered herself to the will of her *kana*. Time decelerated to a crawl in the world of the five senses, while beneath its skin the Sisters clashed at blinding speed. Kaiku's fractional hesitation had afforded Phaeca an advantage. Only when she had cast aside all doubts and had realised that her friend really meant to kill her, that this was a fight for her very life, did she lend her will to the conflict and begin resisting in earnest.

But by then it was too late. Phaeca had undermined her, laid traps that foiled her attempts at constructing defences. Kaiku constructed labyrinthine tangles only to have them come apart at a single tug. She built snares to delay her opponent and watched them fall to pieces when they were sprung. By the time she had got her barriers up, Phaeca was already behind them, and Kaiku was forced to abandon them and back away further. The assault was relentless, furious; she crumbled under it. Phaeca was not as good as Cailin, but she was still better than most Weavers, sliding and shuttling like a needle. And Kaiku had been taken totally by surprise, had still refused to believe it even when she *had* realised what was happening.

Phaeca burst through the holes in Kaiku's stitchwork and reached into her body, grasping, encircling her heart, sewing into muscle and bone. Kaiku screamed in horror, a wordless mental anguish at the violation, the knowledge that she had no way to fight back now and that this cry would be her last.

Then the pain hit her. Phaeca was tearing her apart. She had done it to others before, and always wondered what it must have felt like, the kind of agony they would suffer in the instant before they died. Now she knew. It was as if her every vein and nerve were being pulled forcibly from her flesh, sucked out like tendrils through her skin to be cast away. The torture was incredible, overwhelming . . .

. . . and suddenly gone.

She was alone in the Weave. Phaeca had disappeared, with only an aching pulse of sadness left in her wake.

Her mind settled again, reorientating her senses. She left the Weave, her *kana* turning inwards and scouring her for damage. Her red eyes refocused and the light of dawn in the forest filtered back.

There was a weight atop her. A booted foot braced against it and shoved it off. Asara. She reached down and helped Kaiku up.

'I had no choice,' Asara said. 'It was her or you.'

She forced herself to look at Phaeca. The Sister lay face-down, her hair bloody. Shot through the neck.

'It was her or you,' Asara said again.

Asara's voice was dim and tinny in Kaiku's ears, cushioned by a numb blanket that had settled on her. Her vision had narrowed, the periphery hazed. She felt fractured from her surroundings, barely aware. Around her, gunshots and cries, denting the whine of the blood in her ears. She could not reconcile the figure lying before her with the woman she had known. The fact that this husk of flesh was here did not equate with the certainty that she would never see nor speak with Phaeca again.

'Kaiku, we have to go,' Asara was saying to her. Then, turning her so that she was looking into her eyes. 'Do you hear? We have to go *now!*'

She could see over Asara's shoulder, into the trees that surrounded the village. Of course, of course. The retaliation. From the foliage, white shapes were slinking, muzzles wrinkled and teeth bared. The emyrynn were coming. Their hospitality had been abused.

'Where is Lucia?' someone cried. 'Where is Lucia?'

It was that name that brought Kaiku out of her daze. With a whimper, she moved to flee into the camp and search, thinking only of the need to protect her. Asara grabbed her arm.

'She is there,' Asara said, pointing. And indeed she was, with Doja and a half-dozen soldiers clustered around her. Tsata and Heth were approaching, Peithre carried in Heth's arms. Kaiku saw him and motioned towards Lucia, then ran that way herself, with Asara following.

Phaeca . . .

Kaiku shoved the grief away. She could not allow herself to think on it now. There were others whose lives would depend on her. Lucia was all that mattered.

The emyrynn were coming from all around the village, but they appeared in greatest number at the point where the camp lay against the outermost edge. They sprang through the leaves, sleek and graceful, their white fur pristine. Such beautiful creatures, but their faces were sharp now, grinning in animal rictus, and there was deadly purpose in their steps. The soldiers were firing into the undergrowth, rifle balls clipping purple stems and ricocheting off tree trunks with a splintering of wood. They hit nothing. The emyrynn appeared in glimpses, and each glimpse showed them to be ever closer to their prey.

'Fall back!' Doja cried. 'Protect Lucia!'

'Which way?' Asara called, addressing Lucia, who was gazing into the middle distance. 'Lucia, which way do we go?'

'They're so angry,' she whispered.

Kaiku wiped her eyes with the back of her hand and moved Asara aside. 'Which way, Lucia?' she asked, gently. 'We have to leave.'

At the sound of her voice, Lucia's focus shifted to her. She trembled for a moment, then flung her arm out and pointed into the trees. 'That way.'

'Fall back!' Doja cried again to the soldiers who were retreating towards them, loosing shots into the trees. And with that, Lucia and her retinue ran, away from the village, and the forest closed around them.

The emyrynn broke cover with a harmonic cascade of piercing howls. They burst out into the open, sprinting on all fours, moving like liquid. Their curious musculature gave them a disconcerting gait, rippling them left and right in a sinuous charge towards the men who were covering Lucia's retreat. Those who still had powder in their chambers fired off what shots they had, but all of them missed. Some turned and took flight at the sight of the creatures; some stayed and fought. The outcome was the same. The emyrynn tore into them with surpassing savagery, gouging at faces with their small, sharp antlers, ripping at throats with their blade-like teeth. They bounded onto their prey, bore them to the ground like hunting cats, then shredded them while they were helpless. Their white fur became stained dark red, their muzzles wet with blood. They revelled in the slaughter.

Lucia and Kaiku hurried into the forest, the centre of a

stumbling cluster of soldiers who fought to protect them from every side. There were perhaps ten soldiers left now including Doja; also with them went the three Tkiurathi and Asara. Kaiku's eyes were blurring with tears that fell from her lashes with the jolting of her feet on the ground, but she did not notice. She was seeing past them. The forest could not obscure her vision; it had turned to a transparent mass of golden sinews, and within it she saw the emyrynn stalking. Hundreds of them, converging on the village.

'Kaiku, can you see them?' The voice was Asara's.

'Yes.'

'Are they coming after us?'

Kaiku looked. She had dared to hope that vacating the village might curb their wrath, that the emyrynn merely wanted their unwelcome visitors gone. But now she saw, as the last of the soldiers who had stayed behind were killed, that some of the emyrynn had set off in pursuit, following the trail Lucia and the others had left.

'Yes,' she said.

There were scattered emyrynn ahead of them and to either side as well. Some were moving away, either ignorant of their presence or uninterested. Others lay in wait in hollows or in the branches of trees, plainly hoping for their victims to come near. Though some of the creatures seemed content to leave them be now that they were driven off, others had decided to hunt them. There was no way they would be able to escape without further bloodshed.

'Can you speak to them, Lucia?' Kaiku asked. 'Can you explain?'

Lucia did not hear her. She was sobbing and panting, propelled along by Doja's strong arm, tripping on branches and roots. She seemed seized by some fear that she could not identify, gazing around wildly like a madwoman, fleeing without hope of escape.

Kaiku breathed a curse. They had no choice but to go where Lucia led them, and abandoning the village had robbed them of any place to make a stand, however futile. The low, slanting light of Nuki's eye forced its way dimly through the canopy, but the trees were too dense here to see far, and only Kaiku could spot the emyrynn as they darted nimbly through the trees. The forest still resounded with the fading echoes of their comrades' screams, and the only other sound was the scraping of twigs, the thump of boots and the rush of exhaled breath as they raced away from the emyrynn village. That, and the endless, monotonous tapping in the distance that had plagued them for days.

Gods, what were they hoping for, anyway? That the emyrynn would turn around and give up? That was a slim chance indeed. They would run, they would fight, and after that they would die. The odds were impossible. But there was nothing else left to do.

'There are two of them, ahead and to our left,' Kaiku called, as she sensed their approach. The soldiers shifted their blades, ready to receive the creatures; but Kaiku got to them first. Though there was something of the spirit world in them, they were not as hard as demons or Weavers to overmatch; but they were awkward and unfamiliar, and it took time to engage them, longer than she would have liked. She would be unable to deal with more than a few at a time.

She used her *kana* to reach inside their minds and stun them into unconsciousness. She was reluctant to kill them if she could help it.

'They have been dealt with,' she said.

'Any more?' Asara asked, as they scrambled up an incline thick with bluish bracken, shepherding Lucia awkwardly onward.

'Three from behind,' Kaiku said. Her heart sank as she saw them arrowing through the forest. 'They will catch us in a few moments. Three from the right. Two ahead.' She grimaced. 'I cannot protect you from all of them.'

'Then you take the ones that are following,' Doja said tersely. 'We'll handle the rest.'

The soldiers had slung their rifles back over their shoulders and drawn swords by now, for ranged weapons were useless in the confines of thick undergrowth. Despite Kaiku's warning, they were still not prepared for the emyrynn when they attacked. They expected to be able to hear the stirring of leaves, the rustle of bracken as their enemies neared; but the emyrynn were like ghosts, and made no sound at all. They sprang as if from nowhere, took down two of the soldiers, ripped out their throats in a single bite and were gone before anyone could lay a blade to them.

'Keep going!' Doja cried, as some of the soldiers faltered. The wounded men were still flailing, gurgling out their last. 'We cannot stand here!'

In the forest behind them, three bright blooms of fire ignited. Kaiku turned back to Doja, her eyes hard. Now that they had shown their intentions beyond all doubt, she would not be merciful to these creatures any longer.

The five remaining emyrynn attacked all at once. The soldiers had a few seconds to prepare at Kaiku's cry, and then the enemy were among them in a blur of white and a flurry of teeth. Asara, faster than most, ducked under the leap of one of them and divided it neatly in half along its midriff; Kaiku incinerated another. Between them, the soldiers took down a third, but as the remaining two disappeared they left behind one man dead and another with a stump for an arm, spewing blood. There was a scramble to get a tourniquet on the wound, during which the group's onward motion collapsed: they would not leave one of their wounded behind when there was still a chance of saving them.

'More! All around us!' Kaiku barely had time to shout before the emyrynn were among them. They had seemed to appear out of nowhere, even to her Weave-sight, a dozen of the creatures flitting suddenly into existence. She saw Tsata slashing with his gutting-hooks, darting between the emyrynn's antlers, protecting Heth and his burden Peithre. She saw Asara dodging and slashing, her movements fluid, honed by ninety years of practice and a perfect metabolism. And she saw the soldiers fighting, and Doja being savaged, and Lucia fallen to the ground where another of the creatures was about to pounce on her . . .

Kaiku was about to obliterate the threat to Lucia when she was knocked aside, crashing into a tree trunk with the weight of an emyrynn, its teeth fastened in her shoulder at the collar. Too many of them; she hadn't seen it coming. She screamed with the pain. Blood pumped between her attacker's teeth as it bit deeper into her flesh. Then her *kana* reacted, seizing the creature and flinging it away from her with enough force to break its back against a thick bough. She clutched her torn shoulder, blood pulsing through her fingers. Her body was already repairing itself, but it was sapping vital resources she needed to protect others, and she was already looking to Lucia, a terrible fear gripping her heart. She would be too late, too late to save her from the emyrynn now.

But then a new sensation bore down on her, a terrible, crushing presence that drove her to her knees with its fury. She looked up, and blanched as she saw it.

The beast. The vast shadow that she had met a few nights ago was back, its colossal bulk swelling up to the treetops. Its bellow, midway between a roar and a screech, shook the earth and blasted a hurricane through the forest, sending men and women and emyrynn alike tumbling and scrambling. The trees hissed and rattled as the wind wailed through their branches. Kaiku was blown back into the base of a tree, the breath squeezed from her lungs, her hair whipping around her face. She gritted her teeth against the agony from her shoulder, eyes shut tight, fighting down the urge to shriek. The creature was a black wall of rage in the Weave, a power that Kaiku could not hope to match. Her *kana* recoiled from it, retreating, curling up inside her.

Silence. The hurricane died all at once, faint skirling gusts chasing away through the trees to nothingness. Leaves drifted slowly earthward, spiralling clumsily.

Kaiku opened her eyes. The site of the ambush was strewn with bodies, men and emyrynn alike. Bloody swatches of white fur lay alongside torn corpses. She saw Asara getting to her feet, her blade hanging loose in her hand. Tsata and Heth crouched protectively together over the prone Peithre. A few soldiers were stirring, but not many. The emyrynn were gone.

At the edge of the carnage stood Lucia, staring up into the face of the beast. Its shape was hidden from sight by the trees, and by the darkness that it exuded like smoke, but it was still possible to make out its size. Small, glittering eyes regarded her. She was a tiny morsel to it, minute and insignificant; yet she stood there alone, and it glared down on her, the heavy soughing of its breath faintly audible, as slow and massive as waves on a beach.

Gradually, the survivors of the massacre rose, their gazes pinned to the monster. All except the Tkiurathi. Kaiku stumbled over towards Lucia, her hand clutching her shoulder where her wound was sealing itself, but as she neared Tsata he looked up at her, and his eyes were wet. The shock of that stopped her for a moment. She had never seen him weep before. Then she glanced down at Peithre, and saw that she was dead. They had protected her from the emyrynn, but in her weakened state the exertion of being carried so violently had proved too much. Heth was bent over her, his shoulders shaking. Kaiku met Tsata's gaze once again, but her eyes were bleak and she had nothing to give him; then she staggered away, towards Lucia.

Lucia was swaying slightly as Kaiku came to stand near her. She did not dare get too close, afraid of breaking whatever spell held the beast in check. Lucia's eyes were rolled up in her head and flickering with movement.

'Gods, what has happened here?' she whispered, though she said it more to herself than to anyone else, and expected no response.

Lucia surprised her. 'It is an emissary,' she said, the words barely formed as if she spoke them in a dream.

Kaiku thought for a moment. 'Of the Xhiang Xhi?' she asked.

'Leave our dead,' Lucia murmured, 'and follow.'

Kaiku closed her eyes. She had been sure to memorise the names of each and every man and woman in the party before they set off into the forest, for she had believed that many would not live to leave it and they would need to be commended to Noctu after their deaths. As long as she had their names, the place where their bodies lay meant little.

She raised her head and met the expectant faces of the survivors, Doja was among the fallen, and those who believed in leaders looked to her now.

'We leave our dead,' she said, her voice almost breaking as she spoke. 'We leave our dead and follow.'

It was several hours later that they came across the entrance to the Xhiang Xhi's lair.

Kaiku remembered little of the intervening time. She trudged dazedly through the forest with the rest of them, in something like a state of shock. The beast led them, always ahead, a colossal shadow that was never quite seen, a fraction too distant to make out in detail.

She wept as she went, mainly for Phaeca but also for the other men who lay behind them and Peithre, whose body Heth carried and refused to leave. She had kept herself at a distance from the soldiers, out of habit – she was a Sister, and she could no longer easily mix as she had in the past – but the suddenness of their deaths, the frightening savagery of the emyrynn, had shaken her badly. She knew enough of war and killing, but she was not inured to it entirely.

Other thoughts had briefly intruded on her misery. Thoughts of the beast that they followed, and how it had not been attacking her that day but that it had for some reason been *protecting* her from the spirit that had taken Lucia's shape. It had prevented her from being lured away; her, and her only, for the other soldiers had been left to their fate. Why was that? Why had *she* been treated differently?

Then there were the memories of the moment she had shared with Tsata, and her argument with Asara. Both were decisions she had to face, matters of huge importance to her; and yet for now she could not bring herself to care about them. All she wanted to do was to get away from this gods-cursed forest and never look back.

But there was one more challenge yet, and it was Lucia who had to face it.

They would have known when they came to the boundary of the Xhiang Xhi's domain even if Lucia had not told them. The air was thick with the presence of the great spirit, a charge in the air that made the fine hairs on their bodies stand on end. It came from a tunnel mouth sunk into a hillock, on either side of which stood twisted old trees like pillars. The beast crouched atop the hillock, obscured by undergrowth, sapping the day's light from the air.

'You can go no further,' Lucia said to them all. She appeared sharper now, her mind clear. 'It is up to me now.'

Nobody argued, not even Kaiku. She knew it would come to this. Lucia made no ceremony about it, merely looked over her shoulder at the seven ragged figures that remained of the twenty-four that had followed her into the forest. Her eyes lingered on Kaiku's for a moment, and she tried a smile; but it felt false, and it faltered, so she turned away and walked into the tunnel. They watched as the darkness consumed her, and then she was gone.

At first they were listless, unsure what to do or what to say. Then they began to settle themselves to wait: the three surviving soldiers together, Tsata and Heth with their burden, Kaiku and Asara both sitting alone.

After a time, Kaiku got to her feet and joined the Tkiurathi.

NINETEEN

There was no light in the tunnel, and Lucia was forced to feel her way along it. Her fingers trailed over the moist soil of the tunnel wall, bumping occasionally against protruding roots. It was silent. The babble of the spirits and the animals was quiet. Nothing existed except the Xhiang Xhi.

She wished she could stay here, in the peaceful dark, where there were no voices to plague her. To rest, to sleep in this precious hush just for a single night, would be a prize beyond anything she could ask for. To be this clear-headed forever, not to be burdened with the knowledge that outside this oasis of calm lay chaos, and that even if she survived this she would have to return to it. A place where her thoughts were fogged and a thousand whispers clamoured for her attention, and to even interact with humankind was a struggle to focus.

But it was only a wish. There was no sanctuary for her. She went on through the tunnel, until a short way onwards she saw a ragged oval of grey, with roots hanging across it like a curtain. She pushed through them and stepped into the domain of the great spirit.

It was a gloomy dell that she found on the other side, a hollow surrounded by thick forest which leaned overhead to make a roof of tangled branches. The ground was marshy; ridges of turf rose out of the water, dividing it into brackish pools full of weeds, and thin mists hung in the cold, still air or slunk close to the earth. An occasional tree grew in the dell, ancient and knotted, its leaves brown and dead.

She could sense the spirit here, a vast and brooding melancholy, its attention fixed upon her. The force of its presence was oppressive, the magnitude of its power beyond comprehension. She had spoken with many of the land's oldest spirits since that day when she had descended into Alskain Mar, deciphering the ways of their kind; but this was a thing apart, older than the rocks, older than the rivers, older than the forest it dwelt in.

She waited. Though she was afraid, she was armoured by fatalism. Her life had led to here, and she was as ready as she could possibly be. If it all came to nothing, then that was the way it would go. She could do no more.

Nothing stirred.

After a time, she took off her shoes and walked forward, picking her way from the edge of the dell along a bank of earth towards a tuffet that poked out of the marsh. Chill water welled up between her toes as the soft grass sank beneath her feet. When she reached the tuffet, she knelt there, and laid her hands upon the ground. She bowed her head and let her breathing slow, readying herself to enter the trance-like state necessary for communication with the spirits.

((There is no need, Lucia. I am not as the others are))

She tensed. The voice had been like the sigh of a dying man, a breath of air through a dusty temple. In all her life, a spirit had never *spoken* to her before. Contact had always been achieved without language, a primal, empathic exchange. It was a meeting on the most basic of levels, because it was the only way beings utterly alien to each other could reach some sort of understanding.

((I understand you)) said the Xhiang Xhi. Her thoughts were as transparent to it as if she had said them out loud. *((They are as children to me, and lack wisdom. They do not know how to think as you do))*

She felt dizzied. Children? Heart's blood, this being saw the other spirits as children? What kind of fool had she been, thinking that she was ready for the Xhiang Xhi? She dared not consider what might happen if she had tried to meld with it as she had with the others.

Slowly, she opened her eyes and looked upon the spirit. It

hung in the air before her, a slender wraith of mist, an elongated wisp of humanoid form like a shadow cast at sunset. It had hands, with spindly, attenuated fingers, and something that might have been a head, but it shifted and blended with the stir of the murk, so that Lucia could see only impressions of it. Perspective was skewed: it appeared near and far all at once, tiny and massive, and its aspect shifted with its movements and frustrated her efforts to decide. It was ever the way with the spirits: they could not manifest themselves in ways that human senses were entirely comfortable with.

((Stand)) it said to her. *((Do not abase yourself before me. I have no need of worship or respect))*

She did so.

((You need not fear to speak, Lucia))

And indeed she did not fear it, not in the way she had some of the other spirits, the ones who were angry and capricious and who had met her with malice or resentment. What she did fear was its terrible sorrow, the heartbreaking sense of tragedy that seeped from it. She was afraid that it might let her know the source of that sorrow and pass its grief on to her, and that was something she would not be able to bear.

'How old are you?' she said eventually. She wanted to test its responses before she asked what she had come to ask, even though she was sure it already knew her purpose. But there was a way for things to be done, and she would bow to that.

((I existed before the first of you stood upright, before the land was formed, before the moons were born. I existed when this world was but dust, and before that. There is no measurement I can give you that would have meaning. I am not like the other spirits you know: they were formed of this land, but I was not. I came from elsewhere, and I will go elsewhere once again when this world is swallowed in fire and its moons turned to ash))

Its voice, like the stirring of dry leaves in her skull, arrived amid fleeting images, spectral glimpses of star-studded void with gargantuan spheres of breathtaking colour turning slowly, and bright, bright flame swelling to consume them. Then, as quickly as they flitted across her consciousness, they were gone, leaving her wide-eyed, her breathing quick, her pulse fluttering. The Xhiang Xhi swirled restlessly in the mist.

'Are you a god?' Lucia asked at last.

((I am not a god)) it replied. *((What now you call gods you may come to call by other names. Some you will lose to myth; others may be more real than you imagine. It is not my place to reveal them. There can be no understanding for you of the things you speak of, though that may come with the passing of ages. For now, you have only interpretation, and that will change as you change, sometimes taking you closer to truth, sometimes further away. Your race is young, Lucia; and like infants you cannot fully comprehend what you see))*

Lucia accepted this with a slight nod of her head. Her mind had gone blank. Now that she was here, in the presence of the great spirit, she found that words were eluding her. For long seconds she stood mute, a slight figure in torn and muddied travelling clothes, her blonde hair in disarray.

((There are things you need to know, Lucia)) the spirit said at last. *((You seek to make war to save your homeland, but you do not yet realise the threat. I will show you))*

'Show me,' Lucia murmured, and the dell and everything around her disappeared.

She was standing on a vast plain of black rock, rucked with ridges of shattered stone and scattered with smouldering rubble. The air rippled with heat, scorching her lungs, shrinking her flesh. Wind screamed past her, throwing dust and pebbles and pushing boulders end over end, making her clothes flap furiously against her body. It stank of sulphur and poison. At her feet, a massive chasm roiled with magma, underlighting the contours of her face in infernal red. Other chasms scratched their way across the plain, and the earth shook sporadically like the shivers of some sleeping leviathan.

Lucia was shocked by the panorama and the chaos of the

gale. She knew, somehow, that she was not really here, and she believed it had no power to harm her; but her instincts said otherwise, and she stumbled away from the chasm, gazing wildly around for a rescuer.

The lava ran from a distant range of volcanoes, so broad and high that their tips were lost above the thick blanket of brown vapours that roofed the world. Muted red glows blazed up there, amid thunderous concussions as the volcanoes erupted endlessly. Other mountains, seemingly dead and cold but just as gigantic, loomed around her, and where she could see across the plain to the horizon it seemed much too near. Lightning flickered in the clouds and struck the earth, faster than she had ever seen, a dozen times a second and more.

'What is . . . what is this place?' she said against the howl of the wind.

((This is the home of your enemy, thousands of years ago, before it was destroyed. This is the moon which you call Aricarat))

The Xhiang Xhi's voice came from inside her head like a rattle of twigs.

((It is not a place for your kind. The air here would choke you. The temperature would melt the flesh from your bones. The wind would pick you up and dash you to pieces. The very atmosphere would crush you like an egg))

'Why have you brought me here?' Lucia gasped, her eyes beginning to tear in horror.

((To show you)) the spirit said again.

'Show me what?'

((Your enemy))

Lucia looked around helplessly. 'I see nothing.'

((You are hampered by the limits of your senses. Use the ability that makes you unique. Listen))

And so she did. With some effort, she began calming herself, sinking slowly down into a trance of stillness. Practice had made it possible, even amid the maelstrom that whipped around her, to turn herself inward and create a core of quietude to retreat to. She sank to her knees, only now noticing that her feet were still bare. She laid her hand on the hot rock, and listened to the heartbeat of the moon.

As careful as she was, the sheer violence of Aricarat was still overwhelming: the burning veins of lava tubing, the swirling core, the constantly changing surface that crumbled and was remade by earthquakes and volcanoes. The raging fury of creation stripped raw and made terrible. She retreated, drawing herself away in fear of being destroyed by the power of the sensation. She could not allow herself to be subsumed in that.

Delicately, she sank back into the trance and began again, and this time she was more tentative. Among the roar and screech of this awful place, she began to make out thoughts. Thoughts as slow and massive as continents, drifting beneath her, processes too colossal and complex for her to even begin to fathom. The ruminations of a god.

'I hear him . . .' she said hoarsely, tears spilling from her eyes. 'I hear him . . .'

((Now, look)) the Xhiang Xhi urged, and she cast her eyes upward to where a white glow was growing rapidly behind the clouds, speeding from horizon to horizon, growing from dim to unbearably bright in the span of a second.

'The spear of Jurani,' Lucia whispered to herself. Then something burst through the clouds, a sun flung from the sky, and there was a sound like the end of the world. Lucia screamed as the fireball of its impact hit her.

When she came to her senses, she was lying on the tuffet in the Xhiang Xhi's dell, her face and hair dirty where she had fallen. After a moment to orient herself, she stood shakily, facing the spirit once again. It still hung in the mist before her, veiled from clear sight, a long-fingered wisp like some childish sketch of a nightmare. Drifting, shifting, its dreary emanations oppressing her.

She took a few breaths to compose herself, then raised her head.

'That was the moment when the gods destroyed Aricarat,' she said. 'When the army led by his parents, Assantua and Jurani, made war on him; and his own father, the god of fire, destroyed him with his spear.'

((*That is your interpretation. Muddled with myth, but holding a core of truth, as many legends do*))

She frowned. 'But I was told of it by the spirit of Alskain Mar.'

((*The spirit of Alskain Mar is not old enough to remember nor wise enough to understand. Spirits know much, but their experience is narrow*))

This was new. It had never occurred to Lucia that spirits could be wrong. She knew them to be wilful liars at times, but she had always had faith in their superior lore. To hear that even *they* were deemed benighted by this entity shook her deeply.

'And what is *your* interpretation?' she asked, almost fearing an answer.

((*You would not understand mine. Your knowledge is built on the knowledge of your ancestors, slowly accreting towards truth. That is the way of your species. At all times you believe you know all there is to know, and that which you do not know you explain in other ways. Yet later generations will laugh at your ignorance, and do the same, and be laughed at in their turn. Understanding must be reached gradually, Lucia. What answers I would have for you, you would not believe even if you could comprehend them*))

'Then what can you tell me?' Lucia asked, spreading her hands in supplication. 'What is it I must know?'

((*You have learned much already, but not enough*)) the spirit replied. ((*You know that the fragments of Aricarat that fell onto your planet carried with it fragments of the entity that resided there. You know that this being had enough remnant influence to create the Weavers, and that they carry out its work with no knowledge of what controls them. But you do not understand the Weavers' intentions. You think they want to conquer. But conquest is not their aim, merely a stage in Aricarat's plan. They will not spread beyond Saramyr. They will not have to))*

Lucia waited in dread. So many certainties were falling into ruin around her. The Xhiang Xhi loomed in the mist, becoming darker.

((They are changing your world, Lucia. They are making it more like their master's home. They are preparing it for his arrival))

Lucia saw again, suddenly, the blasted plain and brown clouds, tasted the sulphur in the air, and a weakness swept her. The buildings that the Weavers had erected, the machines, the pall-pits: these were the tools by which they would make the world dark and poisonous. From Saramyr they would spread a miasma over the whole of the Near World, and across the great oceans that none had ever crossed except the mysterious explorers of Yttryx; then even the strange and distant lands beyond would be swallowed, and Nuki's eye would never again gaze down on the world, for it would be forever concealed from his sight.

((There is no word in your language for what they are doing)) the Xhiang Xhi was saying. *((Other cultures in other places far, far, from here have a name for the process, but it would be meaningless to you. You need know only this: if you do not stop the Weavers, one way or another, your world will end))*

Lucia's pale eyes were cold as she looked into the mist. 'Whether by Aricarat's plan, or by that of the other gods.'

((You are perceptive for one of your kind. The spirit of Alskain Mar was right in that, at least. Once, Aricarat was powerful, a great presence in the Weave. If he returns he will again make war on what you call gods. They fear him. The spear of Jurani may strike this planet too))

Lucia's jaw clenched. It took some time for her to realise that she was furious.

'Then the gods are spiteful,' she said, 'that they should make us pay for their ineptitude. They should have made certain of their enemy the first time.'

((Even gods make mistakes)) the Xhiang Xhi replied. *((Your people have a story, of the Grey Moth and the Skein of Lament, that attests to your belief in that))*

'And where are the gods now?' Lucia cried.

((To that I have no answer)) it said. *((Their ways are beyond me, just as mine are beyond you. All things are transient, all things dwarfed by matters of greater scale. Perhaps your war is beneath contempt in the eyes of such beings. Perhaps the acts you commit in the name of your gods go unnoticed. Or perhaps they watch your every move, and they wait for reasons of their own. I do not know. The gods do not interfere unless they must))*

Lucia bit down on her frustration. Anger was an emotion that was almost foreign to her, but she felt it now. So many had died to bring her to this point, the culmination of her purpose, and now she learned that all their strife was to correct an error of judgement made by the gods themselves, and that the gods might not even be present to see them.

No. She would not believe that. When she was a child, the moon sisters themselves had sent their children to save her from the shin-shin. More than once she knew Kaiku had been spurred by the Emperor of the gods into actions she would not otherwise have committed.

And yet . . . what if the moon sisters were merely spirits that had no connection with the goddesses of the moon at all? It was entirely possible that they had saved Lucia for reasons of their own. Spirits were capricious in general, and the Children of the Moons were insane by human standards. What if Kaiku's dreams were only that: dreams, evoked by faith?

The gods don't control. They're more subtle than that. They use avatars and omens, to bend the will of their faithful to do their work. There's no predestination, no destiny. We all have our choices to make. It's us who have to fight our battles.

Her own words, spoken to her friend Flen back when he was still alive. And there was the crux: avatars, omens, subtlety. Never allowing certainty, never allowing their believers to know for sure, never providing anything that could not be accounted for in other ways, as coincidence or delusion. Heart's blood, did they *purposefully* shroud themselves? Did they enjoy the torment of anxiety and bewilderment that their inconclusiveness caused in their followers? Was it better to be like the Tkiurathi, to worship no gods at all but the memories of their distinguished ancestors?

Or were the gods like distant parents, allowing their children to make their own mistakes and solve their own problems? Teaching them that they could not rely on anyone but themselves, intervening with only a guiding nudge here and there? Even when there was *everything* at stake?

But then, thought Lucia with a vertiginous plunge as her perspective shifted, perhaps theirs was not the only world that the gods ministered. Perhaps they were only a tiny, insignificant mote among the stars, one of uncountable cultures, each one squalling for attention in the emptiness.

The cruelty of that drove her to her knees.

((You can never know, Lucia)) said the Xhiang Xhi. *((One way or another, certainty would destroy you))*

She stared at the wet grass of the tuffet.

'Tell me,' she said eventually. 'What hope is there?'

((There is hope)) the spirit replied. *((For Aricarat's plans have gone against him in some ways. He did not expect the Sisters. He did not expect you))*

'But we are Aberrants. We came from the blight he created. A disease of the land, that kills crops and twists children in the womb.'

((The blight is not a disease of the land. It is a catalyst of change. Aricarat does not want to kill all life on the planet; he needs you still, and will for a long time yet, until he is entirely restored. People and plants and animals will die, but some will adapt and survive and recover. He is changing the flora of Saramyr, and he is changing your people))

'Changing us?'

((Changing you so that you can live in the new world he will make. So that you can breathe the air that is poison to you now. The Sisters can already do it to a limited degree. Over time, the change will accelerate. More of you will be born Aberrant. As the air turns more hostile, only those Aberrants who can breathe it well will survive, and their children will inherit that ability. Eventually, only the Saramyr will remain: the blight will be what saves you. All other countries will die, and the witchstones there will be excavated at leisure. By your people))

Lucia closed her eyes, and saw the images as the spirit spoke. A tear ran from the edge of one eye.

'Then how does that offer hope?' she asked.

((You offer hope. The Sisters offer hope. He did not know what he was unlocking when he meddled with your kind. His interference has provoked changes that would not have otherwise occurred for millions of years, if ever))

'Then what are we?'

((You are the next stage. You have torn the veil of ascendancy: the divide between the base world of the physical and the world beyond the senses. In the eyes of the gods, it is the line that marks the end of your infancy. You achieve this in one way, the Sisters in another. It matters nothing. Beyond that point, you are no longer as you were. You are the first of the true transcendents of humanity))

'Cailin was right,' Lucia whispered. 'All this time, she was right.'

((Indeed)) the spirit replied. *((I would have ensured safe passage for you and the Sisters, though I extended no such courtesy to those who had not breached the veil. One of you fell, however, and I could not prevent that))*

She raised her head. 'What about the Weavers?'

The Xhiang Xhi seemed to recede in her vision, melting into the mist. *((They are not as you are. Their abilities come from their Masks. From Aricarat))*

'But if Aricarat created the Aberrants, then why were the

Weavers killing them?' Lucia protested. She did not want to believe any of this, and was fighting to find holes in the spirit's logic.

But the Xhiang Xhi was relentless. *((It was necessary, to safeguard their rise to power, to prevent beings such as you and the Sisters from existing. They failed at that, in the end. They will stop killing Aberrants in time, and begin breeding them selectively instead))*

'How do you *know* this?' she cried.

((Because it is the only course of action that makes sense)) the spirit replied, and she was defeated. She could not argue with such an entity, something older than recorded history, which dwarfed her understanding so completely that she was fighting to assimilate even the limited snatches of information it fed to her. She dared not think of how much it was not telling, how much lay outside her experience. Maybe, if she knew, she would be as sorrowful as it was. Perhaps ignorance was better. How small they all were, in the final analysis.

She got to her feet, dishevelled and haggard, and stared into the mist at the vague and swaying shape of the Xhiang Xhi.

'I beg you,' she said. 'Help us. Help us stop all this coming to pass.'

She felt the Xhiang Xhi regarding her, there in its chill and gloomy dell.

((I will help you)) it said. Then, after a pause of moments that felt like hours: *((But there is a price))*

It was dusk when Lucia emerged from the tunnel.

Nobody noticed her at first. They had sunk into grief, and sat wearily on the forest floor beneath the unwavering gaze of the shadow-beast that hunkered atop the hillock. Most of them had fallen into an exhausted slumber, for here, in the presence of the great spirit, the nightmares were held at bay.

Kaiku awoke to the touch of Tsata's hand on her shoulder. She looked up at him. Sometime over the past hours, she had cried herself to sleep with her head on his thigh where he sat. She raised herself, brushing her hair back behind one ear, and followed his eyes to where Lucia stood.

Then she was scrambling to her feet and rushing over. She gathered Lucia in a tight embrace; but the words of relief that were forming were never spoken. Lucia remained rigid, her arms by her sides. Kaiku backed away, searching her face quizzically.

'Lucia?'

The three soldiers were getting to their feet now, coming closer, warily, as if afraid of her. Asara had stood also, but she watched from a distance.

'It is done,' Lucia said, her gaze shifting minutely to meet Kaiku's. Her voice was flat and expressionless. 'We have been granted passage out of this forest. The beast will guard us.'

'Lucia?' Kaiku said again, the word a question. She tried to smile, but it faded into uncertainty. 'Lucia, what happened?'

'The spirits will aid us when the time comes,' Lucia said bitterly. 'That is what you wanted, is it not?'

Before Kaiku could protest, Lucia addressed the group, overriding her.

'We must return to Araka Jo. I do not wish to stay in this place an instant longer.'

Her tone precluded any further questions, and she did not give anyone the opportunity anyway. She walked away from Kaiku, leaving her bewildered and hurt, and headed into the trees. With nothing else they could do, the remnants of her retinue followed, one by one, as night fell across the Forest of Xu.

TWENTY

The great city of Axekami loured in its own miasma.

The exhalations of the Weavers' constructions had a strange weight to them, a persistency unlike that of smoke. The main bulk of it rose above the city in a roiling cap, slanted by the breeze across the plains so that it leaned eastward; but it also sank to mist the earth, and to spread outward along the ground. At its edges it was a diffuse haze, but still it appeared to permeate the air from horizon to horizon, a suspicion of something amiss that was too subtle for the eye to define. There were always clouds around Axekami now, which was unusual for winter when the skies were traditionally clear. Occasionally they unleashed a brown rain which smelt powerfully of rotten eggs.

The Imperial Quarter was a spectre of its former glory now. Its gardens went untended, its fountains murky and unclean. Its trees had shed their leaves and they decayed on the flagstones and cobbles. The townhouses that had once been occupied by the nobles and high families of the Empire had been gutted, their fineries long since stripped, occupied now by swarms of the destitute. The wide thoroughfares were all but empty of traffic, and shuffling vagrants meandered in the overgrown parks or the scummed water gardens.

Yet though the heart of the place was gone, small sections of its past remained. Shops and wholesalers stayed open, eking a living from what they could get into the city to sell, barely able to afford the guards that prevented them from being robbed. A thin trade from the rest of Axekami kept them alive. The alternative was to abandon their property and move, but few had the money or the opportunity now.

They weathered the troubles as best they could, and hoped for better days.

One such shop was owned by a herbalist, who once had enjoyed a reputation as the best in the land. His father and grandfather before him had been appointed as suppliers to the physicians of the Imperial family, as had he in his turn. After the Weavers had taken Axekami, and the Imperial family was no more, he had refused to give up his ancestral premises. Even when the physician to the Lord Protector and Blood Koli offered him a place in the Imperial Keep, he had refused. Apart from his determination to keep his shop, he had little love for the Weavers, and he trusted them not at all.

So he remained here in the Imperial Quarter, and the physician came to him to buy what he needed, arriving in a black carriage gilded in gold, escorted by guards with rifles. The guards took station outside the shop while he went within.

The physician, whose name was Ukida, was thin and frail, with lank white hair combed across a balding pate and rheumy blue eyes. Despite the infirmity of his appearance, he moved like a man half his age and his hands and voice were steady and sure. His robe hung awkwardly on his spare frame as he walked up to the counter of the shop, passing rows of jars and cloth bags half-full of powdered roots. Most of the shelving was bare. The lanterns lit to aid the grim daylight only served to add to the depressing atmosphere, for they reminded Ukida that there should have been no need for them at such an hour.

He and the herbalist – a stout, rotund man with a whiskery moustache and a brisk, efficient manner – exchanged a few friendly words before a list was passed between them, and the herbalist disappeared into his preparation room to grind the necessary quantities. Ukida waited, tapping his fingers on the counter, looking idly about the shop.

'Master Ukida,' said a voice. 'You are looking well.'

The sound of his name startled him: he had thought the

shop empty. He located the owner of the voice, appearing from a doorway that led into the back of the shop. She walked towards him, and his eyes widened in recognition.

'I have been waiting a long time for you,' she said. 'Three days.'

'Mistress Mishani!' he exclaimed in a hiss, too shocked even to bow. 'What are you doing here?'

'I have come to ask a favour of you,' she replied, her narrow face sallow in the bad light. She was not dressed in her usual finery. The robe she wore was battered and dirty, made for travelling, and her hair was worn in an unadorned ponytail and tucked into the back of her robe to disguise its length, the deception concealed by a voluminous hood. Tied tight against her small skull, it made her look faintly rodentine and not at all noble.

'You will be killed if they find you,' Ukida said, then added: 'I could be killed for just talking to you.' He glanced nervously over the counter, where the herbalist had been.

'He knows,' Mishani said. 'He remembers the days of the Empire, and he is loyal to them. I guessed you would come here eventually, so I asked him to let me wait for you.' She gave him a wry smile. 'This was always the only place you would come to for supplies. You were most insistent, even with my father, that you would settle for nothing but the best.'

'Your memory is good, Mistress, but I fear your judgement is not. You are in great danger in Axekami. Did you walk through these streets alone? Such madness!'

'I know the risks, Ukida. Better than you do,' Mishani replied. 'I have a letter for you to deliver to my mother.'

Ukida shook his head in alarm. 'Mistress Mishani, you would risk my life!'

'There is no risk. You may read it, if you wish.' She drew the letter from the sash of her robe and held it out to him. It had no seal.

He looked at it uncertainly. Mishani could tell he was deciding where his loyalties lay in this situation. On the one hand, he was blood-bound to Mishani's family, and that meant her as well; she was still officially part of Blood Koli. On the other, all the retainers knew that Mishani was no longer welcome within that family, and her father would most likely have her executed if he caught her. At the very least, she would be imprisoned and interrogated. Her involvement in the kidnapping of Lucia was generally known now, though never officially ratified, as was her hand in the revolt at Zila several years later. The Weavers would show her no mercy if they found her, nor anyone who had abetted her.

'Take it,' she urged him. She was recalling how he had nursed her through childhood illnesses, tended to her scratches and grazes. He would not betray her; of that she was sure. The question was whether he would help her.

Reluctantly, he took the letter and unfolded it. There was no indication of the recipient or the sender, only a dozen vertical rows of High Saramyrrhic pictograms.

'It is a poem,' he said. *And not a very good one,* he added mentally.

'That it is,' said Mishani. 'Please, give that to my mother. You need not even say it was from me. Nobody will know.'

'The Weavers will know,' he said. 'There are no secrets from them.'

'Do you really believe that?' Mishani asked him. 'I would not have thought you prone to their scaremongering.'

'They can pluck the guilt from a man's mind,' Ukida said.

'Only if they have reason to look there,' she replied. 'Trust me, Master Ukida. I have lived alongside the Red Order a long time. I know what the Weavers are capable of, and what they are not. There is a risk, but it is small. You are my only hope.'

Ukida studied her carefully, then folded up the letter and bowed to her. 'It shall be done,' he said tightly.

'You have my deepest gratitude,' Mishani said. And with that, she returned his bow, purposefully choosing a more humble attitude than she should have. She knew him:

arrogance would not play well, even though he was still her servant. He seemed faintly shamed by her action.

She departed through the doorway to the back of the shop as the herbalist returned, his timing impeccable. Ukida paid for his supplies and left, the letter carefully concealed in his robe.

Muraki tu Koli sat at her writing desk in her small room, her quill scratching and jerking in the light of a lantern. The lack of windows meant that she took no account of day or night, and she had little desire to see the murk-shrouded disc of Nuki's eye anyway. Aside from the occasional meals that she took with her husband, she rarely left this room. She was nearing the end of her new volume of the adventures of Nida-jan, and she was lost in the world she had created, spurred along by the unstoppable momentum of the story. A part of her still felt bitter at the necessity of haste, for she took great pride in her work and she resented that matters of the real world had conspired to make her rush it; but though unpolished, her tales still had an energy all their own, and she lived for that.

She did not hear Ukida's chime outside the curtained doorway, nor did she notice him enter uninvited. Her retainers had learned not to wait for her to reply, for she never did. He simply entered, bowed, and placed a letter on the edge of her writing desk. He cast an appraising eye over her, noting that she was very pale and looked consumptive. Bad air, bad eating habits, no exercise, no sunlight. She would sicken soon. He had told her so, and had dared to tell Avun too, but he had been politely ignored. With another bow, he withdrew.

Muraki continued writing. It was several hours before she stopped to ease the cramp in her hand, and then she noticed the letter and wondered how it had got there. She picked it up and unfolded it, read what was within. There was a short interruption in her breathing, a soft intake of surprise. She read it again, crossed out several of the pictograms, read it once more and then burned it to ash in the lantern. Then she sat back at her desk and stared at the page that she had been writing.

After an hour, she got up and went to find Ukida, her soft shoes whispering as she went.

Avun tu Koli entered his study with a wary tread. It was dim and cool in here, the swirled *lach* floors sucking what warmth there was from the room. There was little furniture but a huge marble desk before a row of window-arches that looked out across the shrouded city, and a few cabinets for storing paperwork and stationery. He kept his private space orderly and spartan, like his life.

He glanced around the room, unconsciously furtive in his movements, then, satisfied that it was empty, he slipped inside and let the curtain fall behind him.

'Welcome back, Avun,' Kakre croaked, and Avun jumped and swore.

The Weave-lord was standing behind his desk, but Avun had somehow not seen him there. His eyes had skipped over the intruder, a blind spot in his mind.

'You seem unusually nervous today,' Kakre observed. 'You have good reason to be.'

'Do not try anything foolish, Kakre,' Avun warned, but there was little strength in his voice. 'Fahrekh's actions were nothing to do with me.'

'Convenient, though. Oh, indeed,' the Weave-lord replied, shuffling around the edge of the desk. 'What excellent timing he possessed, to strike just after you had done your level best to exhaust me.' He cocked his head to one side, the gaping corpse-Mask tipping in a grotesque parody of curiosity. 'Where have you been, my Lord Protector?'

Avun calmed himself, regaining his composure. Like his daughter, he valued the ability to control the expression of emotion, and it was a measure of how scared he was that Kakre had noticed his fear.

'I went to Ren to discuss the construction of a new pall-pit there,' he said.

'And was that not something you could have left to an underling?'

'I wanted to be there personally,' Avun replied, walking further into the room to assert that he was not afraid, that he had nothing to be afraid for. 'It is well to keep myself involved in small matters as well as large. It helps me to keep perspective.'

'Here is your *perspective*,' Kakre hissed. He cast one withered hand towards Avun, and the Lord Protector's insides wrenched as if twisted. The agony made him stagger, but he gritted his teeth and did not scream as he wanted to.

'You thought my anger might calm if you got out of my way for a few days?' Kakre snarled. 'You thought I would *forget*, perhaps? That my addled mind would not remember what you had done when you returned? Like Fahrekh, you underestimate me greatly.' His fist clenched, and Avun did cry out this time, and dropped to one knee. His pate was sheened with sweat and his face taut with pain.

'I knew . . . you would make . . . the wrong assumption,' Avun gasped.

'I think I know you well enough, Avun, to be confident that you were conspiring with Fahrekh to kill me,' Kakre said. 'Treachery is second nature to you. But you chose the wrong victim this time.'

'I . . . it was not . . . I . . .' Avun could barely manage a breath now. Kakre was increasing the pain, and it was like knives had been shoved into his guts and were slowly revolving.

'More denials? I could search your thoughts to find the truth, if you would prefer,' the Weave-lord offered. 'Though I am not as precise as I used to be. The results could be . . . unfortunate.' His dead face stared passionlessly from beneath the shadow cast by his hood. 'It would be easier just to kill you.'

'You *cannot* kill me,' Avun spat. Loops of crimson spittle hung from his narrow chin.

'Would you like me to try harder?'

Avun's teeth were pressed together so tightly that it was an effort to force them apart to speak. 'The Weavers . . . die with me . . .'

Abruptly the pressure on his organs loosened. Not much, but enough to let him breathe precious air easily again. He sucked in great lungfuls, on his hands and knees now. Blood dripped from his mouth onto the floor.

'Interesting,' Kakre said, his tone flat. 'And what did you mean by that, my Lord Protector?'

Avun delayed his answer for a moment, savouring the respite, choosing his words carefully. They meant the difference between life and death. He wiped his mouth with the back of his hand and glared up at the hunched figure who stood over him.

'There is nobody else who can lead your armies,' he said.

'Is that the best you can do?' Kakre mocked. 'Pitiful. There are many subordinates, generals of the Blackguard who would be eager to take your place.'

'And who chose those generals? I did. And I have been systematically removing all the *good* ones from positions of power for years now.'

Kakre was silent. Avun got one foot beneath him and rose unsteadily, clutching his thin stomach with one hand.

'Search their records, if you wish,' Avun said. 'None of them have any real experience of mass warfare. They are peacekeepers, men whose expertise is policing our cities. The old generals were useless since we had Aberrants and Nexuses to fight with, so I got rid of them. You did not pay close enough attention to that, Kakre. It is well to keep yourself involved in small matters,' – he managed a red-stained grin – 'as well as large.'

Still the Weave-lord said nothing, merely regarding him from within the dark pits of the Mask's eye-holes. Avun stumbled to his desk and leaned one arm on it, supporting himself. He felt like he had swallowed broken glass.

'Remember the first months of this war? Remember how your armies were slaughtered by the generals of the old empire? That is how it will be again, if you kill me. There is nobody to take my place.'

'We can find one,' Kakre said darkly, but he sounded uncertain.

'Can you? Do you know what to look for in a leader?' Avun shook his head dismissively. 'No matter. It would take time for them to familiarise themselves with your forces, to assemble a power structure. Time you do not have. Your breeding programmes fail to provide you with enough Aberrants to both control your territories and attack new ones. And the more you produce, the faster your armies starve. You need the Southern Prefectures, and you need them before Aestival Week. We will be hard pressed to do so as it is. If you get rid of me, your chances drop to nothing. And then begins the slow decline of your forces, and the Empire will take you apart, piece by piece, feya-kori or not. You can invade a city with your blight demons, but you cannot occupy it. For that you need armies. For that you need *me!*'

He raised himself to stand erect again, keeping the pain from his face, and turned his dull, reptilian eyes upon the Weave-lord.

'The new pall-pits are operational. The feya-kori are ready to be called. We need to work together or your precious monasteries will fall like Utraxxa did.'

With that, he walked boldly out of the room. The few steps it took him to get to the curtained doorway of his study were heavy with terror: he expected to be struck down and tortured. But then he was at the curtain, and through it, and though he felt Kakre's seething frustration and anger like a palpable thing, he knew he had won this round.

TWENTY-ONE

Kaiku slid the screen closed on the celebrations throughout Araka Jo and looked across the room at Cailin.

'They are in rare spirits tonight,' Cailin observed.

'They are idiots,' Kaiku said rancourously. 'Like goats, blindly trusting in their herders.'

It was dusk, and the night insects were beginning their discordant chorus in the undergrowth, all but smothered by the cheers and raised voices and fireworks that arced over the rim of the mountains. The house of the Red Order was quiet in comparison. Most of the Sisters were out in the village or up at the temple complex, overseeing the festivities that had erupted at the news of Lucia's return.

'You are angry,' Cailin said.

'Yes,' Kaiku replied. She was not wearing the attire of the Order: she had come here directly after their arrival, having found the folk of the Libera Dramach waiting for them, warned by scouts of their approach.

'About them?' Cailin motioned beyond the screens.

'Among other things,' Kaiku replied.

Cailin was standing, lantern-light falling on one side of her painted face. A table sat against one wall with mats tucked underneath it, but she did not bring it out or invite Kaiku to sit. There was a hostility to her that Cailin did not like.

'They think this is a triumph?' Kaiku snapped. 'They think we return in splendour? We straggle back, only a handful of survivors, and all they care about is that Lucia has returned, and with her she brings some . . . *promise*. That is all. No word of elaboration, nothing that might justify all those deaths, *Phaeca's* death. She will not speak a word of what went on in that forest, except to say that the spirits will aid us when the time comes.'

'She means hope to them,' Cailin replied softly. 'They do not care about the cost. They feared to lose their figurehead. Their saviour. They may be foolish, but they are desperate too. If we had lost her, we would have lost the hearts of the people.' She watched Kaiku suspiciously. 'I am grateful to you, Kaiku. Once again you have excelled yourself. You brought her back alive.'

'I am not certain I care for your gratitude,' Kaiku said.

Cailin descended into icy silence. She would not rise to that. Let Kaiku say what she wanted to say; Cailin would not trouble herself to draw it from her.

'You should not have sent Phaeca with us,' Kaiku said eventually. But her tone was quieter, and Cailin surmised that even this was not the true cause of her ire.

'You should not have agreed to have her along,' Cailin countered. 'I note you did not protest overly at her inclusion.'

'She was too sensitive,' Kaiku murmured. 'It drove her mad. Maybe she would have recovered when we got out of that gods-cursed place. But she should not have been there at all.'

Cailin let this go past. She did not have anything to say to it. None of them had any idea about what the Forest of Xu was like before Lucia and the others had entered. Placing blame was useless. Cailin felt Phaeca's death as keenly as Kaiku did, though for different reasons: she grieved to lose one of her precious Order, Kaiku grieved to lose a friend.

'And Lucia?' she asked. 'How is Lucia?'

'Different,' Kaiku said, pacing restlessly around her side of the room. 'Cold. Taciturn. But since she visited the Xhiang Xhi, she has been clear of mind. She is no longer dreamy or unfocused. If she is unresponsive, it is because she wants to be. I do not know which way I preferred her: they are equally bad.'

The agitation of her body language was increasing. Cailin knew that she would soon come to her point, that she was delaying the moment. She was afraid to speak her mind, perhaps. But Kaiku's nature would drive her thoughts into the open eventually.

'I must know,' she said suddenly. 'The Red Order. I must know.' She stopped pacing, faced Cailin and said bluntly: 'What are we doing?'

'We are saving Saramyr.'

'*No!*' Kaiku voice was sharp. 'I want the truth! What happens afterwards?'

Cailin's tone was faintly puzzled. 'You know this, Kaiku.'

'Tell me again.'

Cailin studied her for a moment, then turned away from the lantern. 'We take the place that the Weavers have occupied. We become the glue that holds our society together.' She turned her head to meet Kaiku's eyes. 'But there will be no conflict between us. We are not as the Weavers. We would not kill each other at our masters' behest, nor would we use our abilities to assassinate our masters' rivals. We would have no masters.'

'And in such a way could you hold the whole of Saramyr to ransom,' Kaiku said.

Cailin regarded her steadily. 'Is that what you think we will do?'

Kaiku gave a short, humourless laugh. 'What does it matter what I think? The nobles will think that. The Empire cannot be run when its power lies in the hands of the Red Order. Are the nobles to believe that we would act out of charity? That we would dedicate our lives to being their mouthpieces, their messengers? We are not blood-bound to anyone, and hence we can do as we choose. Do you think they would stand that for long?'

'They would have little option,' Cailin said. 'Granted, we would be able to extract certain concessions, but not more than the Weavers took. We do not need lives as the price of our power.'

'No, Cailin. They are too clever to fall for that, and you

know they are. That is not security enough. Eventually, their fear of us would make them depose us. And I will wager that whatever plan you have for the Sisterhood is geared towards making that eventuality impossible. Even if it means deposing *them* first.'

'Your accusations are becoming insulting, Kaiku,' Cailin warned. 'Remember to whom you speak.'

Kaiku shook her head. 'I have heard you talk about how the Sisterhood are higher beings than men. I do not for one instant think that you would willingly be a servant to anyone. You are lying, Cailin. You have an agenda.' She brushed her hair back behind her ear. 'Otherwise, you would not have let the Weavers take the throne. You would not have let Axekami fall into ruin. You would not have let all those people die.'

Cailin was a thin, severe line of black against the blue light of the night that glowed through the paper screens. 'You have been speaking with Asara, I see.'

'No,' said Kaiku. 'I speak to her as little as possible. I have been thinking, though. It is all very obvious if I proceed from the premise that you – like everybody else in this damned world, it seems – are merely out for your own advantage.

'If we had resisted the Weavers at the first, if we had warned the nobles and lent our strength to their cause, they might have stopped all this from happening. But what would we gain? The nobles would have averted a terrible danger, and, once their lesson was learned, they would never let beings such as the Weavers – beings such as *us* – anywhere near a position of power again. Aberrants would still be Aberrants: despised, outcast and hunted. Lucia would have been executed.

'But what if it were different? What if the Weavers shattered the Empire? What if they were allowed to become a threat so terrible that *anything* would be preferable to them? What if the only way the Empire could be saved was by an Aberrant empress and by the Red Order? How could they refuse to let us be part of their new world then? Everyone already accepts that Lucia will be Empress if we win this war; and you have been making very certain that she holds you in the highest regard all these years. The Red Order will rise as she does. I imagine that the Red Order would rise even without her now. You have played your hand well.'

Kaiku stared hard at the Pre-Eminent. 'The Weavers had to crush the people so that they would accept us, and we let it happen. Maybe we even helped it along.'

Cailin gave a dismissive flick of her fingers. 'Of course we helped it along. Do you really think the Libera Dramach could *ever* have resisted the Weavers? Even with Lucia on our side, we would have gone the way of the Ais Maraxa, cut down as soon as we showed ourselves. The high families needed to be united against the Weavers, and that would never happen unless they were under real and direct threat. So yes, we wanted the Weavers to take the throne, no matter how many lives it cost. It was the only way to get the nobles on our side, to make them see what was good for them. Such is the art of politics, and its results are not measured in lives but in who gets to write the history books.'

'So we manipulate them as the Weavers did,' Kaiku said, and lowered her head. 'We are the lesser of two evils, Cailin. But we are still evil.'

Cailin laughed bitterly. 'Evil! What do you know of evil?' Her laughter faded, and her face took on a hateful expression, her voice deepening. 'Evil is a village stoning a seven-harvest child and leaving her for dead in a ditch. Evil is being left to fend for yourself when you are afraid of even going to sleep in case the fires come, wandering from town to town, a slave and later a whore because you have no home, because each time the burning comes you have to run, you have to run into the wilderness and scrabble for roots and starve or the men with knives will come and kill you! Evil is the look in their eyes, those ignorant bastard *cattle* who populate this land, as they despise you for being Aberrant!' Her voice had risen to a shout, but now it dropped, and was hard with scorn. 'They can despise me, Kaiku. But they will fear me also.'

Kaiku was silent for a long time. The two of them faced each other across the room.

'I will help you destroy the Weavers,' said Kaiku. 'And after that, it is over. I want no part of you or your Order, Cailin. I see now that you are not what I was looking for all this time.'

She slid the screen open and left, shutting it behind her. Cailin stood alone, listening to the celebrations outside.

Barak Zahn found his daughter sitting on the roof of a temple.

It was a flat roof, made of white stone. Figures guarded the corners, eroded away to mere lumps; it was otherwise featureless. A stairway led up from beneath. Lucia was sitting inches from the edge, with her arms wrapped around her legs and her knees drawn up to her chin, looking out into the night.

When Zahn emerged and saw his daughter like that, he was momentarily at a loss for what to say. When he did speak, the words came awkwardly.

'The guards below told me I might find you here,' he said, redundantly.

She turned to look at him and smiled over her shoulder. 'Father,' she said. 'Come sit with me.'

Puzzled by this response, which was at odds with the one he had been expecting from the accounts of those who had spoken with her recently, he did as she bade, and settled his rangy frame next to her, dangling his legs over the edge of the roof.

'Everyone is happy tonight,' she said. The lights from the lanterns below were glowing strings in the pale blue of her eye. The dirt paths of the temple complex were bright and stalls were busy. People talked and drank or wandered down the slope on their left, towards the lake. Music drifted up to them from an unseen band.

Not knowing what to say to that, Zahn looked at the moons. Aurus was full in the north, dominating the sky, and Iridima peered out from behind it like a sharp white blister.

'I am glad to see you are recovered,' she said. 'I missed you.' Gods, she was a beautiful creature, so much resembling her mother. It made him proud to think that she was his child.

'Your relatives will have to do better than that to get you from me,' Zahn said, his lips twisting into a grin.

'I have spoken with Oyo,' she said. 'It will not happen again.'

Zahn blinked. 'You did what?'

Lucia gave him an innocent look.

'But you did not even know it was her!' he exclaimed. 'Even *I* am not certain.'

'I knew,' she said calmly. 'It was obvious.'

'And you accused her? You have only been back a few hours!'

'I did not accuse her,' Lucia said, unfolding her legs and dangling them alongside his. 'I said to her that if you should die in the future, in any manner I found suspicious, I would disown Blood Erinima.'

Zahn was open-mouthed for a moment, then he laughed heartily and shook his head in disbelief. He had never known Lucia to be this assertive. 'Heart's blood, you really *are* getting to be like your mother. Whatever happened in that forest, it certainly lit a fire in you.'

'Yes,' she said quietly, her eyes drifting to the horizon, to the north, where the Forest of Xu lay beyond the mountains and beneath the moons. 'Yes, it did that.'

Asara came to Kaiku's house in the dead of night. Kaiku had known she would. Kaiku was waiting for her.

'Sit down, Asara,' she offered as an invitation, motioning to the mats she had laid in the centre of the room. There was a table next to them, with bitter tea and wine and other spirits, as well as several snacks and small cakes. A proper reception for a guest; something that Kaiku rarely bothered with, if ever, and doubly strange to Asara since she had turned up unannounced. Trebly so, since she was under the impression that Kaiku hated her.

Asara stood just inside the door for a moment, caution evident on her face. Then she knelt on one of the mats, arranging herself elegantly. She had bathed and dressed and reapplied sparse touches of eyeshadow, and she looked perfect, as ever. Kaiku wore a simple black robe of silk belted with gold, her hair damp and raked through with her fingers, as casual as if Asara were her sister and had dropped around for a gossip.

Asara looked frankly uncomfortable as Kaiku offered her tea. She had wine instead. Kaiku had the same, then sat cross-legged on the mat opposite.

'What is all this?' Asara asked.

Kaiku tilted her shoulder in a shrug. 'I felt like it.'

Asara's unease was not abated at all by that.

'I envy you sometimes, Asara,' she said conversationally. 'I envy the way you can change. How you can start again at any time. That is a wonderful gift, I imagine.'

'Are you mocking me?' Asara asked. It was impossible to tell by her tone.

'No,' Kaiku said. 'I mean it.'

'Then you have nothing to envy,' she replied. 'We do not learn from our mistakes. Age lends no wisdom, only removes the enthusiasm for foolishness. You could change yourself a thousand times and you would still dig yourself the same holes to fall into.'

Kaiku's eyes lowered to her glass. 'I was afraid you might say that.' She took a sip.

'Kaiku, are you in some kind of trouble?' Asara could hardly believe that those words had come from her mouth, but there was something in Kaiku's manner that moved her.

Kaiku raised her eyes, and her lashes dislodged a tear from

each eye to run unevenly down her cheeks. Asara almost reached across the gap between them to touch her arm in comfort, then stopped herself.

'Everything is falling apart, Asara,' she whispered, her throat tight. 'I cannot hold it together. I cannot hold anything together any more.'

Asara, shocked, could not think of a thing to say.

'I watch my friends die and I am powerless to prevent it,' she said. 'I have been fighting for almost ten years and it has gained me nothing. What good is victory? All I will succeed in is removing the only reason I have had to keep living ever since my family died. I will destroy the Weavers and be left with nothing. Nobody I can trust, nothing I can believe in. Everyone proves false in the end, every ideal is a sham. I am not fighting to make my life better, I am just fighting to stop it becoming *worse*.'

'This is not like you,' Asara said at last. 'You are stronger than this.'

'Am I not allowed *limits*?' Kaiku cried. 'Gods, how much am I expected to take before I go the way of Phaeca?'

Asara did not comment on that. She was not sure whether Kaiku blamed her for the death of her friend or not.

Kaiku wiped her eyes with the sleeve of her robe. 'Oh, this is ridiculous,' she murmured to herself. 'I can hardly expect you to care.'

'But I have . . . contributed to your sorrow,' Asara said, wringing her hands in her lap. 'Forgive me.'

Kaiku shifted herself so that she was kneeling, and she put her arms around Asara and held her closely. Asara, still perturbed by Kaiku's mood, returned the embrace. After a moment, it stopped feeling unnatural.

'I cannot hold you in enmity, Asara,' she said. 'You have been a friend to me, in your way.'

Asara let out a sigh, battling down an emotion that she did not wish to experience again. She held Kaiku for a long while, until she was sure she had herself under control, and then said: 'I will not hurt you again. I promise you that. I am selfish and cruel – more than you know – but I will not hurt you again.'

She heard a sob from Kaiku, and then she drew away; and Asara saw that Kaiku's eyes were red, and not only from weeping.

'It is done,' she said.

Asara's heart jumped a beat. She stared at Kaiku, not daring to believe.

'A small thing,' Kaiku said, 'Some kind of process that was not working as it should. I made it work.' Her face saddened a little. 'There has been too much death in this world. I would take this one chance to bring life. It is all I can do.'

When Asara still appeared stunned, Kaiku sobbed a laugh and wiped her eyes. 'Do not just sit there gaping. You are fertile. Go back to your husband.'

Asara exhaled a shuddering breath, and her eyes filled and spilled over. 'Promise me,' she whispered. 'Promise me you will never tell anyone of this. Of what you have done.'

'You have my promise.'

'I will never forget this, Kaiku,' Asara said tremulously. 'In all the emptiness of this world, you will always have me, for what that is worth to you.'

'It is worth much,' Kaiku said, then reached over and stroked her cheek, wiping a tear across her skin. 'I have never seen you cry,' she said thoughtfully.

Asara caught her hand and held it against her cheek, her eyes fluttering closed. Then she got to her feet and went to the door. She slid it open, looked back, and was gone, closing the door behind her.

An hour later, she had stolen a horse and was riding east, to the Tchamil Mountains and the desert beyond.

TWENTY-TWO

The gate of the Imperial Keep stood open during the day to allow in and out the traffic necessary to keep such a vast building running. Carts of food, heavily guarded against the starving masses outside, rattled in and returned empty. Others came with jars of wine and spices, vats of cleaning fluid, bolts of cloth; and not a few of them with unconscious men, women and children concealed inside, slender vagrants from the Poor Quarter to be delivered for the Weavers' delectation.

There were Blackguard and a pair of Weavers at the gate, as always. They watched over the traffic, the Blackguard checking permits, the Weavers looking for any more subtle dangers: concealed bombs and the like. They stood hunched on either side of the wide entranceway like ragged gargoyles, immobile as they went about their invisible task.

Inside his carriage, the physician Ukida fidgeted nervously as they approached the gate.

'They have removed the blessing on the arch,' Mishani commented, staring out of the window. The arc of gold above the gate had indeed been smoothed clean.

Ukida made a vaguely questioning noise out of politeness; he was not listening to her, obsessed as he was with his own fear. Mishani looked away from the window and over at him.

'You will give us away, Master Ukida, if you do not control yourself,' she said sternly.

That stung him, and he made an effort at composing his demeanour, which made his state more obvious rather than less. He wished he had never taken the letter from Mishani in the first place. He should have just refused her. What could she have done? Taken him to face Imperial justice? Ha! There was no empire, and certainly no justice, and she would be arrested herself if she tried. Why had he not thought of that before, instead of clinging to his old notions of honour and ties of allegiance? If he had done so, his Mistress Muraki might not have commanded him to set up this deception, and he might not be in great peril of losing his life.

Hindsight was a cruel thing, and it crowed and gloated at him now as they drew up to the gate and one of the Blackguard approached the door of the carriage.

'Master Ukida,' he said in acknowledgement. He was a good-looking young man, wearing the dark bandana and leather armour that was the uniform of the Blackguard. 'Who is this?' he asked, his eyes shifting to Mishani, who sat meekly in the back of the carriage.

Ukida glanced nervously over the Blackguard's shoulder to the Weaver there, whose coral Mask was turned towards them.

'An assistant,' he said, brandishing a sealed roll of paper which he handed to the guard. 'Just temporary, you understand. Mistress Muraki is ill, something quite unusual, and has need of this one's special knowledge of such conditions.'

Mishani met the Blackguard's inquiring gaze calmly.

'May I?' he asked, indicating the seal. Ukida motioned hastily for him to do so. He broke it open and began to read.

Mishani waited, her anxiety carefully internalised. Ukida was plainly jittery. She could only hope that the guard would not think matters suspicious enough to act upon: to call the Weaver, maybe, or to detain them while he checked the validity of the permit he held. It was written and signed and sealed by Muraki tu Koli herself, granting entrance to the Keep for Ukida's new assistant.

'Mistress Muraki is not too ill to write, I see,' the Blackguard said. A taut beat of silence passed as he looked from Ukida to Mishani. 'That is good news,' he finished, and the tension slackened. He handed the permit back to Ukida and made a small bow to them both. 'Master Ukida. Mistress Soa. Please go on in.'

Ukida was perhaps a little gushing in his thanks, but the Blackguard was not paying attention now. He waved their driver on and was already heading toward the next cart in line.

Mishani allowed herself a moment of relief as they passed across the courtyard. That was one obstacle down. Now she had to contend with the possibility of being recognised, and the certainty of meeting another Weaver before she could get to her mother. If Shintu smiled on them, they might just make it through with her mother's permit. If not . . .

She looked out of the window. The courtyard was busy as always: men and women hurried to and fro; manxthwa lowed and nuzzled one another; arguments and exchanges went on at the feet of the double row of obelisks that led from the gate to the Keep. At least here it was not as downtrodden and dreary as the rest of the city, though there was something of a fierce industry in the manner of the people who came and went, as if they were eager to be done with their task so that they might get away. In the gloom of the overhanging miasma, the golden, sculptured slope of the south wall towered above them, intimidating in scale. They passed down a gentle ramp into a wide bay swarming with attendants, and there they disembarked and went through a guarded doorway reserved for nobles and important retainers which circumvented the subterranean servants' quarters. The guard barely glanced at them.

They ascended a set of stairs and entered the corridors of the Keep proper, a multitude of elegant *lach* passageways and many rooms, from huge and grandiose halls and galleries to tiny and exquisite chambers. Ukida led and Mishani followed, adopting an attitude appropriate to her rank as a physician's assistant. She felt curiously buoyant despite her fear, in a literal sense as well as an emotional one. She had been forced to alter her appearance beyond wearing the correct dress to make herself convincing in her role. She had cut her hair.

She had thought it would be much more of a wrench than it turned out to be. Her hair had been long since she was an infant, and ankle-length since adolescence. It was the feature she was most proud of. It lent her gravitas, for its sheer impracticality bespoke a noble existence, and she had thought it as permanent as her small nose or her thin eyebrows. But nobody would believe a physician's assistant would have hair so long: for one not born to nobility, it was immodest.

And so it became an impediment to her seeing her mother, and in such a light expendable. Mishani was always deeply pragmatic and little given to sentiment. Though she barely recognised herself in the mirror now, she knew that to be a good thing. With her hair worn up, her whole aspect was changed, and at a glance she seemed a completely different person. Some artfully applied make-up, shifting the emphasis of her eyes and cheeks and mouth, completed the deception.

We all wear our masks, she had thought to herself as she had put on the final touches.

She had not realised the weight of her hair till now, and the sense that came from her neck and scalp that there was something amiss was fractionally irritating. She wondered if she would get used to it, in time. It was shoulder-length when worn straight, but it was too similar to her old style that way, so she had arranged it with pins and combs so that it piled up and around her head in a style associated with educated women of low birth.

There would not be many in the vastness of the Keep that would know who she was, even without the changes she had wreaked upon herself. Still, as they neared the Imperial chambers, there would be more and more retainers of Blood Koli, and the danger would increase.

But first, they had to face the Weaver. She could only hope that her mother's plan would work.

Mishani had to chide Ukida for hurrying several times as they made their way through the corridors. He was sweating and plainly agitated, and Mishani cursed his inability to conceal his terror. It did not take a Weaver to know that something was wrong; if anyone asked, she had advised him to put it down to his anxiety at Muraki's condition. Ukida had assured her that her mother had feigned illness these past few days, and his own false diagnoses had confirmed it. Muraki had left strict instructions that she was not to be disturbed today by anyone but Ukida and the assistant he would bring. The retainers and the Weavers had been informed, so there would be no surprise at Mishani's arrival.

And yet it would take only the smallest thing to go wrong, and disaster would befall them. It was not only Mishani's life and Ukida's that were at stake here. Mishani knew far too much about the plans and dealings of the Libera Dramach and the high families in the south, and if she were caught those secrets would be ripped from her mind by a Weaver. What she was doing was selfish and irresponsible, but she did not care. She was going to see her mother. Whatever the cost.

They made their way up several sets of stairs, taking less travelled routes whenever they could. Once Mishani had to grab Ukida's arm and feign interest in an ornamental vase that was set in an alcove, so as to avert her face from a woman she thought she recognised. But most of the servants here were those who came with the Keep when Blood Koli took it over, so they did not know her; and the corridors were quiet, for there were no nobles or their retinues to populate them. The Imperial Keep was all but empty of guests now, though Ukida spoke darkly of the upper levels where the Weavers lived.

'We are nearing the section where the Imperial chambers lie,' he muttered at one point. Shortly afterward, they saw a boy of fourteen harvests or so, who spotted them and ran away in the direction they were heading.

'I was afraid he would not be there,' Ukida said, taking

what solace he could. At least so far, the plan was working well.

They dawdled for a while, pretending to examine a tapestry but ready to move if anyone should come; then, when Ukida judged that enough time had passed, they continued down the corridor to where the Weaver would be.

The Imperial chambers were guarded much more strictly than the rest of the Keep. It was impossible to maintain maximum security in such a huge building, when the day-to-day running of the place required ingress and egress on such a scale. But the Keep was designed so that certain sections could only be accessed by a small number of entry points, and these were where the vigilance was greatest. Each entry to the Imperial chambers was watched over by a Weaver, and Weavers could steal the thoughts from a person's mind.

The corridor ended in a stout door. Before it stood a Weaver with a Mask of silver, fashioned in the countenance of a woman. Mishani sent silent thanks to the gods that it had not been Blood Koli's own Weaver; but then, why should it? Weavers did not belong to families any more.

Just as the Weaver came into view, the door behind him opened and Muraki tu Koli appeared, supported by the boy they had seen earlier. Ukida sped up and hurried towards her. Mishani hesitated a moment at the sight – *Mother!* – then followed him.

'Mistress! What are you doing out of bed?' he cried as he approached.

'Ukida,' she said in a voice barely above a whisper. 'I am so glad you are here. I felt ill . . . I had to take some air.'

'I have brought the assistant you asked for,' he motioned at Mishani, but Muraki did not even look at her. 'Come now, back to your bed. I will take you.'

Ignoring the Weaver, they headed past him and into the Imperial chambers.

'Wait,' rasped the voice behind the silver Mask. It was turned towards Mishani.

'What is it?' Ukida said, and by good fortune his fear made his words come out as authoritative snap. 'She has to rest; she should not have been wandering.'

'I do not know this one,' the Weaver said, meaning Mishani.

'I asked for her,' Muraki said. 'Let her pass.'

'A moment . . .' said the Weaver, and Mishani knew with a sinking feeling in the pit of her stomach what would come next.

She felt the Weaver's influence brush her mind, detestable tentacles slithering over her thoughts. She shuddered. He could not fail to see her as she really was, to dredge up memories of her life in Blood Koli. Frantically she tried to hide her past beneath a muddle of images, but the images that came to her were the junks in the harbour at Mataxa Bay, or pictures of Lucia and Kaiku and incidents that would only make her identity more obvious. She stared, transfixed, into the black slits of the silver Mask, the woman-face hiding its disfigured owner; heard the wheeze of his breath and was touched by the decay of his mind.

Then the sensation was gone. 'Enter,' the Weaver said, and Ukadi put his hands on her shoulders and led her away swiftly. The door closed behind them.

'Heart's blood . . .' she murmured to herself. 'He did not see . . . he did not see . . .'

She kept her head lowered as they turned a corner and went along a short way. Fortune was with them and they saw nobody. Ukadi held aside a curtain and ushered Muraki and Mishani through, and when he let it drop they were alone together.

The room was a small bedchamber, with only a single bed near to a window-arch that looked out past the arm of one of the great stone figures that lunged from the Keep's sloping walls. A veil had been hung across it, muting the already muted light. There was a table with a slender book on it, and two chests of drawers in a matched pair.

A difficult silence passed as mother and daughter looked upon each other for the first time in a decade. The resemblance between them was remarkable.

'You cut your hair,' Muraki whispered.

'I had to,' Mishani said. 'It matters nothing. I can grow it back.'

Muraki reached out and touched it carefully. 'It looks odd. But it suits you.'

Mishani smiled and turned her head away. 'I look like a peasant. I will be taking it down as soon as I possibly can.' Studying the veiled window-arch, she said: 'I read your books. All of them.'

'I knew you would,' her mother replied. 'I knew it.'

'The Weaver . . .' Mishani began, a question on her face.

'They are there to root out those who mean harm to the Imperial family. You, apparently, do not. Not even towards your father. They read no further into a person's thoughts than that. To do so would be . . . violation. It is dangerous. They have accidentally killed guests that way, or driven them mad, until Avun forbade it.' She glanced uneasily around the room. 'I would not have let you come if I had been able to leave myself. But I cannot leave. Your father sees to that.'

'I told you I would not take refusal,' Mishani said. 'I would have tried anyway, with or without your help. The risks are acceptable to me.'

She motioned to the bed, and they sat down on its edge next to each other.

'There are things I want to say to you,' Mishani replied. 'Things that must come from my lips, not from a coded poem. We are on two sides of a war now, Mother, and one side or the other must win eventually. Whichever of us is on the losing side will not survive, I think. We are both of us too involved.'

Muraki was silent, her hair hanging across her face. She had always hidden behind her hair: straight and centre-parted, it concealed her, leaving only a narrow gap for her eyes and nose and mouth.

'I have wanted to see you for so long,' Mishani said. 'I pictured throwing my arms around you, laughing with joy. But now that I am here, I find that it is as it always was. Why are we this way with each other?'

'It is our nature,' Muraki said quietly. 'And no amount of time can change that.'

'But I saw you in your writing, Mother,' Mishani said. 'I saw your heart in that. I know you feel as deeply as anyone, *deeper* than most. Deeper than Father.'

Muraki could not meet her gaze. 'My writing can express my soul better than my words or actions ever could,' she said. 'There is comfort there. I am not afraid there.'

'I *know* that, Mother,' Mishani said, laying a hand on Muraki's. It was clammy and cold. Startled, Muraki looked at her daughter's hand as if it were something that might bite her. Mishani did not remove it. 'I know now. There are many things I did not see before. Like the code in your poems, they took me too long to understand.'

The words came quickly from them both: there was a sense of haste in their meeting, the knowledge that the danger was far from past. They could not waste time when it was so short and precious. Neither of them had ever spoken this directly to the other before.

'I am older now than then, and much has passed in between,' Mishani said. 'When I was young, I thought you weak and distant. You were a shadow of a woman in comparison to my father. I did not even think of you when I went to Axekami to join him at the courts. It did not occur to me that you would care.' She met her mother's eyes briefly, before Muraki became uncomfortable and broke the contact. 'I was a callous child. You deserved better.'

'No,' said Muraki. 'How could you have realised that? Do we not judge everyone by how they act towards us? You cannot be blamed for my failings, daughter. If you thought me aloof, it was because I did not hold you as a child, because I did not touch you or speak with you. If you thought me weak, it was because I did not make myself heard. There is . . . passion in my imagination, passion in my books . . . but there I can shape the world as I will it. The world outside . . . is stultifying, and awkward, and I am shamed when I speak and afraid of people . . . I am embarrassed by attention . . .' Realising that she had trailed into a mumble, she recovered herself. 'These are my failings. They have been with me since I was a child, since I can remember. It is not what I want for myself – that is in my books – but it is how I am.'

Mishani squeezed her hand gently. 'But every book you have written has made me feel more that I have wronged you. So I came to you now to make amends. To ask you to forgive me. And to tell you that I am proud of you, Mother.'

Muraki's expression was one of incomprehension.

'Do you not see what you have done?' Mishani said. 'You dared to make yourself a spy for us, you risked yourself by sending Chien to protect me all those years ago.' Muraki put her hand to her mouth at this. 'Yes, I surmised that much before he died. Father's men got to him. But in the end, if not for him, if not for *you*, thousands of lives would have been lost in the Xarana Fault. Things could have turned out very differently. In your quiet way you have contributed more than we could ever ask.' She took her hand away. 'And yet still we remain in two different worlds, and soon one of them will end. That is why I am here, that is why I risk all this. There are some things that must be done, at any cost. My spirit could not rest if either of us died and . . . you did not know.'

'I had not realised my child could be so reckless,' Muraki whispered, but a smile touched the edge of her lips.

'It is a new experience for me too,' Mishani grinned. She felt as if a heavy stone had been lifted from her chest. Even if she was caught now, it did not matter so much. It was done, and could not be undone. 'Perhaps nature *can* change with time.'

'Perhaps,' said Muraki, then got up and went to the window-arch. She brushed aside the veil and looked out.

'Daughter, I love you,' she said, her back to Mishani. 'I always have. Never doubt that, though I may not show it, though we may never have the opportunity to speak again. I am glad you came so I could tell you. We should not have left these matters so late.'

Mishani felt tears start to her eyes. She knew how much it had cost her mother to say those words, and to hear them for the first time in her life was ecstasy.

'Now listen to me,' she said, turning away from the window-arch and letting the veil drop. 'I have much to tell.'

And she spoke then of Avun's plans and schemes, of hints he had given and the intentions that he had expressed. She told of his failed plot to unseat Kakre, of the imminent creation of more feya-kori; of the true numbers of the Aberrants and the dire situation that the Weavers were in, how they faced starvation unless they could take the Prefectures by the next harvest. Mishani did not interrupt, filing every word in her memory, and as her mother went on she realised that her visit could turn out to be far more valuable than even she might have guessed: for this was information only days old, reaching her without the delay of months that was necessary in the publication of a book. She was staggered how much her mother knew. Avun discussed everything with her, it seemed, and the little snippets she had managed to secrete in her stories were only those few long-term events that she thought might still be relevant by the time they reached the hands of those she meant it for. In five minutes Muraki told her more than the entire spy network and the Sisterhood put together had managed to learn in four years.

'Lord Protector!' Ukadi suddenly cried from outside the doorway, and mother and daughter froze. Mishani went numb with the force of the sadness that struck her. Being discovered by her father was one thing, with all the lives that would be cost by her foolishness in coming here; but what was worse at this moment was the knowledge that now she and her mother had to part, that they would likely never meet again, that these precious handful of minutes out of ten years were all they would ever have.

'Go!' Muraki hissed, and Mishani hesitated, taking her mother's hands, gripping them. 'Go!' she urged again, terror in her eyes.

'I heard she was walking about,' said Avun. 'I must see her!'

'She is being attended by my assistant,' Ukadi was saying beyond the curtain. 'Please, it would be best if you . . .'

Mishani leaned forward quickly, kissed Muraki on the cheek, and whispered in her ear: 'You were the strongest of us all, Mother. My heart will always be with you.'

Then she got up and swept towards the doorway, just as Avun came through the curtain. Mishani made a deep bow, still walking, and passed by her startled father with her head down as he held the curtain aside for her. Due to the difference in height, he only saw the back of her head. It was an incredibly rude thing to do, and Avun's shock prevented him from reacting for a moment; then, as he opened his mouth to call her back, Muraki cried: 'Avun! Avun! Come here!'

The volume of his wife's voice, which was never more than a whisper, made him forget the servant immediately and hurry into the room, where Muraki embraced him and kissed him with an affection he had not witnessed in years, and she did not let him go. She drew him down onto the bed, and there she made love to him for the first time in longer than he cared to remember.

So surprised and pleased was he that he entirely forgot about the physician's assistant until long after she had left the Imperial Keep; and yet later he found he could not shake the insidious feeling that, even though he had not seen her face, he knew her from somewhere. But he could never recall quite where.

TWENTY-THREE

Word from Mishani reached Araka Jo a day later, via a Sister who operated secretly out of Maza. She was an important relay for the spies in Axekami, and Mishani went straight to her after leaving the capital. Her news caused great commotion. Nobody had known where Mishani had gone, only that she had departed Araka Jo some time before, saying that she was attending to business of her own. When the upper echelons of the Libera Dramach learned what she had done, she was denounced as being reprehensible for placing them all at such risk; but it was Cailin who defended her, who pointed out that great risk had brought great reward, and the information she had given them was priceless.

A meeting was called immediately, and plans were put forward, many of which had been fermenting over the previous weeks and had been discussed in other meetings beforehand. Finally consensus was reached. There was no more room for delays. The time for action had come.

It was the morning after that meeting when Kaiku made her way down the trail to the south of Araka Jo, and found the Tkiurathi village in a state of busy preparation. They had conducted their own meeting last night, in the wake of the one with the Libera Dramach. Each individual had been asked to make their own choice as to whether they would follow the course suggested by the council. Kaiku had come to find the results of that.

She wandered through the Tkiurathi village, exchanging gestured greetings with a few men and women that she recognised. It was not hard to guess how the decision had gone. Blades were being sharpened, rifles cleaned, supplies made ready. They were packing for a journey.

There was a simplicity to this place that Kaiku liked: the smell of the cookfires, the *repka* yurts which looked like huge three-armed starfish lying between the trees, the sense of ease in the interaction of the tattooed folk. They seemed so untroubled in their daily lives, even now, even knowing that they were heading into something that they might well not come back from. Laughter came easily to them when they were together. Some of them were breakfasting, taking from a communal pot, exchanging food from their plates. Even this small act of sharing made a difference, something so natural to them that they must have long ceased to think about it.

She remembered a conversation she had had with Tsata long ago, in which he said that the Saramyr way of life resulted directly from their development of cities and courts and all the things Kaiku associated with civilisation; Tkiurathi shunned all that. Now that she had seen them, the way they interacted as a group, she wondered whose philosophy was better in the end.

Kaiku asked after Tsata by making his name a question, and was directed towards a rough circle of Tkiurathi who sat talking and drinking from wooden cups shaped somewhat like pears or pinecones. There was a large bowl in the centre from which they took refills. Heth was there, too; he noticed her first, and hailed her by name. The circle broke to leave a space between Tsata and Heth, and she smiled her gratitude as she sat down and was immediately handed a cup by a woman she did not recognise. The woman took a new one and filled it for herself.

She managed a general greeting in Okhamban in response to the one she received, then took a sip of the liquid. It was warm, and spicy and fiery on her tongue.

'Daygreet. Have I interrupted?' she asked Tsata, but her presence had cause barely a lull in the conversation, and they were already back to their discussion.

'We are working out final details of our departure,' Tsata said. 'It is not anything of great importance.'

'They agreed, then?'

'Without exception,' Heth said on her other side.

'There was little doubt they would. It is a matter of *pash*,' Tsata explained.

'Gods, it seems such a short time since we came back,' Kaiku mused, then she glanced at Heth. 'How are you?'

'I grieve,' he said. 'But Peithre has been returned to her people. I am thankful for that.'

Kaiku nodded, closing her eyes. In the Forest of Xu, Heth had refused to relinquish Peithre's body until he had brought her back to the village. In the end, he and Tsata had gone separately from the others, for her corpse, even wrapped as it was, had begun to reek of decay. But still Heth would not bury her or burn her. Kaiku did not know what the rites of honouring the dead were in Tkiurathi culture, but she was sure that there had been something beyond mere companionship between Heth and Peithre.

'Our course is set, then,' she said. 'One way or another, I think we come to the last movement of our war.'

The meeting of the day before had been coordinated, via the Sisters, with Barak Reki tu Tanatsua and several other desert Baraks in Izanzai. Mishani's information had been shared among all, though its source had been kept carefully secret for fear of compromising Muraki. Its most pertinent and pressing aspect was this: that the Weavers planned a massive surprise assault upon Saraku in the near future. Saraku, the centre of debate and administration, formed the heart of the Empire's resistance as well as being where most of the nobles and high families resided. If Saraku were to fall then the Weavers would have an all but unassailable foothold deep behind the frontline. From there, they could strike at Machita or Araka Jo, or demolish the marshland cities to the east. Once the Prefectures were secured, they could overwhelm Tchom Rin at their leisure.

But there was hope as well. For if the Weavers could be kept out of the Prefectures until the harvest could be gathered, then the tide might turn.

'But we will not be able to keep them out,' Cailin had said. 'Not even with the information we have. We may be able to turn back the assault on Saraku, but they will strike at us again elsewhere before the summer. Unless they are forced to devote some of their forces to defending their territories. We must prove to them that nowhere is safe. We must attack Adderach.'

Cailin had been the loudest voice advocating an attack on Adderach since Kaiku's visit to Axekami, but now she found she had support at last. Lucia's return had given them hope, a belief that they could face down the previously invincible feya-kori. And with their morale so restored, they were a little more inclined to consider the prospect, however uncertain or unlikely, of ending the war in one strike. They knew now that the Weavers' forces did not number as many as they had believed, and that the Aberrants and Nexuses were disastrously overstretched: the Weavers were using them as an attacking force and relying primarily on the Blackguard to keep order in the cities. It was entirely possible that Adderach would only be lightly defended, for it sat deep in enemy territory and was undoubtedly protected by the Weavers' shields of misdirection. The Weavers had consistently shown themselves to be inept at tactical thinking, and Adderach was one place they would certainly not have let the Lord Protector look after. Cailin had cleverly slanted her pitch so that the chance to get at the Weavers' witchstones – which was her primary concern – was barely mentioned. Whether they were successful in that or not, the idea of destroying their enemy's most prized fortress was too tempting to pass up. And there was an even sweeter aspect to the plan for the high families of the western Empire. None of their troops would be going.

Thus the decision was made and agreed: a three-pointed

attack upon the Weavers. The forces of the Libera Dramach and the western Empire would deal with the Saraku assault. Meanwhile, the warriors of Tchom Rin and the Tkiurathi, along with a number of Sisters, would make their way to Adderach. The desert folk would have the most arduous task: a trek along the mountains lengthwise to reach Adderach from the south. The Tkiurathi and Sisters would go by sea, passing through enemy-held waters to land north of Mount Aon. If all went well, the Weavers would be looking south, to the army of desert warriors; and they would not see the attack from the north until it was too late.

But first there was the problem of getting the ships. Lalyara, to the west, was the only feasible option if they wanted to get to Adderach at roughly the same time as the desert folk. There were ships there enough for the Tkiurathi. But a week ago, the port had been blockaded by Weaver vessels. They made no move to attack, only to prevent anything entering or leaving. The Libera Dramach had guessed what the Weavers were up to even before Mishani confirmed it.

The Weavers' next target was Lalyara. And if they got there before the Tkiurathi did, then half of the assault on Adderach had failed before it had begun.

Later, Kaiku and Tsata walked together in the forest. Kaiku needed some activity to keep her mind off their imminent departure. She knew that time was short, and she was chafing to be away; but organising supplies and equipment to send nearly a thousand men and women to war was not an easy matter, and would take more than a few hours.

It was bright and still and cool, and their feet crunched on twigs as they wandered. They talked idly about things of little importance. Kaiku was trying not to think about the possible consequences of making Asara capable of breeding, and she had fretted about Lucia for so long that she was getting tired of her own voice. They did touch on her feelings about

Mishani's disappearance and her subsequent revelations, but Kaiku was not overly concerned about her friend. Since she had not known Mishani was in danger until she was out of it, she experienced nothing more than a vague sense of relief. It certainly went against Mishani's character to do something like that, but the fact that Kaiku had not seen it coming only served to remind her how little contact she had had with her friend these past few years, and that saddened her.

Kaiku was acutely aware that this was the first time that she and Tsata had been together alone since their kiss in the Forest of Xu. After that, the death of Phaeca and Peithre and the terrible events surrounding them had made any amorous notions seem wan and forceless amid all the grief. But there was something in Tsata's manner today, some coiled tension, that expressed itself in quick glances and half-taken breaths to start sentences that never came. There was an urgency in the air, a sense that this might be the last few moments of peace before the storm broke and swallowed them all, and there were things that had to be said between them that would not wait.

Eventually they found a spot where the land humped up and met the lake shore, dropping a dozen rocky feet to the water, which glittered in the sharp winter light. Distant junks cut slowly towards the horizon, and hookbeaks hovered on the thermals, questing for fish. Kaiku and Tsata sat side by side on a fallen tree that had been partially claimed by moss, and beneath the gently waving leaves of the evergreens they came to the moment they had been putting off.

Tsata looked at his hands, caught in an agony of indecision that was so plain that Kaiku had to laugh a little. It broke the tension: he smiled in answer.

'Your kind are never good at hiding your feelings,' Kaiku said. 'Say it, then.'

'I am afraid to,' he replied, then looked up at her uncertainly as if to gauge her reaction to this. 'I fear I still do not know your ways, and you Saramyr place such store by etiquette.'

'Most of us do. I seem to find it less important than they. Mishani is always telling me how uncultured I am.' She looked at him with tenderness in her eyes, both wanting and not wanting to hear what he would say. 'Honesty is better.'

'But that is one of the things I cannot understand about your people. Though you say you want honesty, you seldom do. You are so in love with evasions that honesty makes you uncomfortable.'

'Stop hedging, Tsata,' she said, not unkindly. 'It does not suit you.'

Eventually he shook his head, as if ridding himself of some annoyance, and clasped his hands together. Kaiku noticed how the pale green tendrils of tattoo that ran along his fingers meshed beautifully when he did so.

'I cannot do this your way,' he said. 'If this were—'

Kaiku ran out of patience. 'Tsata, do you want me or not?'

The bluntness of this surprised even him. He turned towards her, and in the instant before he spoke she fixed the image of him there, preserving the final moments of flux before certainty solidified their relationship one way or another. This picture she would keep in her mind, as insurance against his reply.

But the reply, when it came, was: 'Yes.'

A breath passed.

'Yet it is not that simple for you,' he continued. 'Is it?'

Kaiku's head bowed a little, her hair hanging down across the left side of her face, screening her from him. 'Simplicity is something that my people do not do well,' she said.

She felt betrayed by herself, suddenly angry. Gods, had she not waited for this moment for long enough? She knew how she felt about him. She had known it, without admitting it to herself, since those weeks they had spent together in the Xarana Fault four years ago, hunting Aberrants and spying on the Weavers. It had not been a sudden thing, but something so gradual that she had trouble identifying it. In the time he had been away across the sea, she had almost managed to dismiss it as a fancy. Almost. Since he had come back, since that kiss in the forest, she knew it for what it was. Yet in some matters he was so hard to read, and she could never be certain if that feeling was reciprocated. Not until now.

But it was nothing like she had imagined. Instead of a flood of joy, relief, *release*, she felt only an awful weariness, a sour negation of possibilities. Now she knew beyond doubt that he wanted her, she came up against all the barriers that she had carefully constructed in her heart over the years, shoring them up each time she had been wounded. She found that she had built them so well that they would not come down easily.

'Tsata, I am sorry,' she said. 'You deserve a better response than this.'

He looked down at his hands again. She straightened, brushed her hair back behind her ear and turned to him, taking one hand and clasping it in both of hers. She tried to find words that would not be mawkish or hurtful, but she had never been good at expressing herself in this way.

'I want you also, Tsata,' she said. 'I *do*. That is small comfort to you now, I think, but I want you to know it. Do not doubt that, whatever else.' She was lost again for a moment, before beginning on a new tack. 'Since the beginning, everything I thought good and stable has collapsed. My family, my friends, my . . . relationships. The Sisterhood has failed me, too. Perhaps even the Libera Dramach cannot be trusted now; I cannot let myself be sure.' She gripped his hand harder, willing him to understand. 'I was beginning to feel love for Tane when he was taken from me; I was betrayed by Saran – by *Asara* – just as I had allowed myself to believe that there could be something between us. There were men in between, whom I did not love so fiercely, but they, too, ended in betrayal or disappointment.'

He had raised his head now, and was looking at her.

'Each time I let something or someone close to my heart I am left with a new scar,' she said, a pleading note in her tone, seeking to make him forgive her. 'I want to be alone, to need nobody; and yet I see Asara, and what that has made of her, and I know that is no way to go either. But I cannot bear another wound, Tsata. I cannot bear to let myself love you, and then have you killed in the conflict to come, or to return to your homeland and leave me, or to find another woman. Your people do not believe in exclusive pair-bonding.'

'No,' he murmured. 'But you do. And for me, that would be enough.'

She frowned. 'What do you mean by that?'

'It is hardly unheard of,' Tsata said. 'My people have lived near Saramyr settlements for a thousand years. Tkiurathi have paired monogamously with Saramyr before. Some have even married. It is a matter of personal choice, of redefining the *pash*.'

'And you would do that for me?'

'I would,' he said. He stared out across the lake. 'I had been . . . unsure for a long time. I would have spoken of these feelings then, even when I did not know if I wished to do anything about them. But that is our way, and it is not yours. I knew it would cause you confusion and in all probability would have driven you away, so I stayed silent. I did not know if we could ever be together; I thought our cultures too fundamentally different. But then, in the forest, when I saw you defend us against the soldier, when you refused to leave Peithre fallen . . .' he trailed away, and then turned and looked back at her. 'That was when I knew.'

And now she felt it, like a physical pressure spreading outward from her chest, a warm swell that filled her. It struck her so suddenly that she had to exhale, a short huff of air that turned into an involuntary smile. But it lasted only a moment, for she forced it down again, knowing what it meant, knowing what it would lead to.

But do I have a choice? she thought. *If I turn this man away, this man whom I know I can trust more than anyone not to deceive me, how will the rest of my life be?*

She bit the inside of her lip gently and closed her eyes. Could she live that way, ever guarded, secure and numb? Or was that the beginning of a downward slope from which there was no return? If she came through this war she faced a long, long span of years. Not even the Sisters knew how long. Maybe forever.

And if you let this man into your heart, could you stand to watch him age when you do not?

She would not face that question now. It had occurred to her before in a more general sense, but it was too vast to deal with. What was the alternative? Again, there could be only one: to shut herself off, to be alone forever, barriered against the world. Cloistered, with the Red Order the only safe company, who would be similarly ageless. That was no option, either. All ways led to pain in the end; it was only a question of time.

'Time,' she murmured softly, so quietly that Tsata barely heard it. Puzzlement showed on his face. 'Give me time . . . to think about this.'

He was about to speak again, but he thought better of it. Instead, he withdrew his hand and got to his feet, and she rose with him. They stood together, caught in an instant of prolonged parting and neither wanting to leave it that way; then Kaiku kissed him swiftly on the lips and withdrew into the forest, leaving him behind. She did not look back. She did not want him to see the tears gathering in her eyes.

The Tkiurathi travelled fast and light. By evening they had stripped their village of everything they needed for their journey to Lalyara. Cailin had arranged for the ships at their destination to be stocked with the provisions necessary for what would come afterward. In less than a day, the village was hollow and empty, the fires doused and the *repka* tied closed, awaiting their return. They were gathering in a valley north of the temple complex, ready to depart at dusk. Dozens of Sisters would be travelling with them, including Cailin herself. Kaiku was going too.

After seeing Tsata she spent the rest of the day hurrying around her house, finishing last-minute preparations and ensuring all was in order. She did not know whether Mishani would return soon or not, so she had to prepare the place for a possible period of vacancy. She cleaned and tidied, packed and repacked, prayed briefly at the house shrine, prepared food and ate it in quick, nervous bites. In truth, she needed to be doing something to stop her thinking. Her course was chosen now. She would not turn from it. She was heading to Adderach, the birthplace of the Weavers. Her oath to Ocha, taken long ago, demanded that she do so. Everything else – *everything* – could wait. Her business was with the Weavers, and if there was any chance of ruining them, of breaking their power, then she had to take that. Her family's spirits would not forgive her otherwise.

In a fit of bitterness, she debated whether or not to take the dress of the Red Order with her or just burn it there and then. But when it came to the choice, she was reluctant to destroy it. Though it represented an allegiance she no longer felt, she could not deny the sense of authority and power it conferred on her, and she would need all the courage she could get in Adderach. In the whole length of the war, she had never been into battle without it.

Very well, then, she thought. *I will wear it again. Until the Weavers are gone.*

The last thing to take was the Mask from the chest where it lay. She snatched it up in one swift, disgusted motion and stuffed it in her backpack. Then she shut the pack and secured it.

She was about to depart when she heard a chime outside, and went to open the door. It was Lucia, with two Sisters behind her as guards.

'May I come inside?' Lucia asked. Kaiku invited her, waited to see if the Sisters intended on coming also, and when they did not, she slid the door shut. The room was all but bare, the minimal furniture having been put away. Lucia crossed the floor, stood with her back to Kaiku for a moment, and then turned around decisively.

'You are leaving?' she asked. 'Now?'

'I was about to,' Kaiku said.

'I only heard about it a short while ago,' Lucia said.

'You were at the meeting,' Kaiku said. 'You knew the Tkiurathi were going.'

'I did not know *you* were going,' Lucia replied. 'Were you intending to leave without telling me?'

Kaiku studied her. Lucia's light blonde hair was growing out a little, after years of her keeping it boyishly short. Kaiku wondered what this meant, or if it meant anything at all, or if anything meant anything any more.

'I did not think you would be interested,' Kaiku said truthfully, and was surprised at how cruel it sounded.

The look on Lucia's face showed plainly how deep she felt the barb. 'That is unfair, Kaiku.'

'Is it? You have not seemed to want to know me since your visit to the Xhiang Xhi. What had I done to deserve such treatment?'

'You should know more than anyone that I have . . . *matters* to deal with,' Lucia replied. 'I would expect a little more latitude.'

Kaiku was bewildered by her tone: she sounded nothing like the Lucia she knew. She was much more strident.

'Forgive me, then,' said Kaiku, tossing her a casual apology that had no weight to it. 'But how am I meant to know when you will not talk to me? Before we entered the forest, you were at least *you*, even when you were not lucid. But since then you have changed. I am not sure who you are or what you want now.' Her voice softened as she realised she was being harsh; the emotional rigors of these last days and her nervousness at the prospect of leaving had made her callous. 'What happened to you in there?'

It was the concern in the question that caused Lucia to crumble. Abruptly she seemed to shed her thorny exterior and become once again the Lucia of old. She told Kaiku of what the spirit had said to her, of the true purpose of the Weavers and the veil of ascendancy. But she made no mention of the price that the spirits' aid would entail.

Kaiku listened. It all seemed curiously unimportant to her, and revelations that should have shocked her barely penetrated. The scale was too large: it did not interfere or impact upon her sworn purpose. But Lucia's evasions were obvious, and when she was done, Kaiku said: 'There is something else you are not telling me.'

'That is between myself and the Xhiang Xhi,' Lucia replied.

That brought them to an impasse for a time.

'I am sorry for being rude,' Kaiku said eventually, with sincerity this time. 'You are under a great deal of strain, and you cannot or will not share the burden. It was ungracious of me to leave without saying farewell.'

'Let us forget all this,' said Lucia. 'I want you to know that I did not mean to treat you badly these last few days, and that all I said to you in the emyrynn village still holds true. You have always cared for me, and I for you. I do not wish our last goodbye to be tainted with rancour.'

'What makes you think it is our last?' Kaiku asked. The question was phrased with enforced lightness, to counter the thrill of dread at Lucia's words.

Lucia did not answer: instead she approached Kaiku and embraced her gently. It was worse than any reply she could have given.

'Lucia, what is it?' Kaiku whispered, suddenly terrified. 'What do you know that you are not telling me?'

Lucia released her, and her pale blue eyes were full of sorrow and pity.

'Goodbye,' she whispered, and then she walked away.

Kaiku wanted to call after her, to demand an answer to her question, but she could not think of a single thing to say that might change Lucia's mind. Some part of her did not want to rupture the purity of the moment with anger and shrill entreatments. She felt crushed by the pressure of something invisible and inevitable that she did not understand, and by the time she had recovered herself the door had slid shut and Lucia was gone.

Kaiku stood in the emptiness of the house for a time. It felt like a tomb now, and she could not bear to be here. She snatched up her pack and shouldered it, and she left her house to head to the valley where the Tkiurathi were meeting.

As she walked away up the dirt street, she was suddenly conscious that it might be the final time she ever saw the place. She did not look back.

TWENTY-FOUR

The journey from Araka Jo – around the north edge of Lake Xemit and west, skirting the south of the Forest of Xu – was made with all haste, but even with Mishani's information they had no certain date when Lalyara would be attacked. It was clear by their actions that the Weavers intended to destroy the fleet trapped in the harbour. The Tkiurathi hoped to get there in time to fight their way through the barricade of Weaver ships and away. Then warning reached them several days from their destination that the Weaver force had been sighted, and was moving quickly towards Lalyara. The rest of the journey was taken at a punishing pace; but the Tkiurathi were extraordinarily fit, hardened by the dangers of their homeland, and they covered ground fast when they needed to. They reached Lalyara a mere hour before the fog began to descend, and preparations commenced immediately to launch the vessels waiting in dock.

But quick as they were, they were not quick enough.

Explosions. The creak of timber and the turbulent slap of water against the stone of the dock. Men and women calling to each other, hurrying past Kaiku; the sense of huge movement as one of the enormous ships pulled away from its pier to her right, the deep splash as the discarded gangplank plunged into the sea. An uneven pattern of gunfire speckling the distance. Salt in the air, cold spray on her face, the scent of burning and blood and everywhere the terrible, choking fog.

The feya-kori had arrived.

The docks were in chaos. Sailors clambered along the

shadowy rigging of their vessels, obeying hollered instructions. The junks were looming silhouettes in the haze. Tkiurathi clattered up gangplanks, cramming onto the decks of the ships while dockhands hacked hawsers free and the coastal wind caught rising sails to belly them outwards. Kaiku steadied herself against the buffeting flow of men and women and looked to the north with red eyes, penetrating the murk.

There they were, on the crest of a distant slope, rising over the northern wall of the city with all the inexorability of a tidal wave. Two of them, the same two that had demolished Juraka and Zila, their forms black, seething tangles of Weave-threads. Their drear moans drifted across the rooftops as they pounded the wall to rubble. And though she could not see, she knew that the Aberrants were swarming in.

Something rushed overhead and she flinched; it hit a warehouse a few streets away and obliterated one of its walls. Out to sea she could hear the sounds of fire-cannon. The coastal batteries were shelling blind, foiled by the feya-kori's miasma. Weaver ships had drawn in closer now, no longer content to be a blockade and with little fear of the guns; their Weavers were their eyes, and they rained destruction on the city, using a new kind of artillery that was heavier and more explosive than the kind the Empire had used in years past.

But less than half the junks had set out yet, and there were still many to go.

Kaiku sensed the incoming shellshot from a fire-cannon, instinctively calculated its trajectory and realised that it would hit square on the docks. She was about to deal with it when one of the other Sisters got there first: its momentum dissipated in mid-air and it dropped into the waves.

Another one, and another: two of them coming in at once. She took one out in the same way as her companion had, careful not to break the shell and scatter the jelly within, which would ignite on contact with air. The second one was similarly repulsed.

Two more; and two more on top of that. The Weaver ships had got their range now.

Three of the missiles dropped harmlessly; the fourth did not. In haste, one of the Sisters braked it as it looped over a ship that was almost ready to set sail. It dipped and smashed into the mast, blowing it to splinters. Sailors and Tkiurathi on the deck fell clutching their faces and bodies as they were pierced by shards of burning hardwood; the mast collapsed in a slow topple, trailing smoke from its blazing sails. The men beneath did not have space or time to get out of its way. The ship descended into confusion: some evacuated, some fought to help the wounded, and meanwhile more artillery was coming in, whispering through the fog with deadly speed.

((This cannot stand)) said Cailin to Kaiku privately. *((The Aberrants are approaching fast. We cannot defend against both them and the cannons))*

((Then we should get out there and give those ships something else to deal with)) Kaiku thought fiercely, the message expressed in a blaze of images: burning ships, dying men, blistering hands and melting Masks.

((Agreed, I want you on the next ship. The first of our vessels are already beginning to engage the enemy on the sea))

Kaiku sent her a defiant jumble of emotions in response, indicating that she would go when she was gods-damned ready and that she would not be ordered by Cailin. But in her heart, she would be glad to get off the dock where she was little use for anything but intercepting the enemy's missiles. Defence was not her style.

((Then I am asking *you, Kaiku))* Cailin said irascibly. *((Will you take the next ship?))*

((I will)) she said, because at that moment she spotted Tsata racing up a jetty, and her last reason for staying was removed.

She pushed her way through to the ship that Tsata had boarded. To the north, the feya-kori were engaged in their usual mindless destruction of anything and everything around them, but they were cutting a very definite swathe towards the docks. Shellshot cut through the air overhead, but it was going long and none of the Sisters were interested in stopping it. It smashed into the domed roof of a temple and stove it in with a blaze of smoke and flame.

Another missile got through the Sisters' defences, this time because the sheer volume of artillery was too much for them. It hit the docks in the midst of a swarm of people, most of them Tkiurathi. The explosion ripped bodies apart, sending mutilated limbs skidding across the cracked flagstones, men clawing at their blinded eyes and women flailing on the ground, waving cauterised stumps of flesh that used to be arms and legs.

Kaiku squeezed her eyes shut for a moment, appalled, but she had no time to spend on horror or sympathy, and she pushed on through to the gangplank. Men stumbled past her, supporting the wounded from the burning ship. She smelt the reek of suffering, mixed with the vile, poisonous odour of the feya-kori's miasma, and she used it to fuel her hatred. Breaking free of the crowd, she slipped up the jetty and on to the junk.

There was little space to move on the deck. The sailors were shouting at the Tkiurathi to get below, but few of them obeyed. They were not seafarers, and they did not like the idea of being trapped in a box of wood which was in danger of sinking at any moment. She sought out Tsata, but it was hopeless amongst the mass of tattooed and camouflaged folk.

Other ships were being freed from their moorings up and down the dock now. The remaining craft were filling fast, and Kaiku guessed they would depart close together, for the sailors knew they could not afford to wait any more. The report of cannons bellowed through the air, seeming nearer now than before.

And then suddenly the docks were alive with gunfire as the soldiers of Lalyara opened up on the first of the Aberrants.

Sailors on board Kaiku's ship roared the order to cast off, and the sails unfurled along the mast as ropes pulled tight. Tkiurathi on board sought targets for their rifles as the Aberrants appeared.

Massive ghauregs led the charge, smashing into the defenders on the north side of the docks and throwing them aside like broken dolls. Shrillings tore in after them, warbling in their throats as they pounced here and there, taking down men and savaging them; and skrendel slipped between, biting and strangling. They overwhelmed the primary defences by sheer suicidal force. Even after four years, Saramyr soldiers found it hard to stand against an enemy that cared nothing for their own lives. Then the Tkiurathi on the ships opened up, and the predators were cut to pieces in a shredding hail of rifle balls. But the range was long, and some of them survived to engage the remainder of the soldiers. A dockside cathouse, empty now, took a direct hit from one of the Weaver cannons and vomited fiery rubble from its façade. Swords were drawn, rifles barked, and the soldiers fought as best they could, but they knew their cause was hopeless. They were giving their lives so that the ships could get away. They had been ordered to hold this spot and they would die doing so.

Now Kaiku could feel the slow, massive movement of the junk as it caught the wind and the last of its hawsers were cut free. She shoved through the crowd, her mind divided between the communication of the Sisters and the incoming missiles. She let her *kana* seek Tsata out, following the link between them, the bonds of emotion that existed in a palpable sense within the Weave.

She found him refilling the ignition powder in his rifle from a pouch, just as the pier began to slide away. Another boat to their right had launched ahead of them, a huge, swaying shadow in the murk as it gathered speed. Tsata did not see her as she approached; he was intent on priming and aiming again, picking off the Aberrants that were invading the docks.

One of the junks was not fast enough to escape the tide of teeth and claws, and the creatures swarmed up the gangplank onto the ship; but then it began to move, and the plank fell free, pitching the creatures into the sea. Those few on board were killed, but they took three times their number with them.

Kaiku frowned as she bent her concentration towards a fresh volley from the Weaver ships. There were fewer missiles coming in now, as the Weavers turned their cannons to the junks that were trying to run the blockade; but one of the feya-kori had accelerated in its rampage towards the docks, smashing through the buildings of the city. Though slow, it was not slow enough for Kaiku's liking, and it seemed to know that the ships were escaping and was heading right for them.

Then the pier was behind them and they were out in the harbour. Some of the Aberrants were throwing themselves at the junks, bouncing off their hulls and into the water, where they swam raggedly away. Others were pushed over the edge of the docks by the headlong rush of those behind them.

But they were out of the Aberrants' reach now. The last of the ships had pulled away, and those soldiers that were left on the docks – including several dozen Tkiurathi who had not made it aboard in time – were cut to meat by the Weavers' creatures. The sight was mercifully shrouded by the fog, which gathered ever thicker as they gained distance on the carnage.

There was a moment's respite in the bombardment from the sea, during which Kaiku laid her hand on Tsata's bare shoulder. He was wearing a sleeveless waistcoat of grey hemp, as ever, stitched with traditional patterns. He did not turn, but he laid the hand of his other arm across hers as he stared at the fading outline of the dock.

A burst of alarm across the Weave shocked her out of her brief calm, and she turned her attention to it. It was one of her Sisters, noting that the approaching feya-kori had changed direction, and was no longer heading for the docks but had angled itself out into the sea. Kaiku heard the furious hiss from the fog, the angry boiling and bubbling of the salt water as the feya-kori touched it. A wave rocked the junk to their left, and then Kaiku felt the swell pass underneath their vessel too.

She went cold as she saw the black Weave-shape of the demon ploughing through the waves. It was going to intercept them.

A mournful groan came from the mist, terrifyingly close, and it spread panic across the deck. The ship that had left dock ahead of them was still close on their starboard side. The mist thinned in a swirl of wind and the vast shape of the demon reared out of the water, trailing spray and steam and drooling poison. It rose up, its yellow eyes muted and baleful in the haze, and raised both its enormous arms above its head; then it came down with a thunderous rush of air, onto the junk next to Kaiku's.

She could not help joining in the cry of horror from her ship as the feya-kori smashed the hull of their neighbour in half, breaking its back in one great lunge. The noise was tremendous; the water detonated as the demon's arms plunged through the junk and into the waves, blasting spume and spray in a great cloud. A wave humped under their vessel, tipping it sickeningly. Kaiku grabbed the railing, thinking that they would capsize; several people were knocked overboard. Then the tipping slowed, and with a vertiginous plunge it pitched the other way with enough momentum to fling a few more shrieking into the sea. Kaiku was crushed against the railing by the people sliding across the mist-wet deck behind her. She could not take her eyes from the ruin of the junk as its two halves keeled towards each other, its sails burning from the touch of the feya-kori, shedding blackened bodies and live men and women as its horrible, inexorable tilt steepened.

The bow half did not have time to sink; the feya-kori

reared up again, and smashed it to flinders with sullen brutality.

Kaiku looked away; but she could not avoid the sight, for it was there in the Weave, and she was aware of everything around. The death-cries of the three Sisters that had been on board pulsed over her.

Their own junk levelled out, cutting through the waves, leaving the demon behind in the midst of the wreckage. She could hear the bellowing of the captain as he shouted incomprehensible commands at his crew, bullying them into action. The wind was tugging them onward, out towards the harbour mouth, and they were picking up speed. The feya-kori made no move to follow. They had reached water that was too deep for it. Instead, it turned towards the dock with a long, low moan, and was slowly swallowed by the fog.

The Tkiurathi on deck fell silent. The wind whipped around the rigging, flapping the edges of the fanlike sails. There was no question of going back for survivors. The feya-kori could still be about, and they would not be able to outrun it a second time. A dawning grief settled on the ship.

But the silence did not last long, for the cannons began again somewhere ahead of them, and incoming shellshot began to splash into the sea.

'Cannons ready!' the captain bellowed.

((Find and engage the Weavers)) instructed a Sister who stood at the captain's side. *((Blind their ships))*

Kaiku could see the ragged line of vessels now, strung out across their path, beacons of golden light in the Weave. Some of the Sisters' ships were already on the other side of the line, some slipping through, and at least one sinking in flames. The closest enemy was waiting in the water ahead of them: they would pass it to their starboard side if they kept on this tack. It was flinging cannon fire with spectacular inaccuracy in their direction.

There was no Weaver on board.

((This one has already been dealt with)) Kaiku informed her Sisters. *((Instruct the captain))*

She offhandedly destroyed shellshot that was looping near, then returned her attention to the enemy ship. The men on board were aware of them: the captain's voice had carried even through the fog, and the creaking of the ship as it hauled its massive weight across the waves could be heard. But the fog hid everything.

Kaiku held her breath as they cut alongside it. It loomed close, so close that Kaiku, with her Weave-sight, could not believe that the enemy did not see them. She could pick out the individual men on the ship, could sense their anxiety as they gazed out into the murk to catch a glimpse of their adversary. Others were busy loading cannons.

Then, a skirl of wind, and the mist parted; and she saw their anxiety turn to horror as they caught sight of the huge shadow gliding past them.

'Starboard cannons!' the captain shouted. 'Fire!'

The junk's artillery engaged with a deafening multiple roar, and the side of the enemy ship erupted. Grapeshot riddled the hull, scoring a long and splintered scar down its flank. The fire-cannons threw flaming slicks along its deck, into its sails, sending the crew into a shrieking panic as their hair and skin was coated in burning jelly. There was an enormous explosion on the far side of the ship, blasting a rain of splinters outward and leaving a gaping wound there. In one point-blank broadside the enemy was fatally damaged, and what retaliation they might have made was abandoned in the futile rush to save their craft.

Kaiku's ship slid by and away, leaving their opponents listing hard and already beginning to sink, fading in the gloom.

'Are we out of danger?' Tsata murmured to Kaiku.

'Not yet,' she replied, 'Two more are moving to intercept us. These two have Weavers with them. They can see us.' She paused for a moment. 'One of them is changing direction toward another one of our craft.' She checked the waters again, listening to the reports of those Sisters that were through the line. Distant explosions boomed through the fog. 'Once we have tackled this one, we will be out and in open sea.'

'Can we evade it?'

'I think not,' Kaiku replied. 'We are laden more heavily. Spread the word; we may need rifles ready.'

Tsata tipped his chin and passed on her words in rapid Okhamban to those nearest to him, who then began to do same to their neighbours.

'Do not disturb me now,' Kaiku said, feeling the approach of the Weavers. 'I need to concentrate.'

She abandoned her senses almost entirely, leaving only enough to maintain a vague awareness of her surroundings, and sewed her consciousness fully into the Weave. She meshed with two other Sisters who were on board with her, constructing defences, fortifying their position with traps and barriers and labyrinths in preparation. They worked with a beautiful and unthinking concinnity. Kaiku found herself suddenly thinking that she would miss that when she abandoned the Red Order for good.

Then the Weavers were upon them, and battle was joined.

While the invisible conflict was conducted on a plane beyond their abilities to register, the men and women on board the junk peered into the fog. One of the Sisters had not entered the fray, for she was the captain's eyes, and she relayed to him the position of the enemy. A distant creaking could be heard now, and the rustling of sails. The captain's brow was taut. He knew that to come through this with any hope of surviving the long sea journey ahead, they could not afford to be greatly damaged. There would be no port between here and there to effect repairs. They had to win this match outright.

*

Seconds crawled slowly by on the ship, but in the Weave they lasted much longer. Kaiku darted back and forth in flurries, harrying the three Weavers with spirals and tangles while the other Sisters spun new defences in front of the old. They were gaining ground steadily, bewildering the enemy and forcing them to retreat, then consolidating their position and pushing forward again. One of the Weavers was a weak link, and Kaiku attacked him mercilessly. She guessed that he was retaining a portion of his consciousness to instruct his captain. They did not have the luxury of a spare combatant. It was that Weaver whose inefficient mazes Kaiku went for, tearing them to shreds, chasing him back towards his own vessel, which left his companions exposed unless they retreated themselves. By unspoken consent, she was the aggressor here, and her Sisters lent her cover and support. Slowly but surely, the Weavers were being beaten back.

'They are angling for a broadside,' murmured the Sister who accompanied the captain.

The captain cursed under his breath. He struggled for inspiration, but none came. Since each captain knew where the other was, they might as well be tackling each other in daylight. There was nowhere to run and hide. With what he knew of the Weaver ships, he guessed that he had a roughly equal chance of winning out in a broadside, but he doubted he could come away from it without wounds to his junk that would sink it sometime during the subsequent voyage. The artillery was loaded, the men ready. All he could do was wait and hope.

Though she was occupied almost entirely with the slip and sew of the combat in the Weave, Kaiku was peripherally aware of the two golden ships, their outline drawn in millions of threads, that were gliding steadily closer to each other. Kaiku had guessed what the captain knew: they would not get away from this without damage and loss of life.

By now she had the measure of these Weavers. They were young and clumsy and arrogant, making foolish mistakes which she exploited. The ships were lining up with one another, excruciatingly slow in Weave-time. Soon they would be level, and firing would commence.

It was time to abandon caution. She sent an instruction to her Sisters, and the Weave erupted in response, a blizzard of threads lashing everywhere, random and impossible to follow. The Weavers recoiled, having never encountered this tactic before, unsure of how it might harm them.

But it was not meant to harm; it was meant to distract. Quick and subtle as a blade, Kaiku slid towards them.

'Enemy to port!' hollered the lookout, as the hulking ship emerged from the mist. It was coming in at a distance, too far away to allow boarding, its flanks bristling with sculpted fire-cannon like gaping metal demons. It hove alongside, approaching from the opposite direction, a rapid succession of portholes and shadowy figures holding rifles. Waiting, like the sailors of the Empire, for the moment when all cannons would be face-on to their enemy.

'Fire!' came the cry from the Weaver ship, at the same time as it did from the captain of the junk; and at that moment, the entire port side of the enemy craft exploded. It heeled drastically, its cannons blasting into the water and passing beneath the keel of Kaiku's junk. The sailors slid howling over the gunwale and into the sea. And now its unarmoured deck was presented to the junk's artillery, which smashed it to ruin in a blitz of smoke and fire and sawdust.

It was all over so quickly that those aboard ship could barely believe they had escaped unscathed. The Tkiurathi rifles had not fired. They watched as the wrecked boat plunged into the water, sucking down those who had survived the initial assault, and like the other two boats they had seen in ruin it slid away from them and was masked once more by the murk.

Kaiku blinked, looked about the deck and met Tsata's gaze with her crimson eyes.

'You?' he asked.

'They should be have been more careful where they stored their ammunition,' she said.

And the ship sailed on, while the mist thinned around them and finally broke to a clear winter's day. The open sea was all around, sparkling under the gaze of Nuki's eye, and the ships of Lalyara were there, twelve of them, sailing at a swift clip towards the horizon.

TWENTY-FIVE

The Lord Protector Avun and the Weave-lord Kakre stood together on a balcony on the south face of the Imperial Keep. They were looking over the city to where the Jabaza and Kerryn met to form the Zan, in a place called the Rush. Once, on the hexagonal island in the centre, there had stood an enormous statue of Isisya, facing towards the Keep, but no more. In other times, Avun might have been glad of its loss, for he could not easily bear its accusing gaze. Today, though, he felt that it would not have troubled him. His spirits were high, and all was well.

Even Kakre seemed pleased with him. The sight of the Weavers' many mechanised barges gathering along the rivers of the city was an impressive one indeed, as was the horde of Aberrants that were being brought from their pens underground and herded on board by the black-robed Nexuses. And this represented only the tail of the undertaking: most had already departed eastward, upstream along the Kerryn and down the Rahn. From there, the troops would skirt the Xarana Fault and loop west of Lake Azlea, and then south into the enemy's territory, towards Saraku. The feya-kori would join them en route, six of them in total, including the two that had assaulted Lalyara several weeks ago. Those two were hardier now; they needed less time to recuperate in their pall-pits. The blight demons, it seemed, got stronger with age.

The prelude was done. The forces of the Empire, rocked by defeats at Juraka and Zila and Lalyara, did not know where the next strike would come from. Their armies would be spread in an attempt to cover the greatest amount of ground.

Avun would cut through them like a sword and strike into their heart. By the time they could get their troops to Saraku it would be too late: the Weavers would hold the line of the River Ju, cutting off the marshland cities of Yotta and Fos to be despatched by their forces in Juraka. And after a short recuperation during which they could easily hold a city like Saraku, they would strike west, and nothing the Empire had could stand against them. At best, they could scatter into guerrilla armies, dogging the Weavers' efforts; but the Weavers would have the harvest, and the armies would be starved out and hunted down until nothing remained of them.

It would be over then. The desert lands could not stand alone. Their fall would swiftly follow.

Even the Weave-lord seemed happy today; or at least as happy as it was possible for such a creature to be. He was satisfied at Avun's progress now that action he deemed worthy was being taken. He had always been impatient with Avun's tactics, and had wanted to go in for the kill as soon as the feya-kori were first brought under their control. Avun allowed himself a wry smile. Idiots. If not for him, they would have been in a much worse situation by now.

Thoughts of that made him consider his encounter with Kakre, when he had convinced the Weave-lord of his worth. Kakre appeared to have forgotten about it, or was pretending to. It didn't matter. Kakre had been outmanoeuvred. Removing Avun would cause him far too much trouble, and it was trouble he could ill afford with time growing so short.

But more pleasing even than this to Avun was the behaviour of his wife. Since that day of her frankly miraculous recovery from sickness, she had seemed a different person. In public she was as quiet and meek as ever, but when they were alone she was no longer so demure. There was passion in her now, and after years of showing no interest whatsoever in him sexually she was suddenly, while not exactly wild, at least far more voracious than she used to be. In its absence, Avun had convinced himself that he did not need bedplay. He had always possessed torpid sexual appetites: he was slow to rouse and indifferent to the lures of a woman. But he had found, after so long, that the pleasures his wife's body might provide were immensely attractive again. He was loth to admit it to himself, but he felt more of a man for it.

Tomorrow he would depart, along with Kakre, to join the Weavers' army as their general. But first he had something else to look forward to. Until recently, he had all but needed to command Muraki to join him for meals; now, to his delight, she had asked him to come to one. She had something to celebrate, and when she told him he felt like celebrating too.

At long last, she had finished her book.

The wind whipped through the Tchamil Mountains, chasing itself among the barren peaks and valleys that formed the spine of Saramyr. The men of the desert had kept to the lower altitudes, for in winter there were snow and blizzards in the high passes; but still the ground was frosted and bitter, and they huddled in thick furs around their fires and listened anxiously to the dark. The land was cool and sharp as well-polished steel beneath the combined glow of Iridima and Aurus, and the sky was thick with pinpricks of starlight.

The desert army were seven thousand strong, all told, and they spread down the mountainside in a great clot of tents and lanterns. They had lost perhaps five hundred so far, all of them to Aberrant attacks. The cries of the beasts echoed across the peaks even now, some identifiable as ghauregs or latchjaws, others entirely unfamiliar. It was hard going to take an army through this kind of terrain, but the folk of Tchom Rin prided themselves on their endurance, and they travelled light and wore little armour. Rivalries between soldiers sworn to different families had dissipated out of the need for unity and cooperation in this hostile place, and they had made good progress. But the Aberrants' attacks were becoming more and more coordinated now, and by day gristle-crows wheeled overhead, cawing hoarsely.

The Weavers knew they were coming, and they were watching and waiting.

Reki walked slowly back through the camp towards his tent, a lean and thoughtful figure, the wind flicking his hair about his face. His boots crunched on the lifeless, stony soil. He was running over events in his mind as he had a hundred times before, examining them, turning them to consider from all angles.

The council with the nobles of the Empire and the Libera Dramach had been remarkably quick, all things considered. For the first time Reki had really appreciated what he had taken for granted all his life, that the Weavers, and latterly the Sisters, provided something so valuable that they simply could not ever go back to the way things had been. Men and women from Araka Jo, Saraku, and Izanzai had talked to each other face to phantom face via the power of the Sisters, though almost nine hundred miles separated them. A conference had been carried out, with terms and suggestions bandied back and forth, in less than a day. Without the Sisters, it would have been a labour of months, whether by an exchange of letters or by attempting to assemble them all in one place. He understood then, truly, why the Weavers had become so indispensible to his ancestors, and how they had come to the situation they had were in now.

When the desert folk's part in the plan had been laid out, Reki had agreed without much fuss. Unbeknownst to the Sisters, he had been intending something very similar anyway. It had become clear to him that they were fighting a losing battle in Tchom Rin. If they were content to merely defend against the Aberrants, then eventually the Weavers would come up with some way to overwhelm them, whether by new types of Aberrant, by demons, or by sheer weight of numbers. It was prudent to attack while they still had strength to do so. His scouts had traced the Aberrants from Izanzai, seeking a source to strike at. All those who had returned came back with the same news. Though they could not find the exact place, they knew the general area, and it was in the vicinity of Adderach. Reki had not been surprised.

And so, while he had been in the midst of plotting an assault on Adderach, the Red Order came to suggest he did exactly that. Yet he could not shrug an uncomfortable suspicion that the Sisters thought he and his men expendable, and that they were merely intended as a decoy.

Well, let them think what they would. He would show them how desert folk could fight. And they had Sisters too, gathered from the dozens scattered across Tchom Rin, to defend them against Weavers and to get them through the barrier of misdirection surrounding the mountain monastery.

If Reki could dispose of the threat of Adderach, then they would no longer be beleaguered on two fronts, and they could turn all their attention to Igarach in the south. If the Sisters' intelligence was accurate, then they needed only to hold the Weavers off till next winter; and with Adderach out of the picture, it could be done.

And then there was Cailin's assertion that maybe, just maybe, getting the Sisters to that witchstone might be enough to end this war. That was a prize worth trying for.

He picked his way between campfires, returning the greetings of the soldiers as he neared his tent. He was discomfited tonight, a subtle notion that something was amiss. Posting extra guards and sentries had not eased his fears. He tried to shake it off, to return his mind to matters at hand, but instead he found himself drifting, as he so often did, towards thoughts of Asara.

Trust is an overrated commodity. One of Asara's favourite sayings. And she should know. For he was beginning to suspect that trusting her had been something of a mistake.

He had not known peace since she left him all that time ago, heading to Araka Jo on some secret purpose of her own. At first, he had been tormented by not knowing, mocked by possibilities; and then, when that had become too much to bear and he had sent his spymaster Jikiel to find answers, he had been racked with guilt at betraying her. But now things were even worse. He had thought his love could withstand anything that Jikiel might discover about his wife's past, but when the spymaster returned it was with news that was entirely unexpected.

Asara *had* no past.

His initial reaction was to dismiss this as evidence of the spymaster's limits. After all, he had to fail sometimes. But Reki had had experience of Jikiel's abilities, and he could not convince himself of it in the end. The spymaster was far too good to come up blank like that. If he could not dig out the truth of any matter, then Reki was convinced that there was no truth to be had.

But of Asara, he had found nothing. Her family name, which she had said was Arreyia, yielded no answers. It was a common enough name, for it was very old and had spread widely. Saramyr names ranged from those derived from archaic Quraal, like Asara and Lucia, Adderach and Anais, to more modern ones which arose after Saramyrrhic had evolved, like Kaiku and Mishani and Reki. There were other Asaras, of course, but none matching her description, her talents and her circumstances. Jikiel had heard of a spy called Asara tu Amarecha who had worked for the Libera Dramach in recent years, but he discounted her eventually. She was not desert-born, and Reki's Asara certainly was, unless a person could fake their bone structure, their skin colour, the shape of their eyes.

Jikiel had probed the limits of his spy network as the puzzle became more intriguing. Whispers and hints were followed up and came to nothing. He sought information from those who had met her in the Imperial Keep during the time she had first seduced Reki, but they had no answers to give. He asked in places of learning, for she had been incredibly knowledgeable and well-travelled for one so young and it hinted at a childhood of study or adventure or both, but no clues were found. He worked on the assumption that she had changed her name, maybe even that she had disguised herself with a different manner, different hairstyles and clothes. He was adept at seeing through such basic deceptions. And still, nothing.

Eventually, he had exhausted all possibilities and was forced, shamefully, to admit defeat. In the end, he could report only this: that the woman who was to become Reki's wife had not appeared to exist prior to that day she turned up at the Imperial Keep.

Reki was still thinking about the implications of that when he walked past the guards outside his tent – not noticing the wry grin that one gave to the other – and found Asara waiting there.

The tent was tall and wide enough to stand up in, but inside it was bare and spartan except for a thick bed of blankets and a lamp placed on the groundsheet. The lamp threw light up and onto the curves of his wife's face and body, capturing her as she half-turned at his entrance. The surprise at her presence and the breathtaking beauty of her robbed him of speech for a moment.

'I promised I would be back, Reki,' she said. 'Even though it meant I had to track you through the mountains.'

He opened his mouth, but she stepped towards him and put a finger to his lips. The scent of her and the touch of her skin was intoxicating.

'There will be time for questions later,' she said.

'We have to talk,' he murmured, some remnant memory of his previous sour thoughts inspiring the need to protest, however feebly.

'Afterward,' she said. She kissed him, and he gave up any more attempt to resist. He had yearned for her every instant she had been gone, and now that she was here he could not restrain himself. Their kisses turned to caresses and took them onto the bed, where they sated their passions with one another long into the night and past the dawn.

When Avun arrived at the room where he and Muraki shared their meals, he barely recognised it. The table of black and red lacquer was surrounded by four standing lanterns, the flames burning inside metal globes with patterns cut into them to allow the light through. Exquisite drapes had been hung over the alcoves, hiding the statues there. A brazier of scented wood smoked gently in the far corner of the room, providing heat and a subtle fragrance of jasmine. No longer did the room seem cold and empty, but warm and intimate. The meal was already served, bowls and baskets steaming on the table, and Muraki knelt at her place, dappled by the light from the lanterns.

'This is wonderful,' he said, unexpectedly touched.

Muraki smiled, her eyes averted downward, her face half-hidden by her hair. Beyond the three tall window-arches at the back of the room, it was utterly dark: no stars or moons could penetrate the canopy now.

He settled himself, kneeling at the mat across the table from her. 'Wonderful,' he murmured again.

'I am glad you approve,' she said quietly.

'Will you eat?' he asked. It had become one of their rituals. At first, because she was always reluctant to dine with him, and later, as a wry joke between them at the way she had been. He began to take the lids from the baskets and serve her.

'It is done, then?' he asked. 'The book?'

'It is done,' she replied. 'As we speak it is being taken to the publisher.'

'You must be relieved,' he guessed. He really had no idea how she felt at any stage of her writing, for she had never discussed it with him.

'No,' she said. 'Saddened, perhaps.'

He paused in the act of spooning saltrice onto her plate, puzzled.

'I thought you were celebrating?'

'I am,' she said. 'But it is a bittersweet day. That was my last Nida-jan book.'

Avun was confounded by this. It was as if she had told him she was giving up breathing. 'Your last?'

Muraki nodded.

He passed the plate to her and started taking food for himself. 'But why?'

She was sliding on her finger-cutlery. 'His journey has run its course,' she said. 'It is time, I think, to begin anew.'

'Muraki, are you sure about this?'

She made a noise to the affirmative.

'Then what will you do? Will you create a new hero to write about?'

'I do not know,' she replied. 'Maybe I will stop writing altogether. Today, Nida-jan is ended, and all things are possible.'

Avun did not quite know how to gauge his wife's mood, and was careful in his words. Though he had always found Muraki's constant writing a source of irritation, he found himself unable to imagine her any other way, and now that it came to it he was not sure he *wanted* her to stop.

'Are you doing this for my sake?' he asked. 'I would not have you change yourself for me.' The hypocrisy of this passed him by entirely.

She met his eyes for a moment with something like amusement. 'It is not for you I do this, Avun,' she replied. 'Too long I have lived in the safety of my own world and ignored the one that surrounds me. Today I have closed my world away, and I am ready to face what is real.'

He set down his plate, hiding his wariness. He was unsure whether to be glad or worried about her decision. Writing had been such a big part of her life for so long that he was afraid she might not cope without it. And he would not be there to watch over her; there was no way he could delay the movement of the Aberrant forces now, even if he wanted to. After all the effort he had spent to make himself indispensible to the Weavers, he could not back out. Kakre would shred him.

'You must tell me,' he said, to cover his thoughts. 'How does it end?' He poured each of them a glass of amber wine.

'It ends well for him,' she said. 'He finds his son at last, in the Golden Realm where Omecha has taken him. There he wins him back after facing Omecha and beating him in a game of wits. They return to their home, and the son acknowledges Nida-jan as his father, for only a father's love could drive him to seek his son even beyond the realms of death. And so the curse laid upon him by the demon with a hundred eyes is lifted.'

'It is a good ending indeed,' Avun said. And yet privately, he wondered. For it was no secret to him that she had been mourning the loss of their daughter in her books, mirroring her grief in the actions of Nida-jan, and this sudden turn to happiness made him suspect that something had happened which he was unaware of.

'Come to the window, Avun,' she said, picking up her glass of wine and holding out her hand to him across the table. Surprised by her uncharacteristic impetuousness, he took up his own glass and rose with her. Together, they walked across the room to the window-arches that faced out over Axekami.

In the night, the miasma overhead could not be seen, and Axekami seemed peaceful. Lights were lit, tumbling down in profusion towards the Kerryn and the River District. Not as many as there had been in days gone by, but enough. It was almost possible to believe the city was beautiful again.

Muraki turned to him. 'While I was dreaming, you have become the most powerful man in Saramyr, my husband,' she said. She kissed him deeply, and there was a hunger in it that made him dizzy. He wanted to have her then and there, but he did not yet dare to do so, did not trust that he would not embarrass himself by overstepping the mark. Presently, she drew away from him, her eyes searching his, and she took a sip of wine, regarding him over the rim of her glass. He slid his arm around her tiny waist. His wife's words made him burn with pride. It was true: he had done all this, he had made this of himself. He sipped his own glass as he surveyed his conquest, the great capital of Axekami, and he was content.

It took him only seconds to realise that the wine was deadly poison, but by then it was far too late.

The first he knew of it was the awful tightening of his throat and chest, as if he was choking on a bone. His hand came free of Muraki and went to his collar; his other, absurdly, still held the glass out of instinctive reluctance to drop it. He could not draw breath. Gaping, he staggered backwards and tripped on his heel, falling to the floor. The glass shattered in his hand, cutting it badly. His chest was a blaze of pain as if he had swallowed the sun. His lungs would not respond to the urging of his brain, would not expand to fill with oxygen.

Wildly, in blind animal panic, he reached for his wife, but Muraki was standing by the window, her face shadowed by her hair, and she was not moving to help him. His eyes widened in horror and disbelief. That appalled gaze still rested on his wife when his body went slack and his life left him.

Muraki regarded him for a long time. She had expected tears to come, but there were none. She had expected, at least, to be consumed by remorse or guilt, but she felt none of that either. If she were writing this scene, she thought, she would not do so with such a dearth of emotion. Real life was infinitely stranger and unpredictable than the one she lived in her imagination.

She turned away from her husband and looked out over the city once again. She could smell the oily tang of the miasma, overpowering the jasmine from the brazier. She had never quite become accustomed to it. Her lips tingled where the poison wine had touched them, but she had not let it past into her mouth. Simple enough to procure poison from Ukida: she had only to order him, and he obeyed. He was loyal enough to keep her secret and not to ask what it was for.

She glanced at the corpse of Avun again, trying for some last time to stir something in her breast. The newly awakened passion for him had not been faked by her. She had wanted to enjoy what she could while she could, and she wanted to make him happy too. After all, she thought he deserved that much before she killed him.

She realised what would follow now. The Weavers would take their revenge, would scour her mind agonisingly until they knew all about her code, and about Ukida, and Mishani's visit. They would know their plans had been compromised, and would alter them.

That could not be allowed to happen. From the time she had decided to murder her husband, she knew she would have to die too. She had found that knowledge an immensely liberating sensation.

Thoughts of her daughter brought back words she had spoken during those precious minutes when they were together, a few short minutes in ten terrible years – ten years for which Avun had been responsible.

We are on two sides of a war now. Mother, and one side or the other must win eventually. Whichever of us is on the losing side will not survive, I think. We are both of us too involved.

She was right. She always had the gift of cutting to the point. So let it be Muraki on the losing side, then, for she could not bear the thought of her daughter suffering such a fate.

Avun had indeed been clever in arranging the Weavers' power base so that so much relied on him. He had carefully guarded his battle tactics, kept them close to his chest, and ensured that there was nobody else in a position to easily succeed him. His death would be a major blow to the Weavers, at the time when they could least afford it. And from what she knew of Kakre, she did not think he would turn back from his assault now, no matter what speculation might arise as to what happened in this room tonight. The Aberrants would move according to plan, and their enemies would be waiting for them.

Would it be worth it, in the end? Only the gods could say. There were no certainties in the real world.

She gave a long sigh, and her eyes turned to the night, the impenetrable blackness with no moons and no stars. What a cold and dreary prison her husband had made for her. She much preferred her dreams.

She drained her glass, and soon she was dreaming once more.

TWENTY-SIX

Nuki's eye was sinking in the west, igniting cottony bands of cloud. The surface of the River Ko glittered in fitful red and yellow. It had been unseasonably hot today, but the folk of Saramyr were glad of it, for winter was drawing to an end and it was their first hint of a spring to come. Now the temperature dropped as Nuki retreated towards the far side of the world, afraid of the tumult that the moon-sisters would bring when they took the sky. For tonight the moons' orbits would cross at shallow angles, and they would drag screeching fingers across the darkness. There would be a moonstorm, and a particularly long and vicious one.

It would be a suitably apocalyptic backdrop, Yugi thought, to the battle that was to come. He stood holding the reins of his horse on a rise a little way south of the river, and looked to the north. Waiting for the Aberrants.

The lands to the north and south of the Ko were rolling downs, a gentle sway of hills that ran from the Forest of Xu twenty miles to their west to peter out on the shores of Lake Azlea, a similar distance to their east. In between was the Sakurika Bridge, a sturdy arch of wood and stone that spanned the river. It was a plain construction, not as grand as many in Saramyr, and little used. Its abutments, spandrels and parapets were painted in faded terracotta to blend with the honey-coloured varnish on the wood, but beyond that there was no decoration. It had been built during a campaign in the far past to facilitate troop movement along the west side of the Azlea, but no road had ever been laid to it. The thin strip of land sandwiched between Xu, Azlea and the Xarana Fault was considered too perilous back then to merit

346

a tradeway. Still, it had been maintained all this time, for it was the only crossing-place for this river east of the forest, and wide enough for twenty men abreast.

And it was here that the forces of the Empire hoped to halt the advance of the Weavers.

Yugi felt sick. He wished he could smoke a little amaxa root to take the edge off his fear. Instead he surveyed the scene below him, the sea of armour and blades and rifles. Several artillery positions were dug in on the hilltops to either side of the bridge, densely packed with mortars and fire-cannons and even old trebuchets and ballistae that they had managed to acquire. The flat ground in between was thick with soldiers, representing almost all of the remaining high families and the Libera Dramach. Their banners hung limp in the failing breeze.

A barricade of spikes had been built along the centre point of the bridge, and behind it soldiers waited. Beneath their feet, well hidden inside the arch, were enough explosives to blow the bridge to matchwood.

'Gods, I can't stand this waiting,' Yugi murmured to those nearby: a few generals, a black-haired Sister that might have been a twin to Cailin in her make-up, Barak Zahn, Nomoru, Mishani and Lucia. Horses shifted and whinnyed restlessly; there was the creak of leather armour and subdued coughing.

'Are we certain that they are coming this way at all?' Mishani asked. It was a measure of how tense she was that she asked such a redundant question; she already knew the reports of the scouts.

'They are coming,' said the Sister, whose irises were red.

Yugi glanced down at Lucia. Her expression was bland. The enemy had to be on time. There were better places in which they could have met the Aberrants, places further south where they could mount ambushes and which were far more defensible than this. But they would not win without Lucia, and it was at her insistence that they chose to meet the threat here. This, their scholars promised, was the night

of the moonstorm; and it was on this night that the Aberrants – whose steady and unwavering advance had been
marked by scouts all along their route – would reach the
river. This night, in this place, Lucia would draw the spirits
to the defence of their land.

They could only pray that Lucia knew exactly what she was
doing, for without the intervention she had promised their
stand would not last for long. Thousands upon thousands of
lives were staked on the word of a girl barely into adulthood.
Yugi thought they could be forgiven a little nervousness at
this point.

Mishani, not for the first time, was asking herself why she
was here at all. For someone who prided herself on her self-
control and level-headedness, she seemed to have been
remarkably rash of late. First her visit to Muraki and now
this.

*But if not for my rashness, we would not have even this
chance*, she thought. *Oh, Mother.*

She took a steadying breath to keep down the tears. No,
she would not cry again. The thought of that last meeting still
burned her with grief, but she was glad, at least, that she had
made amends to Muraki. If she died today, she would have
done that much.

Had she known then that her mother and father had
already been dead for weeks, her grief would have been
keener still. But the Weavers had been careful to keep that
matter secret.

In the end, Mishani thought, it came down to Lucia.
Mishani and Kaiku had been her guardians throughout her
childhood in the Fold, and they had acted as elder sisters to
her. Though time and circumstances had made them distant,
they still had that bond. But Kaiku was needed elsewhere,
and Mishani could not bear the notion of leaving Lucia to
face this alone. She knew how easily manipulated Lucia was,
and there was nobody here who truly cared for her except her
father Zahn, but he would be down in the battle. Mishani

could not contribute much to war, but she could stand alongside Lucia. She felt that it would be dishonourable to abandon her.

Once, she had almost killed the young Heir-Empress, when she brought her a nightdress which she thought was infected with bone fever. When it came to it she had backed out; but she still felt responsible for harbouring the intention, and she had come terrifyingly close to executing it. She owed Lucia this, at least. And if Lucia fell, there would soon be little left to live for anyway. As with her visit to her mother, this was something Mishani had to do, no matter what the risks. A moral need that would not be overmatched by sense or logic.

You are getting impulsive in your old age, Mishani, she told herself wryly.

There was a cry from somewhere to their left, echoed by another voice closer by. The lookouts with their spyglasses had seen something on the horizon. A few moments passed, during which Mishani felt her blood slowly chill, before the Sister spoke.

'Our enemy has arrived,' she said.

Zahn exchanged glances with Yugi and the generals, a grim understanding in their eyes. Zahn was overall commander of this force, by consent of the council of high families. The generals mounted up and began to disperse to their positions. Yugi looked at Lucia, who did not acknowledge him, then he swung on to his horse, and pulled Nomoru up behind. Zahn put his hand on his daughter's shoulder, and her gaze shifted to him.

'We will do a great thing this night,' he murmured. 'Be strong. I will return to you; I promise you that.'

She nodded, her face set.

'Keep her safe,' he said to Mishani, and then he launched himself up onto his horse. He sidled the mount over to Yugi's, and the two of them clasped arms. Nomoru turned her scarred face to Lucia and Mishani and regarded them with an impenetrable stare, then both Zahn and Yugi spurred their horses and she was carried away, down the hill and towards the front.

Lucia and Mishani were left together on the hill with the Sister and a group of bodyguards. They watched and waited.

Night was drawing in as the Aberrants came, pounding through the twilight in a filthy tide of teeth and claws. They swept across the downs like the shadow of an eclipse, at a speed just short of a headlong run. Even at such a pace, they were virtually tireless, and could travel all hours with very little rest. More than once the Weavers' ability to move armies so quickly had surprised the forces of the Empire.

There were no gristle-crows in the sky. Like Lucia's ravens, they were useless at night, for they could not see well without the sun. And so the Weavers had no warning of the army ranged across the south bank of the Ko until they were close enough for the front ranks to be able to see the artillery on the hills.

The guiding minds of the Weaver forces were safely protected amid the mass of expendable soldiers. Nexuses were scattered about, riding on Aberrant manxthwa. With them rode Weavers, to whom the Nexuses signed when they had information to pass on from their connection to the Aberrants. The Weavers then penetrated deep into their servants' minds, through conditioned channels that made it an easy process, and learned what the Nexuses knew. They conversed among themselves along the Weave and then gave their orders to the Nexuses, never knowing that they themselves were in turn enslaved by the will of the witchstones and of the moon-god Aricarat. Through such a chain of command were the Weavers' affairs conducted.

The passage of information throughout the Aberrant army from the moment that the forces of Empire were spotted took less than a minute. The reaction was immediate, and unexpected. The high families had predicted that the Aberrants would slow, to take stock of the situation. But they did not know that Avun was dead, and that Kakre was in command here. Kakre had a different way of doing things to Avun.

He sent his orders, and the Aberrants charged.

Thousands of animals bayed and roared as they were goaded into a berserk rage by their handlers. The colossal swell of noise washed over the downs and reached the soldiers of the Empire. They stood grimly along the river-bank, on the flanks of the surrounding hills or packed thick on the bridge. They would not dishonour themselves by showing fear, but they felt dread settle on their hearts as they saw the hills aswarm with an army that vastly out-numbered theirs. They thought of their families, of moments of joy and pleasure, of things left undone. Some of them felt regret at their mistakes and hoped that the gods would find them worthy when they came to the Golden Realm. Some of them regretted nothing, and waited coldly for the end. Some of them felt the fire in their veins and thirsted for combat. Some felt noble, proud to be part of this; some were angry at throwing away their lives when they could have run and seen another day, another month or year, and honour be hanged.

But none of them broke ranks, and none of them shed a tear, and none of them showed their weakness. Though some sweated and trembled, though some fought to keep down the contents of their stomachs, they held at the riverbank as the Aberrants raced towards them, each second bringing them closer and closer.

And closer.

The air was torn by the scream of a firework as it spat into the twilight, trailing dazzling white fire; then the artillery opened up.

The first salvo drew a billowing line of fire across the downs, and ripped the leading edge of the Aberrants apart. Broken bodies spewed into the air in clouds of dirt and flame, shrapnel tore away limbs and sliced through hide. Those that survived the concussion and the heat were knocked to the ground where they were crushed by the stampede. The entire front line collapsed and was driven into the earth by the predators behind, who ran on through the blazing slicks left by the fire-cannons. A second salvo followed the first, pitched shorter. Shellshot sprayed burning jelly, mortars maimed and blinded, and heavy trebuchets lobbed bags of explosives that clattered to the earth amid the horde and then erupted, sending flailing corpses in every direction. The Aberrants were a target that was impossible to miss, and each shell or bomb accounted for a dozen or more. Hundreds fell as a result of those initial salvos, but they were a drop in the ocean. And the tide kept on coming.

The artillery continued firing without cease as the Aberrants reached the Ko. No longer were they aiming at the leading edge of the horde; instead, they placed their strikes carelessly into the heaving mass, confident that it was impossible to miss. The deafening barrage faded into a background noise, a constant roar of slaughter; the ground became a bloody trench of body parts, the soil red and churned and scorched. But the soldiers of the Empire had a greater concern: the Aberrants were upon them now.

The creatures swarmed onto the Sakurika Bridge or ploughed into the river, not slowing for anything. The spiked barricade across the bridge's centre took care of the first few dozen Aberrants before it collapsed: they simply threw themselves onto it with nauseating force until it cracked beneath their weight. Their brethren swarmed over their impaled corpses.

The soldiers of the Empire were ranked across the bridge to meet them. Riflemen stood behind kneeling swordsmen, aiming over their shoulders. A volley of shots cut the first row of Aberrants down like wheat. Then the swords swung, and battle was joined.

The fury of close-quarters combat was terrible. The huge, shaggy ghauregs tore into the soldiers, flinging them off the bridge into the water, or else picking them up and biting off their heads. Skrendel wound along the parapets of the bridge to insinuate themselves in the ranks of the defenders, scratching and biting, blinding and strangling. Shrillings filled the air with their insidious ululations as they pounced and tore with their claws. Other creatures fought too, nightmare things of bony hide and jagged tooth, beasts that were too strange or uncommon to be recognised as a species.

The soldiers cut and sliced, but hand-to-hand the Aberrants had a great advantage. The shrillings' natural armour turned sword blades away; the ghauregs' tough skin and thick pelt made it hard to cut them deeply, and even then nothing short of a strike in a vital organ would take them down. Skrendel were too fast to hit easily, and the soldiers were crammed too tight on the bridge to make wild swings for fear of hitting each other. The Aberrants pressed forward as the soldiers fought and died. The bridge became greasy with gore and cluttered with bodies as the men of the Empire were pushed back.

And, in the river beneath, the Aberrants were swimming across.

'It is time, Lucia,' Mishani murmured.

Lucia ignored her. She could see what was going on below as well as Mishani could. From their vantage point on the crest of the hill, the battle seemed strangely removed and insignificant in the last of the light, the deaths too distant to be real. Nuki's eye had gone now, leaving only a soft blue glow in the sky through which the stars were visible. The three moons, all of them full, had risen from the same horizon and were converging slowly. There was something eerily malevolent in their steady movement, heavy with purpose.

Four guards stood around them, doing their best not to glance at Lucia or the Sister who stood by her. Mishani waited for a reaction to her comment, then turned her head to regard the young woman at her side.

'Lucia, it is time,' she repeated.

Lucia slowly met her gaze, a deep sorrow in her eyes. For a moment, Mishani was struck by an awful thought: that Lucia would confess it was all a sham, that there *were* no spirits coming to their aid. But what she said instead was almost as worrying.

'Whatever comes after, Mishani, think well of me,' she murmured. 'I made a choice that nobody should ever have to make.'

Mishani did not reply. She sensed that she did not need to. There was no time to discuss this, anyway, for the Aberrants were almost across the river now. The soldiers on the south bank were riddling them with rifle balls as they swam, but there were too many of them to stop.

Lucia bowed her head and closed her eyes.

The change in the atmosphere was swift and immediately noticeable. At first, Mishani thought it was the onset of the moonstorm, somehow beginning before the great satellites had aligned. But though it was similar, it was not that. The air tautened, stretching across the senses and bringing with it a sense of dislocation, a faint notion that the eyes and ears had become detached from the mind. The wind began to pick up, at first in sporadic gusts and then rising to a fitful bluster, whipping back and forth. Lucia's cropped blonde locks, now grown a little wild, began to lash against her cheeks; Mishani's newly cut hair did the same, escaping the jewelled combs she had used to tame it. She had the impression of movement on the periphery of her vision, slender, shadowy figures darting between the guards that surrounded them. But they were phantoms, and when she tried to catch them with her eye they were not there.

The surface of the river became a chaos of ripples, coldly glinting frills chasing each other with the switching of the wind. The Aberrants swam through, oblivious, cutting across the slow current of the Ko.

Then there was a howl, rising above the battlefield, and the first of them disappeared under the water.

The river was suddenly alive with a white churning. The Aberrants began to bay and shriek and hoot as their companions were sucked down, and the white froth turned pink. Spectral shapes, sinuous like eels, arced and slid among the Aberrants. They curled and swept and plunged, encircling their victims in the knots of their bodies and dragging them under as they dived. The Aberrants thrashed and twisted, but it did them no good. The river spirits caught them all, and none survived to reach the other side.

Some of the Aberrants, their fear of the spirits overriding even the urging of the Nexuses, tried to brake themselves at the river bank; but the momentum behind them tumbled them over, tripping those that followed, and in a clutter they slumped into the water. Hundreds more fell in that way, to be drowned in the Ko, until the Nexuses managed to gain control of the horde and check their assault. Gradually, the headlong rush dissipated, and the Aberrant army was still. Their only way to cross now was the Sakurika Bridge, and only a finite amount could cram onto that at once. The artillery, relentless, continued to pound them without mercy; but the animals paid no attention to the carnage being wreaked upon them, and whenever a hole was blown in the horde more simply moved in to fill it.

Seeing their enemy halted and frustrated, the forces of the Empire raised a triumphant cheer, echoed by the guards who stood on the hilltop with Lucia and Mishani. They gazed at her with fear and wonder and a kind of adoration, and though she did not see it through her closed eyes she sensed their emotion.

'I'm sorry,' she whispered, so quiet that only Mishani heard it; and Mishani felt a chill clutch of trepidation take her.

The air crawled with invisible conflict as the Sisters and Weavers engaged. The scope of their combat was immense. Not only did they seek to kill each other, and in greater numbers than had ever matched before, but they sought to manipulate the battlefield as well. The Weavers probed tendrils towards Lucia, trying to find her even though she, by dint of her unusual abilities, was invisible to them. They reached towards men's minds, to persuade generals to make rash choices, soldiers to turn on their brethren, to shift their fire-cannons so that they fired into their own allies. The Weavers were trying to take down the artillery positions that were accounting for so many of their troops, for they had no ranged weaponry to fight back with, but the Sisters worked to foil them, and thus far they had been successful.

Still, there were too many options, too many possibilities. Sooner or later, something had to get through.

Yugi, Nomoru and Barak Zahn watched the battle on the bridge from horseback. They were down near the river bank, in the thick of the men but out of reach of the fighting. Here, a circle of soldiers and a Sister was gathered round a sapper who crouched with his lantern at the end of a fuse. The fuse was threaded through a long, thin pipe that was buried just beneath the turf. It emerged from the end of the pipe near the bridge, where it was connected to a package of hidden explosives. Detonating this one would detonate the others that had been placed around the structure, and bring the bridge down. In case anything went wrong, there was another sapper nearby who had a secondary fuse.

The Aberrants were cramming onto the bridge now, and though they were gaining ground the soldiers made them pay dearly for every inch. The boards of the bridge were slippery with fluids, and the combatants stumbled as they fought. Terrible wounds were sustained on either side as blades and claws chopped through flesh, sometimes severing cleanly, more often not. Men were opened to the bone from armpit to thigh, shrillings tore away faces from skulls, ghauregs were hamstrung and crippled. Up close, the savagery of man against animal was unparalleled.

'Pull them back,' Zahn said to the Sister. 'Prepare to blow the bridge.'

The Sister wordlessly passed on the order to another of her kind, nearer the front, who advised the general that she accompanied. The rising wail of a wind-alarm signalled the retreat, and at once the soldiers on the bridge began to back away, allowing more of the Aberrants to crowd in.

'Light it,' Zahn said to the sapper, who touched the flame to the fuse. It hissed into life and disappeared into the mouth of the tube, burning its way along the darkness within. Elsewhere, the secondary fuse was also being lit.

The soldiers had retreated to the south edge of the Sakurika now, and they pressed forward again, bolstered by riflemen who picked off the taller ghauregs with headshots.

The fuse sparkled its way through the tube, across the arch and up one of the spandrels of the bridge, accompanied by another which burned up a different route. Two tiny lights in the darkness, racing towards a single destination. With the bridge down and the river impassable, they had only the feyakori to worry about, and the blight demons had yet to make an appearance.

The second fuse caught up with the first, and they reached the hidden package at the same time.

And went out, inches short of the end.

Yugi's vision was not sharp enough to see the fuses being extinguished, but it was not long before he realised that the bombs had not gone off. He saw the line of soldiers at the far end of the bridge bowing under the press of predators, and knew that it was about to collapse.

'What happened?' he cried. 'Where's our gods-damned explosion?'

'The Weavers,' said the Sister, her red eyes unfocused. 'Heart's blood. The Weavers got to the fuses before we could stop them. They slipped past us. A trick . . . a trick that we did not know they had.'

Yugi looked back at the bridge in horror, and finally the line broke and the Aberrants surged through. They spread like oil onto the south bank of the river, and there they began to kill.

TWENTY-SEVEN

'Destroy it!' Yugi cried. 'We need that bridge down!'

The Sister to whom he was addressing this barely heard him. She was already immersed in the effort to do just that. Though the fuses might have failed, the Sisters could detonate the explosives themselves easily enough; in fact, they could tear the bridge apart without the need for explosives at all. It had always been intended as another backup in a situation such as this.

But the Weavers had guessed how crucial the Sakurika was to the Empire's battle plan, and they had got there first. By spinning false images of themselves, they had duped the Sisters into thinking that all their opponents were accounted for, when in reality several of them were slipping unnoticed through the Weave to the bridge, where they found the explosives and choked their fuses. The Sisters had not expected such deftness and cooperation in their enemy, and it had cost them. Before they could react, the Weavers had stitched a defensive position around the bridge, abandoning their attempts to influence other parts of the battlefield in favour of consolidating there. The Sisters swarmed around them, probing at them, feinting and retreating, but they had meshed solid and they were impenetrable. The Sisters had met their match.

'We cannot,' said the Sister who stood near to Yugi. 'We cannot destroy it.'

Yugi swore, looking over the heads of the soldiers to where the Aberrants were carving bloody swathes into the ranks. Close in, the predators had the advantage of greater strength; the secret to victory lay in keeping them at a distance, where they could be hammered by mortars and fire-cannons. He glanced back at the hill where Lucia stood, but it was too dark to see her now.

What is she waiting for? he thought angrily. If those river spirits were the best she could do, then they were all doomed.

'The artillery,' Zahn said. 'They are making for the artillery.'

Yugi looked, and saw he was right. The Aberrants were cutting a path towards one of the hills where the artillery positions were steadily massacring Aberrants on the far side of the river. Their push was costing them dear, for it was exposing them to attacks from the flanks, but by sheer weight of numbers they were winning through.

A portion of the artillery had been turned toward the bridge now; through the Sisters, word had already spread about the failure of the explosives. But any shells that came near were plucked from the air by the Weavers and fell harmlessly into the river.

Yugi and Zahn looked at each other stonily. 'Defend the artillery,' Yugi said. 'I'll take back the bridge. We have to hold them on the north side.'

Zahn nodded. 'May Ocha and Shintu favour you,' he said, and then spurred his horse and rode away, accompanied by his bodyguard. Yugi could hear his rallying cry as he went, and other soldiers began to join him as he raced to intercept the enemy.

Yugi looked over his shoulder at Nomoru. 'Can you get a position on the riverbank to hit the explosives?'

'They're hidden under the bridge. And it's dark. Won't be easy,' Nomoru said. She slid down from the saddle behind him. 'I'll try.'

'Don't forget the Weavers. They can stop a rifle ball.'

'We will be ready,' said the Sister. 'They can intercept shells, but a rifle ball is smaller and faster. We could get it through.'

Nomoru shouldered her rifle, cast a disparaging glance at

the painted woman, and then looked up at Yugi. Her eyes were flat.

His gaze flickered over the radial scars on the side of her face. 'I'll send up a signal rocket.' He patted his belt, from which hung a small and innocuous cylindrical tube. 'Don't hesitate.'

'I won't.'

They paused a moment longer. There was something left to be said, but neither would say it. Then Yugi spurred his horse towards the pennant of the Libera Dramach, which was raised near the mouth of the bridge.

As he forged through the troops, smelt the stink of sweat, of cured leather and blade oil and smoke and blood and death from upwind, he could not shed the feeling that he was dreaming all of this. The withdrawal from amaxa root – he had not had the opportunity to smoke any tonight – and the presence of the spirits charging the air suffused everything with a muffling haze. It seemed as if they were all complicit in some sort of game in which the stakes were trivial things instead of lives. He simply could not encompass the sheer number of people who would die here today, who had died already. This kind of slowly settling unreality had threatened him in the past, but he had never been a general in a battle of such scope before. War was too big for him, and his only defence was not to think about it at all.

He reached the pennant. Faces were upturned in the green wash of moonlight, looking to him. It seemed easier to do what he had to than to consider it any longer. He raised his sword and shouted:

'Libera Dramach! We're taking back the bridge!'

The roar of approval, full-throated and bestial, was loud enough to shock him. His senses sharpened, his blood began to pound, and the haze disappeared. Suddenly, he saw everything with an incredible clarity. The wind lashed against him, blowing the rag tied around his forehead like a streamer.

'Forward!'

The soldiers surged around him in an intoxicating wave, and he was borne along on its crest, unable to stop a fierce cry rising from his own lips. The ranks before them either parted or joined the charge. The Libera Dramach collided with the Aberrants in a brutal smash of bodies and blades.

Yugi was one of several mounted men, and they rode behind the leading edge with their rifles at their shoulders, using their height advantage to shoot the Aberrants at close range. He primed, fired, primed, fired, drawing the bolt on his weapon with fluid ease between each shot, controlling his mount with his knees. His shots smacked into their targets with shattering force, spewing ribbons of dark blood: a ghaureg went down with a hole in the side of its neck; a feyn took a neat headshot and went limp; he put three in the hump of a rampaging furie before he got something vital and killed it. He did not have time to think about anything but aiming and shooting until his rifle clicked dry and he was forced to break open the powder chamber and refill.

He was in the midst of doing so when there was a shove from the side, and his horse toppled into a group of men with a neigh of distress. Yugi's rifle fell from his hand as he fought for balance, but somehow his mount righted itself. Only long enough, however, for the ghaureg that had forced its way through the soldiers to grab the horse's head in both hands and break its neck with a sharp twist.

But it had chosen the wrong adversary of the two to attack first. Yugi's blade flew from its scabbard and he hacked downward with all his weight behind it. The ghaureg's arms were cut through at the elbows, and it flailed backward, roaring in pain, until someone drove a dagger into the glistening black nexus-worm in its neck.

Yugi did not see the demise of his opponent. He felt the tip of the horse as it went over, and tried to scramble free of the saddle. By good fortune, he managed to jump aside and tumble as the horse crashed down, and he fetched up against the legs of a soldier who dragged him to his feet before he could be trampled.

'Are you hurt?' came a gruff demand. He shook his head, and the man patted him roughly on the shoulder. 'Then come on! We've got a bridge to win back!'

Heartened and strangely touched by the soldier's bravado, he grinned and shoved his way forward, with the other man closely accompanying him. At the point where the armies met, the battle lines were like liquid, flowing uneasily as men or Aberrants fell and the victors surged into the gap. Down here, in amongst the press instead of above it on horseback, the reek of sweat and the claustrophobia was overwhelming; Yugi was too charged with adrenaline to care.

He saw a man killed in front of him, and there in his place was a chichaw, a nightmarish thing like a giant four-legged spider, its head thick with curling horns like a ram's and with a long, beak-like jaw full of tiny teeth. He stepped into the gap left by the fallen man, his sword already sweeping a cold arc in the moonlight, trailing spatters of its last victim's blood.

The Aberrant lunged at him, lashing its forelegs, which he belatedly noted were edged with chitinous blades along their length. He pulled his body aside and they glanced across the leather armour on his chest, cutting a deep groove but not getting through; and he turned his sword stroke so that it hacked one foreleg off. The chichaw recoiled automatically at the pain. He used that instant to gather a great lateral swing into the creature's flank, opening it along the side so that its internal organs crowded out in a great steaming spume. It collapsed, juddering, in the throes of shock and imminent death.

A flash of movement on his right among the chaos of swords and teeth. He turned in time to see a furie charging him over the bodies of the fallen, a wall of muscle and tusk; but the corpses shifted beneath its weight and it stumbled, and then a great overhand chop from the soldier at Yugi's side severed it nearly in half. It slid in a broken heap at Yugi's feet, the sword still stuck in its ribs. Yugi wrenched the weapon out and threw it back to his saviour, who offered him a quick salute of thanks and was then swallowed by the fray.

Yugi lost track of time after that. His past and future contracted to a single instant in which he was *still alive*, where the aching of his body was a distant and dull nothing and his muscles and mind were geared only towards his blade. He cut and slashed, not out of conscious desire to kill but because it would make them stop trying to kill him. He moved along lines drawn by years of practice, dodging and slashing and parrying without thought as to where the next strike would go, not daring to imagine how close he had inched by death since this battle had begun, for to do so would break his nerve and crush him. At some point, he became aware of wounds on his body, deep cuts that he had felt as tiny nicks, dribbling warm blood across his skin. He ignored them. He could do little else.

And then a gap appeared in the moon-drenched phantas-magoria of horrors that faced him, and he saw the end of the bridge, a mere dozen metres away.

The sight of it caused him to pause. How long had he been fighting? How far had they come? He became aware of the yells and screams of men all around him, but there was a predominant tone which sounded like defiance. Their assault had been bolstered by other troops, men eager to lend their blades to a winning cause, and the rally had multiplied and invigorated the soldiers. Now, as the bridge neared and the Aberrants on the south of the Ko were being cut off from their reinforcements, the other soldiers pressed in with new zeal to drive the creatures against the river bank and into the water. The spirits embarked on a fresh frenzy, drowning any living thing that came within their reach. Yugi could taste cold, wet dirt on his lips. The air was becoming tighter still now, seeming to pluck at them, to lift them upwards. The moonstorm would soon be upon them.

Yugi wanted that bridge. With a cry that was more like a shriek, he fought on, and his men fought with him.

Nomoru ran low through the dark forest of soldiers on the south bank, careful to stay behind the lines of riflemen that loosed shot after shot over the river. Far behind her, there was the churn of combat on one of the hills, where Zahn was making a stand against the Aberrants that had made for the artillery position. Now that Yugi was steadily advancing to plug the mouth of the Sakurika Bridge, the creatures were finding themselves becoming isolated and were steadily being whittled away on all sides. Nomoru could not see over the heads of the soldiers, but she heard the reports, spreading from the mouths of the Sisters, out through the troops.

Idiot, she thought. *He will get himself killed.*

She was thinking of Yugi. She had not imagined him as one for heroics – and indeed, she suspected that the stories being circulated were more than a little exaggerated for the purposes of morale – but it bothered her. As she slipped along the river bank, accompanied by the clip and stutter of rifle fire, she wondered how she would feel if he *did* die. Probably very little, she had to admit. Their affair so far had been pleasurable, but no more than that. She was a woman who had grown up amid the depravity and impermanence of the Poor Quarter of Axekami, and her heart was thickly calloused because of it. Death did not really affect her. She did not allow any feeling to dig in deeply. It was not a conscious decision, but it was her way and she had never felt it necessary to examine that or try to change it. She existed on a constant level, untroubled by spikes of wild happiness or terrible sorrow. She was a survivor, and survival was a business best enacted without the luxuries of emotion.

She brought her concentration back to the matter at hand. She had gone some way along the river bank now, heading away from the bridge. The explosives had been secreted carefully: that meant that they presented a very tricky target, concealed as they were in the corners of the stonework. Nomoru, with a sniper's instinct, had taken account of where they were and was making for the angle that would present the best shot.

Well, that was not strictly true: the easiest angle to fire from was right at the side of the bridge, but there was no way she was going to be that close to the Sakurika when it went up.

Judging that the time was right, she slipped through the riflemen. The bank dipped sharply towards the water, and she clambered carefully down it and settled herself into a crouch, so that she was below the level of the guns firing over her head. The River Ko, a mere foot or two away, was quiet now, though the ripples of its surface still flocked this way and that with the unpredictable wind. Nomoru gave it an uneasy glance. The river spirits were still down there. Nomoru had a suspicion that if she so much as touched the water they would take her too.

She put it out of her mind and allowed herself to relax. She ignored the threat of the river, the fusillade ripping over her head, the oppressive atmosphere of the oncoming moon-storm. She ignored the endless barrage of artillery bombardment, and the distant sound of swords clashing and the bellow of ghauregs and furies. She set her rifle against her shoulder.

Gods, it was dark. The greenish, steely light, bright as it was with the clear sky and the three moons out, was barely adequate. When the moonstorm began, she would hardly have a hope. She calculated where she thought the explosives were, sighting past the near spandrels and up into the corner of one of the further ones. There; it had to be there. She shifted her aim slightly, sighting on another spot. There too. She could not see them in the shadow, but unless they had moved somehow, that was where they were. She only had an angle on two of them; the rest were obscured by the architecture.

Most would have said it was an impossible shot. But Nomoru liked a challenge.

The conflict between the Weavers and the Sisters around the bridge was so intense that Yugi could physically feel the atmosphere crawl. He looked more like some golem of the earth than a man now: he was caked and gloved in blood and muck, his muscles fuelled only by animal fury. They had stopped aching now: he had gone beyond tiredness. His strikes were unsubtle and clumsier than before, but enacted with more viciousness than he had believed himself capable of. His ears rang with the cries of men and he felt their burning adulation. Some faint, rational corner of his mind knew that they were inspired by him, but it was not clear why that was. He knew only that he fought in the forefront of a great column of soldiers that had carved its way deep into the clot of Aberrants on the south bank, and that at some point, as he wormed his boot through the slither of corpses to find solid ground, his foot came down on wood instead of dirt and he was on the bridge.

The realisation triggered something hitherto forgotten. Nomoru. He reached for the signal rocket at his belt, but the instant he took his attention away from the battle he almost lost his hand to some whip-tailed creature and was saved only by the intervention of one of the men who fought alongside him.

'The bridge! The bridge!' someone was crying, and a great cheer went up. Then Yugi felt himself propelled from behind as the soldiers of the Empire surged forward.

'No! No! Hold here!' he managed to shout, but his voice was overwhelmed. A clot of Aberrants on the bridge collapsed under the force of the surge, pulling one another down as they fell. Yugi tried to resist, but it was too much. He could only ride the crest of the wave.

He beheaded a ghaureg with a two-handed swipe, then twisted to break a skrendel's jaw with the pommel of his blade.

In the frenzy he lost what it was he was trying to remember: there was no time for anything but combat. Trapped in a seething, whirling world of chaos and madness, Yugi managed only swift episodes of sense in among the blur of constant movement, and at some point he realised that they had managed to make it a third of the way across the bridge, and that the Aberrants were being driven back by the soldiers of the Empire, who fought with a primal elation at their own heroism.

Where would it end? Would they push onward into the Aberrant horde, into certain death, driven by a false sense of invincibility? Yugi did not know, and he could not have resisted it even if that were the case. It had gone too far to stop now.

But there was another enemy here, one he had not accounted for. He only realised it when the man to his left suddenly keeled over, fitting and spewing blood from his mouth and nose. The man who tried to help him did the same.

Weavers.

He felt the wrench as his muscles clamped up on him. He had experienced that agony before, in the Fold when he was forced to watch powerlessly as his friend and leader, Zaelis, shot himself. Then it had unmanned him. Now it was worse. It was no mere paralysis, this; he felt himself juddering, in the preliminary throes of a seizure. Soon the contractions would intensify to a strength sufficient to break bones, to crush organs. He fell, cushioned by the rough hide of his dead enemies, his eyes rolling wildly.

And suddenly it was gone, the grip loosened. Stamping feet were all around him. Blood dripped from his lips. But he was not dead. Somehow, through some twist of battle in the invisible realm, the Weaver that had been about to kill him had been distracted, forced to divert its attention elsewhere. But he could hear the shrieks around him as other men died, saw someone collapse nearby, milky foam frothing from between clenched teeth.

He did not need to think. Anything, anything was better than the touch of a Weaver. He wrenched the signal rocket from his belt and tore off the cap of the cylinder. On its top was a strip of coarse paper, which could be struck against another strip on the bottom of the cylinder, lighting the fuse through friction. He struck it.

A rain of sparks spewed from the cylinder. Lying in an island of burning white light on a shallow heap of corpses, surrounded by the pounding feet of soldiers, he held the rocket out shakily.

The ignition powder caught, and it shot upwards into the night with a scream, crisping the flesh on his hand with the backwash of heat.

Nomoru had observed the troops of the Empire as they battled their way onto the bridge. When she saw the rocket, she saw also that it had come from near the front of those troops, and knew that it had come from Yugi.

It did not give her an instant's pause. She fired four times in rapid succession, priming in between each shot: two at her secondary target as a decoy, and two at the largest package of explosives, the one which Yugi had intended to detonate in the first place.

The Sisters were true to their word, and were ready at the signal; but even with the Sister's best defence, the Weavers took out the first two rifle balls, stunning them in mid-air before they reached their target.

Two, however, was not good enough.

The Sakurika Bridge exploded, annihilated in a terrific bloom of flame and smoke all along its length. It blasted great tracks of white spume along the river, and sent wheeling planks of wood and lumps of stone high into the night, to splash into the water or to fall amongst the armies on the banks. Those men and Aberrants who were on the bridge when it was destroyed were obliterated instantly, and to either side dozens fell with burns or other injuries, or were thrown down by the concussion. The violence of the eruption rolled over the downs and echoed away into the night.

The author of that destruction put down her rifle, and looked at the pitiful shreds of wood that were left, their ends ablaze. She considered saying something, a few short words to herself in memory of the man she had just killed. But it would be pointless, and so she kept silent. She slipped up the bank and ducked under the riflemen, and was lost amid the ranks of the soldiers.

Zahn had finished off the last of the nearby Aberrants when the river lit up in fire. He reined in his horse, panting and wet with sweat, and looked down the hillside. Behind him, the fire-cannons and mortars still boomed, and the trebuchets creaked, flinging missiles which tore ragged chunks out of the endless expanse of predators on the far shore. It was safe now; the bridge was down at last. The enemy was trapped on the north side of the Ko. They could only retreat out of range and try to find another way around – a journey of many hundred miles, for they faced the Forest of Xu to the west and Lake Azlea to the east – or wait to see how long the spirits of the river would hold against them.

Then he heard a cry from the men around him, and he saw that the Weavers had unleashed their greatest weapon at last.

They rose over the crests of the distant hill, shadows against the horizon, but their incandescent eyes could be seen even from miles away, and they shone in the dark. Slowly they lumbered closer, their silhouettes growing as they ascended the hill, towering to the height of great siege-towers.

Feya-kori. Six of them.

Mishani and Lucia stood together on another hilltop. A light rain began to fall, chill droplets brushing against their skin and soaking into their clothes, blooms of darker colour spreading across the fibres.

'Yugi is dead,' said Lucia, her eyes still closed and her head bowed. Mishani looked questioningly at the Sister, who nodded in confirmation. The news glanced off her. It was mere fact, meaning nothing. She would find time to grieve when she could, but Yugi had never been a great friend of hers.

'The feya-kori are on their way,' said Mishani, her words caught up and lost in the wind. She looked at the sky, where the moons were drifting together. Clouds were boiling out of the air, sucking inward to the point where they would meet. Mishani felt her senses twining tighter and tighter; the storm was only moments from breaking.

'I know,' said Lucia.

The rain gathered in intensity; the wind picked up, keening across the battlefield. The feya-kori's moans drifted through the air as they approached.

'Lucia . . .' Mishani murmured.

'Not yet,' she replied.

'They are getting close, Lucia.'

'Not *yet*.'

The downs were ripped with a terrible shriek, making Mishani shudder, and a jagged fork of purple lightning split the night. The sky exploded in a thunderous roar. Wind howled, jostling them, and the rain drove down hard enough to hurt. Lucia lifted her face up, tilting it to receive the full force of the downpour. Above them, the moons formed an uneven triangle, scratched with churning clouds.

Her eyes flickered open.

'Now.'

TWENTY-EIGHT

The men surrounding Lucia fell back from her with oaths of terror as she called, at last, the full force of the spirits to their aid. Even Mishani stumbled away, shocked at the thing she saw in Lucia's place. Nothing physical had changed, but her aspect had warped. No longer were her features pretty and naïve in appearance, but sly and evil and chilling. The air became flat, difficult to breathe, tasting of iron. Mishani looked around her and saw that it was not only Lucia who had changed: the soldiers' faces were narrow and hateful, the Sister's painted countenance was shrewish and full of spite. Subtle whispers, promising half-imagined horrors, hissed in Mishani's ears. Flitting figures massed thickly in the moon-shadows. The presence of the spirits twisted perception, and never had it been so strong as now.

Lucia was standing still, her arms loose, her face upturned to the barrage of the rain as if it were a balm, blinking rapidly against its fury. She was soaked to the skin. Mishani, small and light as she was, had to fight to keep steady in the wind. She shielded her eyes with her hand and looked on fearfully. Steam was wisping from Lucia's clothes now, thin trails of vapour that congealed and thickened until Mishani realised what she was seeing.

Something was rising out of her.

The Xhiang Xhi unfolded from Lucia's body like the wings of some mythical demon, spreading and looming, its impossibly long fingers giving it the appearance of some vaporous and skeletal bat. A thin chalk figure, a shadow cast in mist, it was attached to her lower back like a ghostly incubus, covering her with the parasol of its hands. Its face was a blur, its size defying the eye as it seemed to change with every new angle. The soldiers cringed, and some of them ran, unable to take the overbearing weight of its presence.

Mishani would have run, too, if not for Lucia. But she had sworn to herself that she would not desert the child she had once thought of as a sister, and so she stayed, caught between honour and dread.

The feya-kori unleashed a long, discordant drone across the downs, loud enough to rattle swords in their scabbards. They had sensed their adversary and were issuing a challenge.

The Xhiang Xhi raised its hands, splaying its spindly fingers wide; Lucia opened her mouth, and the answering screech that came from her blasted outward like the concussion of a bomb, making Mishani clamp her hands to her ears, staggering back under the force of it.

The armies stilled. The artillery fell silent. The night was darkening as a blanket of cloud boiled out from the triad of moons, its underside flashing with lightning. There was a rumbling in the earth, at first so low that it could not be heard, but growing ominously louder. The wind had roused to a gale strong enough to push men over, and the armies of the Empire and Aberrants alike were thrown into disorder. Mishani fell to her knees in the mud, bracing herself as best she could on the hilltop. Lucia's bodyguards slipped and slid and held onto each other for support. Only the Sister stood firm against it, the pressure of the wind diverting around her and leaving her untouched.

The Aberrants went scrambling aside as the feya-kori walked through them on all fours. Some of them, blown by the wind or trapped by the press, were crushed like beetles, or burned by the noisome filth that dripped from the demons. The feya-kori drove on through the tempest, not slowed by it in the least.

The rumbling had become huge now, and the earth trembled in small judders. The soldiers cried prayers to the gods and almost broke ranks to run, but their generals barked at them and their legendary discipline held them in place.

The sky shrieked and boomed. A crooked tine of lightning struck the flank of one of the feya-kori, blowing a hole there, spraying acidic muck in great gobbets over the Aberrants below. The demon groaned and crabstepped sideways; then it continued onward, toward the river. The ooze from its body was seeping inward to close the wound in its side.

Mishani looked on, huddled low against the storm and slimed in mud, as more lightning came flashing from the clouds in strikes as fast as the flicker of a snake's tongue. Each one was accompanied by a resonant explosion that battered the ears and made her cringe. The world was turning to madness: everywhere was noise, the crashing and keening of the sky, the ceaseless bellow of the earth, the shaking of the ground, the shoving of the wind and relentless lash of the rain. And all this made worse by the disorientating influence of the spirits and the moonstorm combined, leaving her scared and paranoid. If she had had anywhere to run to then, even her honour would not have kept her by Lucia's side; but there was nowhere to go.

The feya-kori were being hit again and again, rocked by the lightning. And now their advance faltered, for the blows hurt them, and though they forged on towards the river they stumbled and flinched under the barrage. Mishani, staring through the sodden mesh of her hair, could see faces of spirits in the lightning, leering sketches in jagged light burned onto the darkness, slow to fade. And not only that: the wind's howls had changed tone now, becoming more and more like voices, distorted mutters, cooing and shrieks of nonsense, barely definable but intimating some kind of language.

Gods, let it stop, let it stop!

But though the lightning could slow the feya-kori, their wounds closed again. And though the wind could batter and shove them, they were too massive and too solid to be toppled. They came onward, towards the river.

Far back in the ranks of the Aberrant army, hidden from sight, the Weave-lord Kakre worked, surrounded by his retinue of ghauregs. His mind was largely gone, the connections in his brain fused and muddled by the impossible task of overseeing six feya-kori. Yet while he was with the demons, as part of this gestalt of Weavers, his faculties still held together. He had been subsumed into the whole, borrowing from it heavily. When this all was over and he was released from the net they had woven, he would be left a gibbering lunatic.

His judgement had gone awry long ago. Reluctant to relinquish power, he had given himself the most important position among those Weavers that pooled their abilities to call and guide the initial pair of blight demons. He had done so again with this larger gestalt, and it had been far beyond him, far beyond the powers of any one Weaver; but they would not know that until afterward, when they disentangled themselves. For now, he was entirely occupied with the feya-kori, attempting to steer them to his will.

The strikes that hurt the demons hurt Kakre also, as they did the other Weavers of the gestalt, who were hidden around the battlefield. Kakre cared nothing for the pain, however, nor for the Aberrants his demons were trampling. Without Avun, the Weavers did not see the need to preserve their troops so carefully; after all, their numbers were overwhelming, and even the great army ranged against them could not have held them off if it were not for the spirits brought into play.

But the feya-kori knew what to do about that. Though Lucia could not be touched by the Weavers, the demons could sense the Xhiang Xhi like a beacon.

Yes, Kakre saw the girl's plan, oh indeed. The Xhiang Xhi *was* the Forest of Xu: it had become so much a part of that place that it could not possibly leave its home without a host to carry it. And as it was a beacon to the demons, it was also a beacon to the spirits; Lucia had had to bring it here so that the spirits would flock to it.

He wished his predecessor had killed her when he had the chance. But even the best efforts of the spirits thus far were not enough to destroy his demons. The feya-kori were made strong by the blight that spread through the land, even as it weakened their opponents. Perhaps they were too strong to be stopped by any force left in Saramyr. They had only to get to Lucia, and it would all be over, the Empire's last hope gone.

Behind his Mask, Kakre's ruined face twisted in an idiot grin.

The rumbling became unbearable, and the earth split.

The noise was colossal. The ground was shaking so violently now that the soldiers were falling over, grasping at each other for support. The artillery juddered out of position; mortars went toppling. On the north side of the Ko, a vast slice of land suddenly dropped away, plunging downward with a grinding roar and a billow of dust. Hundreds of Aberrants pitched squealing into its depths; an instant later a great fan of magma blasted out, high into the night, a pyroclastic fury of black smoke and flame.

Mishani, near-mad with terror, could not be sure if the fearsome cackling visage she saw in the fire was real or imaginary.

The smoke of the explosion spread across the battlefield, whipped and torn by the wind. As the magma splashed to the ground to scald and kill, Mishani thought she saw shapes moving in the smoke, swift darting things like monkeys. At first she imagined they must be skrendel, but they moved with a jerky flicker, never seeming to be quite where she thought they were. They passed among the Aberrants, springing upon them, bending to bite and springing away again. The Aberrant predators were in a panic: even the Nexuses could not control them now. And still the earth shook and smaller rifts spread across the downs, slumped trenches of broken grass and turf.

The smoke blew clear in one patch, and the purple stutter of lightning illuminated the uncovered scene for a moment. Nothing moved there. It was as if the Aberrants had all frozen in place. It was only when she saw one of them crumble that Mishani realised they had been turned to earth, sod effigies of themselves, by the bite of the nimble spirits.

The ground split again, this time beneath one of the feya-kori. With a wail, the demon toppled, and the chasm swallowed it with another fountain of magma.

The armies of the Weavers were being slaughtered. The wind had turned to knives and was cutting the predators and their handlers to pieces. The land was bucking and heaving, and within the smoke that belched from the chasms deadly spirits moved. Lightning played, killing dozens wherever it touched. Only the Weavers remained safe, their defences too strong to be easily tackled.

But through it all came the feya-kori. One of their number had fallen, but they had reached the River Ko now, which seethed as fleeing Aberrants were drowned by the spirits there.

She cannot hold them back! Mishani thought wildly. *All this, and she cannot hold them back!*

Lucia was motionless, unaffected by the rain or the wind or the shivering of the land. Her face was still uptilted, her eyes now closed, her arms hanging limp at her sides. It took Mishani a moment to notice that her feet were not touching the ground, but that she hovered an inch above it. Only the Xhiang Xhi moved, its fingers flexing as if it were a puppeteer, its wispy body writhing slowly above its host. The moons glared down upon them from behind the churning mess of tattered cloud, as lightning raked across the feya-kori again.

Then the demons halted, right on the bank of the river.

Behind them, their army was being decimated. Many were scattering as their handlers died and they reverted to their animal instincts. The demons paid no attention. Their burning eyes were fixed on a single spot, something invisible which had arrested their progress.

Mishani squinted against the storm, and she *could* see something there. A strange glittering in the rain on the south bank of the Ko, a shimmer in the air as if the veils of droplets had turned to crystal. The soldiers were retreating from that spot as the phenomenon became more pronounced. It separated into three, the light tightening and hardening into form and shape.

Mishani knew what was happening before it was finished. She had heard this tale from Kaiku, long ago.

They were the mad spirits of the moonstorm, the offspring of the goddesses that ruled the night sky. The Children of the Moons had come.

They towered over the soldiers of the Empire. In Kaiku's story they had been twice her height, but now they had manifested themselves as giantesses, forty feet tall, the same as the demons they faced. They wore the form of women, clothed in decayed grandeur. Their robes were of exquisite finery that had fallen into ruin, and from their wrists and elbows hung ancient artifacts that swung gently as they moved. A cold glow exuded from them, like the brightness of their parents, casting a grim and unforgiving light, and their hair was like feathers. But it was their faces that were most terrible, for their features were smooth like partially melted masks of wax, and they blurred and shifted. Only their eyes were stable, holes of utter black through which might be caught a pulverising glimpse of eternity.

The discipline of the soldiers broke at last and they ran from the monstrous entities. But the spirits were not interested in them. Their abyssal eyes were turned upon the feya-kori, and from beneath their robes they drew thin blades which shone with a cruel luminescence.

Lightning flickered and the sky shrieked as the demons and the spirits faced each other across the river. Then, as one, they plunged in.

The clash was brutal and short. The feya-kori had greater numbers and strength, but they were ponderous in their movements, and the Children of the Moons flowed around them like liquid. The feya-kori swiped and swung, beleaguered by the insignificant attacks of the river spirits, but they could not hit the Children. When the counterstrikes came, the effects were devastating. Mishani saw one of the whirling spirits cut the forelegs away from a feya-kori, so that it toppled face-forward into the river. Another was sliced in half along its midriff and fell into two pieces, the water steaming and bubbling as it toppled. In moments, the five feya-kori had sunk, and the Children of the Moon stood alone.

But they were not alone for long. Scalding vapour rising from their back and flanks, the demons rose out of the Ko with defiant groans, their bodies whole again, rejoined where they had been sundered. The water was turning black with the poison of their presence. The Children, their reactions unreadable, stood motionless.

Then the feya-kori attacked: five of them lunging at the same enemy. Though two of them were cut to ribbons and splashed once again into the befouled river, their target could not avoid the rest. The feya-kori slumped onto one of the Children and it was borne under with an earsplitting shriek. Its brethren were upon the remaining feya-kori instantly, chopping them apart with surgical precision; but when the spirit got back to its feet again, Mishani noted how its movements were jerky, its outline indistinct and its aura less bright. The feya-kori had wounded it.

And the demons were reforming and emerging anew, sloughing off the small spirits of the river that were making futile attempts to drag them under again.

The entities met and matched. The splashing of their

combat was like dull explosions under the cries of the storm. Rain-wet blades flickered and darted through the vile muck of the feya-kori, and the demons fell to pieces at their touch; but the spirit that they had hurt was slower now, and one of them caught it with a swipe of one club-like stump, smashing it hard so that it staggered. It guttered like a candle and then stabilised, but its light was noticably dimmer than before. As if it were not quite *there* as much as the other two.

As this was going on, the remaining spirits had not been idle. The Aberrant army had all but disappeared beneath the maelstrom. The ground was scored with chasms, smoke rolled over everything, small tornados roamed and lightning stabbed from the clouds; yet no move was made by the Weavers to retreat. They knew they would not get far if they turned and ran. Their only hope now lay in getting to Lucia, and that meant going through the Children. So they bent all their will to the feya-kori, and the Sisters did their best to harass and distract the Weavers; but between them, there was still a stalemate, and neither had much influence here.

Now the Children of the Moons raised their swords together and screeched. The noise made Mishani shudder and cover her ears. She was sodden and frozen, huddled and filthy, insensible with fear. The Xhiang Xhi raised its own hands, the spindly digits of mist splaying wide, and from Lucia's mouth came an equally inhuman scream in reply.

The effect was immediate. Mishani could hear it even over the storm. The sussurus of the river, hitherto a background murmuring, increased to an angry hiss. She looked down from the hilltop and saw that the rain-speckled surface of the water, churned with spume, was flowing faster now, dragging the white foam and the dark pollution downstream. The noise intensified, underpinned by a low roar, until it had become a rushing torrent, breaking its banks. The river was in flood.

The armies of the Empire – who had settled at a wary distance from the Ko after the Children had appeared –

scrambled to draw back from their positions, but they were too close-pressed to move quickly enough. Some of those at the fringes were caught up in the drastic rise of the river and swept away. Men fought to rescue their companions or fled for cover. The misfortune struck the Aberrants also, but there were none surviving so close to the bank on the north side, and the flood waters merely swept away the dead and those that had been turned to sculptures of earth.

In the river, the spirits and demons faced each other again. Both were noticably struggling against the flow, but they kept their feet. The Children screeched again, and then they struck, cutting through their enemies: five feya-kori went down in pieces.

But this time there was no quarter. The Children allowed them no time to reform. They chopped into the water where the demons had fallen, slicing through the black scum to the sludgy bodies beneath. They squealed in a frenzy, hacking with gleeful cries, their blades throwing polluted water and bits of burning muck in all directions. The river boiled around them, and the slim, ghostly eels of the river spirits thrashed and dodged in between.

Downstream, a small gobbet of filth bobbed to the surface and was carried away for a second before the river spirits enwrapped it and pulled it under. Then came more, chunks of varying sizes that gradually dissolved in the flow.

The Children of the Moons butchered the feya-kori over and over, and the river caught up the pieces and flung them away so that they could not reform again. For almost five minutes the appalling violence continued, until one by one the Children of the Moons stopped cutting, and the river ran clear.

They raised their swords again and gave a scream that could be heard all the way to Saraku, and in response the spirits that were attacking the Aberrant army renewed their assault with savage enthusiasm. The Weavers' defences crumbled as the feya-kori fell: they had invested so much in the demons that their loss tipped the balance. The Sisters took them apart rapaciously, and as they began to fall the spirits turned on the Weavers too, no longer afraid of their power. In moments, none were left alive.

The Weavers were dead, the Aberrant army scattered or destroyed. Gradually, the smoke dissipated and the extent of the carnage was laid bare to the eyes of the soldiers of the Empire. A cheer went up, swelling as it was joined by others, until the sound of it carried over the storm, over the restless tremors in the ground and the din of the moonstorm and the howl of the wind. The cheer gained shape, and became a chant:

Lucia! Lucia! Lucia!

They had stopped the Weavers, crippled their forces utterly. Even if the Weavers could muster another army now, the forces of the Empire would be able to hold them. For they had Lucia, the girl who commanded the spirits. At last, their saviour had revealed her power. With her, they could march into Axekami and take it back. With her, they could do anything.

But only Mishani was close enough to see that the droplets running down Lucia's face were not only rainwater. There were tears squeezing from beneath her lids.

Slowly, the Children of the Moons turned their dreadful black eyes upon the soldiers, and the chant faltered and died.

'Lucia!' Mishani cried. 'Lucia, what have you *done?*'

The first strike of lightning hit one of the artillery positions and annihilated it, destroying the hilltop and everyone on it in a tiara of flame. The second lashed down in the midst of the army, killing a dozen men instantly. The soldiers barely understood what was happening until the shaking of the earth suddenly intensified and it opened beneath them: a long, jagged split ripped the downs, and hundreds of men fell screaming. The wind turned to a localised hurricane, picking people up and flinging them into the river where they were drowned. The army broke down entirely. Soldiers fled, their weapons discarded, crushing each other in their desperate attempts to get away. Thousands upon thousands descended into complete disorder, every one interested only in preserving their own lives against the awful, unknowable forces that had suddenly turned against them.

The Children of the Moons stepped out onto the shore, surveyed the scene of abject panic all around, and began to kill.

The banks of the Ko ran with blood on both sides now. The Children swept here and there with their blades, scything through bodies. Men fell in uneven fractions. The river lapped hungrily outward, flooding ever more, sucking in those who could not escape the torrent. Blackened corpses still crackling with purple electricity lay in ragged circles where the lightning had hit. The smoke was rising again from the gash in the earth, and movement could be seen within it; when it passed, it left turf statues in its wake.

'*Lucia!*' Mishani shrieked from where she lay in the mud. '*Lucia! Stop them!*'

But Lucia could not hear her, and the Xhiang Xhi paid no attention. It waved its hands above its host's head like the conductor of an orchestra. The Sister that had accompanied her as a bodyguard was looking from the carnage below to Lucia and back, uncertainty in her eyes.

A soldier came crawling up the hillside, fighting against the wind and rain, his eyes fixed on Lucia in supplication.

'Save us!' he cried, 'Save your people!'

But Lucia did not answer.

'Why won't you help us?' he demanded.

The Xhiang Xhi reached down to him, encircling him in its huge, spindly hands, and crushed him to a pulp with a cracking of bones.

Mishani screamed as blood spattered her. The horror and shock were too much. Her mind was frozen, her body paralysed.

Then Lucia jerked violently, as if some invisible force had

punched her in the gut. The Xhiang Xhi shrieked, a long, drawn-out wail. And Lucia dropped, falling from where she hovered just above the ground. She collapsed as she hit the earth, crumpling like a ball of paper. The Xhiang Xhi, still attached to her, began to darken and attenuate, reaching toward the west, lengthening like a shadow at the end of the day until it stretched across the whole battlefield and over the horizon, to where the Forest of Xu lay. Then perspective twisted, and it was gone.

The effect on the spirits was immediate: they began to settle and fade. The river went quiet, its flow diminishing and retreating. The smoke from the chasm no longer hung in the air but sank and dispersed. The wind died, dropping from a hurricane to a light breeze. The lightning stopped.

Silence ached. Only the Children of the Moons remained amid the death that surrounded them. Their swords had lowered, and they looked up at the moons above. The clouds were coming apart; the unreal sensation in the air was passing. Even the rain had lessened to a drizzle, and finally stopped altogether.

The moonstorm was over. A shimmer passed across the Children and they disappeared. The three moons drifted their steady way apart in a gradually clearing sky.

Mishani was curled up, trembling, still in shock. The sense that the danger had passed was a relief too precious to believe. She was alive, she was alive, beyond all hope it had seemed. She would have lay there for much longer, if not for one thing: the reason she was even here in the first place.

Lucia.

She crawled on her hands and knees to where Lucia lay. A frail thing, eighteen harvests, her clothing plastered to her body. And red, red blood, soaking her stomach, where she had been shot.

Mishani sobbed her name, gathering her up so that Lucia's head lay in her lap, and shook her. Lucia's eyes flickered open, and they were blue and distant. She tried to smile, and coughed instead. Blood ran over her lips and down her chin.

'I'm sorry, Mother,' she whispered. Mishani knew then that it was not her face Lucia was seeing, but Anais'. Already her gaze was becoming dim.

'Ssh,' she said. 'Ssh, do not speak.' She looked up at the Sister, who was standing over them and looking down. Her make-up had not even been smudged by the rain. 'Can you not help her?' she demanded, her voice shrill.

The Sister shook her head sadly. 'The power that kept her from the Weavers' attentions keeps her from ours as well. We cannot touch her. I cannot heal her.'

'Then what good are you?' Mishani shrieked. The Sister did not answer, and Mishani turned back to Lucia. 'What good are you?' she murmured again, helplessly.

'I didn't know,' Lucia was saying, her eyes roving. 'I didn't know they'd take so many. They took so *many*, Mother. They said they'd only take a few. A few lives to satisfy them. Because they hate us. Because that was their price.'

'Oh, child,' Mishani wept. 'Why? Why did you do it? Why did you agree?'

Lucia coughed again. Her chin and breast were soaked in crimson now. The night had gone still. There seemed nothing in the world but the three of them on the hilltop.

'I couldn't let them down . . .' she whispered.

Mishani began to weep anew at that. Gods, this poor girl, this appointed saviour who had spent every moment of ten years under the crushing expectation of the world. Could she have walked out of that forest a failure, after all the lives already given in her name? No. She had taken the Xhiang Xhi's bargain: a sacrifice in return for the spirits' help. Mishani could only imagine how that had torn her apart.

And now she was here in Mishani's arms, a rifle ball in her. Her skin was grey, her hair in wet draggles. Her slowing heartbeat pulsed in the crook of her collarbone. She was seeing beyond, into somewhere Mishani could not follow.

'Help me, Mother,' she said, her voice trembling. 'I don't want to die. I don't want to die.'

But Mishani could not form a reply. Her throat was locked with grief, her body racked by it, and all she could do was cry as Lucia gave a long sigh, and her last breath was driven from her lungs.

It was some time before Mishani heard the footsteps of Barak Zahn, and she looked up. He slumped to his knees, his face a mask of disbelief. He did not try to take Lucia from her. To do so would be to admit that it was real, that this had really happened, that he had lost his child for the second and final time.

She wondered how historians might one day justify this loss. Would they count it worthy that the Weavers' army had been stopped, even at such a terrible cost? No, there was not even that to offer succour. To destroy the enemy was one thing, but the armies of the Empire were destroyed too. There was barely enough in reserve to defend their lands now. The same could be said of the Weavers, but the Weavers bred armies faster and stronger than humans did. The two forces had wiped each other out, levelled the score temporarily, but the reality was that the Weavers had won in the long term. Without this army, they needed less food. They could survive another two years, perhaps three, on what they had. And in that time they could launch a new offensive, one that nobody could stand up to. The Empire had bought itself a stay of execution, no more.

Everything now relied on one thing. Cailin's plan had to work. They had to destroy the witchstones. It was their last and only hope.

Those soldiers that had survived stood around the tableau on the hilltop: their fallen saviour, her head in Mishani's lap; the broken Barak on his knees; the impassive Sister. They felt the uncertainty that Mishani felt, and they dared not think of the future now.

Among them stood a thin woman with tangled hair and a sullen cast to her face. She watched the scene for a time, then turned away. Grief and death were not new to Nomoru: she had seen enough as a child to last her a lifetime. Her only concern was that nobody knew who it was that fired the shot which killed their beloved Lucia. And beneath that, there was the slightest twinge of embarrassment at her shoddy marksmanship. After all, she had been aiming for Lucia's head.

When dawn came, the battlefield was empty. Starfall drifted down in the aftermath of the moonstorm like tiny flakes of glass, glinting as it caught the sun. The armies of the Empire would search for their comrades and loved ones when Nuki's eye had risen high, but until then they had retreated, unable to bear staying in the abattoir that the banks of the River Ko had become. No carrion birds or flies troubled the corpses: the residue of the spirits was too strong here.

On the north side of the river, amid the uncountable thousands of those that had died, there stood a mound of earth the size and shape of a small, hunched man. Its visage, what there could be seen of it, was a gaping face, emaciated like that of a corpse.

The effigy lasted until mid-morning, when the sun warmed and dried it. It began to crack slowly; and then the Weave-lord Kakre crumbled, bit by bit, until he was nothing more than powdery dirt on the wind.

TWENTY-NINE

Kaiku stood on the foredeck of the junk and looked bleakly towards the grey peaks. She clutched her robe to her chest with one hand, cinching it tight against the chill sea breeze. She could have warmed herself up with a thought, but she wanted to suffer. It suited her mood.

The sky was overcast, and though it was spring there was no hint of it today. A dozen ships swayed at anchor before and behind her. They shed small rowing-boats periodically that ferried back and forth from the drab shingle beach to the south, a slender finger of the Newlands that extended along the line of the coast and stopped just east of the looming, slanted bulk of Mount Aon.

For days they had been skirting the northern edge of Saramyr and there had been nothing but sheer black rock, great mountain walls that plunged vertically into the sea and offered no purchase for a landing. Kaiku had gone to starboard every morning and watched the thin plume of dark smoke from the volcanic Mount Makara drift steadily away to her right. And now here they were at their destination, a bay of stony beaches and hard planes of slate which ran inland for a few short miles before the mountains rose up again. This was where they were to make landfall, where the seven hundred Tkiurathi would disembark and make their way southwest to Adderach.

Their voyage had been favoured by Assantua, it seemed. The moon-tides had gone their way and the winds had been good. And though they had been forced to take a somewhat indirect route – passing Fo on its western side to avoid the heavily trafficked Camaran Channel – and more than once they had been forced to detour while the Sisters cloaked them from the attention of distant ships, still they had arrived on the exact day they had intended to. Or so Cailin assured them, anyway. Kaiku had stopped counting long ago.

The journey had been a miserable affair even before Kaiku had learned of the Empire's pyrrhic victory and Lucia's death. After that, she remembered little, and the discomfort and boredom of their confinement seemed insignificant in comparison to her grief.

She was trapped on this ship. Even her cabin held no privacy, for she shared it with two other Sisters, and that she counted as a luxury compared to the holds of the junks, where the Tkiurathi slept in cramped confinement. She took to wearing the make-up of the Order, because when she did so people tended to leave her alone. Often she was seen wandering the decks at night like some dark spectre, and the sailors became used to the sight after a time and ignored her. The other Sisters mistrusted her; though Cailin had told nobody of their argument at Araka Jo, Kaiku's disdain for their cause was subtly evident, and they sensed this. Cailin was on another ship, and had maintained an icy silence which suited Kaiku.

In her more bitter moments, she found a dark satisfaction in the knowledge that Lucia's death had robbed Cailin of her champion, that the Pre-Eminent must have been furious to learn how her carefully laid plans for the Sisterhood's future had been ruined. But that was small comfort: it was a setback at worst, and Kaiku knew Cailin would overcome it. If the Weavers fell, it would be the Sisters that claimed the victory, and the Sisters that would rise to take their place. Kaiku could scarcely bring herself to care. Why should she concern herself with a world so full of horror and sadness, a world that seemed to exist only to break her heart over and over? She cared only for her sorrow, and nursed it well.

Now she watched the sailors taking the Tkiurathi to shore. They were eager to get off the junks, having been tormented by conditions during the long journey. Though they had endured it without complaint, they hated to be penned in, and the overcrowded ships – much smaller than the massive vessels that had brought them across the sea from Okhamba – were claustrophobic in the extreme.

In less than a week, it would all be over. Seventy miles across the mountains lay the first monastery of the Weavers, and beneath it the first witchstone. Given that they were unsure of the terrain, they could not be certain of the exact timing of their arrival, but they kept in sporadic contact with the Sisters that accompanied the desert forces which approached from the south, and they coordinated in that way. Their activity in the Weave was heavily disguised: each communication was attended by several Sisters to ensure that no hint of their location could be divined. Their part of the operation relied on stealth.

If all went to plan, the Weavers' forces would be drawn out of Adderach to meet Reki's army in the south, whose progress had been well marked. They would not expect an attack from the north, from the sea. Kaiku doubted greatly if the Weavers would extrapolate a threat to Adderach from the daring breakout the Sisters had achieved at Lalyara: for all the Weavers knew, they were simply trying to save the Empire's fleet, and had sailed south to the safer ports of Suwana or Eilaza. Besides, the Weavers did not know that Muraki tu Koli had given away their plans; that much was evident by the way they fell into the ambush at the River Ko.

The prospect of having done with it all, one way or another, was comforting to Kaiku. She did not consider the shades of grey between success and failure: either the Weavers would be destroyed, or she would. She held on to the memories of her family, of Tane, of Lucia, and used it to fuel her hatred. Death would not be so bad now, if it could take her away from the cruelty of this world.

But first there was something she had to do. When they reached the barrier of misdirection that the Weavers would certainly have erected around their monastery, she would have to wear the Mask again.

It lay still in her pack in her cabin, now at the bottom and buried in clothes. At night, it whispered to her, tempting her with promises of her father. It was infused in some way with his essence, an essence that it had robbed from him, as it was also infused with hers now. If she wore it, could she once again attain that peace of her childhood, the comfort of her father's presence, the unthinking security he offered? No, she would not allow herself the luxury. It was a narcotic, offering anything she wanted in return for taking everything she was. But each time she was forced to use it, it became harder to resist, and after so long in such close proximity she had almost caved in more than once, hoping for refuge in its warm folds. Only her sour and venomous abhorrence of the Weavers and their devices kept her from doing so.

But when they came to the barrier she would have to put it on. Though the Sisters were capable of getting through without much effort, there was no guarantee that the Weavers would not detect their intrusion, and the element of surprise would be lost then. The only sure way they had of passing unnoticed was the Mask.

This Mask, this Mask that had cost her family's lives, was still one of the most important weapons they had. There had been no others: those Masks that the Sisters had taken from dead adversaries were too old and powerful to dare investigate, and would kill or corrupt any Sister that wore them.

So it was down to Kaiku. She would have to lead seven hundred Tkiurathi and almost fifty Sisters through the barrier. It would take hours, and she would be wearing that awful Mask all that time.

Her eyes flickered over the mountain peaks, and she sighed. Let it all be over. Just let it be finished.

She sensed somebody by her side, and turned slightly to acknowledge Tsata. He had been wary around her ever since she had learned of Lucia's death, unsure whether she needed him to comfort her or if she wanted to be left alone. There had been little talk between them lately. He had busied himself with matters among his people in the hold.

'How are the Tkiurathi?' she asked. Her voice seemed foreign to her, older than before.

'Well enough,' he replied. 'They know how much is at stake since the battle at the River Ko. They will not falter. The journey through the mountains will restore their spirits after so long trapped in these ships.'

Kaiku brushed her hair away from her face. 'What will you do . . . afterward?' She looked at him. 'When this is all done?'

Tsata held her gaze for a long time before replying. 'That will depend on how things turn after we have reached Adderach,' he said. 'I will not say I have not thought on it, but there are too many factors.'

Kaiku nodded in understanding. It was no evasion; he was being honest. But honest though he was, he had picked up a habit of employing Saramyr ways while dealing with Saramyr, and the unspoken implication was clear. What it depended on was her.

And what did *she* want to do? She had no answer to that. The only person other than Tsata she had left was Mishani, but who could say in what direction their lives might take them? Tsata would probably return with his people, and Mishani would engage herself in something diplomatic which would keep her travelling. But for Kaiku, there was only a void, an emptiness that would be left by the fulfilment of her promise of revenge. In happier times she might have thought of it as boundless opportunity, but now she saw only a frightening loss of purpose.

She felt a surge of resentment. Why *should* he rely on her? Why should her decisions be so important to others? Why, if the world was so determined to wound her, was it so reluctant to let her divorce herself from it?

She realised that she was succumbing to self-pity again, and caught herself. No, she would not go that way. This man at her side loved her, and he was a man worthy of her love in return; it was her fault that she was reluctant to give it, and no one else's. There were things she wanted to say to him, things that nestled so deep in her that she did not know whether they would survive the journey out, the harsh process of speech. Promises, pledges, oaths. Words that were solid and real, to fix her back to the world of light and laughter that she had drifted away from. But everything seemed so frail and ephemeral to her now. She wanted to tell him these truths in case either of them should die in the coming conflict, so that he would not be left unknowing, but she realised also that if they did *not* die, she would have to live with the things that she had said, and she was not yet ready for that.

She could not think on it. It was a decision too great for her in the face of all that was to come. Afterward, let things fall as they may. For now, there was only revenge, and the promise of an ending. The world was glutted with death these days, but it could stand a little more.

'Are you ready?' Tsata asked at length. 'It will soon be my turn to go. I would like it if we went together.'

'I will get my pack from my cabin,' she said. *And my Mask*, she added silently, and heard its glee like a whisper behind a wall.

'I will wait for you, then,' he said after her, as she began to walk away.

She stopped and looked over her shoulder. '*Would* you wait for me?' she asked, and by her tone he knew she was talking about something entirely larger than a simple boat journey. 'How long would you wait?'

'Until all hope was gone,' Tsata replied, without a trace of embarrassment. 'Until it hurt me more to be with you than to be without.'

Kaiku felt something buck painfully in her chest at that.

She found that she could not meet his eye, and that if she stayed any longer under the intensity of that gaze then she would begin to cry. She was so terribly fragile, and she hated herself for it.

'I will not be long,' she said, and left; but whether she meant it in answer to Tsata or in relation to fetching her pack, even she did not know.

It took them six days to reach the Weavers' barrier. Six days before Kaiku put the Mask on again, and for the first time in what seemed like forever, she was happy.

The hooves of Reki's manxthwa crunched steadily over the loose gravel on the floor of the pass. He was watching the gristle-crows circling overhead in the flat light of the dawn, his eyes tight with distrust. The air was dead and still.

He rode with his hand near the hilt of his nakata. His hair was tied back in a short queue to keep it out of his face in battle; it made his scar more obvious. The beige leather of his armour creaked as he moved, and his expression was grim with concentration.

Reki had been keeping in contact with the Tkiurathi force since landfall, and in that time the tension in his men had grown unbearable. The Aberrants had all but disappeared, except for the gristle-crows that shadowed them from high above, out of rifle range. In less than an hour, if the Sisters' estimations were correct, they would be coming up against the Weavers' barrier. The Tkiurathi had already successfully penetrated it during the night, and were lying in wait in the mountains just inside the perimeter. But there was no sign of any opposition. Even the skirmishes that had whittled at his army in those first weeks had ceased.

It was too easy. And this pass was too dangerous: a shallow-sided valley of shale and granite, bulwarked on either side by peaks. After so many days of struggling to find navigable trails through the hostile heights, he should have been glad that they at last had a few smooth miles to walk.

His men had been taxed to their limits by the journey, and they needed a rest, but the pressures of time would not allow it. The longer the day wore on, the more chance that the Tkiurathi would be discovered by roaming gristle-crows within the perimeter of Adderach, and their deceit would be revealed.

So they had to come through this eerily silent pass.

All the scouts he had were scouring the surrounding land, but they reported nothing. He asked the Sisters that travelled with him, but they had no answer. Perhaps the Weavers were consolidating around Adderach. Perhaps even inside it. That would make things extremely problematic. It would be much harder to winkle the Weavers out of their lair if they had settled in to a defensive position, and it would give them time to destroy their own witchstone if it came to a last resort. That, as far as Reki understood, would be disastrous.

Asara rode alongside him, in the midst of the army of desert warriors that moved uneasily down the narrow route through the mountains. Her manxthwa murmured and snorted and shook its head as it plodded, apparently oblivious to the prevailing mood of foreboding.

She was trying to reconcile the man at her side with the boy she had first seduced, long ago, in her capacity as a spy for the Libera Dramach. It was no good. He was no great warrior – his skills lay in tactics, and he never fought in the frontline like some Baraks did – but he certainly looked like one now. Once he had been shy and uncertain of himself; now he was lordly and assured, and people responded to that and followed him.

Asara had watched that change, due in no small part to her. Having a lover and later a wife of such staggering beauty did wonders for his self-esteem. She had been unfailingly supportive and loyal, guiding him towards strength, and he had done whatever she suggested. When he was with her, he believed he could achieve anything, and believing made it so. Four years had passed swiftly for her. At her age, time was accelerating faster and faster. She had the body and face of a twenty-harvest goddess, but the soul of a woman of ninety.

However, things were not as they were. A cloud had gathered over their relationship and was darkening rapidly. He was asking about her past, and he would not let it lie. His love for her was poisoning him. His imagination fashioned dozens of different scenarios that he tested her with to see her reaction: desperate suggestions as to how she might have lived her childhood, as if she might give away some signal when he struck on the right one. It had become an obsession, a worm of doubt that had grown into something monstrous and gnawed him inside, feeding on the magnitude of his passion for her. Had she not won him so utterly, he might have managed to be content with ignorance; but she had long experience of men and their ways, and she knew that this would consume him until he was either satisfied or driven to some mad act. She had known men slay their partners in frustration when in the throes of such torment, or cast themselves from cliffs.

Even a lie would not be enough, now. Soon it would be time to leave.

Her whole life had been a sequence of transitory episodes, always forced to move on as her nature became apparent. Eventually people noticed that she did not become old, or that she healed from wounds uncommonly fast, or that people had a strange tendency to die in any place where she settled. The Sleeping Death had struck several times in the last few weeks, causing consternation among the men and fears of a plague. It was unwise, but Asara was hungry. Hungrier, in fact, than she had ever been. And she knew exactly why; had suddenly, unequivocally understood when she woke in the night less than a week past.

She was pregnant with Reki's child.

Even the Libera Dramach, where her Aberrancy was acceptable and known to some, she must leave behind now.

Cailin would learn in the end that Kaiku had been persuaded into completing her part of the bargain struck with Asara long ago. Asara was beholden to Cailin no more. She had what she wanted. But Kaiku's misgivings at allowing her to become pregnant would be shared by Cailin. It was simply not politic to let Asara breed, to run the risk of allowing her to become the first of a race of beings that could change their outward shape at will.

Asara believed that Cailin would kill her if she ever knew. And kill her children too. So she would never return to Araka Jo, nor ever have any part of the Libera Dramach or the Sisters again.

Then why not go now? said the new voice in her mind, the voice that thought of her child first and only and always. *You have what you want from him. If you make yourself part of this battle, you could die; and what you carry is too precious to lose. You have a duty to survive now.*

But as much as she believed that, she could not leave. There was one thing left to do.

A cry from somewhere in the army brought her attention sharply back to her surroundings, and, seeing that everyone was looking up, she followed their gaze, and saw the Aberrants.

They were swarming down one side of the pass, a heaving mass of claws and fur and hide and teeth; and there, on the other side, more of them, coming from behind as well.

'How did we not see them?' Reki cried, unsheathing his sword. He turned to the Sister that rode nearby. 'How did you not know?'

Her expression was grim; she did not seem surprised or horrified, but resigned. 'They have learned to disguise themselves well,' she said.

Reki shot her a look of disgust and dismissed her with a snort. The sound of rifles was crackling along the flanks of the army as they arranged themselves defensively. The gods only knew what chance they would have against this. The

Aberrants kept coming, thundering down the sides of the pass.

'Stay with me, Asara,' he said; then he muttered a quick prayer to Suran, and the first of the Aberrants reached them.

THIRTY

The pale light of Nuki's eye grew over Adderach, illuminating madness.

The oldest monastery of the Weavers was a testament to the insanity that saturated their kind. Though the other monasteries were similarly chaotic in their architecture, nothing came close to the nightmarish creation that they had raised on the spot where they had first found a witch-stone, where Aricarat had ensnared them and turned them, unknowing, to his will.

It towered at the foot of Mount Aon, built primarily of stone the colour of sand, a bewildering agglutination of forms fused together in a pile that possessed a fractured logic all its own. Domes like bubbles poked out at odd angles from brickwork that varied wildly in size and shape. Walls slumped or curved, perhaps once intended to encircle something but never completed. Surreal statues, dream-images both fascinating and terrifying, were frozen in place, scattered randomly about the surroundings or growing out of the monastery itself. Walkways jabbed from the main body of the structure, half-completed. Spires tipped crazily, corkscrewing along their length.

The monastery sprawled in all directions. Half of the place was derelict, as were the majority of the outbuildings, which were themselves incredible demonstrations of caprice. Most of them looked ridiculous, but some showed hints of genius in their construction that the best sane minds in the Empire had never come close to matching.

Where the Weavers' ideas came from, even they did not know. But just as the Masks took pieces of their owners and passed them on, so did they possess pieces of their progenitor. The knowledge they contained – most of it far beyond the grasp of the Weavers' minds – would reveal itself in dreams and visions and moments of insight that the Weavers could not possibly have attained by themselves. Through the addle of benighted understanding, revelations were glimpsed like lanterns in the fog, some so incomprehensible that they sent their witnesses further into madness, and others lying just on the cusp of reason, that the Weavers might act on. Strange mathematics, unheard-of techniques of manufacture, combinations of reagents that would produce astounding results, patterns of logic: ideas, ideas, ideas.

The Weavers were inefficient conduits for their unseen master, but eventually the results leaked through. For every thousand misfires there was one moment of shocking clarity, and the Weavers built on these. Beneath the anarchy of Adderach there was cold, hard purpose.

The Tkiurathi attacked in the early morning, not long after they received the news that Reki's forces had been ambushed. They had crept inward from the perimeter as the dawn broke, their progress cloaked by the power of the Sisters. When the first of the gristle-crows began to appear, the Red Order deflected them so that they turned away and looked elsewhere. Once a Weaver surveyed their area, his attention crackling over them, but he was easily blinded by his skilful opponents. The Weavers were evidently not on any alert: after all, they had been steadily tracking the progress of Reki and his men for days now, and knew exactly where they were. They were confident of having their enemy safely within their grasp.

As Cailin had hoped, they did not expect an assault from the north.

When the moment came, the Tkiurathi broke cover at a run, howling battle-cries. Kaiku ran in the rearguard with some of the other Sisters. There were perhaps two hundred Aberrants, scattered across the rocky surrounds of Adderach as guards. As soon as they noticed the enemy, they raced to intercept.

Two hundred Aberrants could have done a lot of damage, even to such consummate warriors as the Tkiurathi, but they did not coordinate themselves, instead rushing at the army in clots and drabs. The Tkiurathi took them to pieces.

Kaiku felt a surge of fierce joy at the sight of Adderach, revealed there before her as the incline bottomed out and they rounded an outthrust root of the colossal Mount Aon, which rose into the insipid sky to her right. The proximity of their target and the battle ahead served to stir her from the maudlin reverie she had sunk into ever since she had removed the Mask the night before. Gods, even now she could remember the awful joy of it, and half her mind was telling her to take it from inside her dress and put it on, that she would seem so much more fearsome and formidable wearing it over her face. But she was already wearing one mask, that of the Red Order. She told herself that it was enough to serve her, and held onto that one to stave away the temptations of the other.

She caught sight of Tsata at the fringe of the horde, but then he was gone again. She had only a glimpse of him, his face fiercely intense as he swept toward a rampaging group of furies, and then the Weavers attacked.

The force of it was staggering. The Sisters had not expected such *rage*. Their enemies came through the Weave like demons, with a vigour beyond anything Kaiku had ever faced from them. They were angry at being duped, that much was evident; but more, they were angry that *women* were here, that they had penetrated the sanctuary of man this way and appeared, uninvited, so close to the heart of them. And under that anger they were desperately afraid, because they knew now that they had made a mistake and that their adversaries were close enough to reach their most precious treasure.

That first clash was a brutal one, and the Sisters almost

buckled under the power of it, for they could not devote all their resources to the combat while they were still attending to the physical world in some degree. They were hampered by the necessity of running towards the monastery, and were fighting on the fly. But the Weavers' rage worked against them and made them clumsy, and after the shock of the initial impact the Sisters rallied and fought back, spinning traps and tricks into their path.

Kaiku was guarded by several Tkiurathi, as were the other Sisters, and she took her cues from their movements as to where to place her feet while she looked into the Weave. She was darting and shuttling, meshing with the efforts of her companions, as if she were one of a dozen needles working in perfect unison to knit fabric. She felt a blaze of satisfaction as the Weavers ran into their traps, or pulled up short to avoid them. Those that were too slow became ensnared and were pulled to pieces by the Sisters, or lost themselves in closed labyrinths, leaving their bodies in a drooling, vegetative state while their minds ceaselessly wandered.

Cailin had schooled the Sisters ruthlessly in the tactics they would employ, and Kaiku sensed several of the Order tracing away under cover of the battle to find Nexuses. With the Weavers distracted, the Sisters were free to hunt the masters of the Aberrants through the links that were strung between the nexus-worms embedded in both Nexus and predator. It was a discipline that they had learned from Kaiku. She had been able to do it intuitively the first time she tried, back in the Xarana Fault, but it had proved oddly difficult for most of the other Sisters. Now they had the art of it, and the Weavers were too busy to prevent them. They followed the links back to where the Nexuses were and burst their internal organs. The controlling minds behind the Aberrants faded, and those beasts that the Tkiurathi had not killed ran into the safety of the mountains.

At some point during the conflict, Kaiku noted a diffuse spray of threads heading away from them across the golden vista that she operated in. A call for help, directed south. Just as Cailin had planned.

The Sister to Kaiku's right stumbled, fell with a strangled cry. The Tkiurathi behind her caught her, bearing her up, but Kaiku knew it was useless. The Weavers had got to her. Her essence was destroyed now, and her body was an empty husk, which would soon wind down and stop without the spark of life to empower it.

There were many Weavers here, more than there were Sisters; but the Sisters were better, even with the new tricks that their opponents seemed to learn with every conflict. It would be a hard fight, but it was one they could win. At least until the other Weavers that had been occupied with Reki's forces joined in.

Time was against them. They had to find and penetrate the witchstone before then, or they would be overwhelmed.

Obsessed with the fight, Kaiku barely noticed the deafening tumult of the Tkiarathi, the thudding of feet and the giddy rush of the charge. The Aberrants had all but ceased to be a threat now, and it was only the Weavers that concerned her. But as she neared the monastery, its baroque and twisted spires reaching high above, she began to notice something else. The witchstone. She could feel it, all the way out here, throbbing through the earth. Its power dwarfed the other witchstones she had come across before, a venomous and malevolent strength like nothing she had ever encountered. If they could sense it all the way out here, what must it be like to stand before it? For the first time, doubts began to creep in.

I will ease your mind, promised the Mask that was hidden in her dress, close to her breast.

For an instant she faltered, stumbled a little, and in that moment a Weaver slid at her along the Weave like the thrust of a rapier. It was only by Cailin's intercession that the strike was turned aside: she wrapped the point of the attack in threads like swaddling a hot poker in towels, and thrust it away.

((Kaiku, concentrate!)) came the swift admonishment. Kaiku felt a surge of resentment at being scolded so, and used it to clear her mind of the Mask's whisperings. Hatred was her ally here, no matter whom it was directed at.

Then they were at one of Adderach's many walls, a spot between two wings that snaked away like angular tentacles on either side on them. It was curved and bowed inwards, constructed of uneven layers of brick and what looked like whole boulders suspended in a matrix of mortar. The Tkiurathi were bunching around it expectantly.

((With me)) came the order, and Kaiku and several other Sisters broke off portions of their consciousness from the front line of the battle in the Weave and sent them spinning in Cailin's wake. They sewed themselves along the length of the wall, and it detonated in a blast of sandy powder. It slumped inward on itself, leaving a wide hole, strewn with rubble.

The Tkiurathi headed for the breach and poured inside. Kaiku followed, pulling out of the Weave as she clambered over the shifting chunks of stone amid the flood of tattooed folk. Several Weavers had already fallen, and there were enough Sisters to do without her now.

The morning light brought unbearable brightness to the shadowy interior of the monastery, and it echoed with the sound of the Tkiurathi's feet and voices. Much of the room was covered in debris, but she could see that it was cavernous, and that its walls were built at drastically uneven angles, higher at one end than the other. A great semicircular opening fringed with what looked like human hair led out of the room. There were other doorways, but they were too small for anything bigger than a dog. The twisted perspective made her head hurt.

Then Tsata was at her side, scrambling up from behind and taking her arm. She welcomed the sight of him; together they ran through the debris and onward, where the Tkiurathi were spreading through the building. Small clashes began as they came across those Aberrants that were still trapped inside.

Adderach was just as demented within as without. Rooms narrowed to nothing; doors had been built but no doorways; corridors were like mazes. Every room brought some new strangeness. They came across a chandelier of crystal hanging incongruously over what looked like a butcher's table, with fresh and bloody meat strewn everywhere. There was a sculpture twice the height of a man that was shockingly hideous and yet masterfully crafted, standing in a room that had been built with no doors. It was only revealed when one of the Sisters blasted a hole in the wall. One room was round and sloped down towards a circular pit, and from the blackness came hungry howls. There was little they came across that had any obvious purpose, and certainly there seemed to be nothing like dining rooms or other places of gathering. There was only the evidence of a speedy evacuation: food and rubbish everywhere, fires left burning while stew bubbled over, torches still blazing where they had been dropped. Kaiku had expected to find golneri everywhere, the diminutive servants of the Weavers, but while the presence of cooking equipment and their footprints in the dust suggested that they were around, there were none to be seen.

There were, however, dead Nexuses. Their elongated bodies, freakishly tall and thin and clad in black robes, were twisted in the throes of death. They lay in various contortions, blood weeping through the eyeholes of their blank white masks. Kaiku's stomach turned as she remembered what she had seen when they had looked beneath those masks. Tsata, who had shared her experience, gripped her shoulder reassuringly; she laid her hand on the back of his in acknowledgement.

These, then, were the Nexuses who had been coordinating the small defence force outside. And yet still it all seemed too easy, and there were too few of them.

She rushed from room to room with Tsata and several

other Tkiurathi, often backtracking as they were foiled by the Weavers' architecture, sometimes blasting through the wall when it was possible to do so without bringing the upper levels down on them. She could sense other Sisters there, scouring the corridors above her, hunting their way up to the spires.

Presently, she came face-to-face with Cailin, who stalked into the room from another doorway. Semicircular discs of metal had been embedded in the walls and floor and ceiling of this chamber, their edges etched with markings that Kaiku could not identify. Cailin picked her way across to Kaiku, accompanied by the Tkiurathi that were guarding her.

'This is wrong, Cailin,' Kaiku said.

'Indeed,' she replied. 'Where are they all? Where is the resistance? They are not in the levels above; that much I am certain.'

Kaiku tapped her foot on stone. 'They are below. They have retreated and they are waiting for us to come to them.'

Cailin met her eyes, and it was clear that she had thought the same. The conflict in the Weave buzzed around them, tickling their senses. Kaiku was keeping sporadic checks on it, but the Sisters had matters in hand.

'Can you sense it?' Kaiku asked. 'The witchstone. Already it hampers my Weaving; I cannot see the layout of this cursed place, nor see a way down.'

'There are many ways down,' said Cailin. 'It does not foil me as it does you, but I think that will change as we get nearer.' And Kaiku saw the ways as Cailin broadcast a blaze of knowledge to all her brethren. The answering mesh of information came smoothly back: the Sisters all knew their place, whether it be continuing to fight off the the Weavers, checking the remainder of the upper levels, keeping in contact with the Sisters who fought with Reki or heading downward to whatever lay beneath Adderach.

Abruptly the battle in the Weave collapsed. The Weavers, as one, faded from the field, drawing back into themselves.

The Sisters, bewildered, made to follow, but Cailin forbade them.

((Do not be drawn in. We will descend and face them there))

Adderach was eerily silent. There was no fighting, whether physical or in the Weave. The place was still, but for the pulsing of the witchstone beneath their feet.

'Come,' said Cailin, and she swept away. Kaiku followed, Tsata and the other Tkiurathi with her. They were somewhere near the centre of the edifice, Kaiku knew that much. Other Sisters were heading for other routes down. The Tkiurathi were draining into them too, leaving Adderach and its surrounds empty. They did not have a large enough force to retain a guard on the surface, in case an enemy army should arrive. If they did not succeed below, then their only chance at survival was to get out and away before the Weavers answered the distress call sent a short while ago.

Otherwise, they would be trapped down there.

Asara fired, primed, fired again. It took two more shots to get through the latchjaw's thick skull, but eventually she hit the brain. It slumped to the ground, its great porcupine-like quills shivering as it settled.

Grimed with sweat and dust, she took quick stock of her surroundings and located Reki. He was in the midst of a crowd of men, his nakata drawn but unbloodied; he was well protected. They struggled with another pair of latchjaws, squat monstrosities with fanged snouts, covered in deadly spines. They had stubby feet that protruded before them, their three digits stumpy and clawed; they had no back feet at all, only a short tail which they dragged behind them. Though they were cumbersome, they were fast enough in a lunge and their spiky armour meant that they were incredibly dangerous at close quarters.

She looked around. The floor of the pass was thick with fighting, but the desert warriors' core still held strong, due in no small part to the fact that most of the Aberrants had already left. At first the overwhelming tide of predators had taken a great toll on them, but Reki's generals had wisely kept up the defensive until their reprieve came. At some unseen signal, which Asara guessed had come from the Weavers at Adderach, the larger proportion of their attackers had broken away and headed northward up the pass. But they had left enough to keep the desert warriors busy for quite some while, and the battle continued on. Their situation was not quite so desperate now, but it was far from comfortable.

Reki was casting about for a sight of his wife, and relief showed on his face when their eyes met. She had become separated in the melee; now she slung her rifle across her back, drew a dagger and began to make her way to him, shying away from the swell of conflict as it loomed close to her.

The latchjaws had succumbed at last to their wounds, after taking down three of Reki's men, and his Blood Tanatsua bodyguards were regrouping around their Barak. They parted to allow Asara through. Reki regarded her for a moment, then unexpectedly he embraced her, driving the breath from her. He recoiled with a grunt, looking down at his hand.

Asara took it, concern on her face. There was a deep scratch along his palm, where the tip of the dagger she held had caught him. Blood welled up from within. 'Careful, my Barak,' she muttered. 'You will hurt yourself.' She turned the hand over, then looked up at him with a smile. 'I pray that is the worst of the wounds you sustain today.'

'These men will see to that,' he grinned. 'I even find myself eager to join in at times, but they will not hear of it.'

Asara brought out a bandage from a pocket in her travel clothes and expertly bound his hand. He flexed it; there was still perfect freedom of movement.

'Where did you learn to do that?'

'Don't,' Asara warned, her eyes hardening a little, and the moment of tenderness between them was gone.

Reki opened his mouth to speak, then closed it again and looked away. Now was not the time. He would have answers from her, whatever it took; but that would come later.

A shout of alarm made him snap his head round in time to see five ghauregs powering their way through a group of soldiers, heading for him and his men.

'Get back!' he cried, pushing Asara behind him. His bodyguards arranged themselves to tackle the menace. One of the creatures was taken down by rifles before it reached them; the other four crashed bellowing into their midst.

Reki's bodyguards were the best warriors Blood Tanatsua had to offer, but even they could not easily kill a ghaureg. Reki stumbled and fell as his men were driven back into him. He scrambled to his feet, looking around for Asara but unable to see her in the press. Blades sang: one of the ghauregs lost the fingers of its hand, another one had its leg cut off at the knee and fell. Someone split its face with their sword. Suddenly Reki's bravado seemed ridiculous: he was no fighter, and had no wish to be anywhere near combat if he could help it. But he was no coward either, and he would not run.

The battle had suddenly grown around him. Everything pressed in closer. He cast about for the enemy, but he could not see over the jostle of his bodyguards. A man screamed somewhere. There was a volley of rifle shots. A gap opened in the crush, and he saw a ghaureg on its knees, being hacked to pieces by his soldiers.

Then the army flexed and flowed away from him, and there was space again. The battle was no longer so near. His bodyguards moved to surround him. The ghauregs were dead, and shortly afterward a runner told him that the Sisters had begun to overcome the nearby Weavers and were killing the Nexuses that plagued them. The battle was turning.

Reki listened with half an ear: he was searching, becoming increasingly frantic.

'Where is your Barakess?' he demanded of the people around him. 'Where is Asara?'

But they could not answer him, and he himself had not seen her since the ghauregs had attacked.

In the end, he did not find her. Not even after the battle was over, and the remainder of the army – almost half its size now – forged on to Adderach in the hope of saving their allies there. Grief-stricken, he stayed with a small retinue and walked the corpse-strewn pass, praying to Suran that she might still somehow be alive.

Perhaps he would have found her, if he had been given time. He would have hunted for her over every inch of Saramyr if there was but the faintest shred of hope. Maybe, when he found her, he would have found her with the child that was his.

But Asara knew that. It was the reason she had disappeared into the mountains, and it was the reason she had smeared her dagger in poison. She had taken the unguent from the master poisoner who had collaborated with the assassin Keroki in an attempt to kill her husband months ago. It would be almost two hours before it would be felt, and by the time it struck it would be too late to remove it and too sudden for even a Sister of the Red Order to do anything but watch.

Barak Reki tu Tanatsua spent the last of his life looking desperately for the woman he loved, not realising that she had already murdered him, as she had murdered his sister long ago.

THIRTY-ONE

Cailin, Kaiku and the Tkiurathi emerged from the end of a sloping shaft, and into the sub-levels of Adderach.

Kaiku looked down the corridor that lay before them. It had once been a mine tunnel – that much was evident by the glimpses of rough stone that could occasionally be found – but its surface was almost entirely covered in metal. The walls were thick with black pipes that dripped a noxious liquid; the floor was of iron or some alloy of that. Gas-torches burned with smoky flames, connected by cables that ran along the ceiling.

The Tkiurathi were eager to be on with their task, distrusting their surroundings. They took point, with Cailin and Kaiku just behind and Tsata with them. Kaiku caught his nervousness and laid a hand on his forearm when nobody was looking.

'*Hthre*,' she murmured to him, offering the Tkiurathi pledge of mutual support.

Surprised, he grinned at her. '*Hthre*,' he replied. It did not matter that she had got it wrong, that *hthre* was supposed to be the response and not the offer. The sentiment was what counted, and he found it heartened him immensely in this dark and horrible place.

They hurried down the corridors, following Cailin's directions. Kaiku suspected that the Pre-Eminent did not know exactly where she was going: the witchstone's influence was overwhelming and made it hard to navigate. But that was a double-edged sword, for it also gave them a very definite target. They merely had to head for the epicentre of that influence, and there would be the witchstone.

But they saw no sign of their enemy at all. There were small rooms, like cells, some of them full of noisy devices and others standing empty and apparently without purpose. They looked into them as they passed by, but did not stop. They had other priorities.

They met up with another group of Tkiurathi and a half-dozen Sisters at a junction, swelling their numbers. Keeping in contact was harder now: it was like trying to shout over a hurricane. The brooding energy beneath them was confusing the Weave, sending it into disarray. Kaiku hoped it would hamper the Weavers as much as it would the Sisters, but somehow she doubted it.

The Sisters and the Tkiurathi were descending from above, spreading out through the tunnels of the old mine, an army of ants invading an enemy nest. But still the enemy would not meet them.

Cailin's force was the first to come out of the corridors. The claustrophobic tunnels opened into a massive room, bigger than any great hall ever built in Saramyr. It was circular in shape and flat-roofed, and as the invaders poured in from the tunnel they gradually faltered and stood there, aghast, at the sight.

It was stultifyingly hot and oppressive. The air was tinged with a coppery taste and thick with steam and smoke. There were two upper levels to the room: wide, ringed platforms that ran around the edge, walkways of metal. At ground level, furnaces roared from within their casings, glowing red through the vents at their sides and spewing strange gases. Contraptions clattered and jerked, chattering through cycles of activity incomprehensible to the observers.

Placed in concentric rows around the room were elaborate metal cradles. Hanging amid the cradles' frames were veiny, transparent sacs of flesh that looked like the stomach of some huge animal. Within, there were dark shapes suspended in liquid, lit by a greenish inner glow, visible only as smears from a distance.

Kaiku walked up to one, dazed by the scale of what they had discovered, and knelt down to look inside it.

It was a child, an infant, perhaps three harvests old but out of proportion, its bones too long. Its tiny chest sucked in and out as it breathed the liquid. It was on its side, facing her, and on top of its bald head there was the glistening diamond shape of a nexus-worm female embedded in its flesh. Kaiku could see a face tracked with ridges where the tendrils ran just beneath the skin, reaching to its eyes and mouth and nose, around which thin purple capillaries showed through. Its eyes were open, but they did not follow Kaiku as she moved. They were purest black.

A young Nexus. They grew them here, in these wombs.

Kaiku stared at the thing in the tank, numb. Cailin came up next to her.

'Is this what knowledge their god gives them?' Kaiku said. 'They blaspheme against Enyu herself.'

'That is not all,' Cailin said, motioning across the room.

Kaiku got to her feet and went to where a trio of larger cradles stood. The Tkiurathi were gathered around them, talking in hushed tones. She caught a word she knew: *maghkriin*. It was the name they gave to the beings created by the Fleshcrafters in Okhamba, who shaped babies in the bellies of their captured enemies to make them monstrous killers.

As she neared the cradles, she understood.

It was difficult to tell what the things that hung in the sacs had originally been, nor what they might become. But they moved fitfully, here twitching a leg, there curling a claw. They were baby Aberrants, three of the same species but each one different from the other. One was growing little fins along its arms, another was developing outsize teeth, while the last was a true horror with two three-quarter heads fused together in the centre, its animal features colliding and merging. The sacs glowed from within with the same nauseating light which Kaiku recognised as that given off by witchstone.

She had seen what happened to the Edgefathers who were in contact with the witchstone for too long. She knew how the Weavers changed through even the tiny dose of dust in their Masks. The Weavers were using witchstone to mutate these creatures, who were probably themselves the offspring of mutants. Like the Fleshcrafters, they were shaping their troops. Designing Aberrants through forced mutation and selective breeding. Was this where the latchjaws had come from? The nexus-worms? The *golneri*?

To Kaiku, the noise of the room faded until she could hear only the sound of her own breathing. The hate in her was choking all else. She wanted to lash out, to ruin this place, to kill every one of the Weavers and eradicate their practices from a world she had once loved. She thought suddenly of Tane, the priest of Enyu who had died to save Lucia, a man who had dedicated himself to understanding nature. How this would have destroyed him. All this time, these two and a half centuries, the Weavers had been learning the dark art of subverting Enyu's plans, using these poisonous devices to imitate her processes and turn them to their advantage.

She felt a hand on her shoulder.

'We must go,' Tsata said. Behind him the Tkiurathi were beginning to move again. They crossed the room and out through the far doorway, the Sisters following behind. Kaiku paused beneath the coiled-iron frame, her shoulders tight.

'Cailin,' she said, and the Pre-Eminent, who had been just ahead of her, stopped. She saw the look in Kaiku's eyes, and nodded.

When the last of the Tkiurathi had left the room, the two of them remained in the doorway, like estranged twins, their appearance uniting them in ways that they did not feel. The only thing between them now was a common goal.

Kaiku waved a dismissive hand, and the sacs detonated from within, spewing a green flood. Those that lined the upper levels burst at the same time, slopping forth their embryonic cargo like rough abortions. A great deluge of the amniotic liquid came splashing over the edge of the walkways and washed around the boots of the Sisters.

'I wish you would change your mind, Kaiku,' Cailin said at length. 'Stay with us. We have need of your strength. And there is so much more you could learn from me.'

But Kaiku turned away and stalked down the corridor after the departing Tkiurathi, and Cailin, after appraising the destruction for a few moments more, followed her.

The first attack on the intruders occurred not long afterward.

It was Cailin who sensed it. She was somehow able to filter through the baffling effect that the witchstone produced, at least to a better extent than Kaiku could. Kaiku's *kana* was limited to her line of sight now; the very walls seemed infused with the stuff of the witchstone, and it was extraordinarily hard to try and Weave through it. She had only been given hints of how much greater Cailin's mastery of her *kana* was than her own, for Cailin kept her secrets close; but she was becoming more and more assured that the Pre-Eminent and some of the most proficient Sisters operated in an entirely different league.

What Cailin sensed she rebroadcast with greater clarity for those nearby, and that was how Kaiku learned of it. Garbled empathic impressions of surprise, pain, and combat. Then silence, and the soft ache of death.

Cailin said nothing, but she continued on and the others went with her.

It happened again later, as they hunted through another empty series of rooms. This time it was a bigger group of Sisters and Tkiurathi, and there was a clearer picture. Aberrants, swamping into the corridor, bolstered by Weavers. They were systematically assaulting the Sisters, group by group, taking advantage of the fact that they had to split up to search the complex. This was what they had lured them down here for. They knew their best chance for survival lay in picking the Sisters apart.

But that was not a usual Weaver tactic, Kaiku thought. If they had the strength of numbers, they would have attacked outright. They were delaying until their reinforcements could arrive. They were on the defensive.

As Cailin had hoped, they had been drawn off by Reki's men, and had not left enough of their forces behind to protect themselves from something like this.

As it turned out, the second group of Sisters were not taken down so easily. The Tkiurathi put up a vicious fight, and it was still ongoing by the time Cailin and Kaiku were ambushed.

The Aberrants boiled out of a side-corridor, filling the junction with their bodies and ploughing towards the Tkiurathi, howling. They almost caught the front line by surprise: they had been virtually soundless in their approach, and the Weavers had cloaked themselves from the Sisters well enough that, in this difficult environment, not even Cailin had detected them. But the soft warbling of the shrillings had given them away at the last moment. The Tkiurathi met the charge with their gutting-hooks sweeping.

The two groups crashed together. The corridors were wide enough for seven or eight to fight at a time, but the Aberrants in their frenzy clambered over the top of the combatants to reach those behind. Most found themselves eviscerated as they did so, their exposed underbellies ripped open and their steaming innards spilling out. The front line of the Tkiurathi collapsed under the weight of the creatures and were either dragged free or savaged. But the Okhambans were taking down the Aberrants faster than they themselves were dying. Their twin-bladed weapons, one in each hand, hacked and plunged and parried. The warriors, men and women both, were possessed of an uncanny harmony of movement that kept their blows from interfering with their neighbour's even when they were packed tight like this.

The Weavers had made one bad mistake. The Tkiurathi were born for close combat. Their weapons were adapted to its purpose and their fighting technique tailored to those conditions. Life in the jungle had meant that they had evolved short, fast, controlled movements so that they would not tangle their blades in vines or trees, and they had reactions honed by generations of living in one of the most hostile places in the Near World. Here in the confines of the tunnels they outclassed the Aberrants, who were used to the open spaces of the mountains.

The Tkiurathi were as animals themselves when they fought, primal and ferocious, and they dodged and slashed and killed until they were drenched in the blood of their enemies.

Kaiku and the Sisters dealt with the Weavers. There were only four of them, and the Sisters in Kaiku's group outnumbered them two to one. It was no contest. The Sisters attacked in a whirling chaos of threads and the Weavers' defences could not stand it. They held out briefly and then collapsed. The Sisters ripped into the fibres of their enemy's bodies, and the force released by the sundering turned the Weavers to pillars of fire.

With the Weavers gone, they broke the necks of the three Nexuses who were controlling the Aberrants, and the predators collapsed in disarray, some of them fleeing or attacking each other. The Tkiurathi made short work of the rest.

Kaiku caught sight of Tsata nearby. He was breathing hard, flecked in blood, his eyes sharp with an intensity that she only saw when he fought. A quiet and introspective man in the main, his flipside was this feral killer. She wondered briefly what that meant for the future, how deeply that ferocity was suppressed and whether it might one day be turned on her, if she should stay with him. Was he capable of that? How could she tell? How well, in the end, did she know him?

Tsata sensed her gaze upon him and turned to meet it. She felt a shock of guilt, as if he had realised what she was thinking. Then, expressionless, he turned away, and the group began to move on, deeper into the maze of corridors.

The Weavers attacked them three more times over the next hour. Other groups of Sisters who were searching elsewhere in the complex were similarly assaulted by forces of varying size. Some were overwhelmed and slain; some managed to kill their attackers. Cailin's group, with eight Sisters among them, had the strength to outmatch the Weavers; but some were not so lucky.

Kaiku could sense Cailin's mood growing graver. The Weavers' plan, costly though it was, was working. The invaders' numbers were dwindling slowly, and still there had been no sign of a way down to the witchstone beneath them. They could be running around these colossal sub-levels for hours yet, being gradually whittled away; but long before that, the Weavers' reinforcements would arrive, and flood down through the mine. Nobody thought of giving up and going back to the surface. They were just too close. But the enemy army could not be far from Adderach now.

Reports of other places like the chamber that Kaiku had destroyed came through to them. One group found a huge complex of grim workshops, forges and lathes and whittling benches where the Masks of the Weavers were crafted; but there were no Edgefathers to be seen, for they had all been taken elsewhere, presumably to the same place that the absent golneri had gone. There was also a bigger forge nearby, something entirely different to that of a blacksmith or an artisan: a monstrous, sweltering place with huge vats of molten metal and great moulds, where they found newly-made pipes and cogs and other components of the Weavers' devices. Another found a room full of roaring machines that pumped up and down, and in its centre a pool of bubbling mud that belched foul-smelling gas. Unusually, there was a marked lack of evidence of the Weavers' insanity in these sub-levels: there were no corpse-pits, no wild scrawls or strange sculptures. Here there was only the chill efficiency of machinery, designed by the Weavers and built by the golneri. Aricarat kept a tighter rein on his subjects down here.

Whether by Shintu's will or Cailin's guidance, it was Kaiku's group who found the way down. And they found it held against them.

They were directly above the witchstone at this point: Kaiku could feel it through the great weight of rock beneath their feet. They had reached what appeared to be a wall of metal at the end of the corridor, but which turned out on closer inspection to be a door of some kind. Cailin rested her hand against it and closed her eyes; a moment later there was a loud crunch, and Cailin stepped back as the wall began to part in the centre, sliding into recesses on either side.

The chamber it revealed was dimly lit by a scattering of gas-torches, but it was too large for them to do anything more than offer faint contrast to the shadows which cloaked the far end. It was circular, like the incubation room they had passed through, and its walls were metal and lined with cables and heavy pipes that leaked steam at regular intervals with a soft sigh, as if the mines themselves were breathing. In the centre of the room was a tower of machinery, bristling with cogs and chains. In the tower was a featureless metal doorway.

They stepped into the chamber, spreading out around the entrance, and regarded the strange edifice before them.

'There it is,' said Cailin. 'That is how we get to the witchstone.'

Tsata took a step forward, but Kaiku held out her hand to block him.

'It is too easy,' she said.

Something massive shifted in the shadows at the back of the chamber, moving from behind the obscuring bulk of the tower. There were smaller figures, also, strangely indistinct even to Kaiku's *kana*-adapted eyes.

'Trickery!' Cailin hissed, and swept a hand out. The shadows flexed and a veil dropped from their sight.

Kaiku paled. Twenty Weavers, a dozen Nexuses, and at least fifty Aberrants were emerging from the gloom, sidelit in the faint yellow glow. And behind them came something worse still.

Kaiku had seen giant Aberrants before; she had almost been killed by one on the way across Fo many years ago, and since then there had been reports of them from time to time in the mountains. But this was something altogether more terrible than any she had heard of. It must have been twenty feet high at the shoulder, its skin black and leathery and thick with sinew. It walked on all fours, its feet flat and its bulk enormous to support its weight. Its head was all jaw and teeth, crooked fangs far too big for its mouth, and its twisted muzzle was deeply scarred and torn because of it. It drooled a frothy milk of spittle and blood which drizzled onto the metal floor. Asymmetrical features were warped out of true: a tiny eye was lower on one side of its face than the other, almost upon the ridge of its cheek. A fringe of spikes that were somewhere between fangs, tusks and horns stuck out at random angles, sprouting from the edge of its mouth, its forehead, and its lower jaw. Its back was ridged in the same spikes, as was its tail – which was flaccid and appeared broken – but they were set to no pattern. Rather, they gave the impression of rampant growth, as if its skeleton had thrust protrusions through its flesh wherever it could. At its neck, visible only as a wet patch against its skin, Kaiku could see a nexus-worm.

It was a freak, a beast spawned from generations of creatures breeding in the mines beneath Adderach, where the mutating influence of the witchstone had created horrors beyond imagining. Though much of the mine was sealed for the Weavers' own safety, and it was suicide even for them to set foot in its depths, they had managed to secure this one and tamed it as the guardian of this place. It lived in the chamber just beyond this, through a dark doorway and down a long corridor to a room full of bones and the stench of musk and dung.

The Weavers shuffled to a halt at the edge of the light. The predators stopped also, shifting restlessly. Behind them, the giant Aberrant growled, a rumbling from deep within its chest.

For a long moment, the two forces faced each other across the chamber. Then, possessed by some feeling that she could not name, a mixture of resignation and anger and deep, deep hatred, Kaiku stepped forward. Her hair hung over one painted eye, and with the other she stared coolly at the Weavers ranged before them.

'You are in our way,' she said.

It was like the spark to a powder keg. Both sides erupted in a roar, and the Aberrants and Tkiurathi charged each other.

Kaiku plunged into the Weave, and the scene slowed around her. The golden knitwork figures of the Tkiurathi and the Aberrants became transparent: she saw the clench and tug of their muscles, saw the air sucked into their lungs through gritted teeth, the minute disturbance of soundwaves as their shoes and claws hit the floor. The Weavers came fast, but she realised their tactics immediately. They had divided: half were guarding the Nexuses and the giant beast while the rest attacked. Cailin and the Sisters were with her in the Weave, their own tactics already assigned and agreed in a communication faster than thought. And then Kaiku was spiralling towards her nearest adversaries, drawing two of them in together, and as they hit they burst into a ball of threads and sucked back inward onto each other, a tight knot of conflict that would only untangle when either Kaiku or the Weavers were dead.

Tsata jumped the swipe of a shrilling's sickle claw and struck down with his *kntha*, half-severing its foreleg. His leap landed him some way past the beast, and he left it for his kinfolk behind him while he tackled a ghaureg. In these moments of combat, he felt a stillness unlike any other, a perfection of focus that no other activity could bring him. In the sweep and slice of his gutting-hooks, in the dance of his body as he avoided the blows of his enemies by inches, he found that the chaff of existence sloughed from him like falling leaves from the trees. He was as his Okhamban ancestors had been, and their ancestors, all the way back to a time before civilisation had touched mankind. He was a hunter, a predator, streamlined to that one purpose. There was no fear of death. Death was simply impossible.

The ghaureg reached for him; he ducked under its elbow and buried his gutting-hook to the hilt in its armpit, angling in toward its heart. The creature's reflex was to swipe its arm back at him, but he had expected it and dropped beneath the swing; then he braced his foot against its ribs and in one quick motion he pulled the blade free. Blood sprayed from the wound, and the creature went down.

Rifles cracked behind him, and he saw an Aberrant he could not identify fall with its skull in ruins. The Tkiurathi, out of the cramped corridors, now had space to employ their ranged weapons without killing their own folk. Some of them took down Aberrants from a distance, but others fired at the Nexuses that hid in the shadows, and the Weavers were kept busy protecting their allies.

Kaiku saw none of this: her world had diminished to the frantic scurry inside the Weave-knot, the battlefield between her and the two Weavers. They struck at her hungrily, heartened by their numerical superiority; Kaiku barely fended them off. She spun herself a tight ball of defence in the centre of the knot, sheltering from the Weavers' attacks. They were harrying her instantly, picking at stray threads, trying to unravel her. She kept curled like a hedgehog, building a construct within the confines of her defences. The Weavers, puzzled by this sudden cessation of aggression, were determined to get at her. They wound themselves together and, as one, drilled inward. Even Kaiku could not withstand an attack like that in concert, and her ball came apart, its threads scattering.

Inside was a labyrinth, an insoluble jumble of threads with no beginning and no end, and the Weavers fell right into it and were lost.

Kaiku stayed there just long enough to be sure that they would never get out, and then threw herself back into the fight. One of the Sisters had fallen, but four Weavers had also been taken out of the action. Kaiku let her hate and anger spur her to new vigour. This was a battle they could not afford to lose. Much more than their own lives depended on it.

The giant Aberrant, meanwhile, was making its presence known. It roared and snapped and stamped among the combatants. The metal floor trembled with the impact. Tkiurathi swarmed around it, trying to take it down, but it was too big. Its jaws dripped with blood as evidence of the dozen lives it had already accounted for. The Sisters tried to get to it, to stop its heart or blind it, but the Weavers had made it the focus of their keenest protective measures and there were not enough Sisters to get through.

Tsata was among those who were attacking the monster. His efforts were futile. He ducked in and tried to hamstring its foreleg with his blade, but his hardest swipe made little more than a shallow cut against the creature's hide. Another Tkiurathi to his left made an attempt to get to the nexus-worm which kept the creature under control. The Aberrant swept its head to the side and gored him, then flung him shrieking into the air and caught him in its mouth with a crunch of bones.

Tsata saw the furie charging him out of the corner of his eye, and he moved just in time. The boar-like Aberrant skidded past him, and was taken in the side of the head by another Tkiurathi blade. The force of its momentum tore the weapon from its killer's hand, and it crashed into a heap, bleeding from the eyes.

Tsata looked up at the man who had slain it. It was Heth, his hair wet with sweat, his tattooed face gleaming. He gave Tsata a grave stare and then tipped his head at the roaring monstrosity that was tearing through their people.

'I'll be the lure,' he said in Okhamban. 'You kill that thing.'

Tsata tilted his chin at his friend, knowing that Heth would probably pay for it with his life. Neither of them had the slightest hesitation. It was a matter of *pash*.

Kaiku sensed the wave of alarm across the Weave through the muting effect of the witchstone, and knew what it meant even before Cailin amplified and clarified it. It had come from one of the Sisters in another part of the complex, and its message was simple.

The enemy army had arrived, and were already pouring down through Adderach.

Kaiku felt terror clutch at her. Not at the prospect of dying: death was something she was not afraid of at this point, and part of her would welcome it. It was the thought that she might fail here, when she was so close to fulfilling her oath to Ocha, to avenging her family. She redoubled the intensity of her assaults, but it was hopeless. The Weavers had dug in; they knew what the Sisters knew. They had only to hold out for a few minutes and the reinforcements would be here.

It will not end like this, she told herself, but it was an empty thought. There was nothing she could do about it.

((Sisters)) said Cailin. *((Time has run out))*

And with that came an empathic blaze of instructions. Kaiku did not question them; she had no other inspiration. The Sisters moved as one, breaking off their attacks and whirling into a frenzy, setting false resonances and weaving a screen of confusion. With the portion of her mind that attended the physical battle which raged across the chamber, Kaiku saw Cailin drawing a slender blade from inside her robe. She had a fraction of an instant to wonder what it was she hoped to do with that, when Cailin disappeared.

She had never witnessed anything like it. Even the display Cailin had shown her at Araka Jo, when she had made herself simply *not there*, was nothing compared to this. For as she disappeared, she dissassembled herself in the Weave, her very being coming apart into its component fibres and racing away in a diffuse burst before knotting together again elsewhere. Again, and again and again, she darted back and forth through the Weave, and finally returned to her original position and reappeared.

In the space of a heartbeat she had appeared behind several of the Weavers in rapid succession, so quick that it seemed almost simultaneous, each time stabbing with her blade. Then she was back where she had begun, the whole process enacted fast enough so that it might have been a trick of the brain. But on the far side of the room, in the gloomy shadows, eight Weavers collapsed, pierced through the nape of the neck.

Kaiku was dumbstruck. She had never imagined Cailin capable of such a thing; no wonder the Weavers were caught by surprise. Just for an instant, she had glimpsed the unplumbed depths of her own abilities, what she might be able to do if she took up Cailin's offer and returned to the fold.

But there was no time for such musings now. The Weavers were rocked by their loss, and the Sisters, scenting victory, threw themselves into the offensive.

The giant Aberrant swung its head around at Heth's cry. Even from a being so small to a creature so massive, it recognised a challenge. Its mismatched eyes squinted down at the blurred figure at its feet. This little thing was becoming a torment: already the Aberrant had tried to catch Heth twice, and he kept dodging out of the way. Frustrated, it lunged for him.

Heth moved as the great jaws gaped, and when they snapped shut he was not between them. As the head came down, Tsata darted in from the side, driving his gutting-hook in towards the creature's neck, where the nexus-worm glistened. His blade hit one of the Aberrant's many facial spikes, glanced away, and Tsata was forced to jump backwards to avoid being gored as it raised its head again.

Heth was already running to a new position, and Tsata went with him, keeping himself clear of the other Aberrants that were engaged in battling his brethren. He spared an instant to glance back at Kaiku, but she was anonymous among the other Sisters, and he had no idea how their endeavours were going. He had only this purpose: to bring down the beast. And every time he failed, Heth was forced to make himself the bait once more. But the creature was too well-armoured, making what was already a hard target near to impossible.

His knuckles whitened on the hilt of his *kntha*. He would not fail next time.

The giant Aberrant was following Heth now, ignoring the other Tkiurathi that hacked pointlessly at its legs and tail. Heth glanced over at Tsata, to be sure he was near enough; but in the instant that Heth took his attention away, it struck.

Heth only dodged at all because of the alarm on Tsata's face, but he was a fraction too slow. Though the beast missed most of him, its jaws snapped shut on his trailing arm with a terrible cracking noise. Heth screamed; blood squirted through the monster's teeth. It shook him violently, pulling him over and tearing the rest of his arm off.

Then Tsata was there. The beast's head had sunk low to the ground, and Tsata threw himself at his target. He felt a blaze of pain in his ribs: the thing had turned slightly, and he caught one of the spikes in his side. But he took his gutting-hook and rammed it into the soft, slimy flesh of the nexus-worm, then twisted hard. The beast roared, flexing spasmodically; Tsata was lifted up and flung away. He sailed through the air for a few awful instants and landed in a heap on the hard metal floor with a loud snap.

But the beast buckled. Its legs gave way as the nexus-worm died, and it staggered sideways and collapsed with a thunderous boom, crushing Aberrants and Tkiurathi alike underneath its massive bulk. The death of the worm, so closely tied in with its brain and nervous system, triggered a stroke and a heart attack simultaneously, and after a few violent spasms it gave a bubbling sigh and was still.

The Weavers fell to pieces all at once. The remainder of them had consolidated their efforts as best they could into one defensive force, but eventually it could bear the strain of the Sisters' furious assault no longer. The six Sisters that were left shredded the remaining eight Weavers, blowing them apart from within in a flaming rain of flesh and bone.

After that, it was a slaughter. The Sisters went for the Nexuses next. The black-robed beings went up like torches, silently burning. They showed no indication of pain, nor made a sound, but collapsed into blazing heaps. The Aberrants lost their minds as they lost their masters; some fled, some kept fighting, but the Tkiurathi were still thirty strong and the Aberrants half that now. The remaining beasts were destroyed by the Sisters or by the Tkiurathi, and then there was silence. As if waking from a dream, Kaiku realised that the fighting had stopped.

But a new sound was growing. The roar of an approaching horde, coming from the doorway through which they had entered. The Weavers' reinforcements were here.

'Seal that door!' Cailin cried, and the Sisters responded immediately. The mechanism that drove the metal barrier jerked into life, and the two halves began to slide from their recesses and grind shut. The sounds of the enemy got louder, louder, until Kaiku thought they must surely be upon them;

and then there was a reverberant clang, and the door was closed.

Kaiku turned away, looking for Tsata, and found him kneeling, one arm cradled in the other. She hurried over to him, slowing as she neared. His trousers were black with blood which had soaked into them from the great slick all around him. Heth lay in the midst of that, his yellow skin gone white, his tattooes pallid. His arm had been ripped away, leaving only a wet mess at the shoulder through which a knob of bone showed. He was clearly dead.

'Tsata . . .' she murmured, then realised she did not know what to say. He did not look up. She noticed that his left forearm kinked at an angle, and he was holding it to his chest. 'Let me see to that . . .' she began, but then Cailin swept up to her.

'Kaiku. Come with me now,' she said. She looked down at Tsata. 'The Weavers will not be long getting through that door. We need what time you can give us.'

'You will have every moment our lives can buy,' he said quietly, and still he did not raise his head.

Cailin cast one last glance at Kaiku and then made for the doorway in the tower, where the other Sisters were heading. Kaiku waited there for a short time, trying to think of something to say, something suitable for this parting. But there were no words that could express her sorrow, nothing adequate to ease his hurt. In the end, she turned and walked away without a word. She was last through the doorway, and as soon as she was in Cailin used her *kana* to decipher and activate the mechanism. The door slid shut with a squeal of metal. Kaiku's gaze lingered on Tsata until he disappeared from view.

The elevator began to descend with a lurch, and they went down, down towards the witchstone.

THIRTY-TWO

None of the Sisters spoke as the machinery whirred and squeaked. They could sense that they were sinking by the feeling in their stomachs, but they were encased in the circular metal room of the elevator, and there was nothing to look at but each other. With every passing second, the power exuded by the witchstone was growing, becoming fiercer and more intense. Cailin had not brought the Tkiurathi with them because she believed they would not be able to survive such proximity to the thing; Kaiku wondered now if any of them would. This witchstone was older by far than the one she had destroyed in the mine long ago, older even than the stone that had been shattered at Utraxxa. It was the heart of a god, and merely to look on it might be enough to kill them.

After what seemed like an age, the elevator shuddered and stopped. There was a pregnant silence. Then the doors opened.

The force of the witchstone's presence made the Sisters cry out and recoil, their arms instinctively raised before their eyes as if by blocking the brightness they could mute its strength. The thick metal of the elevator had been shielding them until now; robbed of that barrier, they were blasted by it like a hurricane.

Kaiku fell backwards to the cold, hard floor, breaking her fall with her arm. The Weave was a maelstrom, its churning so violent that it physically pushed her over. She clung to control, trying to ride the chaos before she was swept away by it entirely. The very touch of the witchstone was foul, tainting the golden threads black, a sucking morass of malevolent darkness. The rage of Aricarat was palpable, a hatred pure enough to drive them insane.

But somehow Kaiku held on, long enough to sew a skin around herself, a protective cocoon that screened out the worst of the barrage. She found her level and allowed herself to flow with the maelstrom like a boat on stormy waters. Then she set about rescuing those of the Sisters that had not managed to do so yet. Finally, they were stable enough to stand again; but Kaiku's *kana* was already being taxed, and she knew she could not hold out like this for long.

They staggered out of the elevator and into the chamber of the witchstone.

It was gargantuan, towering almost a hundred feet high and half that in width, filling the cavern. There was no discernible overall shape to it; it was simply a mass, a crooked lump of rock that sprouted roots and protuberances all over its surface, and from those extrusions other extrusions came. It was growth gone mad, multiplying over and over in ridiculous plethora until there was barely any space at all between its branches. Like the other witchstones, it thrust into the wall of the surrounding cavern, melding with it; but unlike the others, its branches were so dense that it was almost impossible to tell where the witchstone ended and the cavern began. It had assimilated itself into its surroundings almost totally.

The nauseating luminescence of the witchstone blanched the faces of the Sisters as they came cringing into its presence, casting stark shadows across the broken floor. Several great roots reared over them, dwarfing them by comparison.

But Cailin straightened herself, her expression made hideous by the unnatural light, and her voice rang out across the chamber.

'Sisters! Cleanse our land of this abomination!'

Kaiku steeled herself and unleashed her *kana* at it. The vast, pulsing black tangle filled her world and engulfed her. The touch of it was like acid, but through the burning she fought to untangle the threads of the witchstone, to find purchase to get inside it. Its radiance was so terrible that even the Weavers had not been able to come near to plant explosives, like they must have done at Utraxxa. The Sisters had only to bore inward and they would be inside the web of the witchstones, able to spread to every stone in Saramyr. But each moment they wasted was a moment closer to that when the Weavers would break through the lingering defences that the Sisters had left on the door to the chamber above. Then the Tkiurathi would be killed – *Tsata* would be killed – and the Sisters would be next. The Weavers would send an elevator full of Aberrants down, and it would be the end.

She gritted her teeth, scratched and picked at the witchstone ferociously, but it did no good. Frustration grew in her. She could find nowhere amid the awful mass that would permit her entry to the thing: its exterior defences were too dense. No Sister had ever Weaved into a witchstone before, and now they found that they had underestimated the difficulty greatly.

Cailin sent an instruction to them all, and they battled their way through the whirling disorder and sewed themselves together. In one slender needle of intent, they thrust at the witchstone, driving into it; but incredibly, it held. They managed to make fractional headway before the point of the needle was blunted and expelled. They struck again, to no avail.

The Sisters began to try anything and everything they could. They attempted to make themselves diffuse, to seep into it like gas through the pores of a membrane; they tried attacking it from many angles at once; they worked at unpeeling it like an onion. Nothing worked. It remained invincible, and their best efforts did not even scratch it.

Kaiku was exhausted. The sheer mental strain of being in its presence was becoming too much, and Weaving on top of that was draining her utterly. What was more, her *kana* was being diverted to repair the damage that was being done to her physical body. She could feel the witchstone's insidious rays changing her, making minuscule alterations, causing tiny cancers and encouraging unusual and unnatural processes into life. Her *kana* was automatically fixing this corruption as it occurred. If not for that, it would not have been long before she became like the elder Edgefathers were: repulsive freaks, warped beyond recognition.

She dropped out of the Weave, and realised that she was on her knees on the rough floor of the cavern. Her legs had been unable to support her any longer. She was gasping for breath, her body aching.

Spirits, no. Not when we are so close. We cannot fail here. Ocha, emperor of the gods, help us now if you can. Help me fulfil my oath. Show me how to end this evil.

And the answer came to her. A possibility so awful that she at first dismissed it out of hand, but then, despairingly, she realised that it was the only chance they had left. She could sense the Sisters fruitlessly battering at the witchstone, and knew that even Cailin's skill could not help them now.

She thought of all that would be lost if the Sisters fell here. Of all the beauty she remembered from her childhood: the rinji birds on the Kerryn, the sun through the leaves of the Forest of Yuna, the dazzling waters of Mataxa Bay. All that would pass into a memory, and eventually even memories would fade. The skies would die. And after the Near World was gone, after their planet had been enshrouded as the Xhiang Xhi had predicted, then Aricarat would spread outward, into whatever was beyond.

It was too much, too much responsibility to comprehend. So she thought only of Tsata. She would save *his* life, if she could. Even if it meant trading her own. For *pash*.

She drew the leering red and black Mask from her dress and slipped it over her head.

'Kaiku!' Cailin shrieked, seeing what she was doing. 'Kaiku, *no!*'

With the Mask on her face, she Weaved.

The world shattered, and there was nothing but delirium and pain. Sense unravelled, connections of logic becoming estranged. There was no Kaiku, no *self* at all; she was a part of everything, subsumed, a curl of wind in a cyclone of derangement.

But she felt a gentle and insistent tugging, drawing her. For no reason she could fathom, it was a comfort, and she went to it. The disassembled parts of her consciousness gradually came together, reaching tendrils of sanity to each other, cohering into a structure around the warm, blessed clot of emotion that attracted them.

Father.

It was him. Or rather, it was the part of him that the Mask had robbed all that time ago, an imprint of his thoughts and mind that Kaiku had subconsciously recognised and gravitated towards. She wished somehow that she could gather it up, treasure it; but it was only a faint recollection, a sensation of trust and safety that she had lost long ago.

That the Weavers had taken from her.

She struggled to gain control of the madness around her. Anger rose within, anger at how this sanctuary had been stolen by her enemies, how her father had been so *broken* that he had poisoned his own family rather than let them fall into the hands of the Weavers. *They* had done that to him. *Them!*

With one colossal effort of will, she dragged herself into focus, until she was Kaiku again.

She was in the Mask, in the fibres that formed the wood and lacquer of the thing. And she was in the witchstone dust, tiny particles of the enormous entity that they had come to destroy. They were part of her surroundings, bending the Weave unnaturally, befouling and violating her. She saw the dementia they engendered, the way they fractured the Weave in such a way that even she found it hard to understand. No wonder that it drove the Weavers mad in the end.

No wonder the Sisters had never dared to attempt this. It was only because the Mask was exceptionally young and therefore weak, and because she had worn it before and was used to it, that she had not entirely shed her mind upon entering; that, and the fact that her father had been here before her.

She let herself sink into the dark threads of the witch-stone dust. These were mindless things, possessing none of the fearsome hatred of Aricarat, and yet they did live. In those little particles were a multitude of infinitesimally small organisms, so incredibly minute that Kaiku could only sense them and not identify them at all. But they possessed a portion of their parent, ingrained memory and power held in suspension. Each one possessed a tiny glimmer of energy, the force that twisted plant and flesh into new configurations. They were like tiny synapses: individually they were nothing at all, but in a group they made connections, and the connections made them greater than the sum of their parts.

And as Kaiku touched them, a flash of understanding bloomed in her mind. How one of these organisms could link with another, how the links increased in number exponentially as the number of organisms increased until they were sufficiently complex to become aware, like the processes of the human brain. How the organisms, multiplying endlessly, became legion, their intelligence and their ability growing as the gestalt entity grew until it was beyond human comprehension. And how the more them that gathered, the greater the energy they exuded, and the more they warped anyone or anything that came near.

Once these things had dominated a *moon*, until the spear of Jurani destroyed it. The god had been smashed, and the pieces had rained down on Saramyr. But the organisms in the rock had survived: senseless, stupid, like newborns once again, but *alive*. And some pieces, like this one beneath Adderach, had been large enough to exert their influence over the weak minds of humans when they were at last uncovered. They discovered blood, which had been absent on the moon; they converted its organic energy to strength, building pathways, altering the rock that sheltered them to better distribute the life-giving matrix, full of the nutrients they needed for growth. They took the designs from the beings that had discovered them. They built hearts and veins and used them.

I know you now, she thought darkly. And with that, she attacked the witchstone.

She burst from the Mask, tearing through the Weave towards the seething snarl of her enemy. She was aware of the shock of the Sisters as she raced past them, and then she hit the skin of the witchstone's defences.

But this time it was different. She had found the tiny threads that connected the Mask to its parent, just as the greater links joined witchstone to witchstone across the land. And she rode those threads, piggybacking them inward, and permeated the rock at last.

The witchstone's alarm was a blare that stunned her. It knew she was here, knew she was inside it. She sensed the billions upon billions of organisms that surrounded her, the crushing foulness of their presence. There, at the core, she found a junction, a nexus of tendrils, each snaking away to another, distant witchstone, assimilating them as part of the matrix, making them nodes in the unfathomable mind that the people of Saramyr called Aricarat.

But then the world around Kaiku began to wrench apart. The threads of the Weave twisted and snapped. And Kaiku realised in terror what was happening, and what had happened to the witchstone at Utraxxa. It had not been destroyed by the Weavers at all. It had realised that it was compromised, and had destroyed *itself*.

No! No! It was not enough that this witchstone should crumble into ruin. It was not enough that they won here today. It had to end now.

And as the witchstone began to tear itself apart around her, Kaiku sewed herself into it and she held it together.

It almost pulled her mind to pieces. The agony was appalling. She was being ripped asunder from every direction at once, and only her will kept her from being shredded into raving lunacy. But she would not let go. She would not let the witchstone come apart. And though the pain was more than she could bear, and the power that burst from her scorched her insides, the witchstone did not shatter. Though it shook and pulsed and deep cracks appeared along its length, though chunks of it rained down upon the Sisters so that they were forced to deflect them, it did not split.

Kaiku, both Sister and Weaver, bound it together. And with the last fraction of her energy, she punched a hole out through its defences from within, a conduit for the Sisters outside. They flooded in eagerly, passing through her and into the nexus at the core of the witchstone; and from there they spread outward, flashing along the links between the other witchstones across Saramyr. Possessing them. Infecting them.

Destroying them.

The first blast of a witchstone's death rolled across the Weave, buffeting Kaiku like a tsunami. But still she held, still she refused to let the witchstone go. She would not release it until she was sure that every one of them was gone. The suffering was unearthly, more than she could take, and had she a voice she would have screamed; but she held on, beyond endurance, possessed of a power greater than she had ever known. The Mask was turned against its master, and she had dominated it and taken its strength for her own. The world around her was frantically trying to twist itself apart even now, wrenching her so that she felt she would burst.

But still she held. Holding on was all she had left now. She knew nothing else.

Another shockwave rolled over her, and another. Aricarat was convulsing, his death throes ripping across the Weave, anguished and terrible and desperate. A vicious, bitter satisfaction sparked in her breast.

Die, she thought savagely. *Die for what you did to me.*

The Weave knotted before her, shrinking to a point of infinite density. A moment before it sprang back Kaiku realised what was about to happen and braced herself for the arrival of the Weave-whale.

It smashed into existence, its sheer mind-bending immensity crushing her. She hung in the Weave, the centre of a web of millions of straining tendrils all trying to break away from her, stretched as if on a rack; and now she was pierced also by the dread regard of one of the monstrous beings who haunted the Weave. She had gone beyond pain: her mind trembled on the edge of snapping, unable to exist in such conditions. The indescribable torment of continuance was all that had ever been, all there ever would be, a timeless hell with nothing beyond it, and all there was left of her was that slender thread of will that told her to endure, and which would not break.

The witchstones were dying. One by one they shattered, pulverised from within by the Sisters.

More singularities sucked and bloomed. More Weave-whales arrived. Kaiku did not even realise. She had gone beyond sense, beyond sight. She was only a force of purpose now, driven far beyond the limits of her body and mind.

The Sisters were returning. She felt them flow through her, and a tiny sliver of comprehension penetrated. The witchstones were all gone, all but the one that she held together that was still desperately trying to pull itself to pieces. It would not bear an invader, though all hope of saving the rest of the network had long passed. It would rather have non-existence.

It is done, Kaiku thought, and she let go.

Tsata and the remaining Tkiurathi waited in the chamber above, hardly daring to breathe. They feared some kind of trick. The great metal barriers were gradually sliding aside, their mechanism activated at last by the Weavers without;

but the scene they revealed was far from the ravening horde that the Tkiurathi had expected.

There were perhaps thirty Weavers there, and all of them were dead. Behind them, several dozen Aberrants fought among themselves, some of them fleeing away up the corridor, others attacking members of different predator species. A dozen Nexuses stood still, their shoulders slack, and even behind their blank white masks it was evident that something had been extinguished inside them. Tsata watched in disbelief as one of them was knocked down and savaged by a shrilling. The Nexus did not react as the beast tore him apart.

'Fire!' one of the Tkiurathi cried, and a hail of bullets ripped into the Aberrants and Nexuses alike. Those Aberrants that were not killed ran howling; the Nexuses keeled over silently and lay still.

Tsata, his broken arm held to his chest, his teeth gritted against the pain, merely stared. Then a cheer rose from the Tkiurathi, a full-throated bellow of victory. They had realised what had happened before Tsata had. The witchstones were destroyed.

All across the land, the effects were the same. The Weavers died, simply falling over like puppets whose strings had been cut. The Nexuses, bereft of instruction, went still and did not move again. Their minds were void, utterly empty, and most stood where they were until they starved to death, unless they were first eaten by the predators that they had controlled or killed by vengeful townsfolk. It took the people of Saramyr a long time to understand what had happened at that instant when a god had been slain, but when they did they rejoiced, whole cities erupting in scenes such as none in living memory could recall; for their world was theirs again.

But for Tsata, there was only one thing that concerned him. The great mechanism that had taken the Sisters away was grinding and clanking again, bringing them back. Bringing Kaiku back to him. He walked over to the doorway to the metal edifice in the centre of the chamber. His brethren gathered around him, their gazes expectant. Finally, the elevator settled with a racket of machinery, and the door slid open.

Five Sisters were there, but they were crouching around a sixth, who lay in the arms of Cailin. Cast aside on the floor of the elevator was a Mask that had split in half. Kaiku's Mask.

Cailin looked up at him, and in her red eyes he saw all that he had to know. Numbness clouded him, killing even the pain of his arm. He took a few steps forward and sank to his knees before the fallen Sister. He had not recognised her at first, but he recognised her now.

Her hair had turned from tawny brown to bright white, and her irises were rich crimson, but it was unmistakably her. Her, and yet not her. She still breathed, but her features were vacant. The life that had animated them had gone. She was not there.

'She gave too much, in the end,' Cailin said quietly, and there was real grief in her voice. 'Nobody could master a Weaver's Mask like that and hope to come out unscathed.'

'Where is she?' Tsata whispered, his eyes filling with hot tears. 'Where has she gone?'

'She is lost to the Weave, Tsata. She has lost her mind to the Weave.'

THIRTY-THREE

The year that followed was a turbulent one.

The restoration of the Empire was not to be achieved in a day; nor would the famine that gripped most of the land disappear overnight. Saramyr was like a wounded animal which had licked its injuries clean of infection: it was healing itself, but it was still weak, and the process was slow and painful.

Against all expectations, there was little civil conflict in the wake of the Weavers' demise. It had been predicted that riots would occur as the redistribution of limited foodstuffs left some areas hungrier than others, that lack of medical supplies and malnutrition would encourage plague, and this would spark further unrest. It was expected that opportunist leaders, demagogues and bandits would rise up to fill the power vacuum before the Empire could regain what it once had lost. But Saramyr was exhausted. It was tired of war and suffering, and there was little enthusiasm for it any more. Even through their strife, the people were prepared to be patient. They had been given a taste of what an alternative to the Empire might be like, and in the light of that they would endure anything to get back the days that already seemed like a fond dream.

Though the high families' armies had been decimated and they barely had enough strength to defend their borders against the roaming Aberrants that were now a feature of the Saramyr wilds, they returned to their lands and were rapturously welcomed. With them went the Sisters. There were few of them left, dangerously few, for despite Cailin's best efforts they had been brought perilously close to extinction in the war with the Weavers. But those few knitted the continent together. And if there were murmurings of dissent at the idea of replacing the Weavers with women like these, they were drowned out by the acclaim. The Sisters, after all, had saved their country where even the high families and the legendary Lucia had failed. Cailin made very certain that everyone knew that.

The accession of Emperor Zahn tu Ikati was due in no small part to the support of the Sisters. Cailin could have thrown her weight behind a more tractable candidate, but she knew that Zahn was the strongest, and she wanted to be sure of being on the winning side. His old treaties with the minor families had held firm even through the war, and the generals knew him as a warrior and a tactician. Though his detractors pointed out that the death of his daughter would leave him a broken man – as it had in the past when he had believed her dead – Zahn's reaction surprised everyone. Though he grieved, he accepted that there was no question this time that Lucia had died and no possibility of her coming back. He became grim and cold, but he did not retreat into himself. Though there was no spark of compassion in him any more, and he was stern sometimes to the point of cruelty, he was in perfect possession of his faculties. The nobles believed a firm leader was what they needed to restore their country. There was the usual squabbling, but Zahn took the throne at the last.

As to Cailin, she lived in the Imperial Keep and nursed her plans. The reconstruction of Axekami went on around her: the destruction of the pall-pits, the rebuilding of the great temples, the dismantling of the Blackguard. But she had little interest in that. She was thinking, as always, of her Sisterhood.

The retreat of the blight across the land meant fewer Aberrants, and soon there would be no more born with the power to manipulate *kana*. The time would come when she would allow the Sisters to breed, under closely controlled conditions and with carefully chosen stock. Without the Weavers, they had no competition in the field of the Weave any more, and she could count them relatively safe. But one day, that might change, and she must be ready for it. The Sisterhood would grow and diversify, and their powers would grow also. They would sink into the fabric of society and become inextricable, even more so than the Weavers had. Who knew what might be possible in a century, in ten centuries? Would they be as gods? Or would they wane and fade into history? Perhaps she would not live to see it; perhaps her *kana* would dry up and she would age and die. Perhaps she would be here until the apocalypse predicted by the Xhiang Xhi would come to pass, engulfing the planet in fire. Or perhaps, even, she would be elsewhere by then.

She thought of the Weave-whales, and what they had left when they departed, and she knew they would not be safe for ever.

And so, more and more, her mind strayed to the empty Weaver monasteries, that had been sealed by the Sisters and surrounded by defences. More and more she wondered about what was inside them, what secrets they might hold that she could use to protect herself and her kind.

More and more, she wondered about the machines.

Two hundred Tkiurathi were left alive of the thousand that sailed to Saramyr in the winter of the war. Seventy of them went back to Okhamba, to spread the word of what had happened. The rest stayed.

For their part in the destruction of Adderach, the Emperor Zahn gave them a gift of land. At Mishani's request, they were mandated a small stretch of the western coast, northeast of Hanzean and just south of Blood Koli's ancestral territories around Mataxa Bay. The minor noble who had owned it had been one of the many casualties of the war, his property annexed by the Weavers. The Tkiurathi built a small settlement there, of *repka* and precarious dwellings raised on stilts and poles, with aerial walkways and rope bridges built between the trees. And there they went on with their way of life, puzzling the local Saramyr with their strange and foreign customs and philosophies.

Mishani was never quite clear why the majority of the Tkiurathi had decided to stay. She suspected, from what she had learned of them, that it was simply a matter of whim, that there was no deeper meaning behind it other than that they wanted to. But for Tsata, it was different. He stayed for a reason.

Mishani had returned to Mataxa Bay after the high families were restored. She was, after all, still the heir to Blood Koli, and with her mother and father dead she was entitled to inhabit her childhood home again. Blood Koli were much diminished, having had most of their power taken away after the restoration of the Empire began. Much of their army had formed the Blackguard and were executed for their crimes. But Blood Koli still held powerful concessions, not least with Blood Mumaka, who had begun to trade with Saramyr from Okhamba again, transporting much-needed supplies from the Colonial Merchant Consortium to ease the famine. Mishani had once considered freeing Blood Mumaka of their obligations to her family in gratitude for what their scion Chien had done for her in the past, but she decided against it now. Blood Mumaka had weathered the conflict overseas; though they were mighty they had not acted with honour. And Mishani, as the head of a high family, needed all the advantage she could get.

Though there was grief and pain at the news of her parents' death, it passed. But there was another source of sorrow that did not heal with time. For Mishani had taken it upon herself to care for Kaiku, and every day the sight of her friend wandering listlessly through the grounds of her house pried open the wound in her heart.

Tsata visited Kaiku every day, travelling from the Tkiurathi settlement. He walked with her when the weather was fine, and talked with her often, though she never replied. She drifted like a ghost at his side, uncomprehending. Mishani watched them from the house sometimes, two distant figures on the cliff edge. His broken arm had healed clean and he was physically none the worse for his experiences in Adderach. But like Mishani, his wounds were of a different kind.

She wished sometimes that Kaiku had died on that day when she destroyed the witchstone. Anything would have been better than this torment. Kaiku was aware of her surroundings, and capable of learning ritual and reaction to certain situations, but inside her mind she was a wiped slate.

Mishani let her roam the house and along the cliffs above the bay on her own. Kaiku had demonstrated that she had enough sensibility to avoid harming herself. She made toilet of her own accord, she ate when she was presented with food, she went to bed and slept when she was tired. But she did not speak, nor did she appear interested in anything, and there was no indication that there was any intelligence left in her beyond the rudimentary logic of an animal. When she was awake, she shuffled around without purpose, or sat and stared at nothing. Her presence was disconcerting, but Mishani tolerated it; and though Mishani was ever busy, she always made time to talk to Kaiku, or read to her. But it had been a long time since she had any hope of bringing her friend back from wherever she had gone. Though Kaiku's *kana* still ministered to her, keeping her healthy and strong and fit, it was attending to an empty house waiting for a mistress that would not come home.

Her hair grew white from the day when she had lost her mind, and her eyes never changed back from their deep crimson hue. The Sisters and Cailin herself did what they could, but that amounted to nothing in the end. Once she had become untethered from her body they had no way to find her in the vastness of the Weave: it was like searching for one fish in all of the oceans.

'She has to make her own way back,' Cailin said to

Mishani. But no one had ever done so, and privately she considered it impossible.

Tsata travelled from time to time, seeking medicines and physicians. The other Tkiurathi would take turns visiting Kaiku in his place. He sought out remedies both Saramyr and Okhamban, and even managed to arrange for a Muhd-taal from far Yttryx to visit and try his exotic techniques. But his chants and potions and crystals did nothing, and Kaiku remained a shell with no inhabitant. Tsata would only try again. After a year, Mishani wanted to suggest that he not exhaust himself over and over in a futile task when there was a life for him to lead. But she felt unworthy even thinking that, and she knew he would not listen anyway. Whether it was some memory of love that he bore, or loyalty to a companion as dictated by his beliefs, he would not give up.

But the spring of the second year since the witchstones' destruction turned to summer, and still Kaiku was not there.

She slept in a bedchamber near the back of the Koli family house, which faced east over the cliffs to the bay. The sun-light drenched her room in the early morning as it shone low across the land, glowing through the wispy veil that hung across her window, and the sultry heat of midsummer began to ascend. The walls were cool stone and the floor was coral marble. She lay on a simple sleeping mat in the centre of the room, and dreamed of nothing.

Mishani and her visitor stood in the doorway, looking in on her.

'This is Kaiku,' Mishani said.

The woman nodded. She was tall and long-boned, with the narrow, sharp features of the Newlands, coolly elegant and beautiful. Her summer robe was light blue and white, and her skin was pale. Her hair was worn in looped braids, a fashion from the north-east that had never caught on in the west.

'Please, leave us alone,' the woman replied.

Mishani agreed without really knowing why. Certainly,

this stranger's appearance at such an early hour was unusual, as was her tale: she was a healer, who had heard of Kaiku's plight and come to help her. She had arrived on a manxthwa-drawn cart, with her two children in the back, a twin son and daughter aged six harvests by the look of them. They were playing with the servants' children in the great tiered garden that ran down to the cliff edge, watched over by retainers.

Mishani felt that she should be suspicious, but could not think of any reason why someone should want to harm Kaiku. And though she did not admit it to herself, she almost hoped someone would. To end this half-life, to release her to Omecha's care, would be a mercy.

When Mishani had left, the healer crossed the room and knelt by Kaiku's side. The sleeping woman's cheek was limned in gold in the morning sun, the fine hairs of her skin incandescent. Her face was unlined, her expression peaceful, her mouth slightly open. For a long while, the healer watched her.

'They say you are lost, Kaiku,' she said quietly. 'That your mind wanders far from your body and cannot trace its way home.' She laid the palm of her hand lightly against the side of Kaiku's jaw, caressing her. 'I have carried a piece of you for many years, and you a piece of me. Perhaps this will help you.'

She bent down and put her lips to Kaiku's, and exhaled. And after a moment the breath became more than breath, a glittering passage of some ephemeral energy crossing between the women, gushing from one mouth to another. It went on for some minutes, longer than lungs could sustain, until finally Asara broke away, drawing her lips softly across Kaiku's as she did so.

Still Kaiku slept. From beyond the window came the high laughter of children.

'Do you hear them, Kaiku?' Asara said. 'My kind grow fast, it seems. Too soon they will be adults, and I will be a grand-mother. I think it appropriate. I am not too far from my first century.' She smiled sadly, looking down at the woman she had once known. Maybe she had once loved her. She could not say.

She got to her feet. 'I have you to thank for them, Kaiku,' she murmured. 'You gave them life.'

Mishani offered her a meal, and they spoke of matters in the distant steppes of the Newlands. She left in the afternoon, taking her children with her.

Kaiku collapsed later that day.

It happened towards sunset, as she was walking with Tsata. They were meandering along a path on the cliff edge, and the temperature had diminished to pleasant warmth, leavened by a breeze off the sea. Since Kaiku never replied to him and conversation was impossible, Tsata had developed a tendency towards storytelling, recounting to her the events of the settlement and the tales of the people who lived there. He had become well practised in making even the most mundane of incidents entertaining, though really it was only himself he was keeping amused.

He was in the middle of such an anecdote when, without warning, she went limp and sighed to the ground. He was so surprised that he was not fast enough to catch her. He squatted down and raised up her shoulders, patting her cheek with his palm and shaking her. She did not respond; her head lolled. He looked around, but there was no one nearby, and the squat shape of Blood Koli's house was far away. He would have to carry her, then.

He scooped her up easily. Her head hung, her white hair – somewhat longer since the day it had turned that colour – spilling down. He tipped her weight, jogging her head so that it lay against his shoulder.

She put her arms around him like a child clinging to its parent and held on tight.

It took him an instant to realise what she had done, what the pressure of her grip could mean. He did not dare to run with her, for to do so would be to break this moment, to shatter the possibility of it.

'Kaiku?' he said, his tongue thick.

She clutched him harder, pressing her head into his shoulder.

'*Kaiku?*'

Her body began to shake, and she was making a small sound in her throat. Tsata's heart jumped painfully in his chest.

She was sobbing, and Tsata was soon crying too, but his tears were of joy.

Kaiku's recovery was phenomenally quick. Though for the first few days she was skittish, prone to taking fright at loud noises and sudden movements, it was as if she had merely awoken from a deep sleep. Her mind was fogged, but it cleared rapidly; and though Mishani and Tsata and the entire Tkiurathi settlement celebrated, they managed to restrain themselves from taxing her too much with their visits.

In less than a week, it was like nothing had ever happened. The bad memories of Kaiku's fugue seemed like some disconnected reality that they had observed but not participated in, and the only reminder of it was Kaiku's hair of pure white and her eyes of deep red, which did not revert to normal even after everything else had.

She could not explain what had befallen her during the time she was away. She remembered only that she had been lost and searching, thinking that she was dead but unable to find Yoru and the gate to the Fields of Omecha. She had no conception of time, only an endless instant of uncertainty, caught in between one state and another. Then she had sensed something that she recognised, some*one* she recognised, a blaze in the Weave that had drawn her like a moth to a flame. And there she found herself at last.

Mishani told her of the healer from the Newlands, but Kaiku could shed no further light on the matter. They could only count her a blessing from the gods. The servants already believed that Kaiku had been visited by Enyu herself, the goddess of nature come to reward the one who had saved her from the Weavers. Others took her icy beauty as a sign that she was in fact an aspect of Iridima, the moon-goddess, who was grateful to Kaiku for slaying her brother Aricarat.

Kaiku did not know. But deep down, where reason and logic held no sway, she had her suspicions.

One evening she sought out Tsata, and found him in the spot where she had woken up, standing a little way off the path at the edge of the precipice. He was gazing out to sea.

A dull heat was thickening the air. The waters of Mataxa Bay were reddening, and the shadow of the cliff was reaching out to the great limestone islands in the mouth of the bay, their bases narrower than their broad tops, which were shaggy with vegetation. Hookbeaks cawed to each other as they hung on the breeze, watching the tiny junks and fishing boats below.

'Do you miss home?' she asked as she joined him.

'Sometimes,' he replied. 'Today I do.' He looked across at her. 'You should come to the settlement with me tomorrow. Many of my kinfolk have not seen you since your recovery, and they are eager.'

She smiled. 'I would be honoured,' she said.

They stood together a short while, observing the distant birds, sharing silent company.

'Mishani has been telling me a great many things,' she said at length. 'How matters have gone in the land while I was absent.'

'And that troubles you,' Tsata said.

She made an affirmative noise, brushed back her hair from her face. 'What did we do, Tsata? What did we achieve in all this?'

'We stopped the Weavers,' he said, but it was unconvincing, for she knew he felt the same as her.

'But we changed nothing. We *learned* nothing. We have merely set the calendar back a little. The Weavers are still here, only wearing a more pleasing form. Like them, the Sisters will one day decide that they no longer need the nobles as much as the nobles need them. The Empire survives, but . . .' She trailed away. 'After so much, the only winner is Cailin. I cannot help feeling that we followed paths of her making.'

'Perhaps,' Tsata said. 'And perhaps we are not right to despair. At least the Aberrants no longer have to hide. All fortune is relative, and the future is brighter than it was. You could consider that an ending.'

Kaiku shook her head. 'No, Tsata. That is what I came to tell you. This is anything but an ending.'

Tsata turned away from the vista, his full attention on her now. Though he had become used to her new appearance, he was still sometimes taken aback by the otherworldly quality it lent her. Those eyes, that hair, were the marks of a place she had been that nobody but her could ever know.

'I Weaved today,' she said. 'For the first time since I returned, I Weaved. And I know now something which the Sisters have not told us, which they have not told anyone. The Weave-whales have gone.'

Tsata's eyes showed his puzzlement. Kaiku had told him of the Weave-whales, but he did not understand the relevance.

'They have been there, in the Weave, since any of us can remember. They were always distant, unreachable, until *we* drew them. You and I, Tsata, when we destroyed the first of the witchstones in the Xarana Fault. But now they are not here.'

'What does it mean?'

'I do not know,' Kaiku said. 'But they left something behind them. Something in the Weave. A construct, a pattern, a . . .' She stalled. 'I cannot describe it. It is incomprehensible. But it is *active*.'

'Active?'

'Imagine a leaf that nods into the surface of a still pool, its tip touching the water. That pool is like the Weave, and this thing is sending ripples. The ripples spread, further and wider, far past where we dare go.'

Tsata frowned. He found always found it hard to follow Kaiku when she talked of the Weave, even when she simplified it with analogies.

'Then what is it?' he asked, feeling ignorant.

'It is a *beacon*, Tsata,' she said, animated. Then she calmed, and looked down to the bay. 'Perhaps it is a message also, though if that is true then I am sure we cannot understand it. But ripples in the pond draw the attention of the fish who swim there.'

'Kaiku, I still do not know what you are saying.'

'I am saying that this war will not be remembered as a fight for the Empire,' she said. 'It will be remembered as the time we came of age. Our conflict has attracted the notice of entities greater than we can imagine. The Xhiang Xhi told Lucia how Aricarat's influence changed us. We learned to meddle with forces beyond our understanding long before our due time. We tore the veil of ascendancy when we were but infants.' She met Tsata's gaze. 'And now our presence is being made known.'

'Made known to whom?'

'To those who dwell in places impenetrable to us. It may be a day, a year, a thousand years or longer; but sooner or later, something will come looking.' She dropped her eyes. 'What that may mean, whether that will be blessing or catastrophe, I cannot say.'

Tsata had no response to that. He did not believe in gods, but he knew enough to respect the world beyond the senses, and her words evoked a subtle dread in him that he could not define.

She laughed suddenly. 'But listen to me. I should be anything but maudlin. Forgive my foolishness. The future *is* brighter, at least for a time. I will enjoy that for now. Cailin can wait, the Sisters can wait, the Empire can wait. Maybe I will leave it all behind, and maybe I will rail against it; but not today.'

He caught her grin and was infected by it.

'I have something to ask,' she said. 'There is one more thing for me to do. I must travel east, to the Forest of Yuna, to a temple of Enyu that sits on the north bank of the Kerryn. Nearby there is a sacred glade, where once I made a promise to Ocha and to my family. I must return there, and offer thanks, and let my family know that they may rest now.' She touched his upper arm lightly, her eyes alive again. 'Come with me.'

'I will,' he said, without hesitation. Then, his expression faltered, and Kaiku became concerned.

'What is it?'

He steeled himself, and asked the question he had been putting off for some days now.

'After you have made your peace, Kaiku, what then?' he said. 'The war is over. The world goes on, and we go on with it. Where will *you* go?'

Her smile returned, and her fingers slid down his arm until her hand lay in his.

'I will go with you,' she said.

ACKNOWLEDGEMENTS

The Braided Path trilogy owes its existence to the following people:

Carolyn Whitaker for persuading me to rewrite the entire first book from scratch.

Simon Spanton for taking a chance on an unknown kid and sage advice throughout.

Nicola, Ilona, Steve, Tom, Gillian, Sara and everyone else at Gollancz who either contributed their efforts or made me feel welcome there.

And lastly my parents, for unconditional and unwavering support ever since they bought me my first typewriter at sixteen. The Braided Path trilogy is dedicated to them, with love.

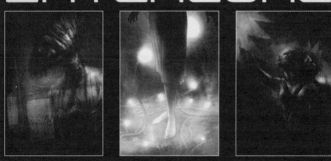